A SECOND DANIEL

BOOK ONE OF
IN THE DEN OF THE ENGLISH LION

4715

BY NEAL ROBERTS

*How can a man be expected to know
where his natural loyalties lie,
if he never knows who he is?*

booktrope

Booktrope Editions
Seattle, WA 2015

Cover Design by Greg Simanson
Co-Editors: Laurel Busch and Martin Jones

This is a work of fiction. Names, characters, places, brands, media, and incidents are either the product of the author's imagination or are used fictitiously. Any resemblance to similarly named places or to persons living or deceased is unintentional.

PRINT ISBN 978-1-5137-0441-8
EPUB ISBN 978-1-5137-0491-3
Library of Congress Control Number: 2015914772

ACKNOWLEDGMENTS

First and foremost, to my good friend and correspondent Brenda James, who alone deciphered the code in the dedication to Shakespeare's sonnets and who, together with William Rubinstein, began the long and arduous — but fascinating — task of introducing the world to the true bard. Also, to Mark Bradbeer and John Casson for both their past work and their excellent new book on the authorship evidence in the history plays.

I'd also like to extend my heartfelt thanks to Myra, Gigi, Joanna Volpe, Jen Nagler, Uncle Jack, Tim and Marie Donovan, the Coxes, Good Cousin Barbara (think screenplay), Nadine (who first brought Mrs. James's work to my attention), John O'Donnell and his cadre of experts (who so improved Noah's execrable Latin), Mom, George, Lily, and all the other relatives and friends who've lent their time, and their moral and literary advice and support to this project.

To my editor, Laurel Busch, I extend my sincerest thanks for her patience and extraordinary skill in helping this most opinionated of writers. To the rest of my great support team at Booktrope, for whom no amount of gratitude is enough, Martin Jones, Samantha Williams, and Greg Simanson, I hope to work with you all as long as I have a book to write. To my wonderful web designer, Willa Cline, many thanks.

And finally, I extend my thanks to Kenneth Shear, Jesse James Freeman, and everyone at Booktrope who took an interest in the project and made it possible to bring Noah and his friends to the world.

To Dad (the first Daniel) and Mom

To Myra, the love of my life and my tireless literary critic and advisor

To Adam & Gigi, the best kids anyone has ever had

PERSONS OF THE STORY

ELIZABETH, BY THE GRACE OF GOD, QUEEN OF ENGLAND,
FRANCE AND IRELAND

NOAH AMES, born MENACHEM, barrister
RACHEL AMES, born AÑES, his distant cousin and first wife
JESSICA, LADY BURLINGTON, their daughter
AVRAM AÑES & SARAH AÑES, his uncle and aunt
BETH FERNANDEZ, his distant cousin

HENRY NEVILLE, the younger, Member of Parliament
ANNE NEVILLE, born KILLIGREW, his wife
HENRY NEVILLE, the elder, knight, his father
CHEERFUL KILLIGREW, his nephew
WILLIAM SHAKESPEARE, reputed playwright, his cousin
WALKER, their footman
LUCY, their maidservant
JULIA, another maidservant

JONATHAN HAWKING, barrister
GRAVES, his investigator
ARTHUR ARDEN, barrister, his friend
ANDRES SALAZAR, barrister, his friend
THE BENNETT TWINS, barristers, his friends

RODERIGO LOPEZ, physician, coroner's assistant, Portuguese ambassador,
    intelligencer
EMANUEL TINOCO, his fellow intelligencer

DON ANTONIO, contender for the Portuguese Throne

ANTONIO PEREZ, former Spanish courtier, object of poisoning plot

STEPHEN RODRIGUEZ, the elder
MARIE RODRIGUEZ-MILLER, his widow
STEPHEN RODRIGUEZ, the younger, their son

EDWARD COKE, Solicitor General for England and Wales
THE LORD STEWARD
GARDNER, Senior Yeoman of the Guard
FRANCIS, Yeoman of the Guard
BARNSTABLE, Constable
CHRISTOPHER MARLOWE, playwright
MASTER TREASURER, Gray's Inn

THE CECIL FACTION

WILLIAM CECIL, LORD
  BURGHLEY, Lord High
  Treasurer
ROBERT CECIL, knight, Secretary
  of State, his son

LORD BLEFFINGHAM, Serjeant-
  at-Law, Judge at Queen's
  Bench

JACK GRANGER, a grain
  merchant accused of
  murder

THE ESSEX FACTION

ROBERT DEVEREUX, EARL OF
  ESSEX
GELLY MEYRICK, his principal
  attendant
NICHOLAS SKERES, his servant
ROBERT POLEY, his servant
PETER, his page

HENRY WRIOTHESELEY, EARL
  OF SOUTHAMPTON,
  friend to the Earl of Essex

ANTHONY BACON, barrister
FRANCIS BACON, barrister, his
  brother

PROLOGUE

SOUTHWARK, ENGLAND
LATE NOVEMBER 1558

UNCLE AVRAM HAS HINTED that his special customer's house across the Thames can be seen from this hillock in the market square, but the only thing young Menachem can make out on the opposite bank is a scary-looking castle looming in the distance. Wherever the customer's house may be, Uncle Avram has promised to take him there to deliver groceries as soon as the sun goes down. Menachem is eager for even this small adventure outside the Southwark food market.

It's nearly dusk, and red clouds streak the sky. Church bells clang in Southwark Priory on the near side of London Bridge, and north across the river in the walled City of London. The rain of the previous evening still dampens the packed dirt under the market, and a few small pools of muddy water dot the ground.

By this time in the evening, business has dwindled. Around the market, each family closes its booth at its own pace, the day's receipts by now fixed in amount, whether good or bad, with nothing to be done about it at this late hour. A cloth is dropped over the entrance to each booth, telling the casual shopper that food can no longer be purchased here.

Uncle Avram, known locally as "Avram the Jew," selects the perfect produce for his special customer. The best specimens have been withheld from general sale all day, stored in special wooden crates covered by a tarpaulin. As he still needs to supplement their quantity, he traipses about the booth scowling, intently studying each potato, each parsnip, each carrot, to ensure it's clean of rot and dirt, and can pass for the most desirable of its kind. He dusts his wares thoroughly, crates the items he's just selected, and loads everything onto his oxcart. The evening air grows chill as he sets about hitching his cart to the ox.

Menachem spies his pretty cousin Rachel peeking and smiling at him around the edge of one of the carts. Though he's lived with Avram and his family for little more than a week, already he seems to have captured her heart. She has a visitor this evening, her stout cousin Beth. As the children have been taught to keep silent whenever Avram fusses about his special customer's order, what ensues is a little dumb show, such as those seen nearby at The Theater and The Rose before the real play begins.

Having apparently noticed how taken Rachel is with Menachem, Beth prances into Menachem's full view with an exaggerated feminine strut, one shoulder jerking forward with each step, and a preening air about her upturned nose. Rachel makes no attempt to conceal her jealousy, and shoves Beth arse first into a puddle, which makes a little *splush* that Menachem finds even funnier for its quietness. Silently, Rachel points derisively at Beth, who lurches to her feet and drags Rachel out of view. A brief scuffle ensues, the only sign of which is an occasional soft slap or rustling sound. The girls reappear, slightly muddier than when the show began.

Uncle Avram finishes hitching together ox and cart. "Ready," he says, winking at Menachem and grabbing the reins. Menachem clambers up and settles in beside his uncle. Aunt Sarah waves goodbye, and the girls follow suit, still eyeing each other warily.

The ox jerks the cart out of a small rut, and Avram and Menachem begin their trip in comfortable silence. As the market diminishes in the distance, London Bridge looms ever larger.

Uncle Avram hands him a long wooden switch. "You keep those people away from the cart," he says, pointing at a painted woman, "and away from the food. Half of them have more money than we do. They are not so poor as they look."

Menachem accepts the switch and assumes a forbidding countenance for their trip across London Bridge, which he soon realizes is not used merely to cross the river. For much of its length, it's occupied by activities beyond the range of his experience. The furtive glances of those involved remove any doubt that such activities are improper, perhaps even unlawful.

A brazen woman, the tops of her breasts exposed, begins to approach the cart but, seeing Menachem's innocent face and Avram's threatening glare, she stops and recedes into the gloaming. Another woman raises her skirts to flash her legs, but then reverses course, realizing there is no business to be had from this cart. Halfway across the bridge's span, a few beggars huddle around a small fire to ward off the coming chill. From the corner of his eye, Menachem spies what appears to be two men grunting and humping beneath an outsized coat so large it must have been made especially for concealment.

He is not as shocked as another child his age might be. Having heard Bible tales of illicit practices, he is strangely reassured to see that they weren't conjured up merely to frighten little children into behaving themselves. He glances at his uncle's face and takes comfort from his sober eye and his steady hand on the reins.

At the far end of London Bridge, it's rumored, one can often see severed heads on pikes. Now, with a new queen about to be crowned, all the heads have been cleared away. Rumor has circulated that the new queen regards such displays as detestable signs of barbarity and that she'll replace them with new heads only under the most pressing of circumstances.

As they leave the bridge, Uncle Avram points to his left and breaks the silence. "Over there is Chancery Lane, where there's a whole building for the conversion of Jews to Christianity." He smiles, shakes his head, and laughs. "Goyim." He jerks the reins, and the cart turns right.

On their left soon appears the walled castle Menachem spotted from the hillock in the market square. Over its long stone wall peer several stone buildings and one tall white tower.

"What place is this?" he asks, his eyes wide.

Avram snickers. "This is the customer's house. We're bringing them groceries."

Menachem whistles softly. "They must be very rich, and happy!"

Uncle Avram shrugs. "Rich, yes." He pauses. "Happy?" He shrugs again, but says nothing.

"There must be a lot of people living here," says Menachem. "Surely, we can't be bringing food enough for them all."

The cart approaches a gate guarded by four burly men wearing colorful uniforms and holding long pointed pikes. As the cart draws close enough for Menachem to read their expressions in the fading light, they seem in no mood for a chat.

Avram slows the cart to a crawl, his posture stiffening. A few cautious words pass between him and the foremost guard. Avram draws a paper from his pocket and hands it to the guard, who examines it though there is barely enough daylight left for reading.

"That's the royal warrant, all right!" says the guard, returning the paper.

Avram pockets the paper and discreetly palms a coin into the guard's hand. The guard takes a step back, at first raising his hand to wave them through. But as his eyes light on Menachem, he shouts "halt!" and smiles sheepishly, evidently embarrassed by his hesitation.

"If you don't mind my asking, Goodman Jew, who's the English boy?" He nods toward Menachem. "I mean … who is he to *you*?"

Avram's head jerks around toward the boy, as though he's completely forgotten that his nephew's been seated beside him the whole time.

"Oh, he's not English," Avram says cautiously. "He's a distant cousin, an orphan, who just came to us from Poland." He leans toward the guard, and whispers something inaudible.

The guard nods gravely, and regards Menachem with pity. Drawing his great head so close that Menachem can smell the whiskey on his breath, he smiles discreetly, winks, and says hoarsely:

"Welcome to the Tower o' London, boy."

Menachem isn't sure what it is about the way the guard has spoken those words, but there is something threatening inside them, as though the Tower of London is not at all a place to feel welcome. The guard takes a step back, and waves them on.

A few manly shouts are heard calling and answering, some from above the wall, some from inside what now appears to be a giant compound of stately stone buildings.

The cart creeps up the cobblestone path to a giant gate of latticed iron. There the ox stops unprompted and waits, as though it has done this before. Chains clank, and wood creaks against metal. Slowly, the gate begins its rise, revealing sharp spikes along its base. Menachem shudders to imagine what such spikes would do to someone unfortunate enough to be caught under them when they drop.

They pass into a tunnel-like enclosure with a latticework iron gate exactly like the first at the opposite end. The gate behind them clanks shut, trapping them in the tunnel.

No longer able to contain himself, Menachem asks quietly, "What are these gates called?"

With a hushed awe that matches Menachem's own, Avram replies, "They're called a 'portcullis.'"

Menachem mouths the word, and whispers, "Are they to keep the Jews out?"

Avram suppresses a laugh, his face reddening. He composes himself, and replies, "No. They're to keep out the goyim who don't bring groceries." He tousles the boy's hair. The gate ahead of them creaks up, and the cart advances into an open cobblestone courtyard.

It is now full dark. No light shines from any building except for a modest stone cottage, also dark but for the glow of coals still smoldering in a tall fireplace beneath a carved wooden hearth, such as one might see in a great kitchen. The cart turns toward the cottage, and a cold breeze runs through Menachem's cloak and up his spine like icy fingers, as though he has passed into some ancient fairy tale where anything might happen.

The second gate thunders closed behind them.

A low fence surrounding the dark cottage blocks the cart's way to the rear door, which means that the crates will have to be carried in one by one. Avram and Menachem climb down from the cart, careful not to stumble in the dark. Avram pulls a torch from the rear of the cart, lights it, and lodges it in a sconce on the fence. He takes a sack of potatoes from the cart, hands it to Menachem, and points to the rear door of the cottage. "I'm giving you one small sack, so you'll have a hand free to open the door."

Just then, a muffled shout escapes a building across the courtyard. A man's voice. Though it sounds distressed, there seems to be no fear in it. Avram turns first in the direction of the shout, then back to his nephew and nods toward the cottage's rear door. "Go ahead. I'll be in soon." He takes a few hesitant steps toward the source of the shout, which has died away in the night.

Menachem turns toward the cottage door, carrying the sack in the crook of his left arm. Apparently the door has been left unlocked by design, as the key has been left jutting out of the lock. He turns the iron knob and goes inside.

He finds himself in a kitchen that must have been left dark and vacant no more than a few hours ago. There is still a stuffy heat inside, along with unfamiliar scents of finely prepared foods. A few droplets of water cling to the base of a pan hanging from a hook above the fresh-water basin. The stone walls have kept the chill wind out, except for the breeze now entering through the open door behind him.

Across a work area the size of his uncle's booth, an archway leads out of the kitchen into an unlit hallway. He closes the door behind him, half expecting his uncle to barge in before it can fully close. The breeze dissipates, but his uncle does not appear. He comforts himself in this strange new place by softly singing a tune he heard Rachel sing just yesterday. Although the lyrics are unknown to him, his wordless and soft young singing voice overcomes the gloom of the small cottage. He places the bag of potatoes on the marble base jutting out of the fireplace.

Sensing a presence behind him, he is too frightened to turn. He gasps, and his eyes go wide.

A cultured young woman's voice emanates from the archway across the kitchen, with a lilt of humor. "If you leave the potatoes so near to the flame, they shall be roasted long before anyone will care to eat them."

Menachem turns, and there, directly beneath the arch, stands a graceful young woman in a rich gossamer dressing gown. The deep red glow of the firelight illuminates her as something in a dream. He wonders fleetingly whether she might not be some beautiful wraith rather than a real woman, but he quickly dismisses the thought, as the bemused stare that holds him motionless is humanly warm and benevolent. Her most striking feature is her long red hair. Not the brassy red that he has sometimes seen affected by fine older ladies, but a rich auburn that reminds him of warm sunshine, newly tilled earth, and roan horses.

She appears to have been interrupted in preparing for bed, as she wears no makeup. Her face is a healthy pink. Though her eyelashes are nearly invisible but for the flimsy shadows they cast on her lids, her dark red eyebrows betray a sharp intelligence and afford her an air of confidence and authority. Perceiving his adulation, she casts him a broad smile with the slightest suggestion of impishness. "Put the potatoes on the wooden board, and bring one to me."

Menachem lifts the bag off the pediment. It is already hot to the touch and, left where it was, would soon have been scorched from the heat of the dying fire. He places it on the board, where he realizes he should have laid it in the first instance, and opens it to remove a potato for the lady.

"What tune were you humming when I came in?" she asks.

Menachem strains to recall whether he was indeed humming before she made herself known. For an instant he cannot recall any part of his life that took place before she spoke to him. Then he remembers Rachel, and the song. "I think it's called 'Greensleeves.'"

"That's what I thought. My father wrote that song," she says wistfully. She steps forward, lifts her skirts off the floor, and perches delicately on a bench facing the fire, only a few feet before him. Although he can feel the fire's heat at his back, all he can think of is the warmth exuding from her.

"Are you a cook?" he ventures.

"No," she replies, "although this is my kitchen. Are you the grocer's boy?"

He bows courteously. "At your service," he pronounces beautifully, just as he was taught by Aunt Sarah.

The Red Lady (which is how he now thinks of her) giggles with delight.

"And what is your name, squire?"

He plays along with her elevated courtliness. "I am known as Menachem, madam."

"And your surname?" she asks. He looks at her, puzzled. She rephrases her question. "Your *family* name?"

"I have no surname," he replies humbly.

"Well," she says, "I can see you are a quick learner, anyhow."

"And what, may I ask, is *your* name?"

She muses for a moment before answering. "You *may* ask, squire. I think that I shall not tell you my first name, for you may not call me by it. But my *surname* is 'Tudor.'" She stresses the word "surname," as though to caress him for attentiveness to his lessons.

Menachem's mind races. He has heard that name before. "Is that not the name of the royal house of England?"

She smiles. "Why, yes, Menachem, it is!" When she says his name, it sounds like *Manokkem*.

After a moment's thought, he ventures: "Are you a relative of the Queen?"

She regards him forlornly. "Alas, I am not. But where is my potato?"

As Menachem is about to hand it to her, she snatches it away, and her coy expression dares him to snatch it back. She is too quick for him, tossing it from one hand to the other, always too gingerly for him to reach. She giggles, and the music in her voice makes her seem little more than a schoolgirl having him on. She raises the potato over her head, and Menachem, not about to be defeated, places a foot on the bench beside her and steps up. Reaching as high as he can, he tugs the potato from her grasp.

He steps back down and sees that her expression has changed in an instant. Now she seems to be fighting off a sadness. Although he doubts it has anything to do with the potato, he kneels before her and offers it back to her with both hands.

She laughs despite herself, and tries in vain to fight the tears forming at the edges of her eyes. She blows her nose into her handkerchief. "You may keep the potato, Squire Menachem."

"Why are you so sad?" he asks, sorry for any part he has played in her dismay.

She tries to speak several times, but no voice will emerge.

"Have you any children?" he asks.

She shakes her head, and the tears well up again. He has put his finger on it. He assures her calmly, "You are young and beautiful, and shall no doubt have *many* happy children."

She draws herself together, and clears her throat.

"Alas," she says, "I am so lowly a person that I lack the authority to make such decisions for myself."

From the corner of his eye, he sees men with torches emerge from a big stone building far across the courtyard.

She sees him notice them. "They're looking for someone."

"For whom, I wonder?"

She laughs sulkily. "For *me*."

The door behind him bursts open, nearly stopping his heart, and lets in a blast of cold air. It's Avram, and he's alone.

"Uncle!"

But Avram's expression is frozen in amazement. His eyes, wide as saucers, are riveted on the Red Lady's face, and at first he seems unaware that his nephew is in the room. Then he kneels reverently, his eyes downcast, and pulls Menachem beside him by the back of his shirt, pressing him down onto bended knee.

"Forgive him, madam, please. He is just a boy who knows nothing."

She smirks. "He has done nothing requiring an apology, Goodman Grocer. But you do him wrong to say he knows nothing." She casts Menachem an appraising eye. "He speaks English beautifully." Her glance darts skeptically from the small, swarthy grocer to the tall young boy whose hair is very nearly the color of her own. "Is he of your family?"

Avram fixes his stare on a place just before the lady's feet. "He is distantly related, madam. His parents lived in Poland, but ... passed away in a fire."

"How dreadful!" she replies. "His English has nothing of the Pole about it. He is *not* Polish, is he?"

"Indeed, he is not, madam. His people went to Poland from Flanders many years ago, but they continued to speak English in their home."

She nods knowingly. "That is because they *are* English, having been deported to Flanders by my illustrious ancestor Edward the First. Is that not right?"

Beads of sweat begin to form on Avram's forehead and glisten in the red light of the coals. "You are correct, madam."

"An achievement of which my family can be right proud," she says sardonically. "How long has he been with you in England?"

"Less than a fortnight, madam."

To Menachem's young eyes, an idea seems to be forming in the lady's mind.

She cocks her head. "In such a brief time, has anyone in your family grown especially fond of him?" Avram evidently has no idea how to respond. "Do not be coy, Goodman Grocer. You know what I mean. Would your wife or children be bereft by his absence?"

Avram is dumbstruck, his eyes now boring a hole in a spot before her feet. Menachem somehow has the strange feeling that his life is being negotiated between the Red Lady and Avram, and that the Red Lady clearly has the upper hand. Avram appears to be drowning.

"Well, madam," Avram shrugs. "We *all* welcome him, but it is the women who seem to be especially fond of him, especially my daughter."

The Red Lady looks askance at Menachem and smiles bitterly, as though she knows him to be the devil himself. "I can understand *that*, Goodman

Grocer." She straightens herself and stands up to her full height, a simple motion that nearly causes Avram to swoon.

She regards Menachem, and sighs. "You are beloved of women. You sing well, and speak beautifully. All in all, you seem headed for an easy life, Goodman Menachem." She brings her chin up to a proud height. "I shall ensure that your life is made *less* easy" — Menachem looks up at her imploringly — "but far more meaningful" — she hesitates — "and important. Goodman Grocer, would your family object to my placing this boy under my protection, in the custody of an educator at Merton College, Oxford?"

"But, madam, there is the matter of his Hebrew religion — "

She waves away his concern. "His private religious practice will be fully respected, and he will be permitted to visit with you and your lovelorn daughter on holidays."

Avram's shoulders fall in relief. Through the windows, torches approach, ever closer to the cottage. The shouts of men can now be heard, some guttural, others belonging to cultured nobility.

"Your name is Añes, is that correct?" she asks.

"It is, madam."

"Well, let's make *his* a little more English," she says pensively. "He shall be known as 'Noah Ames.' Now, will that be all, Goodman Añes?"

"Yes, madam. Thank you, madam."

"You are most welcome. I will send for Goodman Ames in a few days."

The torches are now very close. Menachem is sure that, if the kitchen were illuminated by more than glowing embers, the men outside would have discovered the Red Lady well before now. Down the dark corridor behind the lady, there is a loud banging on the heavy front door, through which a man commands sternly, "Open up, in the name of the Queen!"

Now the lady's eyes open wide. "Go!" she says excitedly, waving them out the rear door.

Avram scoops Menachem violently into his arms and rushes out of the door, shutting it quietly behind him. At first he appears to duck down, but Menachem sees that his knees have buckled beneath him. Avram struggles to stand again, and rushes away toward the oxcart, pulling Menachem behind him by the hand. Reaching the bushes, Avram lowers his head and quietly vomits.

While Avram composes himself and feebly struggles to find a water bladder in the cart, Menachem watches through the windows of the cottage as a strange scene unfolds.

A man and a boy enter through the front door. The man is quite stout, and appears to suffer from a crippling foot injury. Discovering the Red Lady, he claps his hands in relief and collapses into a chair, removing one boot and rubbing his foot, while the boy lights candles throughout the kitchen. The lady's hair is just the color Menachem perceived in the firelight. The man dispatches the boy through the front door. Although Menachem cannot hear the instructions given the boy, he assumes he has been sent to assure the other search parties that the Red Lady is found.

The man's voice is too deep to make out, but the words of the lady, though muffled by the windows, can be heard. "Sir Henry," she says, "I have told you that I will not be kept under guard like a common criminal!" She kneels to massage his wounded foot. "Your gout must be so painful! Poor Neville!" She wags an admonishing finger. "How could you allow yourself to be enlisted on a pointless errand such as this?"

Sir Henry places his hands sympathetically on her shoulders, and peers deeply into her eyes. Although she stamps her foot and turns away, from that point the voices die down, and the lady's words can no longer be heard.

"Menachem," whispers Avram, "come over here, out of the light." He places himself and the boy outside the view from the cottage windows. Sounding exhausted, he points to a stump and says, "Sit." He stoops and hugs Menachem as though he loves him more than his own life, and begins to quake, although whether from fear or relief Menachem could not say. "It is true, what they say. God protects children and fools. Blessed art thou, O Lord our God, the Lord is One." He draws his nephew's face from his chest, holds him squarely by the shoulders, and looks him in the eye.

Menachem can no longer bear the silence. "Who was the Red Lady?"

Avram regards him incredulously. "Who did she *say* she was?"

"When I asked her, she would not tell me her first name, and said her family name is 'Tudor.' But she said she is not related to the Queen." Voice full of concern, he asks, "Will they hurt her?"

Avram regards him skeptically. "Think hard, Menachem. Is that *exactly* what she said?"

"I — I asked her if she was a relative of the Queen, and she said" — his eyes roll up in deep recollection — "'alas, I am not.'"

Although Avram is apparently losing patience, he says indulgently, "Menachem, we are Jews. We live by our wits, or we do not live long. If a lady at the Tower tells you she is named 'Tudor,' but she is not a relative of the Queen, then who is she? You know this. *Who is she?*"

Menachem's furrowed brow slowly relaxes. Much of what he has heard and seen begins to fall into place. Tears stream from his eyes.

"She is the Queen."

CHAPTER 1

THE PLAGUE THAT HAS TERRORIZED the locals, leaving a horrible toll in its wake, appears to be ebbing at long last. Although few families have been left entirely untouched, a palpable relief now pervades the town.

For each of the past two years, the Master of the Revels has ordered the closing of all London theaters during the plague-ridden months of summer and autumn. Starving troupes of professional players have been forced to earn their meager bread touring the country.

But even during the worst years, the plague recedes each winter, allowing theaters to reopen. Most are as unroofed as any papist abbey desecrated at the hands of Henry the Eighth, and a roofless theater is unusable during cold winter months. But The Rose does particularly well then, as its thatched roof blocks the wind over the Thames from sweeping down onto the audience.

On this particular Saturday in February, a chill breeze blusters through the theater windows, bracing but bearable. Every avid theatergoer knows that by late afternoon the frigid wind will shift and stream full gale through the windows, setting everyone's teeth on icy edge.

It's a bright early afternoon at The Rose, and excitement mounts in the crowded house. In a few minutes, Lord Strange's Men will take to the stage to debut a new play: *The Jew of Malta,* by the same Kit Marlowe who penned *Edward the Second.* That play ended with a red-hot poker being shoved up the arse of a deposed king, inflicting upon the monarch an excruciating death and titillating the audience with a frisson of gleeful horror.

One never knows how far Marlowe will go to shock, but his occasionally enthralling verse provides cover for any nobleman wishing to attend. Despite their masks, however, noblemen are required by the demands of gentility to make a show of averting their eyes from his more lurid displays.

Noah Ames now sits beside his good friend Henry Neville in costly seats aside The Rose's stage. From here, Noah can see what the groundlings cannot: Concealed by the makeshift curtain suspended across center stage are many artfully disorganized stacks of gold-painted coins. Kettles and other household items, also falsely gilded, are carefully arranged to appear carelessly strewn among the coins.

"How goes my old schoolmaster Savile?" asks Henry.

Noah smiles fondly to think on the man who taught him how to get along as a secret Jew in a Christian world, while having no such experience himself. "He is well, and happy so long as he can spend all his time writing. I hope his work can be read when it's complete, as his writing seems an unbroken script of undulating waves. Someone once asked to see his travel journal from our European tour, and could not make heads or tails of it. Gave it up in an hour or two."

"I remember everything about that tour," says Henry. "We should write a journal of it ourselves, so that it will not be lost to posterity."

"As a barrister, I have little choice but write ... however haltingly." Noah turns to Henry. "But I did not know *you* to be a writer."

Henry's face reddens, and he looks away. "No, not I."

An actor cloaked in the black gabardine of the comic Jew strides to center stage on the actor's side of the curtain, his face painted into a cunning expression, his eyes sharpened. Smiling briefly at Henry and Noah, he assumes the face of the wicked Jew and tugs the curtain open dramatically, allowing the offstage audience its first glimpse of the gilded trove.

Ooohs and *aaaahs* arise from the groundlings. Noah can see a quite different reaction from those in the balcony, where the wealthy and noble smile into their sleeves at the groundlings' ignorance in crediting these trashy props as a plausible representation of gold.

Although the house appeared to be full until now, Noah notices with curiosity that one of the largest boxes in the balcony remains vacant and dark.

The player hugs a golden kettle, runs his hands lovingly through the clinking coins, and, in what passes for a thick Jewish accent, shouts loud enough to overcome the audience's murmur:

> *So that of thus much that return was made:*
> *And of the third part of the Persian ships,*
> *There was the venture summed and satisfied.*

Henry covers his mouth with his hand and mutters. "Good Lord! Is that how a Jew speaks English?"

Noah replies, cupping his hand over his own mouth. "Who can say? There have been no Jews in England for three hundred years." But, of all people, he knows best the falsity of his own remark. He wonders yet again how no one has ever guessed at his own Jewishness, at least not with any seriousness.

Though sometimes he feels himself a chameleon adapting his color to his gentile surroundings, in truth his concealment requires little effort, as nothing that can be seen in a mirror reveals his Hebrew race. Nor does his manner of speech. Still, one would think that someone as close as Henry to the workings of his inner mind would have suspected him before now.

Barabas, the gold-loving Jew of Malta, is visited by two merchants. To the second, he proudly proclaims,

> *Rather had I a Jew be hated thus,*
> *Than pitied in a Christian poverty:*

He turns to face the audience with a sneer of contempt.

> *For I can see no fruits in all their faith,*
> *But malice, falsehood, and excessive pride,*
> *Which methinks fits not their profession.*

The crowd hisses. At this, Henry slaps his leg, briefly winces in self-inflicted pain, and draws close to Noah's ear. "Marlowe's got it right on that score. Christendom is a *world* of hypocrites." He surveys the stern-faced crowd. "Still, it will not do to have it writ down, or publicly pronounced."

Suddenly, the play comes to an abrupt, unscripted halt, the players standing silently on their marks attempting to remain in character, their respectful attention acutely riveted on the vacant box in the balcony. Evidently, they have been signaled that some dignitary has arrived fashionably late and is now making his or her way in. The groundlings silently turn to see who is so important that his arrival is allowed to interrupt such a long-awaited performance.

Henry leans close to Noah, using the hiatus to complete his thought. "Half of Parliament think Kit Marlowe is a recusant papist. The other half is sure he's an atheist, of all things." He shakes his head. "I half expect the Master of the Revels to shut down this play before its debut has finished."

"What do *you* think Marlowe believes, as far as religion?" asks Noah quietly.

Henry smirks. "Oh, Marlowe worships a god, all right. Trouble is, his first name is Kit."

In the vacant box, a page enters first, bearing a grave expression, comporting himself in a most dignified military manner. A sword with a golden hilt hangs at his side. Even at this distance, Noah can see that the real gold of the handle shames the painted props onstage. The page solemnly lights several candles with a long match.

Henry taps Noah's leg with the back of his hand and motions for him to rise. "It's Essex!" he whispers. Henry gathers his substantial girth and hoists himself to his feet, grimacing in evident pain. Though he is only in his early thirties (he will never give the precise date of his birth), his gout evidently proceeds apace, just as his father's did.

Noah gathers his black robes and rises at Henry's side, awaiting the arrival of the great man. Five more pages enter the box, equally dignified but not nearly so resplendent as the first, and disperse in grim military fashion to either side. The audience murmurs. Next to enter the box are four silent, beautifully attired couples, each careful to avoid looking at the gawping crowd, though clearly aware of its rapt attention. Couple by couple, they assume their seats near the rear of the box until only two seats remain vacant at the front.

Through the box's open entrance, Noah can see a handsome gentleman unhurriedly removing his gloves and nonchalantly handing them to a valet, then jutting his elbow out to be taken by someone as yet unseen. Henry mutters, "Earl of Southampton, that!"

A dazzlingly bejeweled sword handle flashes into view, then a jewel-bedecked doublet. In a breathtaking portrait of noble English youth, the Earls of Essex and Southampton stride proudly into view, arm in arm, smiling broadly. The crowd erupts into deafening cheers and applause. A few hats fly into the air.

The two earls stand abreast at the front of the box. Southampton smiles glowingly at Essex, steps aside, and bows to him theatrically, on behalf of the whole crowd. He rises and, with upturned palms, silently presents Essex to the exultant crowd. The roar grows to a din. Onstage, the players clap, and beam toward the box. Marlowe, now visible to the audience, stands alone and applauds politely, a painted smile on his face that never quite reaches his eyes.

Smiling and applauding, Henry turns to Noah and leans toward him to shout above the noise. "The players applaud the audience. Which is the performance, I wonder? All the world's a stage, and all the men and women merely players."

Essex surveys the assemblage and bows dramatically, his hand flowing before him with utmost elegance. To Noah's amazement, Essex's eye seeks out Henry onstage. Seemingly oblivious to the crowd, Essex rakishly raises his right hand to his eyebrow and shoots Henry an intimate smile. Imperceptibly to all but Noah, Henry flinches. Every eye vainly scans the stage, seeking out the object of Essex's attention, but Henry gives the curious crowd no clue that Essex's attention is directed to him alone. Noah carefully avoids looking toward Henry, who evidently covets his anonymity.

The play resumes, filled with much abuse of Barabas the Jew, which is then avenged by the most abominable acts imaginable. The Jew seems perversely to exult in the Christian abuse he suffers, however much he rails at it (the better to pardon his increasingly vicious crimes). He seems impelled to justify himself aloud, heaping scorn upon gentiles, which includes the whole audience.

It's unclear to Noah whether these endless expositions are spoken for the edification of other characters, of the audience, or of the Jew himself. More than likely, they were written by Marlowe for *Marlowe* to enjoy while watching his audience squirm. Indeed, of all current playwrights, it is Marlowe who cultivates the most intimate relationship with his audience, sometimes caressing his crowd of paying intimates, but sometimes (as now) slapping them in the face.

For each Christian injustice, Barabas exacts a most draconian penalty. He sets one young man against another, to do each other to death. He poisons his own daughter for having had the audacity to become a Christian nun, and then poisons the rest of the convent for good measure. At last, his intended victims turn the tables on him, and boil him in the very cauldron he intended for them.

The play concludes. For this debut performance, the troupe foregoes the usual parting song and dance. Instead, the players take their bows downstage, in groups of two or three, to universal applause.

The actor playing Barabas comes to the fore alone, still wearing his character's black gabardine robes and diabolical makeup. The crowd erupts, simultaneously hissing and applauding, smiling all the while. The player beams, greatly satisfied by the simultaneous condemnation of the character he has portrayed, and approval of his satisfying portrayal. He brings his finger to his lips to silence the crowd. Amid the tumult, his voice now seems small.

"Ladies and gentlemen," he shouts, "I give you the playwright, Christopher Marlowe."

The groundlings erupt in huzzahs. Even in the boxes, everyone rises to applaud. The last holdouts are Essex and Southampton. Although Southampton soon rises enthusiastically, he notices that Essex remains seated. Lighting again on his own chair, he pleads earnestly with Essex, who nods indulgently, and the two rise together, applauding the playwright. Essex's smile toward Marlowe is no less forced than Marlowe's toward Essex. The audience turns again toward the earls' box, and cheers a final time. Ignoring the crowd, the earls depart unhurriedly, chatting amiably with the other occupants of their box.

The groundlings slowly file out, a few imitating Barabas' more flamboyantly villainous gestures to the delight of their fellows. Henry taps Noah's shoulder and arches an eyebrow. "Follow me!" he winks. "Quicker exit."

Henry leads him through a backstage hall past the players' dressing rooms. All doors are open, all lights are lit, and every room bustles with activity. Costumes and makeup are being removed at all points, and Noah's senses are struck with the unfamiliar, slightly sickening smell of greasepaint. At the end of the corridor, a door that has been left ajar lets in a few rays of daylight and a stream of fresh outdoor air.

As Henry and Noah are about to burst into the open air, Marlowe emerges from one of the dressing rooms, a small man, almost petite, boyish-looking, with an undeniably sharp intelligence about the eyes.

Henry throws his hands up. "Marlowe the Magnificent! Honestly, man, I don't know how you do it … so consistently … with such … *panache!*"

Marlowe bows formally to Henry. "Baron. It is always a pleasure to see you, but you flatter me beyond reason." He rises and turns to Noah, gazing admiringly at his face, and smiles devilishly. "Is this lawyer a friend of yours, or did you rather come to serve me with some suit?"

Henry bellows with laughter. "Not on your life, Marlowe. Even had I cause, I would not let it out that you'd got the better of me. This is my old friend Noah Ames, of Gray's Inn."

Marlowe gazes intently at Noah's face, as though he intends to draw it. "Charming."

Henry gushes. "Tell me. Where did you get the idea for a villain who tells the audience his every motivation?"

Marlowe sidles up to Noah and caresses him familiarly from behind. Noah can feel the heat of his reddening face. "Henry," he says urgently, "are we not expected for supper shortly?"

"Oh, that's right," replies Henry. "I nearly forgot. Marlowe, I'd love to discuss this further, but alas we are required elsewhere presently. Congratulations on an excellent play. God give you good e'en." Henry leads Noah to the door by his elbow and nods in smiling farewell to Marlowe, who bows in return.

"Another time, then," Marlowe says. "And please bring Master Ames. I have a few questions for one of his profession."

Noah turns to Marlowe. "Thank you so much, Master Marlowe," he says, and precedes Henry out of the door into the late afternoon.

As they walk abreast, Henry remarks, "Well! Marlowe was evidently taken with your appearance."

Noah smirks. "A good appearance can be a mixed blessing."

Henry looks at Noah askance. "You're not all *that* good-looking."

"No? Well, better-looking than *you*, anyway," says Noah in mock insolence.

"Oh?" says Henry. "Cheeky lawyer! What makes you so sure?"

"Well, let me ask you this," says Noah, drawing himself up indignantly. "Did Marlowe just squeeze *your* arse?"

Henry's face drops into a comical grimace. He guffaws, and takes Noah by the elbow. "Come on. To supper, then!"

Unlike Noah and Henry, who escaped The Rose through the actors' rear exit and now stroll together around front, much of the paying public is still filing out through the front doors. Noblemen depart quickly by private coach, eager to return home before the onset of the rapidly approaching darkness and cold. The groundlings, who left through different doors, now mill about in no rush, enjoying the remains of the afternoon; many reside here in Southwark, unfashionably close to The Rose and the open sewers that run through the district.

Henry points to a particularly well-appointed coach sitting idly across the theater lawn. "That belongs to Southampton." He glances around. "No sign of him or Essex. I wonder why they're taking so long to go." They pass a doorway where the well-dressed page who first entered the earl's box waits patiently for his master to appear, his familiar gold-handled sword gleaming in the sun's late rays. Neither Essex nor Southampton is anywhere in sight. Although they're evidently tarrying inside the theater, Henry comes to a halt, apparently intending to offer a few parting words once they appear. Noah stops alongside, watching the noblemen depart in their beautiful coaches.

*   *   *

Last to leave the theater box, Southampton waits behind Essex, who's abruptly halted short of the door.

"Out of my way, sir!" says Essex to someone standing athwart the doorway.

Southampton peers around his friend at the unwelcome obstruction: a middle-aged man in worn black robes of gabardine which, together with his long nose, longer beard, and gravest countenance, mark him as a Jew. He seems vaguely familiar.

"M'lord," says the man to Essex with a bow, his supplicating posture completely at odds with his obstinate refusal to let them pass, "a moment, if I may. There is the matter of the … indebtedness."

Already a few steps down the staircase, Essex's chief page places his hand on his golden hilt and turns back to his employer for orders, but Essex, with a wave of his hand, directs him instead to usher his remaining guests out of the theater.

Recalling the man's identity, Southampton rushes him, pinning him against the opposite wall, and remonstrates with him in a stern whisper. "Have you no sense, you fool, that you seek repayment from the earl in a public place? Have a care for decorum, man."

The Jew smiles innocently. "I come only for what is mine, m'lord. I have lent my monies to m'lord of Essex for use by Her Majesty's fleet, and members of my tribe tell me that the fleet is in, so my principal is come due, together with my … usances." Now his smile seems more sly than innocent.

"Simpleton," says Southampton. "Know ye not that the fleet is 'in' only when Lord Essex *says* it is?"

The moneylender's smile fades. "Is it so writ, my lord?"

"It *is* so writ, you ignorant man." There's a light tap on Southampton's shoulder.

"We have no time for this, Wriothesley," whispers Essex, pronouncing Southampton's family name "Rothslee." "Permit me to handle it." He deftly takes Southampton's place in the confrontation. A jeweled dagger flashes in his hand. He sets the point to the moneylender's throat and urges it forward, nearly breaking the skin. The Jew's eyes grow wide with horror.

Essex smirks. "I see I have your attention now," he says, obviously relishing the terror. "Your timing couldn't be worse … for either of us, Master Jew. Do you know which play has just been staged here?"

"I … did not see the play, my lord, but it was about a Jew, no?"

"It was about a Jew, *yes*. A filthy, murderous, scheming Jew, who thinks he's smarter than everyone else. Sound familiar, hah?" He pauses, as though considering how best to proceed. "Now, if I so chose, I could toss you out of the theater and tell the incensed crowd who you are, and that you've come to embarrass me into paying you your filthy lucre. You do know what would happen to you?" The Jew seems too frightened to reply. "They'd tear you to shreds."

The Jew nods, barely moving a muscle.

"The next time you try to collect a debt from me in public, or in such circumstances as might cause me embarrassment, I shall ensure that neither you … nor your survivors … shall ever see tuppence." He smiles with self-satisfaction. "Are we of one mind?"

The Jew nods, his shoulders slumping with relief that this misbegotten interview appears to be coming to an end at last.

"Good," says Essex. He grabs the moneylender by the lapels and hurls him down a half-flight of stairs.

The Jew, his fall broken by the landing, leaps to his feet in obvious pain and, without so much as dusting off his robes, bows low enough to scrape the floor, racing down the remaining steps and bolting out of the door.

Southampton observes, "That will teach him to embarrass a debtor into repaying a debt before it's come due."

Essex dusts off his hands, as though he's been handling some particularly odious beast. "While the Jew has caused me no embarrassment, I fear he *has* delayed me at a most unpropitious moment."

CHAPTER 2

AS NOAH WAITS WITH HENRY for the earls to emerge from the theater, an altercation breaks out near the coaches. While it appears at first to involve three or more men, his eye quickly narrows it down to two. A short, swarthy fellow with gray hair at the temples, perhaps a Spaniard, has fallen (or been shoved) to the ground. He's assisted to his feet by an Englishwoman a few years younger, and dusts himself off, glaring angrily at the other man, an unsavory-looking Englishman of indeterminate age with a cruel glint in his eye.

By sheer chance (or for some reason he can never again remember), Noah glances toward the door where Essex's page waits. Still no sign of either earl.

"No, I most certainly will not!" shouts the short fellow with the slightest suggestion of a Spanish accent. "Now, be on your way!"

The Englishman scowls, mutters something inaudible, and takes a threatening step toward the Spaniard. As he brings his right hand around, as though to grab the purse dangling from the Spaniard's hip, he raises his left toward the Spaniard's face. Then something happens that will later prove otherwise than it appears. To Noah, he appears to strike the Spaniard abruptly in the forehead. It's no roundhouse left, to all appearances amounting to little more than a sharp jab.

The effect on the Spaniard is out of all proportion to the weight of the blow. He staggers for a moment and drops to his knees, his every limb twitching. A second later, he falls face first to the hard ground, motionless. The woman who helped him up a moment earlier stares down at him in astonished horror.

"My husband!" she shrieks. "Help me, someone!" But by the time she rises to confront her husband's attacker, he's faded into the crowd as something incorporeal.

Noah rushes to her aid, plowing through the crowd, and Henry limps after him as quickly as he can. The woman cries inconsolably, in great heaves. Noah gently tugs her by the shoulders to get her attention, but she clings to her husband like a vise.

Despite the cold of the afternoon, Noah feels himself perspiring. As he steps back and takes in the sorry sight before him, he notices several things he did not expect. The Spaniard's purse still hangs from his hip. It has been neither stolen nor opened during the fracas. Evidently, this was not a robbery, as it first appeared. Also, there appears to be no blood. By this time, Henry stands beside him, puffing with exertion.

"Damnedest thing!" says Henry, and pats the woman's back comfortingly. "There, there," he intones. With some strength, he firmly extricates her from her husband. "Let us try to help him," he pleads.

As the woman lets go of her husband, two more things become apparent to Noah. First, the man is very obviously dead. There will be no call for a surgeon. Second, although the man's right eye is shut, a single tear of blood has run down across his cheek and now reddens an inch of moist ground. This is the only sign of blood at the scene.

A man shouts from the gathering crowd. "Here comes the constable!"

"Are men so easily killed with one blow?" asks Henry in amazement. "We shall need the coroner's man."

"Oh! Oh, no!" the woman shrieks, hearing this confirmation that her husband is indeed dead. "Oh, mercy! What shall I do? Stephen! Oh, my poor Stephen!"

The constable appears out of the crowd. At precisely the same instant, the breathless Earl of Essex appears from the direction of the theater.

"'Swounds, what happened 'ere?" asks the constable, his deep voice sounding a strange mix of Yorkshire and North London. He sizes up the grieving woman. "Is this your 'usband, meddem?"

Continuing to weep, she nods emphatically.

"Did anybuddy see what 'eppened?" shouts the constable.

Before either Noah or Henry can open his mouth, a cultured voice says, "I saw the whole thing, Constable." The crowd's attention follows the voice. It's Essex. Southampton is nowhere to be seen.

Evidently recognizing that this is a person of some importance, the constable replies, "Beggin' yaw pahdon, suh, but who are you?"

"I am the Earl of Essex, Constable," comes the reply with seeming humility. The widow looks imploringly to the earl, and her cries diminish to whimpers. A constable's assistant draws her aside and manages to open a quiet conversation with her, frequently interrupted by her snuffling.

The constable's eyes open wide, and he takes an appraising step backward. "Essex? Bless my soul, well, of *course* you are!" He waves toward the pathetic scene before him. "'Tis a pity to make your acquaintance, m'lord."

Essex raises his eyebrows. "And you are … ?"

"I am the poor Queen's constable, m'lord. Barn-Stable, at your service," he says, carefully articulating each half of his name.

Essex regards him quizzically. "Barnstable?" he asks gravely, pronouncing the name to rhyme with "constable." "Constable Barnstable?"

A sound like a sneeze erupts from Henry, who turns away, covering his nose with a handkerchief.

"No, suh. 'Barn-Stable.' After the two places where cows and horses … dwell, m'lord." He looks at the corpse and shakes his head. "Right, then. Could we start at the begin — " An assistant whispers urgently into his ear. The constable deferentially holds up his finger toward Essex. "Pardon y'self for just a moment, m'lord?"

Essex nods, a little uncertainly.

When the assistant finishes his urgent message, the constable asks, "Pardon, suh, but, judgin' from your robes, would it be possible to tell if you're a lawya?"

Noah is astonished to realize that it's he who's being addressed. Instinctively looking down at his robes, momentarily unsure what he's been asked, he quickly collects his wits. "I am a barrister of the Queen's Bench, Constable … Barn-Stable."

"Well, then, beggin' your pardon, suh, perhaps you could service a young widow?"

Henry sneezes again, apparently coming down with a sudden cold.

Noah's jaw drops. "I beg your pardon?"

"Well, suh, this lady is in need of legal disputation. Y'know, some bright lawyer like y'self to … persecute 'er."

"Oh, yes, I see. Perhaps you should attend to m'Lord Essex before bothering further with me. His time is infinitely more valuable." Noah bows to Essex, who nods appreciatively.

As Noah steps away from the constable with the intention of comforting the new widow, he glances up at the theater and stops in his tracks. There are no windows through which anyone could look out from either the hall or the staircase leading from Essex's box to the door where the page awaited him. Essex could not possibly have observed the scene he's about to describe to the constable.

Noah motions to the constable's assistant, and hands him his professional card to give to the widow. "I'll be with her in a few minutes," he says, and rejoins the constable and the earl, whose conversation, he sees, has been followed closely by Henry.

"So, it was a robbery gone bad," says the constable to the earl, shaking his head mournfully. "We can't be 'avin' such vilification 'ere in Southwark." He notices Noah rejoining them. "Oh, 'ere he is now!" He says to Noah, "Would you mind going over the contents of the malefactor's pockets with me? Wouldn't want t'be accused of failin' to take anythin' what don't belong to me, now would I?"

"Certainly, Constable," replies Noah, who has begun responding to what the constable *believes* himself to be saying, rather than to what he's saying in fact.

The constable draws a blank paper and a rough quill from his pocket and hands them to Noah together with a stained old inkwell. He removes the purse from the corpse's hip and draws Noah aside to enumerate its contents.

The Earl of Southampton's carriage draws alongside, and Noah can make out the profile of the earl seated inside, observing the proceedings with little interest. From the corner of his eye, he can see that the widow is also watching Southampton; in fact, she's glaring at him, and Noah wonders what connection there can be between the two.

Essex shouts to the constable. "I hope you don't mind, Constable. I should like to leave a man here to see the purse's contents."

The constable scratches his head, and responds as though the earl has requested permission to litter the grounds. "Not at all, m'lord. Please feel free to leave men anywhere ye like."

Essex shakes his head in dismay and speaks a few private words to Henry, who nods and bows. Essex pats him fondly on the shoulder and steps into Southampton's carriage.

*   *   *

Southampton is surprised that Essex takes the seat nearest him, as there's no one else in the carriage who could overhear. But what Essex plans to discuss is evidently so secret that there must be no chance even the driver overhears a word.

"Henry Neville cast me the most incredulous expression," says Essex. "He suspects I didn't see the murder." He sighs. "Well, at least Henry can be relied upon to have the good sense to keep his mouth shut about such matters."

"It's not Master Neville I'd worry about," replies Southampton. "You evidently missed the look of startlement on the *barrister's* face."

"Barrister? Oh, the one with Neville?" asks Essex.

Southampton nods.

"I barely glanced at him." Grave concern surfaces on Essex's face. "Tell your driver to double back at a distance, and stop where we'll be unseen. I want a better look."

As he instructs the driver, Southampton wonders whether he should mention to Essex that the victim's widow once served at Southampton House, or that he saw the barrister send his professional card her way. He decides to keep such information in abeyance. Besides, there's something about the barrister that will interest Essex more. "Unless I'm mistaken," he offers, "that barrister is the one defending Granger against the murder charge."

"Granger? The grain merchant who dissuaded this fallen Spaniard from joining my ranks?"

Southampton nods. "As well as other Walsingham agents." Walsingham, often referred to merely as "Mister Secretary," long served as secretary of the Privy Council, that body of a dozen or so select politicians holding greatest influence with the Queen. Although the Privy Council has a new secretary, Walsingham was also the Queen's spymaster and, since his death less than two years ago, no one has replaced him in that important capacity.

"I want that bastard Granger to swing," says Essex.

"So much is clear, which gives you another reason to mistrust the barrister."

The coach stops on a rise overlooking The Rose's lawn, where Henry, the constable, and the barrister are earnestly preparing an inventory of the contents of the victim's purse, while the widow, seated on a stump, cries inconsolably. A light breeze intermittently carries the sound of her distant wailing their way. Southampton finds the mournful sound pitiable, but Essex seems unfazed.

"The prosecutor in the case against Granger is Coke, is it not?" asks Essex, pronouncing Coke's name as "Cook."

"'Tis."

"He's having trouble finding an eyewitness to place Granger at the murder scene?"

"He is."

"Well," says Essex, smiling slyly, "it's about time Coke found just such an eyewitness. By pure chance, of course." He smirks. "I'll tell Gelly Meyrick to prepare himself."

"But what would Meyrick know about the case?"

"Well, he's my principal attendant, and he's never had the least difficulty seeming sincere when he lies to *me*. I'm sure a past master such as he will find there's nothing to it. Meanwhile, it might be a good idea to find out if Master Barrister there has anything to hide. I'll put my page to the task." He gazes through the window at the figures on the lawn. "Yes, Master Barrister," he quietly muses, "you'll soon have too many distractions to worry about today's little murder."

*   *   *

The man left by Essex to witness the inventory of the victim's pockets is an intelligent-looking blond fellow about Henry's age.

The constable glances meaningfully at the setting sun. "We'll be gainin' daylight soon. If you could just write these things down as I list them, suh." Noah nods and leans the parchment against his hand. Although the pen he's been given is bent and worn, he manages to make it work passably well.

The constable pulls the purse open by the drawstring, reaches in, and draws out a few small items. "Four silver coins, all identical," he intones.

Henry reaches out for them, smiling ingratiatingly. "If I may examine them."

The constable regards Henry skeptically. "And who might you be, suh?"

"I am Henry Neville, Baron of the Cinque Ports."

The constable appears to find the title familiar. "The cannon maker?"

Henry's countenance relaxes. "Precisely, Constable. I expect *you* are a man o' war, to recognize the title."

The constable smiles. "Oh, I've 'et the elephant once or twice." He winks at Henry. "Are you of the Gresham works?"

"I *own* the Gresham cannon works," says Henry. "The barony doesn't bring much with it, unless the Queen were to marry, in which case I'd get to hold the canopy."

"Well, meaning no offense to the Queen, God rest 'er soul, let's hope she doesn't marry some Frenchy or, worse, one of them Spaniards! *Any* papist, for that matter. Those are fine cannon, Master," says the constable, handing the coins to Henry, who requires only a glance at them.

"These are all Spanish pieces of eight," says Henry. Noah dutifully writes: "Four Spanish pieces of eight." Henry hands the coins to the blond fellow, who holds them in his open palm.

The constable reaches in and draws out a handful of current English coins, including three crowns, four groats, and a few pence, counting them aloud and handing them to Essex's man one at a time. Noah dutifully records the number of coins of each denomination.

The constable again reaches into the purse, which is now nearly empty, and pulls out a weathered piece of paper, yellowed with age, its edges bearing the brownish gray imparted by much handling. "Well, 'ello. What are you?" he asks the paper.

"May I?" asks Henry, extending his hand.

Essex's man suddenly grows serious. "Perhaps we should open this before the earl."

"Oh, I think the earl has far more pressing business," says Henry, who takes the paper and deftly unfolds it. He reads it silently, and looks up at Noah, his eyes betraying the slightest hint of concern.

"What is it?" asks Noah.

Henry half smiles. "Nothing of consequence. It's a commonplace letter of introduction requesting the bearer's admittance to places of public gathering. As the bearer is unnamed, this may have passed through several owners. It doesn't tell us much, I'm afraid. I suggest you don't even include it in your list, Master Ames. Let us leave this with the constable as possible evidence." He turns to Essex's man. "Would that be satisfactory to you, sir?"

The man reaches for the paper. "May I, Master Neville?"

"Oh," Henry smiles, "by all means."

Essex's man reads it silently, and nods. "That would be fine. No need to put this on the list. Let's leave it with the constable."

The constable pockets it. "Well, that seems to be everythin'. What say we give the lady the coins and the purse?" He points to Noah's list, which contains but four entries. "She can sign that as a receipt." Noah nods agreeably and hands it to the constable.

Looking disappointed, the constable turns to the widow. Two voices begin together, as if on cue. "Oh, Constable," they say. The constable turns back. Henry and Essex's man have each extended to him a closed hand with a downturned palm.

Essex's man half smiles at Henry and pushes his hand away. "No, no. Master Neville, I must insist."

"But — " splutters Henry.

Essex's man shakes his head. "Orders of Lord Essex."

Henry nods deferentially and drops his hand, returning its contents to his pocket. "Please extend my compliments to his lordship."

"I shall certainly do so," the man assures him, and drops an angel into the constable's palm.

The constable smiles from ear to ear. "Yes, suh. Please be sure to thank his lordship on behalf o' Master Neville."

Noah follows the constable to the widow, who sits alone on a stump, looking dazed and forlorn. The constable hands over her husband's coins and purse, requests her mark on the receipt, blows the ink dry, and offers his services in the event she discovers who killed her husband.

At that moment, the coroner's black coach pulls up, driven by two burly white-coated men. It pulls to a stop, and a small, gray-haired, neatly dressed Spaniard emerges.

"Hmmph!" remarks the constable. "Holdin' a special on Spaniards today."

"So it seems," mutters Noah.

The two assistants dismount and assemble a device obviously intended for carrying patients or corpses. Consisting of two parallel poles about six feet in length with polished ends, the device has three feet of rough gray fabric stretched between the poles. As the assistants lift the earthly remains onto the stretched fabric and deftly transport them to the rear of the hearse, the Spaniard pays his respects to the widow.

"Madam, I am Roderigo Lopez, the physician who has been asked to collect your husband's remains. May I offer you a ride to your residence?" His voice has barely any accent but sounds vaguely Spanish.

"You may," she says wanly, extending her hand.

The Spaniard, who moves far more elegantly than Noah has come to expect of coroner's assistants, helps her rise, escorts her to the hearse, and assists her up the single step, ensuring that she's seated securely inside. He re-emerges and walks over to Henry, who is deep in conversation with Essex's man.

As soon as Henry catches sight of Lopez, he greets him warmly. To Noah's surprise, so does Essex's man, who then excuses himself, bows, and starts across the theater's lawn toward his waiting horse, a beautiful white steed.

"Thank you, Constable," says Henry, palming him another angel. "You have been a great help."

"Thank *you*, suh," says the constable, bowing low and returning to his assistants.

"Come on, Ames," says Henry. "We're taking the hearse home." He turns to introduce Lopez. "Master Ames, this is Doctor Roderigo Lopez, who is much, much more than he appears. Not only is he an expert physician having many important patients, he's also Portuguese ambassador to Her Majesty's court."

Lopez blushes. "Please, Master Neville, you flatter me beyond reason." He turns confidentially to Noah. "And it would be much appreciated of Master Ames if he would keep these matters between us."

"Indeed, sir," replies Noah, having no idea what to make of this man's unusual combination of offices. "It is a pleasure to make your acquaintance."

Henry, Lopez, and Noah join the new widow in the hearse, unaware that they're being watched from a distant carriage that only now draws away.

CHAPTER 3

AS LOPEZ ASSUMES A SEAT next to the distraught widow, Noah and Henry take the bench opposite. The assistants can be heard clambering up and taking the reins. The hearse starts moving mournfully down the path from the theater.

Lopez clears his throat gently. "Madam, where shall we bring you?"

As exhausted as she is, it takes a moment for her to respond. "My husband and I — " She chokes back tears and begins anew. "I shared a house with my husband at Holborn. If you would bring me there." Although, by her accent, Noah does not place her among the nobility, she speaks well and clearly, in a manner often heard among London's most successful merchant class.

He notices for the first time that, although nearly all the blood has drained from her face after today's catastrophe, she is really quite beautiful. Her eyes, though bloodshot, are a chestnut brown, as is her hair. Her mouth, though pursed now in grief, is naturally wide and generous, disclosing a beautiful set of teeth. Her nose, long and elegant, nowhere protrudes more than a finger's breadth from her face. Her figure is indiscernible in the low crouch in which she now sits, but before she entered the carriage Noah detected her shapeliness, a large bust and thin waist. While normally he would berate himself for harboring lustful thoughts about a woman whose husband has not yet been interred, he forgives himself this time, in part because she reminds him in some ways of his lost and beloved Rachel, and he knows from experience that, where thoughts of her lead, he has no choice but to follow.

Lopez flips open the latch of a compartment built into the side of the carriage and draws out paper, pen, and ink. "Madam, I apologize deeply, but I am required to ask you a few questions under these unhappy circumstances."

Noah glances over at Henry, who's uncharacteristically quiet, watching the widow's face closely.

She sighs. "I'll answer as well as I can, but my thoughts are all in a muddle."

"I quite understand," says Lopez, dipping the pen in the inkwell.

Noah interrupts. "Before you proceed, Doctor, please allow me to make a proper introduction. Goodwife Rodriguez, I am Noah Ames, the barrister whose card was given you a short time ago. Do you have it still?"

By way of answer, she holds up the crumpled card that has evidently remained in her hand the whole time.

"Good," he says. "As I witnessed the ... event, I will be unable to act as your counsel in the case, but if you call for me at Gray's Inn, I will be pleased to introduce you to a reliable lawyer who works closely with investigators. This gentlemen sitting next to me is my good friend, Master Henry Neville, Member of Parliament." Henry nods silently, and the widow nods in return.

"Thank you, Master Ames," she replies. "I may come 'round to Gray's tomorrow, if I'm feeling up to it."

"Very well," says Lopez, now that Noah's business is done. "What is your name, madam?"

"I am Marie Rodriguez-Miller." She rolls the second r in "Rodriguez" as effortlessly as a native Castilian. "My husband's name, that is, the name he went by here in England, was Stephen Rodriguez."

"How old was he?"

She thinks for a moment. "I'm not precisely sure. About forty, I should imagine, but we never got much into it."

"What was his nationality?"

"He was born in Spain. A papist, but converted more than ten years ago. A good Protestant now. Church of England. Holds no love for the Pope." She looks down and corrects herself. "Held."

"Would I be correct in assuming you did not recognize the man who struck him?"

A smoldering cloud of anger drifts across her eyes. "That would be correct."

"Can you think of anyone who would wish him harm?"

"You mean 'murder' him? No. He never cheated anyone in his life."

"What was his occupation?"

"He and I are — were — partners in an import-export concern. Before you ask, we export English woven goods to Spain and Portugal, and import whatever happens to be in demand here."

"And what is that, presently?" asks Lopez.

"Pretty much nothing. Our vessels return mostly empty now. Spain is still not one of your great manufacturing nations." She considers for a moment. "Raw materials, sometimes, cotton, and so on. Oils. We have someone down there who assembles whatever cargo he may. We don't track it very closely. Usually, it's enough to make the return trips reasonably profitable."

"Do you own these vessels?"

"Two or three. Three, right now. Sometimes we take space on the vessels of other merchants. Really depends on conditions." She furrows her brow. "What's this about? Are you going into export?"

Noah smiles privately. He likes the way this woman conducts herself. No nonsense.

Before Lopez can form a reply, Goodwife Rodriguez glances out of the window. "Tell your man to make a right turn at the next corner, go down one block, and stop in the drive."

Lopez leans out of the window and speaks to the driver. He resumes his seat, and his inquiry. "Is your business successful?"

At that very moment, the hearse swings around into the drive of an imposing three-story stone house with torches ablaze at the front door, and lit candles in several windows. As it stops, a footman opens the front door, revealing a roaring blaze in a large-mouthed fireplace. Goodwife Rodriguez notices the astonished look of all three male passengers, and the corners of her mouth turn up in a mirthless smile. "What do *you* think?" She gestures to the footman to remain in place, declines the assistance of all three male passengers, and descends under her own power.

The doctor follows close behind, while Noah watches from the hearse. Lopez hands her his professional card, and apologizes for having to take the remains to the morgue for examination. She assures him that she understands, enters the house, and closes the door firmly behind.

Henry sighs. "Reminds me of my wife. If it weren't for her accent, I'd say she too must be Cornish."

Lopez climbs back into the hearse, plopping down on the bench with obvious fatigue. "Where shall I drop you gentlemen?"

Noah considers asking to be dropped off at Gray's Inn, which is very nearby, but thinks that Henry's wife, Mistress Anne, would deem it rude for him to fail to show up, even though it's quite late.

"My wife's place at Lothbury," says Henry. "We're already late for supper."

"Oh, I am sorry," says Lopez with great sincerity. He speaks to the driver, and the hearse starts up again. They begin their ride quietly, lost in the solemnity of the occasion.

"So," says Henry, breaking the silence at last, "how is our mutual friend?"

For a moment, Lopez seems baffled. "Oh," he says, apparently realizing whom Henry is asking about. "Her Majesty is quite well."

"And Essex?"

Lopez shrugs. "He still has me on retainer, but has called upon me little since Secretary Walsingham died."

The hearse pulls up to the Nevilles' townhouse. As Henry and Noah step down and wave to the departing doctor, Henry seems lost in thought. "England shall miss Walsingham," he says wistfully. "I already do, myself. It was quite a shock to recognize his handwriting today."

"When did you see his handwriting today?"

"That note in Rodriguez's pocket. It was in Walsingham's hand. Not just the signature, either. The whole thing. I'm fairly certain that Essex's man knew it, as well."

Noah fumes. It was Henry who persuaded him to omit the note from his inventory of the deceased's pockets. The only remaining record of the note's existence now is the note itself. And *that* now resides in the pocket of a constable whom Noah has already seen accept two gratuities.

Noah makes no effort to disguise the irritation in his voice. "Henry, I would like to speak with you before we go inside."

Henry turns, clearly bracing himself. "Very well."

"Would you care to explain to me what happened today?"

Henry raises an eyebrow. "How do you mean?"

"Please do not insult me. Tell me what happened."

"Noah," Henry says indulgently, "Essex is the man of the hour in England. You saw the audience's reaction to him. Just two years ago, he helped Drake lead the English Armada in its attack on Spain, after the Spanish Armada was defeated off the English shoreline."

"The English Armada?" scoffs Noah. "'Fiasco' would be nearer the mark. That expedition failed to destroy the Spanish king's ability to reconstitute his armada, and also failed to gain the Portuguese throne for the Queen's favored contender. And, which is worse, of more than twenty thousand warriors who departed on the expedition, only about five thousand returned alive."

"But Essex risked his own life, as well," says Henry. "When a leader takes the same risks as his men and suffers defeat, he becomes godlike, an earthly dream reminding people of those who, once in his service, are now in heaven."

"Perhaps if Daniel of the Bible were to interpret their dream, he might show them that their god has feet of clay."

"Let the people have their favorite, Noah."

"*Their* favorite, Henry? Or *yours*? And what shall be justified in the name of promoting the people's favorite? Why, Essex told that idiot constable — "

"Constable Barnstable!" Henry laughs aloud.

"Be that as it may. Essex told him that he'd seen the altercation."

Henry's smile drops away. He avoids Noah's gaze and shakes his head. "He didn't see it." He glances at Noah's face. "You noticed that, too."

"Of course I did. But think what that means. He had foreknowledge of the murder, which means he was *complicit* in it."

Henry nods gravely. "I suppose it's at least *possible* that Essex had no foreknowledge of the crime, but took advantage of an auspicious — "

"*Murder?*" interjects Noah. "Seems unlikely. And what effect might his misleading the constable have on the estate of that poor widow?"

Henry raises an eyebrow. "That 'poor widow,' as you call her, is rich! She probably has more money than we do. I wouldn't be too worried about *her*. Besides, that constable — "

"Don't say it!"

" — couldn't solve a crime if it were a fish that leapt onto a platter for him."

"And then you told me to leave Walsingham's note off the inventory. Why the devil would you do that? To protect Essex?"

Henry seems incredulous. "Now it is you who are not thinking clearly. That wasn't an inventory. It was a *receipt* to protect the constable from any accusation of theft. If you'd listed the note on there, then the constable would have had to give Walsingham's note to the widow, and Essex would have learned it, through his man."

"So?"

"So … we know it wasn't a daylight robbery. What if the assailant was demanding Walsingham's *note*, because it could be produced at a later time, say, to show that Rodriguez had once worked for Walsingham? Would that not make the note a dangerous thing to have? I wasn't protecting Essex. I was protecting the *widow*."

The townhouse door swings open, and a gray-haired footman emerges into the night, blinking as his eyes adjust to the darkness.

"Yes, Walker?" says Henry.

"Oh, there you are, Master Henry. Mistress Anne wished me to ask you whether you intend to join your wife and your guests," he pauses and looks heavenward, "who have been here more than an hour." Henry looks at him askance. "I'm sorry, sir, but Mistress Anne pointedly told me to add that last."

Henry nods impatiently. "Please tell Mistress Anne that I shall be in by and by."

"I shall say so," replies Walker.

"'By and by' is easily said."

"Will the lawyer gentleman be joining us?" asks Walker.

Henry raises his eyebrows, as if to ask whether Noah would like to come in.

"Oh, I couldn't, Henry," says Noah. "But thank you all the same, and please extend my regrets to Mistress Anne."

"You're going to have to do that yourself. If I know her, she won't let a little thing like a murder excuse missing supper."

Noah smiles. "Perhaps I'd better come in for a moment, to serve as your alibi."

"Yes, let's have a spot of sack!"

"Perhaps, but then I really must go."

Walker holds open the door for Henry and Noah. The most exquisite scent of roast goose and turnips wafts through the door as they enter. To Noah's left, about fifteen adult guests occupy a well-lit, well-heated room, and seem well-oiled by drink.

As Henry doffs his outer coat and hands it to the servant, he mutters to Noah: "Mostly Killigrews here. My wife's family. Speak no politics, and, for God's sake, *no religion*. Oh," he engages Noah's direct gaze, "you can talk about the play, but *don't* mention the murder."

Noah nods. "A lot to remember," he mutters.

A flamboyantly dressed young man with dark hair and a receding hairline approaches them. "Henry!" he says in a pleasant voice. "Who's your lawyer friend?"

"Oh, *him!*" Henry shakes his head dolefully. "This is no friend. I've known this scoundrel for thirty years. He's more of an old shoe, really. Gets me out of scrapes from time to time. Noah, this is William Shakespeare of Stratford. He's distantly related, don't you know, through the Arden side."

Noah bows merrily. "Mostly, I just pay Master Neville's fines out of my own pocket, and bury them in the bill."

"Indeed," says Goodman Shakespeare. "He deserves no less!"

Something suddenly occurs to Noah. He asks hesitantly, "Are you the same William Shakespeare who wrote that excellent play last year about the Wars of the Roses? It was at that theater ... " He searches his memory in vain. "Oh, what's the *name* of it?"

"The play?" asks Shakespeare.

"No, the theater."

"The theater," repeats Shakespeare.

"Yes," replies Noah. "What's the name of it?"

"The *Theater*," Shakespeare declares, and waits for a change in Noah's expression. "That's the *name* of it: 'The Theater.'" They share a laugh.

"This could go on all night," mutters Henry. "I need a drink." He raises his hand and beckons Walker. "Fetch me a sack," his eyes dart around the room, "before Mistress Anne sees you." Walker nods and walks stiffly away.

Noah shakes Shakespeare's hand warmly, holding onto it far longer than he is wont to do, and looks awestruck into the playwright's eyes. "That play was ... wonderful."

Shakespeare draws his hand firmly away, though his smile never wavers. "Thank you so much." He looks at Henry. "I still have some things to learn from Marlowe ... and Kyd."

Henry arches an eyebrow at him, but Shakespeare continues. "And Lyly ... and Greene, as well as a *host* of others." He smiles broadly.

"Really, William." Henry sniffs. "Your humility is most unbecoming."

"Oh!" laughs Noah. "*That's* why the play has so many mentions of 'the Nevilles' noble race'! You're a *Neville!*"

"Well, Henry might disagree about my being a Neville," says Shakespeare. "But perhaps you have it. Won't you come and join us?"

"I'm afraid I cannot. Marlowe's play ran a bit late, and I *had* an appointment at sunset for which I'm badly behind schedule, I'm afraid."

Mistress Anne appears, as out of nowhere, her red hair framing her pretty face perfectly, the unmistakable intelligence in her expression intensified by the darkening makeup applied to her eyebrows. "Are you quite sure you cannot stay for supper, Master Ames?"

"Mistress Anne, if anyone could persuade me, it would be you. But, alas," he winks, "I cannot break this appointment."

Mistress Anne leans into him intimately. "I'm sure she's lovely," she whispers, winking in return.

"I *hope* she is!" he whispers.

She arches an eyebrow in feigned shock, and purses her lips. "Sir, you are a scandal!" She kisses him lightly on the cheek. "Leave my house at once."

He bows to her and Henry, then turns to Shakespeare. "I hope to be seeing more of you and your plays."

Shakespeare nods. "I hope so, too."

Outside, Walker waits by the carriage. "Mistress Anne told me to take you home. Gray's Inn, over by Chancery Lane, sir?"

"Yes, thank you!" says Noah, and loses himself in thought all the way home.

As they pull up to Gray's Inn, Walker dismounts and opens the carriage door.

"Need any help up the stairs, sir?"

"No, I don't think so, as I have no bags." Noah reaches into his pocket and pulls out a coin. "But please take this."

"Oh, I couldn't, sir."

"You can, and you shall!" Noah says, smiling insistently. "Let me ask you something. Does Goodman Shakespeare come to the Neville home often?"

Walker snickers. "I don't know as you'd call it 'often,' suh. But I wish I had a few relatives like him meself. Brings a bagful of coins every time he comes to supper, he does. *My* relatives come to supper, too, but they forget the coins. Goodman Shakespeare owns a share of one of them players' companies. Does all right for himself, too, by what I hear."

Noah watches the carriage roll away. He goes up to his rooms, collapses into his accustomed chair, removes his boots, and rubs his aching feet. Resting his eyes for a moment, he breathes deeply in his newfound solitude.

At last, he goes to the cabinet and draws out a golden candlestick, the candle already in place. This is the night of the year when he lights a mourner's candle for Rachel. It was to have been lit at sunset, but he supposes she would forgive his tardiness in light of the circumstances.

He dons the skullcap that he keeps concealed in a compartment in the cabinet, and recites the mourner's prayer almost silently. In the stillness of the room, looking at the solitary flame, the tears come, as they always do.

"I'm doing the best I can, my beloved," he says to the woman in his heart.

CHAPTER 4

BY THE TIME NOAH AWAKENS next morning, the sun that shone the previous day has hidden itself above a thick billow of gray clouds. A one-eyed glimpse through the window reveals that, although the rain has not yet begun, the darkened sky is fraught with its unspent weight. Thankfully, it's Sunday, so there's no court session this morning. He lolls in bed an extra few minutes, mulling over yesterday's varied events until he hears a knock at the door.

"Who is it?" he grumbles, sounding even groggier than he feels.

No answer. In a moment, a letter slips under the door, and a muffled young voice on the other side says, "Courier from Master Henry, sir. I'm to await an answer."

He grabs a robe from his closet, puts it on, and cinches the cloth belt about his waist. He rubs his eyes and opens the door. The young messenger looks to be about eleven years old, and as crisp as Noah feels rumpled.

"Morning, sir! Master Henry says he'd like to come 'round about ten o'clock, if that's all right with you. What shall I tell him?" The boy waits expectantly, cap in hand.

"Well, Master Cheerful, do you suppose it might be a good idea for me to read the note before replying?"

The boy smiles all the harder. "If ye like, sir!"

Noah waves him in. His cheer is quite contagious. "Take a seat."

The boy chooses the nearest chair, and perches on its very edge, as though to sit comfortably would unacceptably dampen his boundless energy.

Noah slits open the letter. Although Henry prides himself on his ability to write in different hands, Noah knows that this particular style of court italic is Henry's favorite when speed is of concern. In any of his handwritings, the ease and flow of his script is as unmistakable as his playful choice of language.

> Dear Counselor Slugabed:
>
> I sent the boy mostly to ensure that you would be awake upon my arrival. He is as sunny in the morning as you are taciturn. If you are dying of some dreadful illness, please give him a note to

that effect and send it back with him. Otherwise, I shall be there by ten to accompany you to Doctor Lopez. It troubles me that I have been unable to imagine how Rodriguez was killed.

Neville

P.S. If the boy does not return promptly, I shall conclude that you have murdered him for his cheerful disposition, and every smuggler in Cornwall will descend upon you in a flash. He is one of Mistress Anne's kin, a Killigrew, and had better be in excellent condition upon his return.

Noah rises, gives the boy twice the gratuity he would have given another messenger, and tousles his blond hair. The boy makes no demure pretense, but examines the coins with eyes wide. "*Thank* you, sir! What shall I tell Uncle Henry?"

Noah considers for a moment. "Tell him you found me singing ... and practicing the dance."

The boy's ingenuous face falls. "Oh, but I *didn't*, sir."

"How much did I give you there?" Noah looks at the coins in the boy's open palm, and extends his thumb and index finger as though to take some back.

The boy's fist snaps shut, and he smiles. "Song and dance. Yes, sir!" he says, and patters down the stairs as lightly as an elf. Noah closes the door, scratching his head.

He relieves himself, washes his hands, brushes his teeth hard with salt, and rinses his mouth with tinny water from the pewter pitcher by the basin. Quite by accident, he catches a glimpse of himself in the mirror. "Oh, this won't do," he says to his reflection.

The widowed Goodwife Rodriguez has said she might call and, though he doubts she'd do so the day after her husband's death, he decides not to risk it. He trims his beard and straightens himself up properly, putting on a fresh set of barrister's robes and leaving yesterday's for the laundry.

Just before leaving, it occurs to him to strap on the dagger given him years ago by Uncle Avram. Closing his robe, he turns to the mirror once again. Though the dagger is entirely concealed from view, he has the most acute feeling of foolishness. A lawyer and a dagger. What a useless combination!

* * *

As England has neither a police force nor a public prosecutor, any criminal investigation and prosecution must be privately conducted, and privately funded.

Since yesterday's encounter with the widow, Noah has decided that the best lawyer to handle the tracking and eventual prosecution of her husband's murderer would be Jonathan Hawking. A recent graduate of Merton College, Oxford, Hawking came to Gray's Inn only two years ago, but his wholehearted dedication to the practice of law has shamed many of his seniors. Like Noah, Hawking does not spring from the nobility, nor even from the highest ranks of the new merchant class, having made his way on merit alone — a daunting task in a day when, with a few notable exceptions, advancement requires either social rank or a great deal of money.

Unlike Noah, who was reared by an academician and largely sheltered from the tumult of London's seamier side, Hawking has emerged from a common upbringing, maintaining contact with sundry questionable persons from his past. However dubious their reputations, their usefulness to the legal practitioner is beyond question. Hawking works informally with several rough-looking men, each of whom ekes out a living in criminal investigations.

On his way down the stairs, Noah is pleased to see that Hawking's door is open and a light burns within. He pauses outside, and sticks his head through the doorway. Hawking sits at his desk, reading documents contained in a thin file. At last, he looks up and his sight comes to rest on Noah's face. "Master Ames," he says pleasantly. "Won't you step in? Please, sit down."

Noah looks around the room, but every chair is covered with books, files, or both. "Where?" he asks pleasantly.

Evidently realizing that his housekeeping has been less than stellar, Hawking shoots to his feet, removes a mixed stack of books and files from the seat of a chair near his desk, and makes a show of brushing it off. "Here," he says abashedly.

Noah sits, and the spindly chair creaks ominously. "I've asked you many times to call me 'Noah,' Jonathan. I wish you would."

Jonathan smiles. "What brings you here this morning, Master ... Noah?"

"Did you hear about the murder yesterday, at The Rose?"

Jonathan furrows his brow. "Yes, something about a man dropping dead from a single-fisted blow. The perpetrator escaped. Why? Has the widow come to you?"

"Worse than that, I'm afraid. I saw it all, and rode in the hearse that drove the widow home. Nice home, too. Very near here, in Holborn."

"What's bad about that? By the sound of it, she can pay a fee for a lawyer and his investigator, too."

"Oh, I don't doubt she can, but I'm an eyewitness to the murder. Unfortunately, I can't take the case, as a lawyer cannot act as both advocate and witness in the same matter. Besides, I'd look a damn fool arguing my own veracity to the jury."

Jonathan eyes Noah skeptically. "Oh, that rule only applies if the lawyer's testimony is necessary to the case. Surely, there are dozens of eyewitnesses to put on the stand. The murder took place in daylight amongst a crowd of theatergoers, for heaven's sake!"

"But what if I were called by the defense?"

"Nonsense," replies Jonathan. "If the defense offered your testimony as part of their case-in-chief, they'd be stuck with your answers."

"And if, in some respect, my testimony were to differ from every other witness's? My veracity would be impeached. No, I could not persuasively argue the complainant's case while the jury is wondering whether I've been lying to them under oath."

Jonathan sits deep in thought for a moment, and shrugs. "So, what are you going to do?"

"If the widow shows up here, which she may do as early as today, I'll refer her to a young lawyer who's been spending his time wrapped up in old cases."

Jonathan nods, then raises an eyebrow. "You mean … me?"

Noah smiles.

"Oh," Jonathan replies flatly. Almost as an afterthought, he adds, "Well, thank you very much for your confidence, Master Noah."

"Just 'Noah.'"

"Noah, yes. Thank you very much."

"You're quite welcome, Jonathan. As I said, the widow may come 'round today, looking for me. If you see her, please tell her I've gone off with Master Neville to see Doctor Lopez, who will be examining her husband's body this morning."

Jonathan smiles, evidently warming to the idea of representing a rich widow in such a high-profile case. "I certainly will. Won't be going anywhere myself for quite a while," he says, indicating a stack of unopened files.

Noah rises. "Right! Good day," he says, extending his hand.

Jonathan reaches over the desk and shakes his hand. "Good day! And thank you, Master Ames … Master Noah … Noah." Jonathan winces.

"Keep trying. It's in there somewhere!"

As Noah leaves, he wonders whether, and when, he's going to inform Jonathan of what is likely to be the most material fact in the case: that Essex lied about witnessing the murder. Such knowledge is almost certainly possessed by a very few people: Noah, Henry, Southampton, Essex's page, and Essex himself. Simply putting that fact into evidence will place Jonathan at the center of a political firestorm. And whichever witness Jonathan calls to testify to it is sure to be torn to shreds by defense counsel. Noah shudders to think that such witness might be himself.

Then again, perhaps the killer will never be found, and all such questions will become moot. That thought raises his spirits, but only for a moment, for it raises an even more troubling question. What if Jonathan needs to know about Essex's foreknowledge of the murder in order to identify and track the killer? His spirits sink again, and he wonders whether he will really be doing Jonathan a good turn by referring the case to him. Where is this all to end?

As he reaches the foyer, he dons his outer cloak and boots. He walks out into the chilly day, and asks one of the inn's staff to bring his mount around to the front of the building. It's still overcast but appears to be brightening a little. He looks south, and spots Henry on his stout roan turning up Gray's Inn Lane. He waves, and Henry waves in return.

Across the dirt path, Noah spots furtive movement behind a big oak tree in the square. Pretending to watch Henry, he keeps the oak in the corner of his vision. Yes, there he is again. A tall, thin man in nondescript brown riding clothes peers around the oak at Noah. In a moment, the movement is gone.

While Noah is glad to have brought the concealed dagger, he suddenly wishes he'd spent some time learning how to use it in a pinch. As he watches Henry approach at a leisurely pace, he wonders whether Henry might also be in danger. Not likely, he decides, as Essex seems to have a soft spot for him.

Then something else occurs to him: What if the man in riding clothes is not Essex's man? Who else might have an interest in impeding this investigation? He tries to dismiss the thought, assuring himself that the man isn't there to spy on him at all. He shivers in the gloom. The day now looks more threatening than ever, although he's unsure whether that's due more to his misgivings than the weather.

Henry rides up to him, and remains in the saddle. Keeping clear of the horse, Noah speaks under his breath: "Did you see that fellow standing over there by the big oak a few moments ago?"

"Where? Over on the square? I wasn't really looking for anyone. Come to think on it, I *did* see a fellow."

"Brown riding clothes?"

"I think so. If it was who I think it was, I've seen him before."

"Where?"

Henry laughs, and points his chin toward the building housing Noah's and Jonathan's rooms. "There! He's one of Anthony Bacon's men. Bacon lives upstairs in this building, you know."

Noah blushes. "I got the distinct feeling that fellow was spying on me."

"Well, I won't say it's impossible, but I think it rather more likely you're suffering delusions of grandeur. Perhaps we should ride over to the Bedlam asylum, and check you in."

Noah shudders to think of the horrors suffered there by London's madmen. "You can't make mirth of that place." He thinks a moment. "So, he's not one of Essex's men?"

Henry seems a bit surprised by the question, and he equivocates. "Well, I suppose, in a sense he *is* Essex's man."

Just then, Noah's horse is brought around. He places pen, ink, and a few papers in the saddlebag, ties it shut, and mounts with one quick motion. He takes a moment to steady the horse's nerves, and sidles up to Henry. Together, they turn about and move south toward the end of Gray's Inn Lane.

As they're about to turn toward Ludgate, Noah asks, "Where are we meeting Doctor Lopez?"

"Well, Lopez lives right here," says Henry, pointing to Mountjoy's Inn, which practically abuts Gray's Inn.

"Then why are we on horseback?"

Henry laughs. "The good doctor keeps a place at St. Katharine Creechurch, north of the Tower. It's where he does his odd business, where he keeps certain … friends, living and dead. That's where we're meeting him."

"I see. But if I may return to our former topic," says Noah, "you said that the fellow in brown riding clothes was Essex's man — "

"I said he was *Bacon's* man. But Essex and Bacon *are* very closely allied nowadays. Anthony Bacon wants very much to be Attorney General, and Essex is quite influential with the Queen."

Noah is confused. "Last I heard, the office of Attorney General is currently occupied. Besides, I thought the Bacon brothers were related to the Cecils, who are known to be at *odds* with Essex."

"They are, in fact. The Bacons are nephews to William Cecil, Lord Burghley, who is both Lord High Treasurer and the father of Sir Robert Cecil, Secretary of State."

"But if Essex and the Cecils *agree* that Anthony Bacon should be Attorney General, then surely he would be appointed."

"So it seems," mused Henry, "as the Queen relies on Essex and the Cecils, and they agree on so little. But, alas, the Cecils are standing in Bacon's way."

"Why?"

"Probably because Lord Burghley wishes his young son Sir Robert to take over his place eventually, and would prefer that Sir Robert have no competition. That's why he asked the Queen to appoint Sir Robert to take over as Secretary of State after Walsingham. Unfortunately, Sir Robert has never really got his hands around Walsingham's spy network, as nobody's sure what happened to his files upon his death."

"To a layman such as I, all these family relations among the powerful sound a bit like nepotism."

Henry laughs. "Noah, even the English *monarchy* is hereditary. But it's much worse than you think. For example, Sir Robert Cecil is married to my wife's cousin."

"So, you are related to Sir Robert Cecil … and his father Lord Burghley … and therefore the Bacons, as well!"

Henry smirks. "You have a mind like a Hebrew scholar, Noah, never knowing when to stop." Noah suppresses the fear of discovery that shoots through him. Henry's keen intelligence sometimes brings him fearfully close to discovering the secret of Noah's faith.

"Of course," Henry resumes, "even leaving Sir Robert aside, there's another reason not to appoint Anthony Bacon as Attorney General. He's not a well man."

Noah shakes his head. "No, indeed. He suffers from the most vicious kidney stones. If you've ever seen him suffer an attack, you'll never forget it."

"Essex and the Cecils are at odds over *everything*," says Henry, "especially relations with Spain. Burghley is for eventual peace."

"And Essex for perpetual war, no doubt."

Henry nods. "More or less."

"So the Cecils cannot stomach Essex."

Henry half smiles. "*No* one can stomach Essex, except the Queen."

"Why does she have a soft spot for him?"

Henry smirks. "Perhaps you'll ask her someday." They reach Ludgate, and pass through in single file.

Noah breaks the silence. "What of Anthony's younger brother, Francis?"

"Francis Bacon may be the most intelligent man you will ever meet. Far surpasses Anthony, but — " Henry pauses, evidently unsure how to continue.

"But?"

"Well, he's a friend of … Marlowe, y'know."

"Marlowe?" Noah cocks his head. "How do you mean?"

"*You* know … *Marlowe*?" Henry moves his hand down to arse level and makes a squeezing motion.

"Oh … *that!*"

"Yes, *that*. Although the Queen couldn't care less about 'that,' she draws the line when it comes to children."

"Oh," Noah's face sours. "Not *children*!"

"Well, I can't say for sure, but Francis is certainly acquiring a reputation on that account."

They turn onto Paternoster Street and pass St. Paul's Cathedral in silence. Well-dressed, grave-looking people are leaving Sunday morning service, eying these two irreligious horsemen suspiciously.

As Noah and Henry move onto Newgate Street, Henry appears to equivocate on some important question, then make up his mind. "I'm going to tell you something because you may eventually need to know." He glances at Noah, and then faces front once more. "You know, if you carry this 'Essex's man' business too far, you're going to oversimplify the world at court. Many people have one foot in each camp. Some people have one foot at court, and the other in another *country*."

"What are you saying, Henry?"

"Don't go dividing up the world into two camps. Court is more a free-for-all, with constantly shifting alliances of convenience, or, as I like to say, of 'commodity.'"

"Does this have any bearing on what we're doing this morning?"

"Oh, yes," Henry laughs darkly. "You do know that Doctor Lopez was on the English Armada expedition?"

"In which capacity? Ship's doctor? Portuguese ambassador?"

As they pull up to the chapel at St. Katharine Creechurch and prepare to dismount, Henry looks Noah square in the eye. "While he was both of those things, he was also a principal investor." Henry holds his fingers to his lips and arches an eyebrow. This is a strange secret. Noah has no idea what to make of it, but he has no hesitation in agreeing not to tell anyone.

Henry dismounts, huffing and puffing. "Really must do something about my weight. I'm afraid I'll cleave my horse in twain if I continue to gain." He feeds a treat to his horse, whose tail swishes in satisfaction.

Noah ties off his own horse. For a fleeting moment, he considers removing the papers from his saddlebag and safeguarding them on his person, but decides against it, as they consist merely of scribe's copies, neither irreplaceable nor particularly sensitive. "Oh, I don't know," he says. "Your mount seems well pleased to carry you."

"He is but young."

As they walk toward the chapel where Lopez keeps his professional quarters, they notice a well-appointed carriage sitting there all the while, with a driver in attendance. The driver opens the door, and out steps the widow, looking grave but ravishingly beautiful.

Henry leans toward Noah. "She beat us here. Look sharp, counsel."

CHAPTER 5

AS THE WIDOW PROCEEDS dolefully toward the chapel entrance, Noah approaches her. Although she has not yet had time to acquire widow's weeds, she wears a thin black veil. "Good morning, madam," he says softly. "I hope you slept reasonably well."

She offers him a half smile. Close up, he can detect the strain in her face. "In truth, I've passed better nights, Master Ames." Spotting Henry, she says, "Master Neville."

"Goodwife Rodriguez," Henry nods. "Have you family at home to help you?"

"Yes, I do, thank the Lord. I have two sons and a daughter, although they are as shocked as I. Fortunately, they have had the presence of mind to do the necessary to sustain life … such as it is." The sadness wells up in her eyes. "Shall we go in?"

Noah knows it would be foolhardy to suggest, however courteously, that her femininity might render her unsuited to the coming task, but he feels he must say something.

"Are you quite sure you're feeling up to this?" he asks apologetically.

"Are *you*?" she asks Noah, one eyebrow raised.

Henry replies for him. "Master Ames means no disrespect, madam. He and I are accustomed to matters such as this, he being a lawyer, and I a justice of the peace."

"Oh? You are a *JP*, in addition to an *MP*?" she asks, evidently recalling that Henry is a Member of Parliament.

"Yes, madam. I serve as a justice of the peace in Berkshire. Our ancestral home near Windsor is known as 'Billingbear.' Perhaps you've heard of it."

"I have, indeed," she says with what small enthusiasm she can muster. "It is reputed to be a socially lively, and very welcoming, place. You should be most proud."

"Thank you, madam." He smiles sympathetically.

As the widow appears quite determined, Noah offers his crooked elbow. "Shall we go inside?"

She takes Noah's arm, lending him an intimate, though forced, smile. The chapel door stands open, and they enter arm in arm. Henry follows close behind, eying the church grounds discreetly.

Lopez awaits them in the central aisle, dressed in coroner's robes and carrying a small black bag with leather handles, presumably for his professional instruments. "Goodwife Rodriguez, I was not expecting you. Once again, please accept my condolences for your loss." She extends her hand. He takes it gently and bows, studying her expression. "Madam, I had intended to show the cause of death to these gentlemen, as they have need to see it. For your purposes, however, I can simply *describe* the cause of death for you here, rather than show it to you. Perhaps it would be best to send your eldest son to identify the remains."

"You are bringing these two gentlemen down to see the wound?"

"Yes," he replies somberly, obviously hoping she will wait in the chapel.

She inhales and exhales deeply. "I will accompany them."

Lopez looks to the two men. Seeing no objection, he turns again to the widow. "Very well, then. Please follow me." He turns smartly and walks at a moderate pace to the rear of the chapel, where a wooden door leads down rustic stone steps.

He lifts a small torch from the wall and turns. "Please watch your step, and hold firmly to the railing. The steps are quite old, and the railing is much more reliable." He descends the staircase, which is only wide enough to permit them to pass singly. Lopez is followed by Henry, then the widow, and finally Noah.

Reaching the base of the stairs, the doctor leads them into a small chamber with an earthen floor and walls of coarse ancient stonework. Although brightly lit by two torches, and redolent of the incense that burns in one corner, the chamber nevertheless retains the cool dampness natural to its subterranean location, and emits a vague combination of odors strongly suggesting the persistent presence of death.

At the center of the room, which is barely large enough to hold them all, stands a wheeled cot, upon which lies a gray sheet atop the corpse. The body is evidently lying on its back, as a bump in the sheet reveals the location of the nose. Noah sees the widow shrink back at the sight, and supports her firmly about the shoulders lest she swoon.

Lopez turns to address them as though a small class of students, clearly respectful of the mortal remains about which he will now hold forth.

"Goodman Rodriguez was a man about forty years old, in very good physical condition. But for the fatal attack upon his person, I expect he would have lived well into old age. I found no sign of heart disease, gout, or any of the myriad other ailments that often accompany high living and advancing age." He pauses to look at the widow, who seems to be holding up fairly well so far. "The cause of death was the violent insertion of a sharp instrument above the right eye that caused him to expire instantly." He lowers his voice reassuringly, and addresses the widow. "He did not suffer, madam. It was over in an instant."

"How can you be certain he died immediately?"

"His heart must have stopped immediately, as there was very little blood. If he had lived for any duration, a wound so deep as this would have resulted in massive blood loss, which would have been evident at the scene. As I personally attended at the scene, I have no doubt that death was instantaneous. Also, from Lord Essex's description of the event, the deceased fell immediately and never again moved. This is all consistent with sudden death. I will now reveal the portion of the face affected by the blow."

The widow does not turn away, although the doctor waits another moment for her to do so. He deftly moves a small corner of the sheet to reveal the eyes from temple to temple. Noah marvels how concealment of the rest of the face makes it possible for the widow to observe without recoiling in horror.

Even regarded clinically, however, this is a grievous wound. The eyeball has been crushed beyond recognition. A yellow fluid, now caked, has evidently leaked out of it, dripping across the bridge of the victim's nose, pooling on his closed left eyelid, and continuing toward the left temple. Although there is small sign of blood, the tiny flow out of the wound has forked into two small rivulets, one mixing with the yellow fluid, the other running in a very thin line across the eyebrow toward the forehead.

Lopez draws a small ruler from his breast pocket and places it vertically by the right temple to demonstrate the depth of the wound. "The lethal instrument was what the Italians call a 'stiletto,' roughly resembling an ice pick. I estimate that the instrument penetrated about four inches into the brain in less than one second." He applies his index finger to the ruler to indicate the point of deepest penetration.

Noah senses the widow's legs beginning to give way at last. He supports her firmly. Although he admires her courage, he expects that, if he had been in her position, he would have rested with a verbal explanation delivered upstairs in the chapel. This really is too much for anyone in her position to bear.

Lopez also notices her swoon. "Madam, there is really nothing more to be learned here."

"I'm not leaving yet. Allow me to identify the body." She braces herself. "I am prepared." Tears well up in her eyes.

After a brief hesitation, Lopez reluctantly pulls the sheet down, revealing Rodriguez's whole face, which is undamaged but for the fatal wound. She looks for a moment, then winces and buries her face in Noah's chest. "That's him," she blurts.

"Have we finished our business?" asks Noah curtly.

Lopez nods.

"Then, let's get out of this awful place."

Noah assists the widow in climbing the uneven stairs ahead of the others. As they reach the top, he can hear Lopez splashing his hands with a liquid smelling strongly of spirits. Noah seats the widow in the foremost pew of the chapel, and draws up a wooden chair for himself. "While I cannot be certain, this has every appearance of a professional assassination. I strongly doubt that the assailant was attempting to rob your husband. To the contrary, the 'robbery' appears to have been a mere feint intended to mislead investigators. Would you accompany me to Gray's Inn, where I can introduce you to the young lawyer I think would be ideal for this prosecution?"

She looks into his eyes, in evident anguish. "Oh, Master Ames. I would much prefer a more mature man such as yourself to handle this."

Noah hesitates a moment, contemplating the inevitable legal issues to be presented by his continuing involvement in the investigation. "I'll ask this young lawyer, whose name is Master Hawking, to keep me abreast of the case. Would that suit you?"

"Have I no choice in the matter?"

"You have *every* choice as to which lawyer to retain, other than myself. Regrettably, for a variety of legal reasons I can explain whenever you wish, it is poor practice for a lawyer to undertake the prosecution of a crime that he himself has witnessed."

"Very well, then," she says, closing her eyes. When she reopens them, they glisten with tears. "Would you escort me to my carriage? I would like a few moments alone. I shall meet you at Gray's Inn within the hour. Would that be agreeable?"

"Of course it would," he assures her, and escorts her to her carriage, gently situating her inside. The driver nods sharply to Noah and shakes the reins. Noah stands before the chapel, watching the carriage draw slowly away and recede into the distance.

Henry steps out of the chapel and pats him on the shoulder. "She'll recover."

"What did Lopez say?" asks Noah.

"More secrets. They shall remain between us?"

"Of course."

"Lopez said that the man who did this had almost certainly been in Walsingham's service."

"How would Lopez know the murderer once worked for Walsingham?"

"He is familiar with some of their methods, as *he* worked for Walsingham. And, remember, as the deceased Master Rodriguez was holding a note in Walsingham's hand, he was likely working for Walsingham, as well."

"Good Lord! Did *everyone* work for Walsingham?" Noah blurts in exasperation.

Henry looks around evasively, but his gaze eventually lands back on Noah's amazed countenance.

"*You?*" says Noah, in startled disbelief.

"Yet more secrets." Henry nods. "Yes ... and for a long time. You must understand, Noah. When Walsingham yet lived — and he died only two years ago — the Privy Council was not divided into factions as it is now. If Walsingham wanted your help, you gave it without hesitation, and without much concern that someone else might object. There was a feeling then that we were all on the same side." He smiles wistfully. Evidently, there is no longer such a feeling of unity. "Anyway, my friend — and confidant — I must prepare for a business meeting tomorrow, to be followed by attendance at Parliament."

"I don't suppose any of you surviving Walsingham alumni have any idea who committed this murder?"

Henry's face turns grim, and he stares at the horizon. "No, and I expect that finding out shall cost us dearly ... all of us." Henry hugs him, mounts his horse with some difficulty, and rides off toward Lothbury.

The churchyard is desolate and the clouds threaten as Noah returns to his horse and impulsively checks his saddlebag. The knot is secure, and he's pleased to see no sign of any attempt to gain access to his papers.

Just as he is about to mount, something thick and leathery strikes him hard on the back of the neck. Stunned, he topples sideways and feels a pair of strong hands lower him to the ground. As the world spins out of control and then turns black, he catches the briefest glimpse of highly polished gold.

*   *   *

Somewhere close by, a horse chuffs impatiently. As Noah opens his eyes and looks around, the overcast sky seems impossibly bright, and the back of his neck throbs mercilessly. Slowly, he begins to realize that he's been bludgeoned. There is no sign of anyone.

Still on the ground, he reaches his hand carefully around to the back of his head. Nothing sticky. He brings the hand back to his face. No blood. Well, that's a mercy.

The horse clops impatiently in place. As his eyes adjust to the daylight again, he realizes that nothing in the churchyard has changed, so that he cannot have been unconscious for more than a few minutes. He has the uncomfortable feeling that his eyes are bugging out of his head, as though he has the worst hangover of his life. As he rises, the pounding in his neck makes him gasp aloud.

He looks at his saddlebag once again, and the knot remains secure. He feels for Uncle Avram's knife in his robe. Still there. He glances around warily as he unties the knot on the saddlebag and makes a cursory examination of the papers. Just as he left them.

Nausea wells up in his throat, and his forehead grows moist with sweat. He places his hand up against the horse, and lowers his head to vomit, but nothing happens. He shakes off the feeling, unties the horse, and mounts. Once again, his neck reminds him that he's been struck hard. He groans as he grabs the reins and directs the horse slowly back toward Gray's Inn, lost in solitary thought broken only by an occasional twinge induced by the horse's jostling.

There are so many possible explanations for this assault. It might have been a robbery. He reaches his hand into his robe. His purse is still there, and jingles when he shakes it. No robbery.

If the assailant didn't want the papers, and didn't want his purse, then what was the point of the assault? Perhaps the assailant was searching for papers that turned out not to be in the saddlebag. That would mean that the assailant opened the saddlebag, whether before or after the assault, and knotted it again precisely as Noah had originally done. It would have been no great feat, as Noah had used the simplest of knots. In fact, Noah had *tied* the knot for the sole purpose of enabling him to detect later whether it had been *untied*.

One thing seems clear: the assailant did not intend to inflict any lasting damage on Noah's person (at least for the present), as he assisted Noah to the ground, preventing any further injury from his fall. He shivers to think that the assailant could have killed him just as easily as he clubbed him.

The possibility remains that this was a warning. By whom? About what? He recalls seeing the glint of gold as he lost consciousness, and now connects it with the gold hilt of the ceremonial sword carried by Essex's page at The Rose. As the page was standing at the door awaiting Essex when the murder took place, he is one of very few people with reason to believe that Noah knows Essex lied about witnessing the murder.

Is the widow in danger? While Noah wishes to keep the assault upon himself secret for the time being, if his silence will enhance her jeopardy, his conscience forbids it. With this worrisome thought, he shakes the reins, picking up the pace in the hope that he'll be waiting at the inn by the time she arrives.

Pulling up to the inn just as it begins to drizzle, he feels sure that a downpour will soon come. He removes the papers from his saddlebag, places them in his pocket, hands off his mount to the stable boy, and goes indoors. He checks his appearance in the looking glass in the foyer, brushes a few leaves out of his hair and off his robe, and smooths back his hair. He's started to feel better, as well, except for the occasional throb in his neck.

He finds Jonathan in his apartment, deep in study, precisely as he left him, although the stack of unopened files now appears noticeably shorter. Just as Noah is about to make Jonathan aware of his presence, he hears both the downpour and the widow's carriage arriving outside.

He strides quickly to the entryway. Through the windows, he can see the widow, no longer veiled, flying up the outside stairs to escape the gale, and the driver quickly slamming the carriage door shut, holding a cloak above his head for what little protection it offers.

As Noah opens the door, Goodwife Rodriguez runs heedlessly into his arms, startling them both. A strong draft of wet wind follows her into the inn and blows her hair forward around her shapely cheeks. Their faces nearly touching, they look into each other's eyes for a long moment, her sweet breath striking his senses as some natural perfume. Although Noah does his best to seem embarrassed, in truth he is tempted to hold her to his body and kiss her on the mouth. Instead, he stands her firmly on her own feet and takes a step back.

"Oh, I *am* sorry," he says. "I'm so *clumsy* sometimes! Please let me take your wet things."

She seems nonplussed for a moment, then quickly recovers and removes her wet cape and hat, handing them to Noah. "Not at all, Master Ames. It was *I* who nearly ran *you* down, not you me."

Noah carefully hangs her wet garments from pegs in the vestibule, spreading them out to give them plenty of air to dry.

"There," he says, "now come meet Master Hawking." As he escorts her to Jonathan's apartment, he notices that the floorboards squeak heavily under his own footfalls, but only slightly under her delicate steps.

He knocks on the open door, and sticks his head through the doorway. "Jonathan?" Jonathan looks up, and smiles expectantly. "I have with me Goodwife Rodriguez, of whom I told you." As she steps into the room, Noah is surprised to see that she once again wears her veil.

Jonathan's eyes open wide. "Oh! Well!" he blurts, rising to clear off two seats this time. "Welcome, Goodwife Rodriguez. I am so sorry to hear of your loss. I expect Master Ames has told you something about me?" He offers the cushioned chair to the lady, while Noah settles for the same creaky one he used on his previous visit.

She sits daintily in the proffered chair in what strikes Noah as a suitable pose for a portrait, a pretty one at that. "Master Ames has told me only that he greatly respects your dedication and intelligence."

"Well, that's excessively kind of Master Ames, I assure you. But I will do my best to get justice in your cause, if you will have me."

Noah sits quietly as Jonathan conducts a prolonged and thoughtful interview of the widow, grateful for the respite, as it gives the throbbing in his neck a further opportunity to recede. At Jonathan's prompting, she goes step by step through the murder and its aftermath, briefly relates everything she told Rodriguez in the hearse, and ends by recounting Noah's pronouncement that her husband's murder was an assassination, not a failed robbery. She makes mention of neither Walsingham's note found in her husband's purse, nor the falsity of Essex's claim to have witnessed the murder. Noah assumes she knows nothing of either.

"So, you were with Master Ames and Master Neville at the … viewing?"

"I was. It was gruesome, but I thought I owed it to my late husband to see it through."

"Commendable. Do you have any suspicion as to who might have done this?"

Noah's ears perk up at this. The widow hesitates, studying her hands, which now work nervously against each other in her lap. She looks up with eyes as wide as innocence, and shakes her head: "I'm sure I have no idea." Her gaze returns to her hands. "If I think of anything else, however, I shall be sure to let you know."

Noah readily recognizes that averted gaze, having seen it on hundreds of witnesses who were withholding something important. He wonders whether it is as obvious to Jonathan, but lets it pass for the moment.

"Very well," says Jonathan, standing up and offering his hand to the widow.

She rises hesitantly. Before Jonathan can raise the question of payment, she says, "Please be sure to send your debit note to my home. I shall pay it at first opportunity."

"We barristers are permitted to accept payment only from a referring solicitor or attorney," Jonathan replies. "Since Master Ames is a barrister, as am I, I propose that you and I deal through Attorney Thistlethwaite, who maintains an office just across the way. I shall instruct him to submit his debit note to you. I will be sure to see a copy."

"Attorney *Thistlethwaite*?"

"Yes," he replies gravely, relieved to avoid further discussion of legal fees with a grieving widow. "He will need to know where you live, of course."

"Quite near here," she says, and draws a calling card from her purse. She writes her residence address on the reverse side and hands it to Jonathan.

"Holborn?" He looks up at her in surprise. "Why, this address is in sight of this inn!"

"So it is," she replies. "That's why I felt free to send my driver home."

Noah speaks up. "With your permission, Master Hawking, I shall escort Goodwife Rodriguez home. She has already had a very hard day."

"Thank you, Master Ames. I was going to volunteer for that privilege, but I really should be attending to pressing matters."

Noah and Goodwife Rodriguez leave Jonathan's room together, treading the same creaky floorboards they traversed on their way in, and return to the vestibule. Noah carefully removes each of her wet things from the pegs on which he hung them, and assays their dampness.

"Well, they're a *bit* better than before," he says. "Shall we try them out?"

Goodwife Rodriguez nods, and dons her cape. Feeling the dampness in her hat, however, she peers outdoors, apparently weighing whether to put it on. A few rays of sun have struggled through the overcast, and it is no longer raining. She carries the hat in her hand.

Noah extends his arm, which she gratefully accepts. They pass Mountjoy's Inn, which Henry earlier identified as Lopez's residence. It's a new three-story building constructed in the fashionable style of the day. Window boxes have been added to the exterior as a welcoming touch, but nothing flowers there in winter.

They turn right onto High Holborn, and walk past several conjoined houses, all in very good condition, with well-maintained lawns. To Noah, the neighborhood confers a feeling of steadfast financial security, while avoiding the ostentation visible in the wealthiest areas of London.

"Have you family, Master Ames?"

"Oh, please call me 'Noah.' 'Master Ames' is generally reserved for people in the process of dressing me down for one reason or another." He purses his lips and puckers up his face, imitating a stodgy man twice his age. In as pinched a voice as he can muster, he says: "'Can you provide the Court with one good reason you should not be held in contempt,'" he looks at her bug-eyed, "'... *Master Ames*?'"

She laughs despite herself.

"Well, I shall be careful to avoid addressing you as 'Master Ames,' at least until you deserve it. In turn, you must call me 'Marie.'" She reframes her former question. "Have you any family, *Noah*?"

He sighs wistfully. "I have a grown daughter. She is … let's see … twenty-four years old now, married."

"Has she a name?"

"Who?"

"Your *daughter*."

"She has."

Apparently unsure what to make of this reticence, the widow moves to another topic. "Have you a wife?"

"No," he shakes his head sadly. "I did, but she left us some years ago."

"She has passed?"

He nods.

"I'm so sorry for your loss."

"As am I for yours." He is touched that this woman, so recently widowed herself, is moved to console him for a loss suffered at such a remote time.

They walk down another seven or eight doors, and turn onto a cul-de-sac dominated by one large free-standing house on the right. "This is it," she announces.

Surprised, he beholds her house in daylight for the first time. For some reason, he finds it difficult to believe that this is the same house at which the hearse dropped her off only the previous evening. He realizes now that he has been so entranced by her appearance, her voice, her sheer *presence*, that he's quite lost track of the nearness of her house to his own lodgings at Gray's Inn.

"Would you like to come in for a moment? I must forewarn you that my children are all here, to lend comfort."

"Perhaps another time. I expect they will not take kindly to meeting a strange man at a time such as this. There is a natural closing-in of the family upon such occasions."

The door opens, and a handsome young man of about twenty sticks his head out. "Mother, Uncle Horace has arrived, and wishes to speak with you."

She smiles at Noah. "I'd better go," she says, her gloved hand grazing his. She turns to the stairs, and her demeanor changes at once. "Uncle Horace, eh?" she pronounces gruffly, lifting her skirts up off the pavement and staunchly climbing the stairs to the entrance. She strides straight into the house past the young man, who nods respectfully to Noah and quietly closes the door. Noah is glad not to be Uncle Horace.

On his way back to Gray's Inn, he spots the man he suspects of being a spy for Anthony Bacon standing by the same oak on the square. No longer wearing riding clothes, he is now expensively dressed, and is looking in the same general direction as this morning.

As Noah passes within fifty feet of the man, a few things occur to him. First, the man is not looking at him, in fact seems heedless of his presence, making no attempt to conceal himself. Second, the man stands only fifty feet or so from Anthony Bacon's window at Gray's Inn, but the object of his interest, which is now somewhere behind Noah, would not be visible from Bacon's window, which might explain why he is standing outside, instead of peering out from the relative comfort of Bacon's apartment.

If the man knows of Noah's bludgeoning, surely he would have taken precautions to conceal himself, and would have been startled to find himself discovered by Noah. Instead, he seems completely oblivious. Nevertheless, Noah cannot entirely discount the possibility that this man and the assailant are involved in different spokes of the same conspiracy.

Preoccupied with these uneasy thoughts, he goes inside and climbs the stairs to his room. As he empties his pockets, he comes across the papers he removed from his saddlebag, and places them face down on the desk. Turning away, something about the papers catches his eye, causing him to turn back at once.

At first he has to squint to see it, but there, at the bottom of the unused side of the last sheet, in a tiny, unfamiliar handwriting, are two words in Latin. He checks the rest of the papers, confirming his recollection that the scribe wrote on only one side of each sheet. Indeed, the small inscription is the only writing to appear on the reverse side of any sheet. And he is certain it was not there when he packed the papers in his saddlebag this morning. No, this writing was applied by the assailant, either before or after the assault.

Caveat causidicus, reads the tiny inscription. He silently translates.

Let the lawyer beware!

He grabs the papers and flies down the stairs, where he's relieved to find Jonathan's door open and the young man still at his desk. In his urgency, Noah knocks louder than intended, which startles his young friend, whose initial annoyance drops away immediately upon seeing Noah's expression.

"Good Lord!" Jonathan exclaims. "You look as though you've fled a ghost!"

Noah closes the door behind him and assumes his accustomed chair, breathing heavily, sweat forming on his brow. "I must speak with you at once."

Jonathan is amazed, and quietly alarmed. "Catch your breath," he says. "I trust the inn is not on fire."

"No," says Noah, unsure how to begin. "You know I attended the autopsy at Creechurch earlier today?"

Jonathan nods.

"Well, I haven't yet told you what happened afterwards in the churchyard, after the widow left in her carriage and Henry Neville rode away."

"What happened?"

"I was bludgeoned into unconsciousness."

"Ah, *yes!*" he exclaims, rising from his chair. "I don't know what to say! I *thought* there was something amiss with you during the interview. You seemed very ill at ease."

Noah relates the facts of the assault to Jonathan. "And, when I returned here to the inn, before surrendering my mount I pocketed the papers that were in the saddlebag. Just now, I was removing them from my pocket, when I noticed an inscription on the back of one of the pages that was not there when I packed them this morning." He hands the papers to Jonathan, pointing out the inscription. "Take a look!"

Jonathan holds the inscription close to his face. "*Caveat causidicus,*" he reads aloud, and looks gravely at Noah. "And you're quite sure nothing was taken? No papers, no money?" Noah shakes his head. "And the assailant deliberately broke your fall?" Noah nods. "Most curious!" There is a moment of silence while Jonathan stares out of the window, gathering his thoughts. "What do you think?" Jonathan asks.

"I think someone is warding me away from representing the widow in investigating her husband's murder. The irony is that I have no intention of representing her."

With trepidation, Jonathan says, "No, but *I* have."

"Yes," says Noah. "And you are likewise *causidicus*. Indeed, the inn is *full* of *causidici*." Noah accepts the papers back. "The more I contemplate this inscription, the more I believe it to have been carefully drafted. The warning might have been crafted to address only me, for example, if it had simply said 'caveat.' But instead it is directed more generally to an unnamed lawyer, presumably any lawyer who accepts to represent the widow in this matter. And by characterizing the object of the warning as a lawyer, the inscription implies that the person being warned is *not* the client. So the client may be safe. Or more precisely, the assailant wants us to think so."

"Us?"

"Jonathan, there is no reason to think that this inscription is not equally directed at *you*, and there can be little question that *you* are in as much danger as I!"

"But why should this case be more dangerous than another?"

Noah equivocates a moment, then makes up his mind. "I have no choice but to tell you something which must remain a secret from all others for the time being. Are you prepared?"

Jonathan's expression is both confused and grim. "Quite."

"When the Earl of Essex told the constable that he saw the murder, he was *lying*!"

"Why do you suspect he was lying?"

"I don't *suspect* it. I know it to be true. So does Henry Neville. When the fight broke out, we were walking past the theater door where Essex would eventually exit. Essex's page was standing across that very doorway with one hand on his golden hilt. Essex hadn't yet emerged. In fact, he was in a windowless area of the theater at the time of the murder, and so *could not* have seen it."

Jonathan is amazed. "But that means ... that Essex knew the murder would take place, and that he approved of it ... and was prepared to lie to cover it up."

Noah and Jonathan agree that, although it still seems possible for the widow to drop the investigation entirely for her personal safety (to say nothing of Noah's and Jonathan's), there can be no assurance that her doing so will render her or her investigators any safer. To the contrary, Essex's mere *suspicion* of an ongoing investigation might make her a target for murder, which seems especially plausible given that Stephen's murder might have been committed to cut off the mere *possibility* of his releasing confidential information.

Furthermore, even if dropping the investigation were to result in the widow's perfect safety (which there's no way to know), she's made clear that she's simply not prepared to give up without a fight.

If Essex were of neither note nor name, of course, they could simply interrogate him, but that would not be possible with an earl, especially one who is also a military hero, to say nothing of a member of the Privy Council, and, worst of all, the Queen's favorite.

Although in theory Queen's Bench, the ancient court entrusted with trial of serious crimes, draws no distinction among Englishmen, in actual practice the gap between its treatment of someone of Essex's stature and an ordinary English subject is an unbridgeable chasm.

Noah and Jonathan agree that there is simply no way of avoiding the established technique for investigating a peer of the Crown, which is from the bottom up. Yet, to employ this method, they need to identify Essex's complicit underlings and, at this point, they know of none.

"From now on," says Noah, "I want all of us to exercise the utmost care. The inn is probably safe for now. As far as I know, even Henry the Eighth did not violate the sanctity of the Inns of Court. But the widow is another story. Jonathan, first thing tomorrow morning, I want you personally to warn her and her footman that she may be in danger from the same possible conspiracy that resulted in her husband's murder, and that neither she nor her children must ever be alone without an adult male escort, discreetly armed. If at any time her male servant must leave her side, please make sure you have someone at the ready to take his place. Needless to say, you are to make no mention of Essex." He scratches his head. "Who's your best man for the job?"

"Graves," replies Jonathan without hesitation. "He's the smartest by far, and plenty rough in a pinch." He smiles. "He's much more than an investigator. He's like family to me. Been with me twenty years, and I wouldn't want to count how many meals I've eaten when he was too careful to let me know there wasn't enough for two."

"Sounds like you're quite fond of him, but are you equally sure of his skills?"

"Have no fear," replies Jonathan. "He's the best. But to put your mind at ease, I'll have an additional man at the ready to back him up, if need be."

Noah nods grimly.

"What's wrong?" asks Jonathan. "That ought to be enough to provide us all with some peace of mind. No?"

Noah considers the question for a moment, and replies darkly.

"As much peace of mind as one can find sitting on a powder keg."

CHAPTER 6

ALTHOUGH JONATHAN IMMEDIATELY APPOINTED his best man, Graves, to track down the murderer of Stephen Rodriguez, four weeks later the investigation has failed to progress. The trail, if there ever was one, has grown cold, as though the nameless assailant appeared out of nowhere, committed his heinous crime, and escaped to the nowhere from whence he'd come. Of necessity, Jonathan and Noah have shifted their attention to other cases.

Now, on a Wednesday morning, they sit at defense table in a large oak-appointed courtroom at Westminster Hall devoted exclusively to serious crimes, awaiting resumption of the Crown's case in a murder trial at Queen's Bench. Noah can tell by the slant of the sun's rays that the judge is already tardy in assuming the bench, no doubt because Crown Prosecutor Edward Coke will be late and has so advised the Court.

"Coke is cooking up a witness," he says to Jonathan. "If I'm right, this could be an interesting morning for our side." Jonathan smiles in return, but says nothing.

Jonathan has become a regular second chair to Noah, and the arrangement has worked well for them both. Noah's practical skills are supported by Jonathan's legal acumen, but even more so by the quality of his preparation, which far surpasses that of any solicitor (or barrister) Noah has encountered. For Jonathan's part, he's learning how to win a case at court, a skill that can somehow elude even the best law student for an entire career.

"There's *company*," says Jonathan, glancing up at the spectators' gallery. "And evidently, *we're* the entertainment."

Searching through his papers, Noah asks, "Anyone interesting?"

"Doesn't look that way." Jonathan sighs wistfully. "Too bad this is not the theater, where one of the gods might appear 'out of the machine' to assist us in solving the Rodriguez case."

Noah smirks, and glances up at the gallery. "*Deus ex machina?* Oh, never seek for that! For when a god makes a personal appearance, he does so strictly for his own purposes. The hero is never more than a pawn to the gods, and quite often ends up dead."

"Cheery this morning, are we?"

Except in the most sensational cases, the spectators' gallery, which could easily hold fifty, remains vacant. This morning, there are twenty people there. At least three are sound asleep. Periodically, an old man wakes with a start from the sound of his own snort, eyes darting about suspiciously, as though someone may be having him on by dropping a heavy book whenever he dozes off. Among the remaining spectators are at least two rustic men in Sunday-best raiment (probably friends of the victim), one veiled widow, and four important-looking gentlemen occupying varying degrees of lesser nobility. Some spectators are indistinctly dressed, members of the common public often referred to as the "great unwashed."

Seven of the spectators, all wide awake, are young barristers who have come to watch Noah practice the art for which he has become best known throughout the Inns of Court, namely, cross-examination.

The interest of the young barristers in the spectators' gallery has been further piqued by knowledge that the Crown is being represented by Coke, who, if rumor is any guide, is about to be appointed Solicitor General for England and Wales. Most fun of all is promised by his reputation for showing the greatest disdain for his every adversary, as though any client of the great Edward Coke obviously *deserves* to prevail, so that anything accomplished by his adversary cannot possibly amount to more than an antic, a mere dilatory bump in the road to Coke's inevitable victory.

Coke's main weakness, surprising for a barrister so expert in trial procedure, is that he's extraordinarily thin-skinned. On the few occasions when he's faced Noah in the courtroom, Noah has got the better of him by engaging in understated ridicule, a practice coming naturally to Noah, and for which Coke provides the perfect foil. Although the younger barristers have insisted that it is Noah's principal object to send Coke into a red-faced fit, which nearly always happens, Noah has denied it, claiming that he is simply doing everything he can do within the bounds of the law to enhance the likelihood of acquittal. As Noah would explain it, Coke's predictable paroxysms of choler are just a side benefit.

In this trial, Noah's client, Jack Granger, is a grain exporter accused of murdering a complete stranger with a cudgel on a wheat field near the Granger home, just before harvest this past September. Unbeknownst to Noah and Jonathan, however, because Granger has persuaded several former Walsingham agents to decline enlistment in Essex's spy network, Essex is determined to have Granger's head on a platter — and intends to use this trial as the means to obtain it.

Yesterday's proceedings consisted of testimony by the local constable concerning the finding of the body, and by the coroner concerning the manner and time of death and the degree of pain likely suffered by the victim. Thus far, the Crown has called no witness placing the accused at the scene of the crime and, based upon the sequence of Crown witnesses so far, Noah strongly suspects that Coke can produce no credible witness to bear that burden.

As it has been established that there were no witnesses located near the assailant and victim at the time of the murder, Noah has instructed Jonathan to bring to court a few items that might come in handy in impeaching anyone falsely claiming to have witnessed the crime from afar.

The entry door swings open, and in strides Coke, a handsome figure, followed by his mousy-looking clerk and a well-dressed man of swinish features who appears to be furtively counting something off on his fingers. Coke, assuming the lectern beside Crown table, theatrically bangs a fat book down on it, and the blow resounds through the courtroom like a cannon shot.

Jonathan appears startled. "You know who that is?" he whispers. "It's Gelly Meyrick."

"Who's that?" whispers Noah.

"Lord Essex's principal attendant," Jonathan observes. "By his appearance here, it's a good bet Essex wants our client convicted."

Noah's mind races. *Why would Essex care about a murder on a farm? Unless … unless he has a grudge against Granger. Or could his grudge be against me?* Either way, this trial is about to proceed. His pulse pounds in his ears.

The heavy door leading from the judge's chambers booms three times, struck from the opposite side by the heel of a powerful bailiff's staff. "Oyez, oyez, oyez!" cries the bailiff through the closed door. Everyone jumps to his feet. The door swings open on the silent courtroom.

There, in no apparent haste, slouches old Lord Bleffingham, squinting as though he's been left in the dark a long time, his wig slightly askew, his head bowed at the neck. He gazes first at Crown table, and then defense table, a momentary frown of irritation passing over his face. Looking down at his judicial robe, he brushes away a tiny piece of white lint, and steps hesitantly over the doorsill into the courtroom toward the bench.

The bailiff enters behind him and shouts: "All persons having business before Elizabeth, by the grace of God Queen of England, come forward, and you shall be heard! God save the Queen!"

"God save the Queen!" the assembled echo as one.

The judge climbs up to his perch, and glances at the spectators' gallery. Spying the group of fresh-faced young barristers, he assumes a threatening countenance. "I need not admonish the spectators that this is a matter of the utmost gravity. A man is on trial for his life!"

Satisfied with the ensuing solemnity, the judge looks to the prisoner waiting in the dock, where Granger, although obviously exhausted by these proceedings and his weeks in prison, stands with admirable dignity, cap in hand. The judge nods to the bailiff, leafs through a leather-bound liber before him, and inks an entry. The bailiff opens a door to admit twelve men who silently assume their place in the jury box. Everyone sits, except three people: the prisoner, Coke, and Noah.

"Very well," says the judge. "Master Coke! Is the Crown prepared to resume its case?"

"Ready, m'lord," booms Coke.

The judge looks to defense table. "Is the prisoner ready?"

"Ready, m'lord," intones Noah. The judge raises an eyebrow, as it is the voice of the prisoner himself that the Court is entitled to hear, not that of a barrister.

"Proceed," says the judge.

"M'lord," says Coke, bowing to the judge. He draws himself up to full height, and turns on the prisoner like an attack dog. "You murdered the victim in cold blood with malice in your heart — "

"That's false!" shouts Granger.

Coke twirls toward the judge. "M'lord, is the Crown to be interrupted after every sentence? This is outrageous!"

"M'lord," says Granger humbly. "If I'm not to be beaten down by the best talker in all England, I need to respond to each accusation as it's made!"

A moment of silence ensues. The judge calmly addresses Coke. "When you fling the fat upon the fire, Master Coke, you must expect a singeing by the flames that follow." Coke winces at the pun on his name. "The prisoner is a grain merchant, not a debating opponent. It seems to the Court that you are needlessly repeating accusations you have already urged several times." The judge raises his hand from the desk and makes a gentle dismissive motion. "Let's move along. This matter should have concluded yesterday."

"Yes, m'lord." Coke turns once more upon the prisoner. "I have in my hand a letter from your good friend Master Meyrick in which he informs the Crown that he saw you club the victim in the head in the middle of that field!"

"*Who?*" asks Granger. "I have no friend by the name of 'Meyrick.'"

"Oh, not your friend *now*, eh? I suppose he's had good and sufficient reason to dispense with *your* friendship!"

"*Never* had I a friend by that name! If he's to make accusations against me, I demand he be sworn, and that I be given a chance to confront him."

"Oh, be careful, Goodman Granger, or he *shall* repeat his accusation under oath."

"Then he'll be damned for his perjury!" Granger turns to the judge. "Meanin' no disrespect, m'lord, but this man Meyrick is lyin' about me, and I respectfully demand to see him lie to me face."

Coke regards Granger with open skepticism, his voice oozing sarcasm. "But Master Meyrick is right here beside me, m'lord, and the prisoner pretends not to recognize him." He turns again to Granger. "Do you deny that Master Meyrick was in the field that day?"

"I do not."

"Aha!"

"I have no *idea* who was in the field that day, as I was not there myself!"

"So you say!"

"I *do* say. And who have you to contradict me?"

"M'lord, the Crown calls Gelly Meyrick to the stand."

"Very well," intones the judge, sounding more than a bit bored. "The bailiff will administer the oath."

As Meyrick nervously steps into the witness box and raises his right hand, Noah looks to Granger, arching his eyebrows inquiringly. In reply, Granger merely shrugs, as if to say he's never set eyes on the witness in his life.

"M'lord," says Noah, interrupting the oath, "this witness is unknown to the prisoner, who respectfully requests a moment to consult with counsel."

From the spectators' gallery comes the barely audible click of a door being discreetly shut. Had it not drawn the judge's attention, Noah wouldn't have given it a second thought, but the judge smiles up toward the gallery, and nods cordially. Noah glances up at the gallery. A muscular Yeoman Warder with shoulders that seem to stretch across the whole doorway now stands on guard, resplendent in the dignified uniform of the Tower of London. Noah looks over at Jonathan, who shrugs, wide-eyed.

"Yes, Master Ames," says the judge. "The prisoner may have a moment to consult with you, but let's move this along."

"Certainly, m'lord," replies Noah, bowing. As he and Jonathan approach Granger, he glances at the gallery once more and sees a small, dark figure sitting quietly in the corner seat nearest the guard. Several seats remain vacant between the small dignitary and the nearest spectators, who are trying not to gawp. Unless Noah is sorely mistaken, the seated figure is Sir Robert Cecil, Secretary of State, who, together with his father William Cecil, Lord Burghley, are Essex's chief rivals on the Privy Council.

Jonathan's eyes follow Noah's. "Well," he whispers, "I prayed for a god to descend, and now one has done so. Best of all, he's one having no use for you-know-who." Jonathan refrains from mentioning Essex by name, as Granger is now listening, baffled by the significance of this dignitary's visit.

"But recall my admonition," whispers Noah. "They appear entirely for reasons of their own." He smiles to his client apologetically and speaks in hushed tones. "I'm sorry for our mysterious chat, Goodman Granger. The gentleman who just entered the gallery is the Secretary of State."

Granger looks stricken, near tears. "Of what interest is my case to him?"

Noah pats his hand. "None, I should imagine. Perhaps he's come to observe Coke at work. Rumor has it that Master Coke is about to be appointed to high office." He returns his attention to the witness shifting nervously in the box. "You're quite sure you've never seen this witness before?"

Granger nods confidently.

Noah steps back and turns to the judge. "Thank you, m'lord. The defense is ready to proceed."

It occurs to Noah that Sir Robert has no doubt had dozens of earlier opportunities to observe Coke at trial. The notion flashes through his mind that Cecil might actually have come to observe Noah himself. Henry would no doubt refer to this as a delusion of grandeur. Still, if Sir Robert *has* come to observe Noah, it likely has something to do with the Rodriguez case ... and with Essex. His stomach turns to think that he's somehow got himself caught between the most powerful warring factions in the land.

Lord Bleffingham nods to the bailiff. As the oath is being administered, Meyrick is solemn. "I so swear," he says grimly, and drops his right hand to his side. His gaze shifts restlessly about the courtroom, finally meeting Noah's stare. A barely subdued fear creeps into his expression.

Coke smiles, suddenly the picture of fellow feeling. "Now, then, Master Meyrick. Please tell the Court what you saw the prisoner do to the victim last summer."

"Objection, m'lord," says Noah loudly, and the judge nods for him to continue. "The question assumes facts not in evidence. Whether the accused did *anything* to the victim last summer remains to be proven by the Crown."

Coke feigns humility. "M'lord, there is nothing wr— "

"Sustained," says the judge impatiently. "Rephrase the question." The judge makes a notation in his liber.

Coke regards Noah angrily, becalms himself, and resumes. "Now Master Merrick ... "

"*Meyrick*," says the witness, obviously weary of a lifelong need for such correction.

"Yes, Master *Meyrick*, I beg your pardon. Please tell the Court what you saw take place between the accused and the victim." Coke looks sharply at

Noah, as though daring him to object. Although the question is slightly objectionable, Noah says nothing, instead betraying the barest hint of a smile.

The witness answers. "Well, it was a warm, sunny day, and the farmhands were about to harvest the field. It was durin' the wheat harvest last year. An *awful* summer fer plague. So many men had gone away to country that there was plenty of work, and too few to do it. So, the wage was pretty good, and — "

Coke interrupts. "Never mind the wage, sir."

Noah addresses the court. "M'lord, the accused objects to the Crown's interruption of its own witness's testimony."

The judge, looking down as though studying his liber, says, "Of course, it is solely the *Court's* prerogative to interrupt testimony. However," he looks to Noah impassively, "I must agree with the Crown that the past summer's farm wage has little to do with the matter at hand. I assume learned counsel for the prisoner also sees no connection between the two?"

Hearing nothing from Noah, the judge nods knowingly and turns to Coke. "Allow *me*, Master Coke," he says, and turns to the witness, who looks more than a little nervous to find himself under the Court's direct scrutiny.

"Master ... *Meyrick*, is it?" The witness nods meekly. "Very well. Please tell the jury anything that you saw take place between the prisoner and the victim that day."

The witness inhales noisily and stands tall, like an actor given the cue to relieve himself at last of long-rehearsed lines. He holds up his right thumb. "First, I seen the victim bendin' over a sheaf o' wheat on the ground. The *second* thing that 'appened ... "

Noah notices the witness assigning a number to each event in his story, as though he's been carefully instructed to mention each.

" ... was the assailant dropped his scythe. The *third* thing ... "

There it is again, Meyrick furtively counting on the fingers of his right hand, just as he was doing upon entering the courtroom ... but now Noah knows what he was counting.

" ... was he picked up a cudgel that was lyin' on the ground next to a ball of twine. Then ... "

Although Meyrick hasn't assigned a number aloud to the next event, he's touching his right thumb to the tip of his third finger.

"... he turned 'round toward the victim. Next, he brought the cudgel up over 'is 'ed and struck the victim in the left shoulder — a *glancing* blow."

The witness clearly pronounced the word as "glonssing," which pronunciation, although commonplace at Oxford, is unknown to men of his class. His thumb moves to his little finger.

"Next thing, the victim turns 'round, sees the killer, and flails his arms." Meyrick raises his *left* thumb discreetly, and continues. "At that point, the victim tries to run away, but he's been scragglin' a tree branch, and so trips and falls flat on the ground." His left thumb lightly touches its adjacent index finger, and his vocal register drops dramatically. "Then, when the victim is on the ground bleedin', the killer bends over and gives him a *killin'* blow." He relaxes visibly, having accomplished his task, and nods proudly to the judge. "And 'at's what 'eppened, m'lord."

Coke looks grimly at the jury to be sure the witness's words have sunk in. Evidently satisfied that they have, he asks: "Can you identify the killer in the courtroom today?"

Meyrick nods staunchly. "I can. It's '*im*. The prisoner." He points straight at Granger, whose jaw drops in disbelief.

"Thank you, Master Meyrick," says Coke. "That will be all."

Meyrick looks about the courtroom, as though anticipating that he'll be prevented from leaving the witness box. Noah looks to the judge, who returns his stare and forlornly rests his head on his hand. Noah smiles respectfully. "Just a few questions, m'lord."

Although Common Law rules of criminal procedure fail to provide the accused with anything that might be called a "right" to cross-examine adverse witnesses, the trial judge may exercise his discretion to permit cross-examination by the prisoner personally. Less often, but with increasing frequency, a judge will extend the privilege of cross-examination to defense *counsel* on the ostensible grounds that a particular accused is too dull-witted to question witnesses effectively.

Bleffingham wags a crooked finger at Noah. "A *few* questions. See to it, Master Ames."

Coke looks positively horrified. "M'lord, I *must* object … "

The judge shoots back: "*Must* you? Cross-examination by *counsel*, Master Coke. 'Tis all the rage, have you not heard? Besides, can you tell the Court what *cognizable* prejudice will befall the Crown if the witness is cross-examined by Master Ames here?"

Coke looks at Noah who, in a split second, has adopted the most infuriatingly submissive posture. Angelic, really.

Coke throws his quill pen down on his book. It bounces off and wafts to the floor. "No objection," he sulks. "But the Crown reserves the right to object to any undignified line of questioning."

The judge makes another notation in his *liber*, and intones: "The Crown need reserve no such right, as the right to object remains available at all times to either party. Proceed … with caution, Master Ames."

"Yes, m'lord." The witness looks frightened half to death.

Jonathan steps up beside Noah, and whispers in his ear. "You might make more headway if you stop looking at him as a shark does his dinner."

Noah nods, purses his lips, and very deliberately relaxes.

"Good morning, Master Meyrick. I am Noah Ames, counsel for Goodman Granger." Whenever possible, he studiously avoids referring to his client as "the prisoner" or "the accused." "Master Meyrick, have you often worked the wheat harvest?"

"I have."

Noah has no doubt that Meyrick's response is a bald-faced lie. Meyrick may have had some farming experience long ago, but Essex's principal attendant would never engage in farm work. More likely, he'd own the farm. Well, a liar is easily led. "With so few men about because of the plague, this harvest must have remained in the earth ... longer than usual. Would you agree?"

"Yes, suh. A good *month* longer."

"And the wheatfield in which the murder took place had not yet been harvested at all. Is that right?"

"Right."

"Was it a level field, or were there rocks or hillocks on it?"

"No, suh. Now you mention it, it was perfectly leveled. Musta took a bit of work to get it that way, too, as the farms about there are stony and rough."

"Master Meyrick, did you run over to the victim after he'd been cudgeled?"

"No, suh. I wouldn't go anywhere near the killer." Meyrick looks at the jury members. "Had a weird look in his eye, he did, like he might do it again to somebody else."

"I see. So ... you left the scene immediately after witnessing, as you called it, the 'killing blow'?"

"Ran like a rabbit in the opposite direction, I did." Some snickering from the jury box. "Oh, I'm not proud o' what I done, but 'safety comes first' is what I say."

"Did you run for the constable?"

Meyrick shakes his head emphatically. "Didn't see one, nor didn't know where to find one. Wasn't from them parts, y'see."

"Yes, I see. Did you speak with the constable who testified before the court yesterday? Constable ... " Noah searches his memory, "Murphy?"

"No, suh. Never did."

"Perhaps that would explain why he never mentioned you. And when did you next return to the scene of the crime?"

"Truth be told, I ain't never been back. Place gives me the willies now."

"Of course!" says Noah, sympathetically. "How far were you standing from the victim when he was first struck, Master Meyrick?"

"About as far as I am from you."

"As we speak, you are standing in the witness box beside m'lord, and I at defense table. Correct?"

"Yes, sir."

"M'lord, let the record show that such span has been precisely measured in this courtroom many times, and that the distance is twenty-five feet."

"Duly noted," intones the judge.

"Would you agree, Master Meyrick? About twenty-five feet?"

The witness regards Noah a bit skeptically at first, and then, as the Court has already ruled, concedes the point. "That's *about* right, sir."

"And were you about the same distance from the killer?"

"Yes, sir."

"How high would you say the wheat had grown by that time?"

Meyrick shrugs. "About three feet, sir."

Noah nods gravely to show interest in the answer. He takes a few steps forward, and taps on the gated balustrade separating the barristers' well from the judge's precinct. It's comprised of straight white balusters spaced about six inches apart, topped horizontally by a polished wooden rail. "Three feet is about the height of this barrier, is it not?"

"It is, sir, far as I can tell."

"Well, let's leave the precise measure out of the question completely. Is this barrier approximately the height of the wheat around the victim and the killer?"

"Aye," says Meyrick, a note of suspicion in his voice.

"M'lord," whines Coke. "This line of questioning by Master Ames leaves the Crown unenlightened."

Noah smiles. "While the defense expresses no view concerning the Crown's claim to be unenlightened, if we are given small leeway, the significance of this line of questioning will soon become apparent." This bit of humor is evidently difficult for the jury, but a few titters can be heard as individual jurors realize that Coke has pronounced himself unenlightened. Coke's face turns a dark red.

Noah avoids looking to the judge, as Coke's outburst was not actually stated as an objection. "Master Meyrick, may I ask you to repeat the individual events you recounted in response to m'lord's question?"

"The whole thing, suh?"

Noah nods. "Please."

Meyrick takes a deep preparatory breath. "First, I seen the victim bendin' over a sheaf o' wheat on the ground. The *second* thing, the assailant drops his scythe." Meyrick's counting on his digits is quite evident, and, for the first time, a few jurors seem to notice. "The *third* thing: he picks up a cudgel lyin' on the ground next to some twine. Next, he turns 'round to the victim. Next, he brings the cudgel up over 'is 'ed and strikes the victim in the left shoulder — a … a … " Meyrick is stuck for the word.

"A *glonssing* blow?" offers Noah, pointedly staring at Coke, whose shade of red further deepens.

"Aye, that's right. Thank you, suh." A couple of smothered laughs come from the jury box. Meyrick's fingers are really flying now.

"Next thing: victim turns 'round, sees the killer, flails his arms. Victim tries to run away, but he's been, uh, scragglin' a tree branch, trips and falls flat on the ground. Then, the victim's on the ground, and the killer bends over and gives him a killin' blow."

"I see," says Noah, who appears to search his memory for something he cannot find. "What was the *fourth* thing, again?"

Meyrick looks at the ceiling, searching his memory, and touches his right thumb to his fourth finger. "Brings the cudgel up over 'is 'ed."

Noah feigns confusion. "Sure that wasn't the *fifth* thing?"

Meyrick seems deep in thought as he silently runs through his mental list of events, touching his right thumb to various fingers. His eyes open wide. "Why, yes, sir. You're right, sir. *Fourth* thing was: the killer turns 'round toward the victim."

The jury bursts into laughter as one. Meyrick is clearly shocked by their reaction, and Coke noticeably crestfallen.

Noah asks, "Would it be fair to say, Master Meyrick, that you have recounted this story more than once before testifying today?"

"Yes, suh," says Meyrick, evidently missing the point.

"To Master Coke, perhaps?"

"Aye, suh."

"Did Master Coke assist you in organizing your testimony?"

"He did very kindly, suh," says Meyrick.

"Was the phrase 'a glonssing blow' first offered by Master Coke?"

Meyrick nods. "It was, suh."

Noah glances up at the jury box, and is pleased to see several jurymen lean forward, listening intently.

"Do you recall using the word 'scraggling' in your testimony today with reference to the victim and a tree branch lying on the ground?"

Coke leans over the table toward the judge. "M'lord, the Crown objects to Master Ames' shameful attempt to humiliate the witness on grounds of his limited vocabulary."

"To the contrary, m'lord," says Noah. "The witness obviously knows a word or two *I've* never encountered." This is met by a brief outburst of laughter from the gallery, which provides Noah with a pretext to look up. Sir Robert leans on the railing, gazing down at him with a bemused expression.

The judge's eyes go wide. He rises from the bench and glowers at the young barristers in the gallery, his face ashen, a frightening move, even made by a temperate old jurist like Bleffingham. The gallery goes deathly quiet.

"So help me God, I will clear this courtroom of everyone in it!" he shouts. To everyone's relief, he resumes his seat. Taking a moment to compose himself, but still glowering, he says: "The Crown's objection is overruled. Master Ames, you will stick to the point!"

"Yes, m'lord," replies Noah. He takes a deep breath. "M'lord, the defense requests leave to ask the witness to demonstrate how one 'scraggles' something on the ground."

Coke is about to speak, but the judge holds up his hand to silence him before he can get a word out.

"*Denied*, Master Ames. The witness will not leave the box." The judge thinks for a moment, and comes up with a solution he evidently finds highly judicious. "But *you* may demonstrate for the witness, and ask him if you are getting it right." No doubt, the judge deems it fair turnabout to allow Noah to make *himself* an object of ridicule by bending and squatting before the jury. Noah is certain he caught the judge smirking furtively toward the Secretary of State while issuing this ruling.

"Yes, m'lord. Please give me a moment."

From defense table, Noah picks up two books and a heavy walking stick of a type often used to ward off beggars. He lays the items out in a roughly straight line on the floor before the jury, where Meyrick will have a good view of them. He places one foot on either side of the line he has made.

"Master Meyrick, please pretend this line of items to be a tree branch, and tell me if I am 'scraggling' it now."

Meyrick looks at Noah's feet. "No."

Noah registers genuine surprise, as he imagined that Meyrick's "scraggling" was merely a mistaken pronunciation of another common word such as "straggling," "saddling," or "straddling." As straddling a branch might in some way have caused the victim to trip and fall to the ground, Noah has now straddled his makeshift branch, but with no luck.

Noah places his feet in a line atop the makeshift branch. "Now?"

Meyrick shakes his head again. "No."

Noah removes his feet from the "branch" and squats down next to it, placing his hands over it. "Now?"

Several members of the jury laugh aloud at the absurd postures assumed by Noah in this guessing game. Even the judge seems to enjoy it, though he hides his smile behind a handkerchief. Noah rather enjoys the process, as levity is an accused's best friend, especially directed toward Crown testimony.

"No, suh," says Meyrick, turning to the judge. "Would you mind my givin' him a hint, m'lord?"

"If the spirit so moves you," replies Lord Bleffingham.

"Walk over to the jury box, Master Ames." Noah does so. "Now, walk towards the 'branch,' and stop just before reachin' it."

Noah stands to one side of the branch. "Like this?"

"Yes, suh. Now move your feet so they aim at me."

"Like so?"

"Aye, that's it. Now you're scragglin' it."

Noah looks down at his feet, and scratches his head.

"M'lord, may we please have the record show that I am standing with my feet about four inches apart, both of them being to the same side of the makeshift branch at an angle of approximately forty-five degrees from the branch. And the toes of both feet are pointing toward the branch ... and are approximately six inches away from the branch." He turns to the witness. "This is 'scraggling'?"

"I *hope* so, suh," says the witness gravely, causing the jury to laugh once again.

Jonathan helps Noah collect the books and walking stick from the floor. By pre-arrangement, Jonathan then precisely reconstitutes the "branch" on counsel's side of the balustrade, making no effort at concealment.

Noah smooths his hair back and resumes his place at the lectern. "Master Meyrick, did the word 'scraggling' also come from Master Coke?"

"Yes, suh," replies the witness, his eyes hopefully scanning the jury.

"And do you recall telling m'lord that the victim 'flailed' his arms upon seeing his armed attacker?"

"Aye."

"Without leaving the box, could you demonstrate for the court how the victim flailed his arms?"

The witness silently turns toward the judge and holds his arms up, as though the judge were about to assail him, and does not move. As an extra touch, his face assumes a fearful expression.

Noah allows a moment to pass for the jury to take in the witness frozen in his stationary position, still as a statue.

"Thank you, Master Meyrick. And have you now demonstrated to us your conception of 'flailing'?"

The witness nods curtly, prompting the judge to say: "Your answers must be spoken, Master Meyrick, as the court scribe cannot record your gestures."

"Sorry, m'lord," Meyrick sheepishly replies. "Yes, that's what I understand to be flailin'."

Noah, eyes downcast, asks, "And this word also came from Master Coke, is that correct?"

"Aye, suh."

At last, Coke speaks up. "M'lord, Master Ames has just spent a great deal of time demonstrating nothing more than that the witness discussed his testimony beforehand with Crown prosecutors," he turns to the jury, "which is both commonplace and perfectly proper. Indeed, the Crown would have been remiss if it had failed to take the witness's statement."

Noah corrects: "To *take* it. Not to *give* it."

The judge regards Noah weighingly. "Master Ames, I trust you have more to show than this."

"I do, indeed, m'lord, and it shan't take more than a few moments."

"Proceed."

Noah whispers to Jonathan, who removes a clean linen sheet borrowed from Gray's Inn that morning, unfolds it, and hands two ends to Noah. Together, they open the sheet and hang it over the three-foot balustrade so that nothing can be seen through the gaps between the balusters. Jonathan discreetly moves the items comprising the makeshift "branch," stacking them out of sight in a corner, and replaces them with a child's blue plush toy in the shape of a dog.

Coke cannot resist. "M'lord, what do we learn from this sheet, other than the deficiencies of the laundry at Gray's Inn?" As every lawyer in the room knows, Noah and Jonathan are of Gray's Inn, while Coke is of a rival Inn of Court called "Inner Temple."

Noah moves away from the lectern, and steps up to counsel's side of the balustrade, so that his lower body is hidden from the witness by the sheet.

"Master Meyrick, when I was scraggling the makeshift branch earlier, what was I wearing on my feet?"

The witness's eyebrows rise. "Boots, suh?"

"And now?"

Meyrick looks to where he expects Noah's feet to be, but his view is blocked.

"I don't rightly know, suh."

"In fact, I could be barefoot right now, wiggling my toes at you, and you would not know it. Is that right?"

"No, suh. I would not know."

"Can you tell if I have folded my robes up to my thighs?"

"I cannot, suh."

The judge glowers at Noah. Noah shakes his head to assure the Court that no such breach in protocol has transpired. The judge seems mollified.

"And what is right here, beside me on the floor?"

"The 'branch,' suh?"

"What makes you say that?"

"Well, that's what was there before you hung the sheet over the barrier, suh."

"In fact, you don't *know* what's down there now, do you?"

"I do not, suh. I cannot see."

"Have we already established that you are standing the same distance from me as you were from the killer and the victim at the time of the murder?"

"Aye, suh."

"I believe you testified that the field was level. Correct?"

"Yes, suh."

"And you also testified that, before the murder, the victim was stooping over a sheaf of wheat on the ground?"

"Yes, suh."

"But you could not *see* the sheaf. Correct?"

The witness's eyes grow wide, and his face loses all color. He begins to sweat. "No." He finds a handkerchief and daubs at his forehead.

"And you also testified that, before the killer picked up the cudgel, it lay on the ground next to a ball of twine?"

"Correct, suh."

"But in fact you could not *see* the twine, could you, as it was on the ground. Correct?"

"Aye, suh."

"And the tree branch that was being 'scraggled' by the victim? You could not see that, either?"

"Correct."

Noah infuses his voice with indignation. "Because it was *on the ground,* and your view of the ground was *blocked* by the unharvested wheat. Correct?"

The witness looks as though he might faint dead away. "I just *assumed* it was a branch — "

"But that was not your *testimony,* was it?"

Meyrick hesitates. "It was not," he admits. His eyes dart toward the door, and he wilts in despair.

"In fact, you did not see the cudgel on the ground, or the twine on the ground, or the branch on the ground … nor even the victim … once he was on the ground. Correct?"

"Correct, suh," echoes Meyrick vacantly. He is now a beaten man.

"Did you in fact witness *anything* of what you have testified to this morning?"

"I must have witnessed *another* crime."

Noah's jaw drops, and he gazes at the witness in disbelief. He turns to Coke, and sniffs: "No doubt the Crown will proffer your testimony in the trial of *that* crime!"

The entire courtroom erupts into laughter and conversation.

Amidst the uproar, Jonathan calmly removes the sheet from the balustrade, for the first time revealing to Court, jury, and witness a blue toy resembling a dog, its eyes crossed in a most farcical manner, its red fabric tongue hanging out stupidly. The jury laughs aloud and points.

Beneath the din, the judge can be heard pounding his open hand very hard on a closed book before him. He stands and points angrily at the toy. "Master Ames, where did you get that *ridiculous* thing?"

Noah looks at the toy, genuinely surprised at its humorous appearance. "I expect it's a souvenir of Inner Temple, m'lord."

This ill-considered remark is about as far as Noah has ever pushed his luck in court, and he's sorry as soon he's passed it. Nevertheless, for a moment the judge can barely conceal his mirth, causing his face to blush in embarrassment, and he resumes pounding the book until the court comes to order. The young barristers in the gallery peer every which way to catch a glimpse of whatever ridiculous thing is lying on the floor before counsel table, but their view is blocked.

"Counsel will approach the bench." Noah and Coke soberly trudge to the bench. "You, too, Master Hawking."

Coke and Noah are both completely abashed. Coke is deeply embarrassed, not only because he now has no witness to place the accused at the crime scene, but also because everyone knows he has attempted to compensate for inadequate preparation by coaching the witness, a tactic which rarely works in the new day of cross-examination by counsel.

Noah's infraction is one of demeanor, which many a judge would regard as more serious than anything Coke has done. A judge will jealously guard his prerogative of running the courtroom, and any counsel challenging the judge's sense of control is setting himself up for severe admonition. Noah is a natural, if understated, showman who must try hard to avoid using his wit to dance rings around others.

Before either Coke or Noah reaches the bench, Jonathan races ahead of them, tears welling up in his eyes. The judge looks very sympathetic.

"What's the matter, Master Hawking? You appear to be winning!"

"Yes, m'lord, but I want to apologize for bringing that … that, silly-looking toy into the courtroom. Master Ames had not seen it before I drew the sheet off the balustrade. You see," Jonathan speaks in heartbreaking tones, "he told me that we would need some innocent-looking object, such as a child's toy, to make a point in the courtroom, but I was not sure why he would need it, so I thought it did not matter how it looked, so I borrowed the … dog … from my nephew's toy chest."

"I see," says the judge, somewhat mollified. "What is his name?"

"'Finerty,' m'lord."

The judge relaxes considerably at the thought of a young child. "Well, you tell Finerty — "

"No, m'lord. Finerty is the *dog*."

"The toy?"

"Yes, m'lord. My nephew's name is James."

"Why did James name the toy dog 'Finerty'?"

"What, m'lord? Oh, just before I gave it to him, for some unknown reason, he asked me what the highest number was."

"And you said 'infinity,' and he changed that to 'Finerty' and gave the toy dog that name?" The judge turns to Noah. "Is this true, according to your knowledge, Master Ames?"

"I can say of my own knowledge that it *is* true, insofar as I asked Master Hawking to bring a child's toy to court today, but that I had no idea it was a silly-looking one. As for the story of Master Hawking's nephew, although I had no knowledge of it before now, I do not doubt it."

"That still does not pardon your inappropriate outburst that the toy is a souvenir of Inner Temple, does it?"

Before Noah can reply, Coke speaks up. "M'lord, that was said in response to my regrettable attempt to poke fun at Master Ames' use of a Gray's Inn sheet in his demonstration. I sincerely apologize to the Court for that. To the extent that there is a friendly rivalry among the Inns of Court, we all know the truth of it."

Noah jumps in before the judge can begin again. "And I sincerely apologize to the Court, as well. I was caught off guard by the toy's humorous appearance, but my outburst was unnecessary and regrettable."

The judge sits back and looks at Coke and Noah with evident disappointment. "The Inns of Court are not Eton and Harrow, gentlemen, nor are they Oxford and Cambridge. And a courtroom is no place to exhibit any such rivalry among members of the bench and bar. As for you, Master Coke, I take it that you have no other witness to offer who can place the prisoner at the crime scene — or you would not have produced this one. Am I correct?"

"Correct, m'lord," Coke replies. "Without this witness, our evidence consists only of the proximity of Goodman Granger's home to the crime scene."

"Owning a home near a field that one day becomes a crime scene is not a crime, Master Coke. The Crown's alternatives are limited. You can either withdraw the charge, or lose by acquittal."

"But the jury might yet convict!" objects Coke in excited, but hushed, tones.

The judge shakes his head. "The jurors would have no *basis* to convict on this evidence. Your witness has not only been impeached beyond revival, which I acknowledge would still leave a jury issue, but he has completely *recanted his testimony*. There is now no evidence in the record placing the prisoner at the scene." He shakes his head even more gravely. "Assuming Master Ames is about to move for a directed verdict," Noah nods, "then even if the jury were to convict on the basis of this record, I would have no choice but to enter judgment *non obstante veredicto*." A "judgment n.o.v.," as it is sometimes called, means a judgment entered by the Court contrary to the jury's verdict.

Coke nods, obviously dismayed. "The Crown will withdraw the charge, m'lord," he says. He bows and turns, about to resume his place at Crown table.

The judge beckons with his hand. "Just a moment, Master Coke. I want you to hear this." He looks at Jonathan, who has regained his composure. "You especially, Master Hawking, because you are the *future*." He turns to Noah. "Master Ames, despite your sometimes unconventional courtroom conduct, I take no issue with your questioning or demonstrative technique. Your demeanor in dealing with witnesses is really quite clever. However, I do have a problem with your little quips and mumblings. At the Queen's *court*, you might receive all sorts of praise and blandishments for your pithy sayings. I have nothing to say about that. But at the Queen's *Bench*, I have a great deal to say about it. Now, you might persuade *yourself* that all your little off-the-cuff remarks are of a piece with your general courtroom manner, but they are not. It is my distinct impression that the single person you care to amuse is yourself, and, only secondarily, any others who might rise to your level of erudition. Your quips may get you into serious trouble yet, Master Ames. See to it."

Having been dressed down so equably, Noah is humbled. "Yes, m'lord. I will think upon what you have said, and will bear it in mind in future. In the meantime, I apologize most heartily to the Court and Master Coke for my offenses."

The judge rocks in his chair a few moments, sizing up Noah's apology. He indicates Coke and Jonathan. "You two gentlemen may return to your respective tables. Master Ames, remain here a moment. Master Coke, I assume you have no objection? You have my word that we will not discuss this case."

"None at all, m'lord."

Coke and Jonathan bow, and withdraw to their places.

"What am I to do with you, Master Ames?" the judge muses quietly. "I'm going to say something, and I want you to frown when I say it. Now that you've put on your little show for your young barristers, I need to put one on, as well. Pretend I am dressing you down."

Noah hangs his head and frowns.

The judge continues very quietly in the hushed courtroom. "Do you have plans for dinner today?"

Noah swings his head slowly from side to side. "No, m'lord. I do not."

"Meet me at Serjeants' Inn at noon."

The Serjeants, an order comprised of the most renowned barristers in the land, whose cases are afforded precedence over those of all other barristers, was established in France well prior to the Norman Invasion of 1066. The judiciary of the most prestigious courts in the land is dominated by Serjeants. This is certainly not an invitation to be declined by someone in Noah's position.

Noah's brow furrows. "May I bring Master Hawking?"

"Perhaps next time. He is still a little young to hear how judges talk amongst themselves. Now, turn and slink back to defense table. You have been admonished." Noah does as he's been told, and glances toward Granger, who is understandably horrified by Noah's moroseness, as he has no idea what this means for his own jeopardy.

"M'lord," pronounces Coke in stentorian voice, "in light of new developments, the Crown hereby withdraws all charges against Goodman Granger."

The judge leans forward. "Goodman Granger, you are free to go. The witness may step down. The Court thanks the gentlemen of the jury. You are dismissed."

So relieved is Granger by the Court's pronouncement that he stumbles, and must be steadied on his feet by the much smaller Jonathan. Regaining his balance, Granger gratefully seizes Jonathan's hand.

"Thank you so much, sir. Thank you. Thank you."

Jonathan's hand is nearly lost in Granger's outsize grip.

"*There's* your man," says Jonathan, pointing to Noah.

Noah is looking up at the gallery, from which the Secretary of State and his guard have quietly departed. Granger approaches him with awe.

"Sir, I don't know how I can ever repay you. I doubt there's another lawyer in all England who coulda done what you did."

"Nonsense, Goodman Granger. There are many. But it has been my distinct privilege to assist you. I've no *idea* how anyone could take you for a killer."

"I s'pose the Crown don't like unsolved cases more than anyone else. And that's what this is. An unsolved case."

"That it is."

"Sir, can I pay you for your services now?" asks Granger, reaching for his purse.

Noah pats Granger's hand away from his purse. "No, no, no. Goodman Granger, barristers are not 'in trade.' Your arrangement is solely with Master Thistlethwaite. It is *his* job, not yours, to make sure that we are properly provided for."

"Very well, sir." Granger turns toward the heavy doors at the back of the courtroom, and tears well up. "Here's something I never expected to be doin'. Walkin' out of this courtroom a free man." He turns back to Noah. "God bless you, sir. God bless you both!"

"And you, Goodman Granger. Best to your goodwife!"

As Jonathan collects their things, Noah watches proudly as Granger walks to freedom through the rear doors. At the same time, in the corner of his eye, he spies the approach of a small, veiled figure. It's the widow from the spectators' gallery, who has evidently descended to speak with him.

"Well done, Master Ames," she says, as she pins back her veil.

It's Marie.

CHAPTER 7

"GOODWIFE RODRIGUEZ!" SAYS NOAH, gently cupping her hands in his own. Although she is obviously still recovering from profound grief at the death of her husband, the puffiness about her large chestnut eyes has disappeared, and her face is now taut and firm, sharpening her well-defined jawline. She also seems to have lost weight, which enhances her striking figure.

"Don't worry, Master Ames. I have not come to haunt you about my case. I merely thought I'd like to see you at work. And I see I am not alone." She points an elegantly gloved finger toward the young barristers remaining in the gallery, chatting amiably as though they just attended one of Shakespeare's better plays. "You have quite the entourage. And, it appears, one that includes a very important young gentleman."

Instinctively, Noah turns to look at the bench. It's vacant. Although the bailiff customarily shouts "all rise" as the judge departs the courtroom, Lord Bleffingham seems to have departed without ceremony. He wonders whether the judge has not rushed off to speak with Sir Robert Cecil.

"Oh, I doubt he came to observe me. Come," says Noah, smiling at his good fortune in seeing Marie so unexpectedly, "let us walk together in the fresh air." He offers his arm.

Before taking it, she says: "Aren't you supposed to appear downcast before your young friends there? You know … to set a good example, as someone who's been taken to the woodshed?"

He regards her with surprise once more.

"Well," she continues. "Those were the judge's instructions, were they not?"

He is, for once, speechless.

"Oh, come now," she says. "You didn't think your little charade could fool an old negotiator like me, did you?"

"I shall be certain to improve my acting skills before trying to put one past you in future."

They begin walking toward the exit. At first he smiles, but then he adopts a suitably grave demeanor as they pass the gallery, which has only partly emptied. They draw numerous inquisitive stares as they pass.

"Well done, Master Ames!" says one familiar young barrister of Gray's Inn, slapping him on the shoulder.

"Thank you," Noah soberly replies.

From behind them comes a young man's voice imitating a young woman: "Yes, Master Ames. *Very* well done, indeed!" Noah and Marie pick up the pace, trying to conceal their own laughter while escaping the general mirth behind them. They step through the doors, and down the staircase into great Westminster Hall.

"How have you been faring these past few weeks?" he asks.

She sighs. "Well, I won't say it's been pleasant. It hasn't. But I've been managing to get our affairs in order."

"*Our* affairs?"

"Yes, this is a *family* enterprise, Master ... Noah," she says, suddenly remembering his preferred form of address.

He smiles at the cause of her hesitation. "You know, I'm thinking of changing my name to 'Master Noah,' as that's what everyone seems to call me."

She smiles again. What *is* he seeing there? More than mere response to a pleasantry. He feels her studying his face in a way that seems vaguely familiar, then is embarrassed to recall that this is how Marlowe looked at him. He blushes.

"Ha'penny for your thoughts," she says impishly.

"These thoughts would cost you far more than a ha'penny. Tuppence, at *least*! Sorry. You caught me woolgathering."

She nods indulgently. "I've sent my children away until Sunday. They're in Surrey visiting their uncle ... for whom I've finally found some earthly use. I need to attend to a few matters here in London, before attending to more overseas."

As they walk arm in arm out into the open air of New Palace Yard, sunshine greets them. The air smells surprisingly fresh and clean for Westminster. It's one of those unusually warm early spring days when the season seems to run ahead of itself, surprising every living thing. The birds have not yet realized it's time to come out and sing, and only the tiniest green buds tentatively peek out onto the branches.

"Well," says Noah. "If I can be of any use to you — "

"Now that you mention it ... Noah, there are a few matters I'd care to discuss with you. Have you plans for dinner today?"

He isn't sure if it's appropriate to tell her he's been invited to dine at Serjeants' Inn, by the very judge who's just dressed him down.

She reads his eyes, or *thinks* she does, and appears crestfallen. "I see. Well, whoever she is, I hope she's very lovely."

"Oh, no," he scowls. "Nothing of the sort. It's just that I'm not sure I should — "

"Oh?" she perks up. "Matters of law and the state?"

"I don't seem to be very good at withholding information from you. Can you keep a secret?"

She looks around mock-furtively and winks knowingly at him, which he finds especially adorable for some reason. He wonders whether it is proper for a recent widow dressed in mourning to look quite this beautiful.

"Cheeky," he mutters. "You know that judge who just admonished me?"

"You mean the one who just *pretended* to admonish you?"

He nods. "He invited me to dine with him at Serjeants' Inn at noon."

She seems surprised. "When did he do that?" Her eyes grow wide, and her mouth falls open. "Why, when he was dressing you down privately, of course! Oh, and *you*, with that hangdog expression!" She laughs. "You men are all alike. Actors all!"

"Might you and I have supper tonight, perhaps?"

She grows thoughtful and studies his face skeptically. For a moment, she says nothing, evidently mulling over some very important question.

"Oh, very well," she concedes.

"Shall I call for you around eight?"

"That would be fine."

"Where shall we sup?"

"I'll have the servants throw something together."

"Oh, no, please," he protests. "I couldn't impose."

"Nonsense," she says. "Eight it *is*, then." She curtsies deeply and turns toward the intersection of King Street and Thieving Lane, where Noah spies several suspicious-looking paupers only a few feet from her path.

"Oh, no, no, no. None of that! I won't have you going on foot near that wretched lane. You'll be molested by beggars and thieves! Didn't Master Hawking advise you to avoid traveling about London without male escort?"

She seems to regard his protectiveness as presumptuous. "I'm going up *King* Street to the Strand. Besides, how do you think I *got* here?"

"You were not in my care when you came here."

"I can take care of myself," she says, and marches off in a huff. After a moment's hesitation, he runs after her.

A few steps away on Thieving Lane, a stooped woman in shabby clothing draws a kerchief about her smudged face, races toward Marie, and snatches her purse away. As the thief tries to escape, Noah, who is already moving at a jog, tackles her with full force. He feels a sharp pain in his left hand as they strike the pavement together. Splayed out in a tangle on the ground, the thief's estimable height becomes discernible, having been concealed until then by poor posture.

Still on the ground, Noah grabs the purse. Although the thief's initial resistance is formidable, as Noah moves to rip off her kerchief, her grip on the purse relents, and she releases it. She grimaces angrily and knees him hard in the chest. As he struggles for breath, she bolts upright, spits, and quickly disappears from view down Thieving Lane.

Marie runs to kneel beside him. "Noah! Oh, why did you *do* that?" she splutters. "Are you hurt?"

The look in her eyes seems downright desperate. The altercation must have jolted back to mind the barely repressed memories of her husband's murder. Noah sits up before he can fully catch his breath, to assure her that he's uninjured. "I'll be fine," he grunts hoarsely.

"Where were you struck?" she implores, eying his full length.

"I am unhurt, I assure you. Merely winded."

"No, your hand is becoming bruised. Look!"

Although the back of his left hand is turning gray, in truth it hurts very little. He rises without assistance, and gazes down Thieving Lane. "Barely hurt at all," he muses, and turns to her. "I am amazed by the ease with which your purse was recovered." Realizing that he's still holding it, he tenders it back to her.

She accepts it more with irritation than gratitude. "Ease? You call that easy?" She shakes the purse at him, tears in her eyes. "Oh, this is a *trifle*, Noah! You mustn't be drawn into fisticuffs on account of such things. You might have been badly hurt. There is nothing of value in it. A few pence, perhaps a shilling."

He turns to her. "No personal items? Nothing of your late husband's?"

"No!"

"Well, I guess that scoundrel thought there might be."

"What do you mean?"

"I do not believe that was a woman. In fact, it was not a beggar. Perhaps not even a professional thief."

She appears perplexed. "What ever do you mean?"

"He was tall and strong, and could have put up much more of a fight than he did. He probably would have got away with the purse, too."

"Why didn't she ... he?"

"Because concealment of his identity was of utmost importance."

Marie seems to consider his point, and then dismisses it. "Oh, rubbish! How could anyone know the thief was not a beggar?"

He taps the side of his nose with his finger. "Have you ever caught a whiff of a beggar? A *real* one, I mean?"

"Of course. They smell as though they've never bathed."

He smiles. "What did *this* one smell like?"

"Like ... nothing."

He arches an eyebrow. "Precisely!"

He hails a carriage coming toward them down King Street, and pays the driver. Marie steps into it, pouting, and sits down. Noah smiles as cheerily as he can manage. "Eight o' clock, then?" She nods contemplatively, and the carriage clops away.

He expects she will no longer be so quick to move about the city without a manservant, which is all to the good. His hand begins to throb, and he rubs it absentmindedly as he turns toward Serjeants' Inn on Fleet Street.

*   *   *

In a private room at Westminster, Southampton listens patiently to Essex's complaints about the insolent barrister, Noah Ames.

"How is it that, in the space of a few weeks, this ... this *nobody* ... has become a double thorn in my side? Who the devil *is* he?"

"He's *nobody,*" confirms Southampton, "just as you have said, Robert." There's a knock at the door.

"Come!" shouts Essex.

Coke enters, eyes downcast, awaiting the inevitable.

"Master Coke," says Essex calmly, his rage barely suppressed. "It was my understanding that you are one of the most skillful barristers in all England."

"It was not I who said so, m'lord," replies Coke humbly.

"Well, and today you've shown good grounds for your humility."

"M'lord, I profoundly regret — "

Essex interrupts him, red-faced. "I have not heretofore urged your advancement on grounds of either your humility *or* your regret, Master Coke. I have rather urged your name upon the Queen on account of your reputation for *winning.*"

Coke bows. "No one wins all the time, m'lord."

"So I see," says Essex, and places his hand on Coke's shoulder as though to comfort him, although to Southampton he seems the serpent insinuating itself with Eve. "Tell me, what is it about this Noah — "

When he cannot recall the name, Coke suggests it. "Ames, m'lord."

Essex is irritated, as though he would have recalled the name himself, given time. "Yes, why does this Noah Ames seem to perplex you?"

Coke sighs. "He may be the most intelligent barrister admitted to the roll, m'lord."

"Oh!" exclaims Essex sardonically. "And *I* thought that was *you*. Perhaps it's *his* advancement I should be promoting." He sighs. "Well, you're Solicitor General now. Perhaps that's as much advancement as you seek."

Coke pauses. "Solicitor General is a rarefied post, m'lord. For a barrister holding that office, there are few offices to advance *to*."

Essex regards him sternly. "There's the Attorney Generalship," he says, patently disappointed that Coke has given up so easily on the prospect of further advancement.

"Yes, m'lord, but its present occupant, Lord Egerton, seems disinclined to vacate it at present."

Essex shakes his head pityingly. "How little you know of the inner workings at court, Master Coke! Egerton is already being considered for Master of the Rolls, which would make him second only to — "

"The Lord Chief Justice," says Coke.

Essex smiles fondly. "Quite correct, Coke. Perhaps there's hope for you after all. *But*," he says pointedly, "we will need to see more and better from you in future, if the Attorney Generalship is to be yours. And you must better protect any witnesses I send you henceforth, Master Coke. Gelly Meyrick is positively *sick* with humility. He wears his not as well as you do yours, you see. You may go now. And gird yourself for the tasks ahead."

Coke bows twice, once to Essex, once to Southampton, and shuts the door quietly behind him as he leaves.

Essex sighs and turns to Southampton. "I'm afraid I no longer put much stock in Coke."

"Because he lost one case?"

Essex shrugs. "A little. But mainly because I sense he has too many scruples and, which is worse, too little worldly ambition, for me to rely upon him when the going gets rough. I need a loyal friend in whoever the new Attorney General will be."

"Certainly," suggests Southampton, "we shall need friends in high places, if we can manage to get them appointed."

"Yes, but not all high positions are equally important. I need the Attorney General in my thrall so I can be sure to put away whomever I need to."

"Anyone in mind?"

"Don't play the simpleton with me, Wriothesley," says Essex.

"I've no idea whom you mean, I assure you."

"Why, the Cecils, of course."

Southampton nearly laughs, but he realizes Essex is serious. "Pardon, Robert, but wouldn't it be necessary for them to commit some crime first?"

"The laws of conspiracy allow the prosecutor to cast a wide net, Wriothesley. It may suffice if one of their co-conspirators commits one."

Southampton shrugs.

"You'll see," says Essex confidently. "We'll catch the Cecils sooner or later and, just as quickly, have them in the Tower."

"Well, if you no longer favor Coke," says Southampton, "whom will you propose to the Queen for Attorney General, assuming Egerton accepts higher office?"

"He'll accept it. He's already asked for it. My next choice for Attorney General would be Anthony or Francis Bacon."

"Oh," protests Southampton, "but they're not your natural allies. They're more natural allies of their close relatives, the Cecils. *And* they lack experience."

Essex smiles cynically. "I assure you, the Bacons are eminently well qualified. They're both highly ambitious, and they've each confirmed to me that they're untroubled by the prospect of prosecuting their own kin."

Southampton raises an eyebrow.

Essex laughs. "They've none of Coke's inconvenient scruples, you see."

* * *

Noah arrives at Serjeants' Inn shortly before noon, and the sun is now warm enough to cause his upper lip to perspire. He wishes that protocol permitted him to remove a portion of his black barrister's robes, but this is neither the time nor the place. As Serjeants' Inn is hard by Inner Temple, he wonders fleetingly whether he'll run into Coke. Instead, as he enters, he nearly bumps into Henry Neville.

"Watch your step, Master Ames. You're early. No need to rush."

"Henry! What are you doing here?"

"I might ask you the same thing, but that ... "

Noah waits expectantly. "But that ... ?"

"But that I know why you've come. I spoke with Lord Bleffingham late this morning. He appears to think quite a lot of you." He shrugs, and looks toward the dining room. "Can't imagine why ... " His voice trails off.

"It's good to know I can always count on your support, Master Neville," says Noah sardonically.

"What? Oh, you can, old man. You know that. By the way, I've neglected to ask you this past week: Has your man Hawking made any progress in the Rodriguez investigation?"

"None at all, so far as I know. I ran into Marie in court this morning."

It takes a moment for Henry to place the name. He cocks his head with a bemused expression. "'*Marie*,' is't?"

Noah blushes. "Well, she calls me 'Noah,'" he responds, as though the widow's informality somehow justifies his own.

"Well, then I suppose *anything* goes!" Henry teases.

They hear a familiar voice behind them. "I might have known I would find you two conspiring against me," says Lord Bleffingham. "So good of you both to come! Welcome to Serjeants' Inn, Master Ames," he says, shaking Noah's hand warmly. Remembering himself, he nods to Henry. "You, too, of course, Master Neville."

Henry snorts a laugh. "I eat here so often, I'm surprised I haven't been elevated to Serjeant!"

Bleffingham smiles. "Well, you are certainly qualified to be a Serjeant, Master Neville, but you need no status greater than you already have to commend you to court. I understand you spoke with Her Majesty just yesterday."

Henry appears mildly uncomfortable with this revelation. "While I may speak to Her Majesty, I am far from certain she hears a thing I say."

"She is no doubt preoccupied," says Bleffingham indulgently. "A great many things must go through one's mind, when one need answer only to God."

Henry smiles at Bleffingham's remark in the most fondly patronizing manner, as though what he's said is so naive as to be charming. "Ah! Ames, we are in the company of the last true believer in the divine rights of kings!"

Bleffingham seems surprised. "Not the *very* last, I should hope."

"Shall we dine?" says Henry. "I'm famished."

"I've reserved a table by the window," says Bleffingham. He summons a waiter, who leads them to a rear table overlooking Inner Temple's fields.

As they take their seats, Henry says in a tone of concern: "What's wrong with your hand, Noah?"

Bleffingham squints at Noah's bruised hand. "Oh, my word. Yes, that looks quite painful! What happened?"

"I am evidently fair game for all, m'lord," Noah says abashedly. "As I've already told Master Neville, I was struck on the back of the neck some weeks ago, evidently as some sort of vague warning. Then, this morning, as I was leaving court with a young widow, someone snatched her purse, and, in compensation for the pains I took in recovering it, left me this little remembrance in black and blue." He rubs his hand lightly.

Bleffingham seems to recall something, and turns to Henry. "Is Master Ames referring to the woman reared as a sister to the Earl of Southampton?

You know, the equestrienne you and I discussed earlier? Oh, what name does she go by now? Gonzalez — "

Henry shoots a glance at Noah. "Rodriguez-Miller. Yes, m'lord. That is she."

What is this? Why would Henry have been discussing Marie with Bleffingham, of all people? And on the very day when Essex's archrival Sir Robert Cecil happens to drop by the courtroom? Although Noah's expression remains impassive, his mind is striving at full tilt.

Bleffingham turns to Noah. "Master Neville tells me that your services have been sought by the Widow Rodriguez. Of course, she was known by the name 'Marie Miller' when I met her some years ago." As Noah makes no reply but listens attentively, Bleffingham continues. "In fact, she was born to the wife of John Miller, the stableman at Southampton's residence. I believe you may find a suspicious resemblance between Marie and the current earl, he being only slightly more effeminate than she." He chortles. "As the current earl's sister was named 'Mary,' you can imagine the potential confusion when it was decided Marie would be reared inside the residence. You appear quite mystified, Master Ames. Did you not know *any* of this?"

"Not a whit, m'lord."

"Her father, Old Miller, was suspected of stabling a horse at the earl's residence for a papist traitor. He was roughly interrogated on the question, threatened with torture, and held at the Tower for months. He was released only upon the traitor's execution at Tyburn. Meanwhile, Marie had become renowned for her beauty, much to the chagrin of the lady of the house. And all the time Old Miller was detained in the Tower, Marie was left to defend her own honor, which she did intrepidly, or so I have been led to believe."

Noah is stunned to hear all this, especially from someone other than Marie. A shiver shoots up his spine. Since Marie was a member of the Southampton household, could she now be aligned with Essex? He thinks back upon her interview with Jonathan when she seemed to be holding something back, and realizes he needs to learn as much as possible from this fortuitous conversation. "I beg your pardon, m'lord. Did you also say she was an equestrienne?"

It's Henry who replies. "She rides like the wind. Has quite the reputation for it. From years ago, of course."

Bleffingham glances toward the entryway, where two Serjeants converse intently. "Excuse me a moment. I must have a word with those two." He rises and walks away. Henry gazes thoughtfully out at the adjoining field, and takes a sip of red wine.

"I see you've known all this for some time," says Noah. "Did it occur to you that it might be relevant to the murder case, so it might be a good idea to share it with me?"

Henry clears his throat. "Yes, it did, of course. After all, Southampton is one of Essex's closest friends — "

"Southampton was with Essex at the murder scene, for heaven's sake!" exclaims Noah in a hoarse whisper. "Marie was reared in Southampton's *residence?*"

"I had planned on informing you a week ago, when I first drew the connection," says Henry sheepishly, "but our paths haven't crossed until now. It has occurred to me that I know the name of someone for Hawking to speak to, who might have knowledge about the murder. But this must never come back to me in any way. It must remain between us that I gave you this guidance."

"Of course," replies Noah gravely.

Henry leans in close, and looks about before whispering a single name. "Nicholas Skeres. But *do* tell Hawking to bring some of his rougher friends along to the interview."

Bleffingham returns to the table laughing. "Oh, those two!" he says, as he sits down.

"M'lord," says Noah, "have you no idea why the Secretary of State came to court today?"

Bleffingham and Henry exchange a knowing glance. The old jurist looks down at his wine, and swishes it about in his glass. "Simply to observe matters, I should imagine. While Master Cecil does not solicit my advice on such things, I expect he may have had a few moments' leisure. I doubt it had anything to do with the Granger case, if that's what you're asking."

Noah immediately recognizes the patent absurdity of the suggestion that Sir Robert Cecil would drop by a murder trial as an idle pursuit. And it's equally obvious that Bleffingham knows why Cecil came to court.

Noah probes. "Do you suppose he came to observe Coke?"

"I doubt it," says Bleffingham. "Master Cecil came to my courtroom to observe Coke before it was decided to appoint him Solicitor General. Since Her Majesty has now decided, however, Sir Robert has no further reason to do so."

Aha! Then, he came to observe me! concludes Noah. And for reasons related to the Rodriguez murder, which would be of no interest to him unless he suspects that Essex is involved. He sneaks a glance at Henry, and detects the expression reserved for those occasions when, in Henry's estimation, he is "thinking too hard." That confirms it. *Robert Cecil is taking my measure.* But to what purpose?

No more is said at dinner about the Rodriguez case or Sir Robert Cecil, but Skeres' name never leaves the very center of Noah's mind.

*   *   *

By the time he leaves on foot for Gray's Inn, which is barely a quarter mile away, Noah is lightheaded, having been introduced to so many judges and joined in so many toasts that his head is spinning from a surfeit of new acquaintance and old wine. Exacerbating his disorientation is the sinking sun that shines directly into his eyes as he walks west on Fleet Street.

As he's about to turn right onto Chancery Lane, he sees a man approaching the lane from the opposite side, also on foot. Although at first the man seems so familiar that Noah is tempted to wave to him, even in his current fuzzy frame of mind something holds him back from doing so. The man is traveling east, coming from the direction of Westminster. There is something *else* in that same direction, besides Westminster, but much closer, something … something on Drury Lane, right there on the Thames. Then it comes back to him. Only two blocks behind the man is Essex House, the earl's principal residence in London.

Two thoughts force themselves together in his foggy brain. This is the man he's seen standing on the square at Gray's Inn, the one Henry said was Bacon's man. And he might be coming from Essex, or at least from Essex's residence.

The man turns left at the same moment that Noah turns right, and the two begin up opposite sides of Chancery Lane. The man apparently has not spotted Noah. Perhaps he would not recognize Noah even if he had, as Noah has probably never been the subject of his surveillance. Noah discreetly drops back, letting Bacon's man pull several steps ahead.

The man walks past Lincoln's Inn, another Inn of Court, as Noah does the same on the opposite side of the lane.

Next they pass Domus Conversorum, the chapel of which his uncle told him, where all Jews in England were supposed to convert to Christianity, at the same time allowing all their worldly goods to escheat to the Crown. It's no surprise to Noah that, given such terms, the chapel appears to be unoccupied. He finds it curious that such an unappealing institution ever had any takers. Nearly all the Jews who availed themselves of the chapel have long ago either joined the Church of England and assimilated into English society, or died off while still in residence.

While Noah is offended by the religious atrocity perpetrated upon his people in this place, at the moment his mind is dominated by thoughts more personal and immediate. In his current haze, it occurs to him that this is the usual ordering of his thoughts, which makes him feel guilty for some reason he'd rather not examine. *In vino veritas.* He must remind himself not to drink this much.

Bacon's man stops suddenly, apparently spotting something worrisome up ahead. Quickly, the man withdraws into a recessed doorway, and slowly and carefully peers around its edge. Noah continues walking as though he has not noticed. In a moment, he spots what has apparently disturbed his unwitting walking companion. The next building on Chancery Lane is Southampton House. Before it, the Earl of Southampton chats with Doctor Lopez, who carries his familiar black bag of instruments and medicines. Through a parlor window behind them, a man with a pronounced scar on his left cheek observes the earl and the doctor.

Noah continues, his pace unabated, looking straight ahead. Passing Southampton and the good doctor, he dreads the possibility that Lopez might recognize him and hail him from across the street. Fortunately, the conversation between Lopez and Southampton is too intense to allow for such camaraderie. Something about Lopez's demeanor seems rushed, as though he wishes to terminate the conversation, perhaps to avoid being seen.

Noah gives the matter some muddled thought. Lopez obviously knows Southampton, yet apparently does not wish to be seen with him. Bacon's man obviously does not wish to be seen by Southampton, or Lopez, or both. Even in Noah's impaired state, he realizes it is probable that Bacon's man is already well known to Southampton, who is, after all, Essex's good friend. So, in all likelihood, Bacon's man is concealing himself from *Lopez*, which makes Lopez something of an outsider. He packs the thought away in a corner of his mind, and continues on his way.

He arrives at Gray's Inn in need of a rest. Although the exercise has helped him to feel a little steadier, he has perspired the whole way and feels uncomfortable in his damp clothing. He's thirsty, too. As he climbs the outside stairs to the inn, something in a window by the dining hall catches his eye. Much as he longs to rest in the quiet of his room, he crosses the lawn to the window where he caught a hint of blue.

"Oh, no," he mutters. There, in all his glory, is Finerty, the cross-eyed blue dog, his lolling tongue pressed against the window.

Noah returns to the stairs and enters the inn. The floorboards in the hallway creak loudly, and he wonders vaguely why they never seemed quite so loud before. Jonathan's door is open. Noah sticks his head in.

"You look as though you've been dragged through the streets," says Jonathan. "Where have you been?"

"Out," replies Noah.

"Oh, well, *that* clears things up nicely."

"Um … the dog?"

"Dog? Oh, Finerty."

"Yes. Finerty. He's on guard in the dining room window."

"So it seems," Jonathan says, grinning.

"Why, may I ask?" asks Noah impatiently.

"Well, you know Bleffingham left the courtroom immediately, before I had a chance to gather our things."

"And?"

Jonathan is abashed. "Three of my friends restrained me, while another made away with Finerty. Next thing I knew, he was … where he is. I'll gather him up later, after everyone's asleep."

"Good." Noah weighs telling Jonathan about the name given him by Henry, but decides against it, as Jonathan might then try to discover where he learned such information. If Jonathan is told sometime the following day, it will be soon enough, and Jonathan will probably not be so tempted to research where Noah has been. "Um, could you wake me just after seven this evening? I need to clean up before I go out."

"You certainly do … unless you're attending a masquerade as a drunken barrister — in which case, you'll need to wear some flourish to distinguish yourself from the *real* drunken barristers attending without costume." Jonathan looks at an open brief on his desk. "I'll be here. Go. That gives you barely two hours' rest. Take my advice, and drink some water that's been boiled."

"Where can I find some of that?"

Jonathan reaches into a bag, draws out a water bladder, and tosses it to Noah. "One can never be too prepared," observes Jonathan. As Noah turns to go, Jonathan says, "By the way, nice job in court this morning." Noah nods his thanks as he leaves, barely able to remember an event so long ago. He climbs the stairs, swallows the entire contents of the bladder, about a quart in all, and only wishes there were more. He drops face first onto his bed, and knows no more for a while.

* * *

It's almost full dark in his room when Jonathan tugs at his shoulder. "Time to get up, old man. I've got to go. Sit up, so I'll know you're alive. Do you feel all right?"

Noah sits up slowly and puts both feet on the floor. He feels surprisingly refreshed. "Strangely enough, I do. Thanks." He flexes his injured hand, which emits barely a twinge.

"Not at all," says Jonathan, closing the door as he goes.

Noah lights a candle, and scrubs up thoroughly. It's even warm enough in the room for him to wash his hair and comb it out. He brushes the sour taste from his mouth with salt and water, breathes deeply, and looks closely at his reflection in the mirror.

"Hmm. None the worse for wear."

He dresses in fresh robes, and plods down the inner stairs, bringing along his walking stick. He puts on a light wrap, and descends the outer stairs into the evening. The night air is fresh and cool, with just the slightest scent of spring left over from the day's warmth. So far as he can tell, no spy stands watch on the square. The evening feels full of promise.

As he turns onto High Holborn, he sees many people out and about. Happy noises spill out of the open windows of several taverns — the clink of glasses, a loud guffaw, a few competing songs. In what seems a mere moment, there he stands in front of Marie's house, which is darker than he expected. He hopes he has not misjudged the time, as there appears to be no one bustling about supper inside. Indeed, there seems to be no one at home.

He knocks politely on the door. A moment later it opens, seemingly on its own, and Marie's face appears, illuminated by soft light emanating from an interior sconce. She bears the strangest expression, a mixture of desire and doubt, of hope and resignation, inspiring a sympathetic swirl of emotions in his own breast. He aches for her. Silently, she invites him in. The place is even darker than it looks from outside. She closes the door quietly behind him.

He barely has time to put down his walking stick before she takes him by the crook of his arm and leads him up the darkened stairs.

CHAPTER 8

IN A MOMENT, Noah finds that Marie has led him into a deserted upstairs parlor dimly lit by two candles in a corner. Through the main window, he can see Gray's and the adjacent Mountjoy's Inn. Yet all is peacefully quiet here. Even with several windows ajar, the jovial sounds of pedestrian and tavern traffic are pleasantly remote. He turns to her, uncertain what's expected of him in the dark parlor.

Her eyes glisten with unshed tears. To his amazement, she leans into him and hugs him tightly. In a moment, her tears come in torrents and her breathing in heaves, as though no time at all has passed since that awful day when her husband was murdered. He places his arms gingerly around her shoulders, and she snuggles into his embrace.

As he can do nothing but silently hold her until the tempest has passed, he revisits the pain he felt upon losing Rachel, and how terribly long it lasted. Indeed, the pain remains to this day, and he feels somehow that Marie is weeping for his loss, as well. He draws her in closer, and they stand there for an indeterminate time in mutual grief. While he's still not sure what will come next, he resolves that it will have to be she who decides when this embrace is through.

When her weeping subsides, she looks up at him, her moist eyes glistening with reflected moonlight. Her expression speaks of embarrassment, but he comforts her with a chaste kiss on the forehead. Though this almost starts the torrent again, she turns away, removes a kerchief from her sleeve, wipes her eyes, and blows her nose gently.

He clears his throat and says quietly, "I know what it's like being strong for everyone else."

She turns and embraces him once again, this time more in sympathy than grief.

"Where *is* everyone?" he whispers.

"As I mentioned, the children are in Surrey."

"And the servants?"

"They made supper, and left it for us. I sent them home."

He leads her away from the windows to a divan, and sits down beside her. As he struggles for the perfect words to ease her pain, she turns to look at him, candlelight reflecting off her clear, questioning eyes. *Ah, well,* he realizes, *sometimes words fail even me.*

She hugs him again, her sweet scent ample invitation to stay in this embrace forever, to die here, if that's what's meant to be. After a brief respite, she rises and adjusts her dress. "Wait here," she whispers in the dark. "I'll fetch us some food."

Noah smiles broadly. "Would you like help?"

"No need. There's red wine over there on the sideboard. Help yourself."

He closes his eyes, listening to the comforting sounds of slippered feet shuffling down to the kitchen, the opening and closing of cabinets, and the clink of plates and silverware. Outside, the sounds of revelry have dissipated, and the night is nearly silent, but for the occasional song of a nightingale.

At infinite peace, he rises, pours himself a cup of wine, and amuses himself by locating his rooms at Gray's Inn as best he can, there being no light in his window there. Although the full moon is rising, the inn casts an impenetrable shadow on Gray's Inn Square. As he takes a sip, furtive movement catches his eye. Try though he might, he cannot find it again. A trick of the moonlight, perhaps.

Behind him, Marie's slippered feet reach the landing. Her footsteps cease, as she hesitates a moment before stepping into the parlor. As she's no doubt bearing a tray with plates and food, he turns to the doorway to help, but, before he can take a step, she glides across the threshold, carrying a tray holding a covered chafing dish, two plates, and silverware. She places it carefully on the table and gazes at him silently, her expression too clouded to read.

Perhaps it's the way the soft light plays about her face, and sparkles in her questioning eyes. Or the way a stray tress has come loose and fallen down to frame her cheekbone. It might be the clean womanly scent of her body as she enters the room, or the bottomless sadness in her eyes that resonates within his own heart. Whatever it is, at that very moment he falls hopelessly in love with her.

He takes her into his arms, and kisses her mouth.

"The food will get cold," she reminds him.

"*Damn* the food," he murmurs huskily.

* * *

Noah awakens in the dead of night, unsure where he is. Now he recalls. They ate the mutton stew she brought up from the kitchen, and she led him to a soft couch where they kissed for a long time and then drifted off together. He has no idea what awakened him, perhaps the lark announcing the morning. But he has no recollection of that.

"Is everything all right?" she inquires, awakened by his stirring.

"Yes," he says uncertainly, and rises. Their plates are strewn about the table carelessly, just where they were left. The large clock on the mantel chimes once, announcing two-thirty in the morning.

He goes to the window. It's still dark, but the full moon has risen high enough to illuminate Gray's Inn and the square. There, beneath Anthony Bacon's window, stand two men in quiet conversation, evidently confident of being unobserved, one elegantly attired, wearing a big floppy hat, and another dressed more plainly.

Marie shuffles up behind him, placing a hand on his shoulder. "That's Bacon. He's often there at this hour."

"Anthony?"

She shakes her head. "Francis. Unless Anthony is a sodomite, as well."

He has no need to ask how she knows Francis is often outside Gray's Inn in the middle of the night, recalling only too well that grief shows no respect for day or night, but rather haunts the wakeful mourner at all hours, enlisting him in his own haunting.

"Who is that with him?"

Marie squints. "Is that Marlowe?" she guesses. After a moment, she shakes her head. "No, not Marlowe, although he's often out there with Sir Francis. Sometimes, they kiss so deeply I wonder they don't swallow one another."

Noah scratches his head, and shakes it in bewilderment.

"So, you don't approve of sodomy?"

"I just cannot understand it. Men are hairy, smelly beasts. Why would anyone wish to make love with one?"

She laughs. "Why, indeed!" she says, and kisses him on the cheek. "I saw Sir Francis hand Marlowe a *letter* a few nights ago. You don't suppose they write love letters to one another like men and women, do you?"

Noah shrugs. "I suppose so. Why not?"

"Well, what would happen if such a letter were discovered? Might it not disqualify someone like the great Francis Bacon for high public office?"

Now that he thinks about it, he realizes it might. For a quiet interval, he's left to his own thoughts.

"Something on your mind?" she asks.

He nods.

"Oh? *A secret?*" She giggles.

He turns to her in the dark. "This is serious."

She leads him back to the sofa, and sits him down next to her. "You tell me your intimate secrets, and I'll tell you mine."

He marvels that, had he fully succumbed to his own lust, she would already know one secret that could cost him his career as a barrister. He smiles saucily, and plays dangerously near the subject on his mind. "Shall I boast to you of my unusual manliness?"

She titters. "If you like."

He laughs and shrugs. "I don't know there's much that's unusual."

She seems to have something to say, but hesitates at first. "Stephen was circumcised, may he rest in peace."

"Was he?" asks Noah, surprised at both the fact and her frank revelation of it.

She nods. "He had some Jewish blood, God rest his soul. He was … discreet about it."

"*Had* he?" Noah feels a sudden kinship with her deceased husband. Although he'd already felt pity, somehow this disclosure makes him feel as though it was he who suffered that murderous blow.

"He always said so. He told me that his family had considered abandoning the practice of circumcision a couple of generations ago, not wishing to be denounced as heretics."

"So, he was papist, and then Church of England, but thought of himself as a Jew?"

"Yes."

"Did he observe any rituals of the Hebrew religion?"

"Only one. Every year, he would … " The words choke her.

Noah touches her hand. "He would light a candle for the dead?" It's too dark to see, but he senses her nodding. A tear falls on his hand. "Common enough. Would you like to do that for him?" he whispers.

"Yes," she says, holding back a sob.

"That can be arranged." He chooses his words carefully to avoid giving anything away. "I do that, too, for my deceased wife."

She places her hand on his shoulder. "Oh, let's do that for him. I so wish to do *something* for him."

"Most people light a mourner's candle on each anniversary of their loved one's death. That would mean you and I could light a single candle to commemorate both our beloveds, as they died on the same day of the year. Let's resolve to light our candle together next year. I'll bring my candlestick here."

She nods and sniffles, seeming a little comforted.

He wonders whether there will ever come a time when he feels confident enough of her affections to reveal his own Jewishness. It would be a relief simply to say it outright, but such a profoundly dangerous revelation will have to wait. This seems the right occasion, however, to reveal to her what he originally intended. "I have a secret, too," he says, "this one touching the manner of Stephen's death, God rest his soul."

As she waits, Noah considers carefully how to couch what he'll say next. He needs to be careful of her feelings, and watchful of any doubts about his honesty that might arise from his having withheld it this long. Even more importantly, he must consider that her simply *knowing* what he's about to tell her might place her very life in danger. Then again, *not* knowing it might be even more dangerous. On the other hand, in the unlikely event she's in league with Southampton and Essex, and she repeats to them what Noah is about to tell her, then both Noah and Jonathan might well pay with their lives.

While Noah considers himself no expert in judging the character of women, it seems clear that Marie genuinely loved her deceased husband, which makes it very unlikely that she would align herself with his murderer. Under ordinary circumstances, he would be inclined to clear up the matter of her connection with Southampton, but now is clearly not the time. She's far too vulnerable. Nevertheless, he can no longer withhold the secret about Essex. Not after they've shared their feelings for each other.

"Marie, that awful day ... you heard Essex say that he'd seen the attack?"

"Yes."

He braces himself for her reaction. "He had not. I know precisely where he was when your husband was attacked. He was still in the theater, and there were no windows providing a view to the place where it happened."

She's silent for a moment. "Do you think he was ... involved?"

He hesitates, as now he's entering the field of speculation, which he knows by training to be a perilously far cry from fact. "I've mulled over that question often this past month, and cannot come up with an explanation that entirely exculpates the earl. There's something else. Your husband had a note in his pocket written and signed by Walsingham, who was the Queen's spymaster until he died a few years ago. Evidently, your husband had worked for Walsingham. Master Neville and Essex's man both thought it best to leave the note with the constable."

"With that *idiot*?"

He nods.

She shivers hard enough to shake the sofa. Though she is preponderantly horrified, he detects an undercurrent of anger, which he can only hope is not directed toward him. He feels awful, having waited so long to tell her.

"There is one bright note," he offers hesitantly, "although I am unsure what to make of it, exactly. Do you know who the distinguished young spectator was, in the court gallery this morning?"

"No."

"He was Sir Robert Cecil, second most powerful man on the Privy Council. His father Lord Burghley is the *most* powerful."

"Truly?"

"Yes, and together they're Essex's most powerful opponents."

"Why did Sir Robert come to court?"

"Although this may sound delusional on my part, I expect he came to observe … me." He turns to Marie. "He knows that you have sought my assistance in investigating Stephen's murder."

"But … what interest would Cecil have in a murder investigation … and why would he come to observe you?"

"I think he already suspects that Essex was somehow involved in Stephen's murder. Cecil may be looking for allies, such as I might be."

"Would Essex's involvement in the murder of a commoner be sufficient to garner Cecil's attention?"

This is an excellent question, and Noah considers it seriously. He couches his reply carefully.

"Probably not … unless the murder were part of a greater conspiracy endangering the welfare of the whole state."

That thought hangs in the air a few seconds.

"I have a couple of confessions, too," says Marie, chafing her shoulders with her hands.

Noah braces himself.

"I lied when I said that we import and export only with Spain. We do a good deal of business with the Netherlands, as well. They're under Spanish domination. So, in a sense, they are Spain."

He smirks. "The Privy Council might disagree, as it's fervently hoped such domination will be merely temporary."

Marie nods, but remains lost in thought. "Also, I saw Stephen talking to Doctor Lopez one time, about a month before … the incident." He turns to her, surprised. "I didn't recognize Lopez when he first came over to me by The Rose, nor all that terrible day. But the next day when I saw him at Creechurch … as he was about to walk down the stairs to the cellar, I saw his profile clearly. Yes, it was him. I'm sure of it."

"Where did Stephen and Lopez speak with each other?"

She seems lost in thought. "This will sound odd, but Stephen brought me in the coach one time to Eton. The boys' school?"

"Yes, I know of Eton. I attended there."

"Oh, then you may know the building. It looked like a headmaster's home … but there were several buildings that could fit that description. We rode up in a closed carriage, and Stephen got out. Doctor Lopez was already standing in front of the building. Upstairs, the windows were open, even though it was still quite cold outside, and there was an awful row going on inside. I heard two voices. One belonged to an older man, and one to a younger. They were arguing, sometimes nearly screaming at one another. Very ugly. All the while, Stephen and Lopez were talking gravely with each other, doing their best to ignore the ruckus. Then, Lopez handed Stephen something, and Stephen hopped back in the carriage, very relieved to get away from the place. He ordered our driver to pull away immediately."

"Could you hear what they were saying?"

"Who? Stephen and Lopez? Not as I recall."

"How about the men arguing upstairs? Could you make out what *they* were saying?"

Again, she seems lost in thought. "Well, they were shouting like mad at one another in Spanish, or what I *took* for Spanish, which I speak fluently. The dialect was strange to me, though, and hard to follow. It sounded almost as though they had a speech impediment, but of course they both spoke in precisely the same way, which usually means a dialect of some kind. I seem to recall the young man addressing the older man as 'father,' and the older man fervidly denying paternity. 'You are no son of mine,' and so on. Come to think of it, I vaguely recall Lopez referring to the older man as 'Don Antonio.' I caught a glimpse of the old man through the window as we pulled away. He looked a dissolute old drunkard. There was a yellow stain on his open shirt. I think it may have been … vomit, but I can't be sure."

Noah recalls Henry saying that "Don Antonio" was the name of the man to be placed on the Portuguese throne by the English Armada expedition. "Could they have been speaking Portuguese?" he inquires.

A moment of silence passes in the dark. "You know, they *may* have been, for I'm uncertain whether I've ever heard Portuguese spoken. Perhaps I *have*, spoken by some toothless old salt, but never realized it was a different language from Spanish. The number of dialects spoken on the Iberian Peninsula seems infinite. One can never be sure when a dialect has assumed the character of a different language, unless one is told. Anyway, as we pulled away from Eton, Stephen showed me a batch of letters that Lopez had handed him, and said that he had to hand them over to a messenger who would be on our vessel leaving for Antwerp the next day."

"Then, Lopez must have known you were withholding information that day in the hearse, when you said you did business only with Spain."

"Perhaps. But, he might have assumed that I'd been deluded into thinking I knew everything Stephen had been doing in our business. So, Lopez might have thought I was simply mistaken. I'm not sure he even knew I'd been waiting for Stephen in the carriage at Eton."

Noah has a lot to think about now. "It also means Lopez was doing an autopsy on a man he *knew* at least in passing, yet never mentioned that to the man's widow. Any other confessions?" he asks.

"Just one."

"Out with it."

"I'm leaving at the end of April for Antwerp. They're not accustomed to having a woman run a business over there, so I have to set things up with my eldest son as the new owner. He needs to be introduced to important people, needs to sign things, and so on."

"How long will you be gone?" he asks, disappointed.

"A couple of months, at least. Probably through the summer. Just getting a favorable wind to cross the Channel can take days, or even weeks."

He's silent, wondering how he will live without her now that she's carved a place for herself in his heart.

She leans forward and takes him by the shoulder. "Don't think me unspeakably cruel. I wanted you to remember me while I'm gone, as I shall remember you. I don't want some other woman claiming you while I'm not present to stand guard. You do see, don't you?" She says doubtfully, "You won't forget me, will you?"

He laughs. "Were I to live forever, I could never forget you."

She hugs him tight.

CHAPTER 9

IN A SPARE ANTEROOM outside the Privy Council Chamber at Westminster, Essex paces nervously, his eyes darting expectantly down the hall.

"I'm sure he'll be here soon, Robert," Southampton assures him.

Essex arches an eyebrow. "He'd better be. It's imprudent to keep Her Majesty waiting, to say nothing of the Cecils and the other jackals on the Council." Before he can speak further, Skeres darts around the corner, heading their way, his scarred face flush, drawn into a sweaty grimace. He bows low to Essex, and hands up a sealed scroll.

Essex glowers at him and grabs the scroll away. "You came straightaway?"

"Aye, m'lord. Doctor Lopez's seal is still warm."

But Essex is above any need to test such a foolish representation. "Skeres," he says, "did he tell you this contains the promised intelligence?"

"Aye, m'lord."

Essex draws himself up in evident satisfaction, and comes close enough to Southampton to whisper. "Wriothesley, please await me here, and keep this scoundrel with you." He disappears with the scroll into the Privy Council Chamber.

To break the tension, Southampton asks: "And how fares the good doctor?"

Skeres shrugs. "His body's in middlin' health, m'lord, yet he strikes me as a man forever sick in his soul. I'd never urge you or m'lord of Essex to trust him a whit."

Suddenly, a woman's derisive laughter rings through the anteroom.

Skeres looks up at him with dread. "Is that — ?"

Southampton nods gravely. "Her Majesty."

Essex emerges from the chamber, his face red, eyes bloodshot. In his hand is the unfurled scroll. He turns sharply on Skeres, upbraiding him in a hoarse whisper. "How dare you tell me that only I have this information? The Queen just laughed in my face. She said she's known it for weeks!"

Skeres bows low, which only infuriates Essex, who begins beating him roundly.

Southampton stays his hand, and tugs him away from the cowering Skeres. "Robert," he says, "did the Cecils laugh, as well?"

Essex scowls. "What does it matter?" he begins, but then trails off. "Now you mention it … no, they didn't."

"Did they seem … disquieted?"

Essex nods thoughtfully. "What of that?"

"One can't be sure," says Southampton, "but it appears the good doctor has been feeding his intelligence to the Cecils before we ever hear it."

Essex can barely croak through his consternation. "But I've been *paying* him for it."

Southampton shrugs. "The Cecils may have been paying him *more*."

Essex calms visibly, and takes a deep breath. "Please rise, Nicholas," he says. "I beg your pardon. I was carried away — "

"I understand, m'lord."

"It is Lopez's loyalty I doubt. Not yours."

"I do understand, m'lord."

"Rise, Nick, please," says Essex, giving him a hand up. "Has Lopez received from Spain any information newer than this?" he asks, indicating the scroll, its seal smashed to pieces.

"Nay, m'lord, but … but one of his main sources of intelligence from the Continent returns from Spain tomorrow evening."

"Who?"

"His name's Tinoco, m'lord. Another little Spaniard."

"Ah, I see. Well, let's see if we can't get Tinoco's new intelligence before Lopez does. *Secretly*, mind you. If the Cecils report his intelligence to the Queen before Lopez shares it with us, then we'll know they're in conspiracy with Lopez." Essex paces thoughtfully. "Invite Tinoco to that tavern you favor in Eastcheap."

"The Boar's Head, m'lord?"

"The very one. Ply him with drink. Get his intelligence and secure his silence with money, threats … whatever works. Report this intelligence immediately — and exclusively — to me and m'lord Southampton." Essex turns to Southampton and smiles smugly, which unnerves Southampton even more than his churlish display of bad temper.

"A well-considered plan," says Southampton.

"Once we can show the Cecils in conspiracy with Lopez, all that's left is to show that Lopez has committed at least one serious crime in England, which no doubt he has. And then we'll have the Cecils where we want them."

Essex hands Skeres a bag of coins. "Show some initiative, Nick, and there's more for you." Skeres nods silently and slinks out the way he came.

Southampton regards Essex skeptically. "You're forgetting one thing, Robert."

"What's that?"

"You still need your man to become Attorney General."

Essex nods smugly. "And who's there to stop us? No one suspects any connection between the Attorney Generalship and a possible prosecution of the Cecils, now, do they?"

Southampton shrugs. "No one ... but perhaps Henry Neville — "

Essex waves away the suggestion. "*Ach*, he's one of *us*."

Southampton makes no reply, but in the back of his mind lurks the recurring image of Neville's friend, the barrister.

*   *   *

Noah prepares to leave Marie's house. She's assured him that her children will not be returning until Sunday evening and that, until then, the servants will be sent home each evening and instructed not to return until noon the next day. That promises Noah three more evenings alone with her, and the mere thought of them puts a spring in his step.

Though his visit with Marie was chaste, to avoid endless ribbing and possible scandal he needs to ensure that no one at Gray's Inn sees him march out of the widow's house, so he leaves by the back door, which is hidden from Gray's by a hedgerow of tall yew trees, and hugs the concealed side of the house all the way to the road. Instead of taking the most direct route to Gray's Inn, he walks a great circle so that, by the time he appears to any inquisitive eyes at Gray's Inn, he will not be approaching from the telltale southwest.

He arrives at the inn about twenty minutes later. Although Finerty stands guard in the same window as he did yesterday, Noah reminds himself that he has important matters to discuss with Jonathan, and no time for frippery. He sticks his head into Jonathan's ever-open doorway.

Jonathan appears to be studying a yellowed land map spread out on his desk. "Noah!" he chirps, then lowers his voice. "How's the widow?"

Noah's jaw drops. He puts his finger up to his lips to silence Jonathan. "I'm sure I don't know what you're talking about."

"And I'm sure you *do!*"

Grumbling, Noah shuts the door behind, plops onto the only uncluttered chair, and leans forward. "And how might you be sure of that?"

"Thistlethwaite was in his office last evening at dusk and looked out of the window, about to hail you, when you" — Jonathan pretends to search his memory — "'vanished from the steps of a private residence,' I believe were his words. I suspected the residence might belong to the widow. Does it?"

"No," he lies. *Thistlethwaite!* After all the legal business Noah has sent his way, one might have expected some discretion.

Jonathan purses his lips skeptically. "Then whose house was it?"

"I didn't come here to talk about where I spent last evening."

"Oh, but *please* do!" Jonathan implores.

Noah regards him impatiently.

"Don't worry," says Jonathan, with a smirk. "Thistlethwaite hadn't mentioned it to anyone else, and I told him he'd better seal his lips if he knew what was good for him. He assured me he would be governed by my suggestion. Oh! I almost forgot." Jonathan smiles. "He sends you his compliments. But I must say that your having left the courtroom with the widow yesterday was quite enough to get tongues wagging about here. Yesterday, your victory in court had you lauded as the conquering hero. But today, on speculation alone you're an object of *worship*! She really is quite beautiful, y'know."

"Why is Finerty still in the window?" asks Noah. Although he hadn't intended to discuss the toy, it now seems a good idea to distract Jonathan from further conjecture about Marie.

"He's not *still* there. He's there *again*! I took him away last night, and put him back in my closet. The same four jesters who stole him in the first instance came in here and took him back. Incidentally, they wanted me to tell you that they're very interested in working with you in any capacity you wish. Anyway, as far as the dog goes, they threatened to glue my boots together if I remove him again." Jonathan looks at his feet. "And I haven't the boots to spare."

"Go get them," says Noah.

"The boots?"

"Not the boots. The *jesters*! I think they might be of some help in the Rodriguez investigation."

"*Oh*! All right." Jonathan rolls up the map, and stuffs it into a cylinder. "I'm not sure they're all here, though."

"Don't mention why I wish to see them, but tell them that, if they don't come, I'll set Master Treasurer on them." Jonathan leaves the room

It's common knowledge that virtually every resident of Gray's Inn is in violation of the rules to some extent, most often by arrears in payment. The treasurer, who is in charge of enforcing rules of all kinds, is known to apply them most strictly against barristers behind in rent.

A few minutes later, what sounds like a squadron of soldiers approaches Jonathan's room and comes to parade rest outside the door.

"Let me *by*," Jonathan can be heard saying, apparently shoving his way through, so he can enter first. "Here they are," he announces. "The four jesters!"

Four broad-shouldered, solidly built young men file in, each wearing one or more items of barrister's attire, but none of them properly dressed. They are all earnest and fresh-faced. Three are blond; one of those is a handsome, confident fellow, while the other two, perhaps a bit more retiring, appear to be brothers, possibly twins. The fourth young man, much darker than the others, is shorter, but still strapping. Together, they could make a good foundation for a football team. Eyes downcast, they all appear contrite.

"Good afternoon, gentlemen," says Noah gravely.

"Good afternoon, Master Ames," they intone as one, sounding like a well-behaved, but strangely baritone, choir at Eton.

The handsome one steps forward. "I'm Arthur Arden, sir." He breathes deeply. "We meant no offense, Master Ames. We all went to see your cross-examination yesterday, and, when you poked fun back at Inner Temple, we got a bit carried away. We'll take the dog down from the window — "

"Let it be," says Noah. "Master Hawking, how much did the dog cost?"

"Tuppence, sir."

As all four fellows prepare to reach into their pockets, Noah nearly laughs aloud. "I'll bear the freight," he assures them, handing four pence to Jonathan. "Buy James a bigger dog." He turns back to the four. "That's not why I called you here."

All eyes but Jonathan's register surprise, and focus on Noah, just as he'd wished.

"Jonathan tells me you gentlemen would like to assist me in a case." This brightens them up. "May I ask you all a few questions?"

Arden glances back at the others. "Certainly, sir."

"Are you fellows satisfied to become good workaday barristers, arguing over wills and indentures the rest of your days?" Unsurprisingly, he has no takers. "Or would you prefer to see what life is like in the rougher trade?"

The four look at each other, and smile.

"What would that entail, sir?" asks Arden.

"Well, I expect you all know that English Common Law is at its very worst in any case of political importance. Would it trouble you to be involved in such a case? Before you answer, permit me to remind you that a political case can make or break a career, especially those as new as yours."

"So, what's the possible benefit, sir?"

"Well, first of all, if you're on the side of the politically powerful, you might ingratiate yourself with that party, gaining a clear path to advancement thereafter. Even if you lose the case, if you're popularly seen as a good lawyer, you can become famous, and people who can readily pay your fees will seek you out when they're in trouble."

"And what would we have *to lose*, sir?"

"Nothing important." Noah smirks, contemplating his own and Jonathan's predicament. "Your careers. Possibly your lives."

There's a thoughtful pause.

"May we talk among ourselves, sir?"

"Certainly."

They file out into the hallway, and the door closes slowly and quietly behind them. In a minute, a soft rap on the door is followed by the four filing back in. Arden speaks first. "Are we to understand that you are already involved in this case, and that you are in need of our help?"

"Yes," Noah nods gravely. "But I am no longer young, gentlemen. I can take care of myself, and am prepared to follow through alone, if need be."

"Well ... we're in, sir."

Noah breathes more easily. "Very well, then. I have a few questions. Are any of you titled nobility?"

The twins and the dark one snort a laugh. Again, Arden speaks for them. "They are not, sir. I am of a noble family, but my branch is not titled. I am a Neville, sir."

Noah's eyebrows rise. "Related to Master Henry?"

"I believe so, sir ... distantly."

"Yours is a noble family, indeed."

Arden's chest swells with pride.

Noah resumes. "How long have you four known each other?"

"All our lives, sir. We went to public school together. With Hawking here, sir."

"Do any of you have athletic skills?"

This draws a general laugh. "We're *all* Eton football, sir. *And* horse."

Noah smiles in return. "Good. Can any of you shoot?"

This appears to shake them a bit.

"*Guns*, sir?" asks Arden.

Noah nods.

The dark one steps forward. "Andres Salazar, sir. I shoot competitively." Although he looks Spanish, he sounds quite English.

"Salazar," repeats Noah thoughtfully. "Is that Portuguese?"

"It is, sir."

"Do you *speak* Portuguese?"

"Fluently, sir."

Noah nods. "That might come in handy. Have you a sidearm here at Gray's, Master Salazar?"

"I have several, sir."

"Keep them clean. And purchase ammunition. I'll pay that bill, too." He turns to the others. "One last question. Is any of you related to a member of the Privy Council?"

Their eyes grow wide. Evidently, they have not anticipated how politically explosive a law case can be. They shake their heads.

"Very well. Thank you, gentlemen. Leave word with Jonathan where you will be for the next few days, even if you go out only briefly. And do not discuss this with anyone else. On your honor, and *for your own safety*! Go now. We will be in touch presently."

They nod as one, and file out, the last one closing the door. Jonathan furrows his brow. "As you've evidently decided we need those four, it appears as though you've learned a few more things about the Rodriguez case."

Noah informs Jonathan about the purse snatching and the thief's disguise and fear of identification, and he summarizes what he's learned — and guessed — about the reasons for Robert Cecil's visit to the spectators' gallery. Finally, he tells him that an unnamed informant has provided Skeres' name without explanation, but has advised that whoever is to speak with Skeres should bring some of his rougher friends along to the interview.

Jonathan asks about Henry's position in relation to members of the Privy Council involved in the affair. Noah explains that Henry is a favorite of Essex and a relative of Cecil, which gives him any number of possible motives for throwing the investigation of the Rodriguez murder off track. While he assures Jonathan that Henry would never knowingly lead them astray or into a trap (of that much Noah feels certain), men trusted by Henry might manipulate him into doing so unwittingly.

They will have to proceed with caution. Step by step, as though planning to mount a particularly difficult case at Queen's Bench, they plot the first serious steps in their investigation. They agree that tonight Jonathan will speak to Graves, the shady but reliable character who's assisted Jonathan in the Rodriguez case since its inception. Tomorrow, they have two calls to make.

And the latter might be dangerous indeed.

CHAPTER 10

AT NOON THE NEXT DAY, as Noah and Jonathan wait for the stable boy to bring their mounts around, each is lost in his own thoughts.

Noah is overwhelmed by the lingering memory of Marie, her sheer beauty and softness. Even though he's washed since leaving her side today, an occasional hint of her scent seems to waft toward him on the fresh breeze. He inhales deeply the warmth of the day, surrendering to the yearning for life she has newly revived in him. While it seems ironic for his Creator to have enriched beyond measure a life now in danger, he cannot help but feel grateful for the strange coincidence by which she's appeared at a moment of increasing peril, like a warning beacon sent to pierce the gray cloud of profane indifference that enshrouds him after so many years alone.

Jonathan has been up since dawn. His eyes are red, not only from the barrister's bane of reading far into the night, but from worry, as well. An hour earlier, as agreed the previous day, Jonathan dispatched Graves to ascertain whether Nicholas Skeres is presently in London, and where he might be found. Although it seemed a simple enough task to Jonathan, Graves reminded him that making inquiries into the whereabouts of someone wishing not to be found is among an investigator's most dangerous jobs, one that can readily lead to a drubbing, or worse. The stable boy brings the horses around, and Noah and Jonathan tie leather bags securely to the saddles.

Jonathan mounts and turns to Noah. "As we'll be retrieving Walsingham's letter from the constable about two o'clock — assuming we're fortunate enough to find he still has it — I told my investigator Graves to meet us down there."

Noah nods his approval, and they begin their progress. As London Bridge is not particularly crowded that noon, the journey takes less than a half hour. Reaching the stone gate at the base of the bridge, they dismount, turn right, and meander through Southwark Priory to the constable's station that guards its western entrance.

Noah leans toward Jonathan. "Now, remember: A man's deficiencies in the English language do not make him stupid. In any event, I'll warrant the constable has wits enough to realize when he's an object of fun, and you must bear in mind that we need his assistance."

"Be assured," replies Jonathan.

"Oh, and there's no need to mention our names, unless we're asked."

As they approach the constable's booth, out comes the man himself, seeming preoccupied. He looks up at the clop of their horses' hooves. Spotting Noah, he smiles and bows. "If I'm not mistaken, you're the gentleman barrister who's been servicin' the young widow."

Jonathan snorts, and Noah arches an eyebrow at him.

"Actually, Constable Barn-Stable," says Noah, placing equal emphasis on both halves of the name, "*this* young barrister is representing the widow in the prosecution of her husband's murder."

Barnstable nods gravely to Jonathan. "Terrible thing, that! Ought never 'ave 'appened. But me and my men can't be all places at one time, can we?"

"Of *course* not," Noah says sympathetically. "By the way, do you recall discovering a note in one of the victim's pockets?"

The constable seems confused. "Why, sir! Had Goodman Rodriguez been *victimizing* people?"

"I was characterizing Goodman *Rodriguez* as the victim. Do you recall discovering a note in his pocket?"

Barnstable stares at the ground, deep in thought. For a long while, he appears to be in a trance.

"Constable?" says Noah, jarring him to attention.

"Why, yes, sir, I do recall a note. I gave it to the widow, did I not?"

Noah pretends to be thinking hard. "As I recall, we made a list of the contents of all the pockets, but handed the widow only the coins and the empty purse."

"Oh, that's right." He snaps his fingers. "Now you mention it, Lord Essex's man come here some days ago lookin' for the same note."

Noah shoots Jonathan a glance. "*Which* of Essex's men? Was it Goodman Wheaton, the one remaining at the scene after the earl left?"

"No, I know the one ye mean, but it wasn't him, suh. I'd seen *this* one before, about town. Must say I don't much like the look of 'im."

Noah nods knowingly. "Did he tell you his name?"

"He did, suh, but, well ... I meet so many people in this job, it's — "

With a look of distaste, Jonathan ventures, "Was it Gelly Meyrick?"

The constable's eyebrows shoot up. "Why, it *was*, young suh. Now look, if he's a friend of yours, I'm sorry I — "

"Oh, he's no friend of *mine*," Jonathan assures him.

Noah asks, "I take it you turned the note over to him?"

"Why no, suh. I'm embarrassed to say I could not find it anywhere."

Of course! Noah realizes that's why the note was sought in his own saddlebag and Marie's purse.

Jonathan asks, "Did you look in your file?"

"Beg pardon, suh?"

"Your *file*?"

"Not sure I take your meanin', suh."

Jonathan is speechless. "Well, how do you keep your papers arranged?"

"*Arranged*, suh?"

Noah chimes in. "I believe my young friend wishes to know whether you customarily store papers found in the course of your job in some special place."

"Oh, no, suh. Too many things to keep track of. But now you mention it, Goodman Meyrick asked me that, too."

Jonathan looks at Noah and shrugs in defeat, but Noah is not prepared to give up quite yet. As he looks at the constable's clothing, something dawns on him. "Constable, do you recall what you did with the note that day?"

"Can't say's I do, suh."

"I believe you put it in your pocket."

Barnstable's eyebrows pop up. "I did, suh? *Which* pocket?"

Noah points to the right pocket of the constable's doublet. "*That* one."

The constable stuffs his hand in his pocket, and draws out a paper that appears to have been through the wars, as though it's been wrinkled and flattened dozens of times. He hands it to Noah. "Is this it, suh?"

Noah unfolds and reads it. "This is it. Why, thank you, Constable, for your customary care." He hands a coin to the constable, who misses the sarcasm completely.

Barnstable's eyes light up. "Why, thank *you*, suh, very much! Tell you the truth, I didn't want to give it to that Gilly man, anyways, even if I'd found it. Um," he beckons with his finger, and Noah leans in toward him, "if you see the earl, suh, you won't mention my givin' that to you, will ye?"

Noah smiles darkly. "I can assure you, Constable, that he will not learn it from either of us. Right, my friend?"

"Most assuredly," says Jonathan.

The constable seems mollified. "It will be just between us, then. Good! Now will there be anythin' else?"

Noah shakes his head. "Nothing today, Constable. Good day."

"Same to you gentlemen." And with that, he bows briefly and disappears into his station.

Noah hears a hissing behind him, as of someone trying to get attention. He turns, but sees no one. Handing the note to Jonathan, he says, "I suppose we need not be concerned that the constable's clothing will be worn out by the laundry."

The hiss returns. Noah turns, and this time spies Jonathan's man Graves partially concealed behind a stone building adjacent to the cathedral. Noah points him out to Jonathan, who seems perplexed.

Graves beckons with his hand. As he clearly has no intention of being lured out of his hiding place, Noah and Jonathan walk their mounts over to him.

Jonathan seems irritated. "What's the matter with you?" he demands sharply.

"I didn't want that constable spottin' me, that's all. Had a small run-in with him years ago. Couldn't understand a bleedin' word he said. Made me feel like mebbe I was crazy. Y'know?"

Noah suppresses a smile.

"Anyway, you two gentlemen'll want to be at the Boar's Head in Eastcheap tonight at eight. Seems to be where Skeres holds court. He don't know you're comin'. At least, I *think* he won't. But you better come with sharp weapons, and no mistake."

"Thank you, Goodman Graves," says Noah with concern. "We shall surely be armed. But we shall only be making inquiries. Do you really think it might come to that?"

"Aye, sir. It may well."

"In that case, we would benefit greatly by your experience, Goodman Graves. You know, it would be prudent for us to have your wits about us."

Graves snickers dourly. "Well said, sir. I'm afeard that's exactly what you'll need about ye. *My* wits. Not that they're so fine as you gentlemen's, but I've been in places so dark … so … *evil* … " He winces in disgust, and his voice trails off.

Jonathan appears unsettled by his response.

"Well," says Graves, "that says it all. I'll be going with ye, Master Hawking." He sighs resignedly. "And you, Master Ames, mebbe you go into the Boar's Head first, all alone. Y'know, just eat and drink, and keep t'yerself. That way, if anythin' … unexpected happens, you'll be in a position to go for help right away."

Jonathan says, "But you'll be coming with me, Goodman Graves. Won't you?"

Graves places a reassuring hand on his shoulder. "I'll be there with ye, Jon … I mean, Master Hawking. I don't suppose they'll want to be messin' with *two* of us." Although Graves offers Jonathan a reassuring smile, Noah can see grave doubt just beneath the surface.

Noah begins to suspect that two — even three — might not be enough to handle Skeres and his men, and considers what to do about it.

* * *

Beneath the hood of a drab woolen cloak stained with years of travel, Noah sits alone at a small table in the main room of the Boar's Head Tavern. Before him are a few small plates of mutton and parsnips, and a large tankard of ale. He has deliberately held his words to the barest minimum. When he's spoken at all, he's done his best to mimic closely the speech of those around him. So far, he seems to be succeeding in drawing no especial notice, but for the mild flirtation of one young serving wench who seems to have detected something pleasing in what little she could see of his face. He hopes she has not espied the mask he has at the ready under his cowl.

Even so early in the evening, the night has turned chill. The innkeeper, a Mistress Quickly, has built a small blaze in a fireplace behind a long serving board evidently being held in reserve for a group not yet arrived. Noah has chosen for himself a table with a good view of the reserved section.

The air in the room is thick. Adding to the smoke of the wood fire is a stench spewed by a weed called "tobacco." A stationary cloud of foul-smelling smoke floats around each of several customers burning the weed in the tip of a long-stemmed tube. By snippets of overheard conversation, Noah has deduced that the tubes are called "pipes" and that the "smokers" are mostly seamen who've sailed the New World under the privateer Francis Drake. Noah finds the acrid smoke obnoxious in the stagnant air, and feels the urge to cough, until some blessed person opens a window.

A large floor-standing clock with a visible pendulum tells the time as quarter to eight. Noah is nursing his ale, occasionally poking a parsnip with his fork, when a group of three men strides in noisily through the rear and occupies the reserved table without hesitation.

First to enter, and well dressed, is the scarred man that Noah saw two days ago spying out a window in the front room of Southampton House. Noah quickly turns his gaze aside and draws the hood more closely about his face. Trying not to look as alarmed as he feels, he prays that the scarred man did not get a good look at him walking past the earl and Lopez on Chancery Street. Next come two serious-looking men. A few moments later, a fourth man staggers in behind them, appearing to be either lame or drunk. *Drunk,* Noah suspects, for he collapses into the nearest chair.

Mistress Quickly wipes her hands on her apron as she greets the men. "And would each of you gentlemen be wantin' a tankard of ale to begin?"

The scarred man stands behind the table and addresses the innkeeper in surprisingly refined tones: "Why, yes, Mistress Quickly. For each of us, except Bob here, who's had enough already."

One side of the scarred man's face contorts into a sneering rictus so hideous it sends shivers up Noah's spine, but the innkeeper takes it as a smile, and smiles in return. The scarred man seems pleased by her response, and bows in a courtly manner entirely out of place in this sort of establishment. Either he has some noble pretensions, or believes such behavior to be expected of him.

The four assume seats facing out at the room, with the fireplace behind them. The scarred man sits at center table, flanked by his two earnest followers, while the drunk, being pointedly ignored, remains at the end of the table where he first plopped.

The blonde serving wench appears with four full tankards, and smiles as she deposits one before each of the newcomers. Although the drunk smiles at his unexpected tankard, the scarred man rises immediately and removes it from his place, pointedly handing it back to the wench.

The drunk is up in arms. "C'mon, Nick. Where's the harm?"

The scarred man, evidently Nicholas Skeres, addresses his drunken friend in guttural tones. "Quit it, Bob. Yer makin' a nuisance of yerself. Now, sit there, and shut up a while!"

The drunk replies with a dismissive wave, gets up, and walks over to the bar, where he quickly finds conversation to his liking. Noah takes a sip of ale, and continues to observe as unobtrusively as possible.

The front door swings open, and in walks Jonathan with Graves in tow. Mistress Quickly asks where they'd care to sit, and whether they've come for supper or to relax over a pint. Jonathan seems uncomfortable as he responds with a smile, and asks who those three gentlemen are at the long table.

Behind Jonathan and Graves, a short, swarthy Spaniard enters alone, and waits wearily for the innkeeper to get to him.

Bob the drunk, who's getting ever drunker at the tap, recognizes the Spaniard and says loudly: "Hey, Nick! Look who it is! Our old friend Tinoco." He points to the Spaniard. "Looks like they'll let *anybody* in 'ere nowadays." Although his words seem jocular enough, they appear to mask a note of tension, perhaps even a threat.

Skeres grabs the drunkard and mutters to him threateningly. "Now, don't be botherin' Tinoco, Bob. I gotta get some information from him — for *Essex*. Got it?" Bob nods woozily, and Skeres returns to his seat.

The Spaniard pointedly ignores the drunk, but removes his hat and bows toward Skeres, who acknowledges with a nod. After a word with the man to his right, Skeres beckons the Spaniard to sit at the end of the table recently vacated by the drunk. "Won't you sit down, sir, and tell us of your travels?"

Tinoco nods, bows to Mistress Quickly as he passes her, and approaches Skeres' table, leaning over it to speak a few words to him privately.

Mistress Quickly leads Jonathan and Graves to Skeres' table, and says apologetically, "These two gentlemen say they have some business with you, sir. Would you like me to seat them here with you?"

Skeres scowls and squints, first at Jonathan and then Graves, evidently dissatisfied that he knows either of them.

In good barrister's form, Jonathan leads by offering Skeres a handshake. "Goodman Skeres, I presume?"

Skeres regards Jonathan skeptically and declines the proffered hand. "Who's askin'?"

"I am Jonathan Hawking, sir. I represent the widow of Stephen Rodriguez, who was murdered some weeks ago near The Rose Theater. Perhaps you have heard of the crime?"

"You a barrister?" asks Skeres with undisguised contempt.

"I am, sir. This gentleman — "

"Where's yer robes?"

Jonathan smiles patiently. "We do not wear our robes at all times, Goodman Skeres. They can become ungainly, as you might imagine."

"Who's *this*?" asks Skeres sharply, referring to Graves.

"As I was just about to say, sir, this is my associate Goodman Graves."

"Graves." Skeres scowls suspiciously, as though remembering the name. "You been askin' after me today, Graves?"

Graves clears his throat nervously. "I have, sir, but only to arrange a meeting between yourself and my master here."

While Skeres deliberately maintains an outward appearance of suspicion, Noah can see that he's satisfied with Graves' answer.

"All right," says Skeres. "Why don't you two sit down a moment?" He holds up two fingers to Mistress Quickly, who draws a pint each for Jonathan and Graves and hands them to the wench.

"So, what can I do for you two gentlemen? Or, more important, what can *you* do for *me*?" His face contorts into a mellower version of his ghastly smile.

Jonathan blanches, but smiles in return. "I was wondering, sir, whether you might have heard anything about — "

"Still peddlin' yer little red jewel, Tinoco?" comes the voice of Bob the drunk, who staggers over to the end of the table, opposite the Spaniard Tinoco. He's quite obviously smashed now, slurring his words and wobbling on his feet.

Although Tinoco remains seated, he looks alarmed.

Skeres' face reddens, and he tells the man to his right to "do somethin' about Bob." The man gets up and draws the drunk away from the table by the collar. They converse quietly. Skeres nods for Jonathan to resume, keeping one eye on Bob.

"Anyway, Goodman Skeres, I was wondering if perhaps you know of anyone in town who is known to carry what the Italians call a 'stiletto.'"

Skeres, though preoccupied with his drunken companion, is startled and unsettled by the question, removing any doubt in Noah's mind that Henry was right in expecting Skeres to have information that might lead to the murderer.

"What?" says Skeres distractedly, then turns to the drunk. "Bob, so help me. Keep your bleedin' mouth shut, or I'll shut it for you." The skin around his neck tightens, and his veins bulge.

He turns back to Jonathan. "No, gentlemen, I'm sorry. I can't help with what you're askin' about." He turns to the drunk again, who is giving a hard time to the fellow sent to subdue him. "Bob, damn you! Shut up!"

Instead, Bob leans around his subduer, and shouts at Tinoco. "What's the matter, you dago bastard? Can't find anybody to murder that smelly *sodomite* Perez fer yer jewel? Why don't *you* do it? Then, you can keep it!"

As the Boar's Head is quickly growing more crowded and noisy, almost no one seems to be paying much attention to the drunk. Except Skeres, that is, who turns to the hearth and picks up a heavy old-style flagon. He rushes the drunk, knocking over a chair and shoving the would-be subduer out of the way. He grabs the drunk by the throat and smashes the flagon across his face with enormous force. Though the drunk is already stunned, Skeres lifts up the flagon again and repeats the blow with enough force to stave in someone's head. Instead, the drunk's head turns with the blow, blood spewing from his mouth and splattering over Jonathan's face and doublet.

Even through this assault, the drunk not only remains conscious, but remains *standing*, daubing stupidly at his mouth with his handkerchief. He tries to say something that sounds vaguely like "what did you do that for?" But the sounds that actually issue from his bloody mouth are not recognizable as words. He sets himself carefully down on the floor and promptly loses consciousness.

Jonathan, stunned, is momentarily oblivious to the crimson fluid dripping from his face. Although Graves pats Jonathan's shoulder for comfort, Graves himself is obviously unnerved.

Noah is uncertain why Graves is so frightened. Although Skeres is obviously ruthless, he does not appear to be a madman. To the contrary, he calmed down almost immediately, and now appears lost in thought, albeit with no reassuring sign of regret. Skeres calmly whispers something to the man who tried in vain to subdue the drunk, and resumes his seat across from Jonathan.

Jonathan draws out a handkerchief and absentmindedly wipes the drunk's blood from his face. To Noah's amazement, he attempts to resume the conversation. "As I was asking, sir — "

Skeres interrupts him. "Gentlemen, I'm afraid our interview has come to an end."

The two men who flanked Skeres earlier now stand beside Jonathan and Graves. The man beside Jonathan takes his arm, and the one beside Graves takes his. Skeres looks sadly at the table before him, and says: "Show these two gentlemen to the Thames."

Noah is aghast at the speed with which matters have spun out of control. Unless he's mistaken, Skeres has just ordered the murders of Jonathan and Graves.

As Noah glances at the front door to see if any more of Skeres' henchmen might enter, he hears the threatening click of a snaphaunce pistol being cocked. In the second it takes him to turn back toward Skeres' table, a Spaniard in a black mask has stepped behind Skeres and now calmly holds a long, cocked pistol to his head.

At first, Noah expects that the Spaniard is the one the drunk called "Tinoco." But *no*. Tinoco is sitting upright in his chair, smitten with fear. The gunman is none other than Andres Salazar, who has interpreted the rapidly deteriorating situation as his cue for action. Noah, who sent a note instructing the jesters to come to the Boar's Head just in case, now takes some comfort from the knowledge that the others cannot be far off.

"Don't turn around," the gunman commands Skeres in a husky voice with a decidedly lower-class London accent. "These men are my prisoners."

"*Who* are your prisoners?" asks Skeres with disgust.

"The barrister and his man," replies the gunman.

"And who the devil are *you*?"

"Well, that all depends. If you tell your two henchmen to unhand my prisoners and resume their seats beside you, *keeping their hands visible at all times*, then I am the attendant of an earl who doesn't care much for *yours*."

"And if I don't?"

"Then I'm the Grim Reaper. And your time is up."

Skeres sneers, although he dares not turn to the man behind him. "Are you goin' to shoot us all?"

"No. Just you. My men will cut your men's throats."

Skeres' two henchmen turn to see that two masked fair-haired men have quietly assumed places behind them, and now hold daggers to their necks.

Another masked young fellow has taken up a position near the slumped-over drunkard, who has awakened, and whose eyes now dart about in terror.

"Oh, so it's four against four," observes Skeres. Everyone in the room stands stock-still.

All the fear and worry that have seethed for the past month in Noah's mind over the safety of Marie, Jonathan, and himself now bubble over into outrage. *Do these people think they're acting with complete impunity, simply because they attend upon the Earl of Essex?*

In a single deft motion, Noah draws his mask down to cover his face and tosses back his cowl. His fury has rendered him heedless of the danger posed by his sudden movement. He steps up to Skeres' table, draws a loaded pistol from his doublet, and places it point-blank between his eyes. Noah is pleased to see that having his head flanked by two loaded pistols causes Skeres to flinch, at last.

"You need odds?" says Noah in a decidedly upper-class accent. "Well, they're *against* you, you coward. Now, *do as my man says*!" Noah glances around quickly at the terrified expressions of friend and foe alike. Evidently, his seriousness is clear to all. He is beginning to frighten himself.

After a moment of unguarded terror, Skeres regains some of his composure, and chuckles quietly. His eyes lock onto Noah's. "Are you the earl? Why'd *you* come? Don't trust yer men to do as they're told?"

Noah shakes his head contemptuously. "I wanted to see for myself if you're as stupid as you are repulsive." To ensure that Skeres does not attempt to delay matters by continuing the conversation, Noah cocks his pistol, and sneers. "Well, *are* you?" He places his finger gently on the trigger, amazed at the realization that he'll pull the trigger, if it comes to it.

Skeres' face contorts into a hideous grimace differing only slightly from his "smile," and nods to his henchmen, who return to their seats beside him, keeping their hands above the table.

Noah shouts. "Everyone stand still until my men are out of here!"

The jesters grab Jonathan and Graves roughly under the arms and shove them out the front door ahead of them. Everyone but Noah, and Skeres and his men, runs helter-skelter out the front door immediately behind them.

Last to withdraw, Noah keeps his cocked pistol pointed at Skeres' head, and backs out the front door. He bursts out into the smokeless and cool night air, never so relieved to be out of any place in all his life. Jonathan, Graves, and their friends have already bolted from view.

Noah sprints for several blocks, strips off his woolen cloak, and trots to the stable on nearby Old Jewry Street, where he, Jonathan, and Graves left their horses. The thought fleetingly passes through his mind that this was where, five hundred years earlier, William the Conqueror established a colony of Jews. He wonders if any of them experienced anything like this evening's events.

As there's no sign of either Jonathan or Graves at the stables, Noah hopes they've been spirited away by the jesters to some discreet location. He earnestly hopes that they are not loudly celebrating their successful masquerade at a tavern somewhere nearby. Even if their youth were so to incline them, he is confident that the experienced Goodman Graves would do everything in his power to prevent it. Considering the resources available to the Earl of Essex, any such indiscretion would inevitably lead to discovery of their true identities, and imminent danger to their careers and lives. Even overcome with such worries, Noah forces himself to wait an interminable half hour before bidding the stableman to bring all three horses to him. He tips him well, but not so well as to make himself memorable.

Noah's own horse is mercifully sleepy. He mounts as gently as possible, and takes the reins of the other two horses, who appear docile enough to be led from horseback. With no hands free, he sincerely hopes to encounter no further excitement on the way to Gray's Inn.

CHAPTER 11

WHEN NOAH ARRIVES AT GRAY'S about midnight, all seems quiet. He takes the horses around to the stable, where the boy awakens at his approach.

"Sleeping on the job, Tom?" Noah asks, with a note of humor.

The boy wipes his hands over his eyes and smiles, accepting the reins of Jonathan's and Graves' horses.

"Sorry, sir, but I've had a bit o' groomin' to do past couple hours. Residents brought in three horses lathered up pretty good. Looked like they'd been rode hard. Got 'em all cleaned up and put away now, though."

As Noah enters the inn, the hallway is illuminated by several more lights than are customary at this hour. Still, the place is reasonably quiet, and he can detect nothing that might arouse the suspicion of outsiders. He finds Jonathan's door unexpectedly closed, with no light shining under it. Before he can knock, a youthful voice behind him says, "He's not there, sir." He turns to see Arthur Arden standing in the dark at the top of the stairs.

Noah squints up at him. "Tom the stableboy said you brought only three mounts back. I take it Jonathan has not returned yet?"

"That's right, sir. He's with Goodman Graves."

"But how did the four of you … ?" Even in the dim light, Noah can discern that Arthur has put his finger to his lips.

"Perhaps you should come up here with us, sir," Arthur suggests quietly.

Noah climbs the stairs and follows Arden into a large, brightly lit room. The scene that greets him is not at all what he expected. Arden's three friends sit on the edges of beds and chairs, faces downcast, arms resting on their thighs, speaking morosely among themselves. Arden closes the door quietly.

"What's all this?" asks Noah. "I would have expected a bit of relief among you. Why all the long faces?" Suddenly alarmed, he asks: "Is Jonathan all right?"

"Jonathan's fine, sir. But, when we left the Boar's Head, Goodman Graves wasn't feeling well and asked to see a doctor. As he looked a bit pale and sweaty, Jonathan insisted we bring him over to Creechurch. Doctor Lopez was summoned from Mountjoy's and examined him, and said he couldn't find anything wrong, but told us to leave him there for the night, just in case he took a turn for the worse."

"And Jonathan remained with him?"

"Yes, sir. Graves was pleading with him to go back to the inn, but he insisted on staying a while. Jon's very fond of old Graves, sir."

"Does Lopez know what events led up to your going to see him?"

"No, sir. When we first got there, Graves insisted we leave all our masks and weapons in our saddlebags, and that no one mention anything to the good doctor."

"And the four of you returned on three horses?"

"Salazar was light enough to double up with me. Is there a problem, sir?"

"Well, no, I suppose, except I brought Jonathan's and Graves' horses here. So, someone will have to fetch Graves from Creechurch when he's released from the doctor's."

"Oh, one of us will do that tomorrow. No worry there, sir."

Noah sits down in a quandary. "I'm not quite sure what to do. Graves seemed all right to you?"

"We're no doctors, sir. He seemed to have a commonplace bellyache. But ... "

Noah arches an eyebrow. "But ... ?"

"Doctor Lopez wasn't sure."

Noah slaps his thigh. "All right. That decides me. I'm going to Creechurch."

"But, sir, Jonathan will probably have returned here by the time you arrive."

"Just as well. If he's already gone by the time I get there, I'll see him in the morning. But I wish to see Graves for myself." He rises. "Get some sleep, all of you. Meantime, however, let me warn you all to avoid being seen all together for a few weeks, and to avoid wearing any of the clothing you had on this evening. As ever, you need no reminding to speak of this to *no one*."

"Will you be spending the night at the inn, sir?" asks Arden hopefully.

Noah suddenly regrets having told Marie he would see her that night. He shakes his head. "I shan't be back tonight. But I *will* be in my room come morning."

* * *

Having failed to find Lopez at Mountjoy's, Tinoco stops at midnight before the sparsely furnished cottage at the west end of Creechurch, standing far enough away to avoid being seen. He does not relish what he's about to do, but, since the incident at the Boar's Head earlier in the evening, his hand has been forced. Through the window, he spies Lopez alone.

Lopez shivers and rises from his chair, stirring the fire, evidently to coax a little more heat. The embers snap at him in protest, glowing a deeper red. Startled, he mutters something like "slumbering nest of dragons."

Tinoco takes a deep breath, steps forward, and knocks quietly.

"Emanuel Tinoco, my good friend," says Lopez softly, opening the door. "Please come in. I'd no idea you were back from the Continent. What brings you here at this ungodly hour?"

"Sorry to disturb you, Roderigo. Would another time be better?"

"Oh, no, no. I've already been dragged all the way from Mountjoy's Inn this evening to see a patient, and it will be some time before sleep returns, if it comes at all."

"Very well, but I will try not to keep you."

"Here, have some wine."

"Thank you very much," says Tinoco, plopping onto a bench without removing his cloak. "I'm afraid I have no new intelligence from Spain, but I have something interesting to show you. First … permit me to ask you something."

Lopez arches an eyebrow.

Tinoco smiles hesitantly. "You know, I don't get involved in your end of the business, and would never ask what you do with the intelligence I bring. But — "

"That's nothing I keep secret from you, Emanuel. You know I trust you. I share your information with Lord Essex."

"*Only* Lord Essex?"

"Only him." Lopez laughs quietly. "He would be quite upset if I were to do otherwise, as he pays me some small monies for it."

Tinoco holds up his palms in protest. "And I would never go around you. You know that."

"I do know it."

"But have you *never* given someone else such information first?"

Lopez regards him askance. "Such as … ?"

Tinoco shrugs. "Perhaps someone on the Privy Council?"

"No," replies Lopez, but then shakes his head equivocally. "Oh, I suppose I might have told one of the Cecils first on occasion, if the matter seemed of some urgency to the English court, and Lord Essex was nowhere to be found. I suppose I do feel a certain … "

"Loyalty?"

Lopez nods. "To England." He smiles abashedly. "Oh, you and I are a pair of old Spaniards, and you probably think me foolish to — "

"Not at all," Tinoco protests. "More importantly," he says, dodging further discussion of the topic, "I have something for you from His Highness King Philip. And then I really must be going. He sends you his kind regards."

Lopez eyes him skeptically. "To dispatch his regards, Emanuel, he might simply have posted a letter. There was no need to trouble *you*."

It's Tinoco's turn to laugh quietly. "Not *merely* his regards, Roderigo. He has sent you a … a trinket.

Lopez is taken aback. "A gift from His Highness?"

"Yes," says Tinoco. "Of course … it comes with a condition."

Lopez's shoulders sag.

"Only one," Tinoco assures him, as lightly as possible. "You see, I need some … " he glances around furtively, "poison, to rid His Highness of a threat, a certain Spaniard who's emigrated to England from the Spanish court with certain … intelligence … that could be damaging." As Lopez seems unable to identify the man from this description, Tinoco gives him another hint. "Someone under the protection of the English Crown."

"Well," says Lopez, "that could be any one of a number of people I know, some of whom I could never betray, such as Don Antonio — "

Tinoco shakes his head. "It's *Perez*," he interjects, disgusted with his own coyness, and thoroughly exhausted by the near slaughter at the tavern. "His Highness would never ask you — "

"*Perez*," says Lopez. "I know the man. He is odious to me. What intelligence has he that could possibly pose a threat to His Highness?"

"That I cannot say … because I do not know. His Highness does not share all such matters with me."

Lopez looks at him disapprovingly and points to himself. "Still … *murder*?"

Tinoco dismisses the objection with a wave of his hand. "*You* would not have to murder anyone, Roderigo. Perish the thought. I merely need from you something that will be certain to work quickly, but such that Perez's … demise will not be recognizable as having resulted from poison."

Lopez nods pensively, as though presented with a professional challenge. "It would have to be handled discreetly. It could not lead back to me … or to you, as we would surely be put to death."

"Rest assured," says Tinoco.

After some moments' equivocation, Lopez shakes his head with relief. "No, I couldn't. Please pass along my apologies to His Highness."

Tinoco removes from his pocket a maroon felt bag secured by a leather drawstring, and places it carefully down on the table in the candlelight. He opens it slowly, and watches Lopez's eyes widen.

It's a large, magnificent oval-cut ruby. Tinoco lifts it between thumb and forefinger, and holds it up to the candle to show it off to best advantage. Its thousand facets disperse the deepest red light in every direction.

Lopez admires it in silence for a long moment, and once again mutters to himself "slumbering nest of dragons."

"What was that?"

Lopez makes no reply, but Tinoco can see that the despair that's weighed him down since the loss of his considerable fortune has given way to an ancient greed.

Lopez rises, opens a drawer in his desk, and withdraws a corked vial. He places it in a small bag much like the one that contained the ruby, and sighs as he hands it to Tinoco. "My poverty, but not my will, consents."

"Then, His Highness bestows this gift upon your poverty, and not your will."

Lopez collapses in his chair. Overcome, he covers his eyes.

Tinoco steals a glance at the window where, at the very edge of darkness, Skeres' scarred face beams slyly back at him and disappears into the night.

*   *   *

At the same moment, Noah draws up to the opposite end of Creechurch. There are no horses but his own in the churchyard. If Jonathan is still here, he has either tied off his mount some distance away or taken measures to conceal it from prying eyes.

As Noah dismounts, he recalls with some discomfort that, when he was last here only a few weeks earlier, he attended the autopsy of Marie's husband, was clubbed in the neck as he prepared to leave, and had a message scrawled on his personal papers while he was unconscious. He resolves to contrive some means to send Essex a message of his own, that he's not discouraged and will not be deterred. For the moment, though, he cannot avoid facing the possibility that Essex's henchmen have taken another underhanded stab at his allies.

Graves is in bed awake, the sole occupant of a small, dimly lit chamber that once served as a monk's cell. Although he doesn't seem to be in much pain, his face is ashen with worry.

Noah takes a seat in a wooden chair by the bed. "Well, what seems to be the trouble, Goodman Graves?" he asks, trying to sound optimistic without appearing indifferent to Graves' condition.

"Thank you for coming, Master Ames. I've just a bit of a bellyache. But it came on kinda sudden while we were still at the Boar's Head, so it occurred to me I might have been poisoned."

"Ah, yes! I recall you looking very disturbed at one point, but I didn't know why."

"It was stupid of me, suh, but I sipped from the tankard they gave me." He shakes his head. "Unforgivable, really, with all my experience." He sighs. "Well, it's me own fault. Once I realized it might have been tampered with, I moved Jonathan's away from 'im, so he wouldn't be tempted. Later on, he assured me he hadn't touched it, which was a big relief."

"Do you really think the ale might have been tampered with?"

Graves shrugs. "Mighta been, sir, but I'll be dashed if I can figger out when they done it. Most of the time, suspicion falls on the alehouse or the serving wenches, but it's never them. They've got too much to lose if they get a reputation for that sorta thing. Nah, woulda happened at the table, sometime when we were distracted, like durin' the beatin'." He grips his cramping belly.

"How are you feeling now?"

"About the same. If they put anythin' in the ale what didn't belong there, I reckon I didn't take much of it. But, tell you the truth, suh, it ain't me I'm worried about. It's Jon. You'll pardon me callin' 'im that, suh, but that's how I knew him when he was comin' up."

"Not at all. By the way, when did he leave here?"

"Short while ago, suh. He wanted to stay and keep me company, but I insisted he go back to the inn. Doesn't do him nor me any good to sit 'round this depressin' place. He seems to have got the wind knocked out of him this time. I tried to tell 'im not to be discouraged by one bad turn like this, but he wasn't havin' any, sir. He looked like he'd been shaken to the core."

"I suppose he was as frightened as the rest of us," says Noah.

"No, suh. That ain't it. Jon hasn't led a sheltered life, and he's seen a lot worse than that drunk gettin' his face bashed in. Believe you me. He's been in spots worse than that before."

"Fear is an insidious thing," says Noah. "It undermines our better judgment. Tying off my mount just now, I had the irrational feeling I was being watched. Suddenly, every window in the church, and every tree in the woods, seemed a pair of eyes fixed squarely on me."

The rising moon illuminates Graves' face, accentuating every wrinkle, making it seem an old engraving. "I know that hunted feelin', suh. When this sort o' thing happens, it takes a good many weeks for it to pass." His eyes take on a faraway look, and he recites words that seem to be remembered from long ago: "'Every breeze a gallopin' horseman; every shadow the Reaper.' That's what my old master used to say when times was bad like they are now."

Noah shivers in the cool chamber. "Sounds like a wise fellow, your master. Is he still with us?"

"Nah. Long past, suh. Still, he died in his bed, somethin' he never expected to do. So, there's some hope in that. Well, like they say, we all owe God a death."

Noah studies the old man's face, unable to escape the feeling that he has more of interest to say about Jonathan. "But Jonathan *must* be reacting to his fear. His very *life* was at risk! If it hadn't been for his friends and a spot of luck, he — and you — might have been lost presently. Such knowledge would affect *anyone* deeply."

"No, suh, if you'll pardon my disagreement. Y'see, Jon was always smart as a whip, suh. I needn't tell *you* that."

"No, indeed."

"But there's always been somethin', well ... *different* about 'im. He always had faith that if he did the right thing, then good things would 'appen from it. Y'know?"

"Optimism," offers Noah.

"If you say so, suh. It's not uncommon for young people, I suppose. But he's always been so ... well, *competent* about everythin' that he's managed to hold onto his 'optimism' long past his friends. I know some of 'em, and, believe me, they gave up on such notions a long time ago."

"You knew his friends?"

"Lots of 'em, suh. Jonathan's folks died when he was very young, and my late missus and I were barren, so we was alone and took 'im in. He's sort of like ... an only son to me, suh." His voice chokes up. He blows his nose. "Oh, I doubt he knows it, suh, and I'm sure he don't think of me as a father, or nothin' ... "

"I expect he *does*, Goodman Graves, even if he doesn't say so."

Tears run down Graves' cheeks, reflecting the moon's watery image. "Well, that's very kind of you to say, suh. But he's so much smarter, and ... *wiser* than I ever was, even as a lad, that he could never really be a son o' mine." Noah nods patiently, exhausted as he is from the day's tribulations. "Anyways, suh. You'll watch out for 'im for me, won't ye?"

Noah places a reassuring hand on Graves' shoulder. "Nonsense, man. You'll be around a long time to do that job yourself."

Graves shakes his head reflectively. "Mebbe, suh, but there's a lotta nasty people attendin' on Essex. I know Jon looks up to you, suh. He'll listen to what you have to say. Lord knows, he won't always take advice. *Anyone's* advice. But he *could* use some lookin' after."

"Of *course* I'll watch out for him, Goodman Graves. Now, you get some sleep. I fear tonight's 'near thing' has unnerved us all."

"Yes, suh. Bless you, suh."

"And *you*, Goodman Graves."

As Noah begins to step away, he hesitates a moment, feeling as though he's forgotten something. Without turning back, he leaves the church and returns to his horse.

*   *   *

As Noah takes a roundabout path to Marie's dark house, he tries to imagine how it must have horrified Graves to realize that his adoptive son was about to be cut off in his youth. Jonathan would indeed have been killed by now, but for acts of bravado whose successful conclusion seems the result of nothing less than divine intervention.

Once again, Noah and Marie go to the upstairs parlor, holding hands, and kissing. Though their touching this night is less ardent, it's even more tender than the last. He explains to her what happened this evening, and she's horrified.

"To think he was doing *my* bidding when he was nearly murdered," she says. "I feel just terrible about it."

"*You*? Your responsibility is as *nothing* compared to mine. I knew the dangers. I should never have brought him into it. The fault is all mine." He kisses her forehead. "I must be back at the inn before dawn."

"Oh, but don't go yet, Noah. I want to know everything there is to know about you."

His back stiffens. "What would you like to know?" He gazes upon her face in the dim light. She's so sweet, so wonderful, almost too good to be true. Though in truth he yearns to tell her of his humble beginnings and his faith, if she were to repeat such information to the wrong ears, such as Southampton's ... Well, at some point, he expects, he'll willingly entrust his *own* life to her, but he simply cannot put Jonathan's life in further danger.

"I don't know," she says. "Is there anything you wish to tell me?"

"Not that I haven't told you already. Why? Is there something you wish to share with *me*?"

She shrugs. "What would you like to know?"

For one thing, I'd like to know if you're in communication with Southampton. But he simply cannot bring himself to ask her. For one thing, it would insult her by showing that he doesn't trust her fully.

She gazes into his eyes in that unnerving way she has of making him think she can read his mind. "Total honesty," she says, "is the foundation of any serious relationship, don't you think so?"

He kisses her, and smiles. "I do. I could never lie to you."

"But do you tell me everything that's on your mind?"

It's never occurred to him that the concept of honesty required him to be forthcoming with anything. It always seemed sufficient simply not to lie. "Except for legal or confidential matters, I do. At least I *think* I do." *Except, says his conscience, that I'm a Jew.*

When the clock strikes half past two, he kisses her as she sleeps, and takes a meandering path back to Gray's Inn. As he passes Jonathan's room on the way to his own, the door is closed, and no light shines under it. He goes upstairs and collapses onto his bed with his boots still on.

CHAPTER 12

NOAH IS AWAKENED about eight next morning by a letter being slipped under his door. Although the sky is cloudy, the room is easily bright enough for him to read it. He slices open the letter with a sharp blade to find it's from his deceased wife's cousin, Beth (or, as she likes to call herself lately, "Elizabeth"), written in her customarily formal style:

Dear Master Ames:

This will inform you that your daughter Jessica, Lady Burlington, has come to live with me in Southwark until such time as she has fully grieved the death of her late husband, Lorenzo Burlington, Baron Cheswick.

Although she has let it be known to me that she does not wish you to be concerned for her welfare (as she has been well provided for by the Last Will and Testament of this selfsame gentleman), I write to you on my own behalf in the hope that you will avail yourself of this opportunity to re-establish the late family feeling that prevailed between the two of you, as she has also let it be known to me that she loves and misses her *papa* very much, and wishes very much to see you, and hopes that you will overlook any disagreements there may have been between you in the past.

Permit me to remind you, dear cousin, that it was the earnest wish of my late beloved Cousin Rachel, *your late wife* and the late mother of Lady Burlington, that you maintain good relations with your daughter throughout your life regardless of any opinions you may believe her to have, and however disagreeable such opinions may seem to you.

In the upper left corner of this letter, you will find my current address. I hope (we hope) to hear from you as soon as your busy court schedule permits.

Yours, etc., Elizabeth

Only those who know Beth well would appreciate the number of jibes contained in this prolix piece of epistolary prose. To Noah's mind, it has been spitefully crafted to throw up in his face numerous things he already knows quite well and can scarcely *forget*, namely, that contrary to his own wishes his daughter has effectively forsaken her religion to marry into the minor nobility, that she now addresses him using the supercilious affectation *papa* (accent on the second syllable, please), that she is of independent financial means and not remotely dependent upon his patronage, that Rachel was his deceased wife (which evidently requires *emphasis!*), and that she asked him to maintain good relations with his daughter.

While he will undoubtedly accede to see Jessica, this family affair will have to wait. His most immediate item of business is to find out how last night's near disaster has changed Jonathan's outlook, and what can be done to improve matters. He refolds Beth's letter and tosses it on the desk.

*   *   *

Noah finds Arthur, Salazar, and the Bennett twins gathered in Arthur's room, wearing the same dour expressions as the previous evening. "Before I forget myself, gentlemen, I thank you all heartily for your great friendship and courage. Without you, we would have met with certain disaster." Noah's hearty thanks are greeted with listless, mumbled acknowledgments.

"Where's Jonathan?" he asks.

Arthur replies. "He hasn't said a word to anybody since he got back to the inn, Master Ames. He slammed his door behind him. Won't open it for anyone."

"I see. Well, I'll go see if I can gain entry."

Jonathan's door remains closed, and there's no sign of life inside. Noah knocks softly.

"Go away." Jonathan's voice sounds very weary.

"It's me. *Noah*. Jonathan, I need to speak with you."

There's a long silence, but eventually Jonathan speaks again. "What have you to say?"

"If you'll open the door, I'll tell you."

"Tell me now."

This is exasperating, but much as expected.

"Actually, Jonathan, I have come to hear what *you* have to say."

This is followed by another silence, this one so long that he begins to wonder whether Jonathan has fallen back asleep. But at long last Jonathan replies.

"I do not think you will wish to hear what I have to say. And I do not wish to say it."

That's cryptic. "*Please*, Jonathan. It's a little embarrassing to conduct this conversation through a door. I shan't sit on your head. If you ask me to leave, I shall do so. But I promised Goodman Graves I would look in on you."

Another long silence is followed by the click of a latch being released. Before Noah can even open the door, he hears Jonathan flop back into bed. He opens the door slightly. Jonathan's barrister's robes are randomly strewn along the floor. His boots have been kicked into a corner and now lie askew, one partially atop the other. Noah enters and sits down on his accustomed creaky chair, leaving the door ajar. Jonathan is in his undergarments with his head on the pillow. His right arm lies across his eyes, shielding them from the daylight.

After deliberately letting a long time pass in silence, Noah speaks. "Close call last evening." It isn't a question, really, so no response is actually required. He awaits the uncertain outcome.

Jonathan exhales deeply through his nose, but otherwise does not move. "I suppose," he sniffs.

"Were you frightened?"

"Of course!" says Jonathan, in a tone suggesting this to be the stupidest question imaginable. "Weren't *you*?"

This is progress. A conversation of any sort is progress.

"I was terrified even before anyone suspected I was there with you!" replies Noah. "Is that what's bothering you? The fear?" No reply. "Anyone in that position would have been scared to death, you know." He feels it his duty to provide a brief justification for his conduct the previous evening. "You know, don't you, that my drawing a weapon was warranted only in defense of those being threatened with death?"

"I suppose," says Jonathan lethargically. He turns onto his left side to face Noah. "What the hell are we doing here?" he intones, opening one eye, the other firmly hidden by his arm.

"How do you mean?" asks Noah.

"I mean, what do we hope to accomplish?"

"Well, we *hope* to obtain justice for — "

Jonathan exhales rudely through his closed mouth, flapping his lips noisily. "Oh, please! There's no justice to be *had* in this godforsaken kingdom. Unless you're a duke or an earl or something."

"Why do you say that?" asks Noah.

Both Jonathan's eyes are open now. "*You* tell *me*! That barbarian thug last night ... the one who smashed his friend's face in, and gave an order to kill me and my investigator for no discernible reason? That pile of dung works for the Earl of Essex. *The Earl of Essex*, for God's sake!"

"Well," shrugs Noah, "*every* nobleman has his agents. They're not always of the finest character."

"The finest character? Ha! But must they be of so low a character that you would use a stick to scrape them off your boot?" Jonathan sits up, and his face reddens. "What does it say about an earl that he employs *murderers*? He threatened to murder a barrister of the *Queen's Bench*, Noah! I thought we were above that in this country. And can I so much as serve a *subpoena* upon the earl to compel him to give testimony?" He holds up an index finger, as though in lawyerly demonstration. "Well, for that I would need court leave. But the court would not *grant* me leave if I sought it!" He impersonates a stuffy old judge, sounding remarkably like Lord Bleffingham: "'Sorry, Master Hawking, but this is the Earl of Flippin' Essex we're talking about. With respect to persons of such *high* estate, a *special* showing must be made' blah, blah, *blast!*" As Jonathan grows more incensed by the second, Noah discreetly shuts the heavy door behind him in an effort to keep the sound inside the room. "So, that *villain* — as well as the scoundrel who *employs* him — is beyond the reach of Queen's Bench!"

Jonathan raises his index finger again. "With *impunity*, he threatens barristers and their assistants for doing their sworn duty. And, but for a little unexpected help last night, he would have *murdered* them with impunity. *Two* murders, in fact! *Three*, if he'd managed to collar *you* before you reached the door. And tack on four more for the jesters, if we hadn't outnumbered Skeres and his men. Don't *you* ever wonder what the devil we are doing here?" Before Noah can form a reply, Jonathan rises from his bed.

"I'll tell you what we're doing," says Jonathan in answer to his own question. "We're *acting!*" His lip curls into a sneer of self-contempt. "Like a crowd of players on a street corner in Bankside. No, more like *The Rose*. But *our* house is so much *statelier* than The Rose! The Rose is made of mere wood, while *our* great theater is fashioned of *stone*! Chiseled old stone made to endure a thousand years! With a massive, soaring roof, and oak-lined walls. Why, they've given us the biggest and prettiest theater in all the realm! Don't you *see*?

"We don't work at justice, we *play* at it! We draft our pleadings and our writs like so many theater scripts. We conduct a trial like a play in an alehouse, based upon half-concealed evidence and theatrical speeches. And we pretend the end result to be justice, when it is *nothing of the kind*! The litigant who hires the best actor *wins*! *Regardless* of any merit to his adversary's cause." Jonathan laughs giddily, which Noah finds worrisome.

Although he's entertained Jonathan's diatribe with equanimity up to this point, he feels impelled to reply. "All very poetical! But who has such a great interest in seeing us 'play' at justice that he would willingly bear the enormous expense?"

"Well, that's the *right* question, isn't it? Who *indeed*?"

Noah furrows his brow. "Surely, you're not suggesting that *the Earl of Essex —* "

Jonathan nods emphatically. "Him — and everyone *like* him! They let us commoners have our Common Law so they can continue with their special brand of *noble* law. Everyone knows that Star Chamber is a court for trying peers of the Crown. They make decisions about each other there like it's a blasted *fraternity*! They take *no* live testimony. And they do not impose the death penalty. *That* privilege is strictly reserved for the commoners and lesser nobles. Oh, I'm not saying a commoner cannot get a fair trial in a case against another commoner. But when it's a *peer* against a commoner, the case becomes 'political,' and that means only one side gets it in the neck, and that's us! So, I ask you again," says Jonathan, throwing his hands up in exasperation, "*what are we doing here*?" He falls back onto his bed, breathing heavily.

Noah is speechless, as the point is quite valid. While it has always seemed to him that the cards have been stacked in any case characterized as "political," yet he's never heard the argument laid out quite so passionately before. He wonders why it has never occurred to *him* to make a cogent argument against gross inequality in the application of English law. *That's the way it's always been,* he's supposed, *so that's the way it will always be.* And he wonders by what silent, insidious process his mind has been subverted into believing that it's the way things probably *ought* to be. Has it just been his own laziness? Or his status as a secret Jew who lacks the privilege of speaking out, and finds it pointless and dangerous to consider ideas he may not express? Or perhaps worse, as someone who's profited by a system of privilege, has he thereby become complicit in it? Although he's always found comfort in the undeniable bromide that no system of justice is perfect, now he sees what cold comfort such notions must be to those *without* privilege.

To be sure, Star Chamber is reputed to be a fearsome place, but that is its reputation among commoners. The nobility, on the other hand, seems to have wiped it from their collective consciousness, hinting at its existence only in dark corners of old stories.

There's a knock at the door behind Noah. He rises and peeks out. It's Andres Salazar. "Letter for you, sir. It was brought by a little blond boy. Says you call him 'Master Cheerful.'"

"Thank you, Andres," says Noah softly. "He's a good lad, but keep him out of the inn for now." He reaches into his pocket, finds the right coin, and hands it to Salazar. "Thank him, and give him this." Salazar nods, and trots off toward the main entrance.

Jonathan now lies spread out over his bed with his arm over his eyes. "Jonathan," says Noah. "I'll be elsewhere in the inn for a while. We'll continue this a bit later." There's no reply. Jonathan has evidently attained the oblivion of sleep.

Noah goes out into the hall, closes Jonathan's door behind him, and thanks Salazar for bringing him the letter. The address is written by Henry, apparently in great haste. Noah returns to his room alone, and slits it open.

Dear Noah:

What the *devil* happened last night? Essex is beside himself.

I remind you that the Inns of Court are under perpetual Crown protection. This is *not* mere formality. Do not leave Gray's until I get there, and do not let anyone else of pertinence leave, either. Just to be safe, don't let anyone in.

I'll be there as soon as I can, a few minutes behind young Killigrew.

Neville

P.S. I've just been given the most unfortunate news, for which you have my deepest condolences. Graves is dead.

CHAPTER 13

NOAH'S HEART RISES into his mouth as he reads the last sentence of the postscript over and over again. *Graves is dead.* For the first time, but surely not the last, he wishes it was Essex who was dead.

But Essex is not alone in deserving blame. Was it not Noah who enlisted Jonathan, and thereby Graves, in this crusade? Did not Noah just reassure Graves of a long future? And did he not promise to protect Jonathan? How can he do that now?

Jonathan's is the only barrister's face to be seen by Skeres and his henchmen. He's a target now, perhaps their *only* known target.

Noah wipes his brow with his sleeve, and tortures himself anticipating what will happen when Jonathan awakens. What if he awakens *right now*? This young man, who has apparently decided his entire career is a charade, will now have to face the bitter fact that he is all alone in the world.

And who must be the one to tell him? Noah begins to sweat profusely, and the world turns white around him. He lowers his head until the feeling of faintness passes. He shuts his door, taps his head against the adjacent wall, and weeps silently.

He will have to live with his responsibility, but Jonathan and his friends must be prevented from leaving the inn. First things first. He wipes his eyes, and rushes down the hall in search of Jonathan's friends.

* * *

A half hour later, Henry arrives on horseback in far greater haste than usual. Beside him, on foot, trots a weary-looking Doctor Lopez, carrying his familiar black bag. Evidently, Henry stopped at Mountjoy's Inn next door, found Lopez at home with his family, and enlisted him to come along to Gray's Inn.

Henry dismounts in obvious pain, and hands off the reins to the stable boy. Leaning heavily on Lopez's shoulder, he haltingly climbs the outside stairs. When he reaches the landing, he balances his considerable weight precariously on one foot, to favor the other. His face is white. Noah swings opens the door.

Lopez bows to Noah. "Please accept my condolences for the loss of Goodman Graves." He smiles wanly. "Master Neville asked me to come examine his foot. Let us bring him over to that cushioned chair." Together, Noah and Lopez assist Henry to a big soft chair in the parlor.

Although Henry sits immediately, whatever small relief he obtains from doing so seems tenuous at best, as soon he furiously struggles to remove his boot and rub the top of his foot. "Are they all here, Ames?" he grunts.

"They are, Henry. But I have a serious problem."

"We'll get to that in a moment, old man." Henry turns to the doctor. "Have you anything for me in that little black bag, Doctor Lopez?"

Lopez regards Henry as though he were a wayward pupil. "We will have to discuss this later, Master Neville. In the meantime, I do have something, but it may not help."

"Oh, just hand it over, Lopez. I'm in agony."

Lopez tugs a drawstring that opens his black bag far enough for a hand to probe inside. He withdraws a small bag containing a white powder, and a small glass graduate with black marks etched horizontally along its side. He turns to Noah. "May I trouble you for two cups of potable water?"

Noah retrieves the water from his room in a wooden cup, and he and Henry watch with fascination as Lopez carefully graduates a few grains of powder, drops them into the water, and stirs the mixture with a tiny spoon. The cup now contains a lumpy whitish emulsion.

"Drink this down all at once," Lopez instructs.

Henry tips the cup high, draining its contents into his mouth. He swallows with a bitter expression and thrusts the cup back to Lopez. "Are you trying to kill me?"

Lopez ignores the remark. Taking the cup from Henry, he hands it back to Noah. "Go and wash this thoroughly right now, before it can be used again." Noah takes the cup back up to his room, and rubs it hard in fresh water until no sign of the white powder remains. He rinses it, and places it back on its hook upside-down to dry.

By the time he returns to the parlor, Henry, though still rubbing his foot gingerly, seems a bit more at ease. Lopez has cinched his bag shut, and is evidently preparing to leave. "I will return later to discuss this health matter with Master Neville. In the meantime, if you are no longer in need of my services — "

"I'm sorry, Doctor Lopez," Noah says, "but I find myself in need of a bit more of your time. If you could spare a few minutes, I would much appreciate it."

Lopez nods wearily. "Very well, but please bear in mind that I was awakened very early this morning when Goodman Graves took his turn for the worst."

Though Noah is unsure what Henry might have mentioned to Lopez about the events preceding Graves' death, he assumes he's been as closemouthed as usual. "What caused Graves to die so suddenly?" he asks.

"He was not a well man," Lopez replies. "His heart appears to have failed him."

"Was he … intoxicated?"

"In the sense of imbibing excessive spirits, I should think not. His mind was completely clear when he was admitted. His only complaint was a bellyache, and I have one of my assistants checking for the presence of likely toxins."

"Such as … poison?" asks Noah.

Lopez arches an eyebrow. "Why do you ask, Master Ames? Was he the object of a plot of some kind?"

"Oh, no, no. But he was an investigator, and I suppose poisoning was an occupational hazard for him."

Lopez regards him skeptically, as though he suspects Noah is withholding something. "I believe his heart failed because of a dose of poison, although which one I'm not sure. Well, we shall find out soon enough, and I shall be sure to let you know." He rubs his eyes. "Was there something else, Master Ames?"

"I'm afraid so."

Lopez furrows his brow. "What is the nature of the complaint?"

Noah is abashed, but proceeds to ask quietly, "Have you any … laudanum?"

Lopez opens his bloodshot eyes wide with surprise. "I have, sir. I hope you have not become addicted to it."

Noah shakes his head. "No, no. Nothing like that, I assure you. I … must soon break the news of Goodman Graves' death to a young man who thought of him as a kind of father. When the young man and I spoke earlier, on another matter, he was already … not himself. Very excitable."

Henry looks up from his foot-rubbing. "Hawking?"

Noah nods. "How did you know?"

"Know *what*?"

"That Graves and Jonathan were like father and son."

"Oh. Well, I didn't know that until you just told me. I knew only what you had *already* told me, that the two worked together from time to time. Did you say 'father and son'?"

"Adoptively, in an informal sense."

"Before you go onto that, Noah, let me ask you something." As though he's just remembered something, Henry turns to Lopez. "Doctor, would you be kind enough to give us a moment alone?"

"Certainly," says Lopez. Noah shows him to the dining room, and returns to Henry in the parlor.

"Yes, Henry?"

"There were three or four young men involved last night. Correct?"

"Yes."

"Was one of them named 'Arden'?"

"How did you know?"

"I didn't, until you just confirmed it. But I did know him to be a friend of Hawking, who is lodged in this building of the Inn. Also, I heard Southampton's description of the ... participants this morning. One sounded like Arthur."

"It *was* Arthur."

"As I thought. Well, I'm afraid you've got yourself a roommate until this business has been resolved."

"Roommate?"

Henry smiles. "Me. You have a side room with a bed. Have you not?"

"I have."

"Well, I'll take it, and pay half your rent. How does that sound?"

Noah is flustered. "Well ... *why*?"

"Couple of reasons. One is that Doctor Lopez is your next-door neighbor, and appears to have a magic potion that works on me. The other is that Arden is a Neville — "

"Oh? Another Killigrew-Neville?"

Henry laughs quietly. "No, actually, he's more closely related to Shakespeare than to me. I will be keeping an eye on Master Arden until Goodman Shakespeare tells me I need no longer do so."

Noah regards Henry skeptically. "Have you cleared this with Master Treasurer?"

Henry smiles darkly. "I've paid him your rent for the next six months in gold, Ames. What do you think?"

Noah resigns himself. "I think you shall be my landlord for the next six months. Only a *Neville* could take a room in one's apartment at an Inn of Court without asking, and simultaneously make himself one's landlord."

Henry snickers at Noah's cynical summary of the situation. "But at half the rent!" He turns serious. "Where is Hawking now?"

"Asleep in his room."

"Send Doctor Lopez back in here to wait with me. I suggest you tell Hawking about Graves' death yourself, but make sure his friends are right outside his door, in case he takes it badly."

Noah stops in the dining room to ask Doctor Lopez to return to the parlor, and gathers Arden, Salazar, and the Bennett twins to stand outside Jonathan's door. He whispers to Arden. "Go tip your hat to your relation, Henry Neville. He's in the parlor. But come right back." Arden nods and walks away. Noah knocks lightly on Jonathan's door. As there's no response, he enters quietly.

Jonathan still enjoys the blissful ignorance of sleep. Reluctant as Noah is to disturb him, he braces himself and does so. "Jonathan, please wake up."

Jonathan squirms and sits up. "What is it now?"

"I'm afraid I have some bad news."

"Oh?" Jonathan squints, his eyes adjusting to the light.

"Very bad news. I'm afraid Goodman Graves has passed."

Jonathan wilts like a flower in the snow. "Oh, God. How?" His eyes open wide. "*How*? Did that dirty bastard *kill* him? That piece of filth? *Did* he?"

Noah is unsure how to respond.

Jonathan leaps out of bed. "He did! Didn't he? Tell me, Noah! *What happened?*"

Noah says quietly, "Heart failure. According to Doctor Lopez, it may have been brought about by poison."

"Poisoned by that filthy piece of dung? He was unable to drown him or shoot him, so he *poisoned* him?" Jonathan starts to giggle. "Was it *arsenic*? *Foxglove*, perhaps?"

Noah is bewildered, his mouth agape. Jonathan's conjectures about the type of poison must be some sort of madcap joke. But, surely Jonathan could not be so callous as to jest upon hearing such news as this! "The doctor does not know yet. His assistant is testing for the presence of common poisons. Calm down, Jonathan. Tell me about him, so that I may pay my respects. I know very little about him." It's a poor feint at conversation in light of the emotions erupting in Jonathan, but Noah is trying to allay his excitement.

"Why didn't the dunghill just toss him in the Thames, where he ordered us *both* drowned last night? Perhaps *then* the judges would have perceived some connection between the blackguard and his crime! But no, no, I'm *sure* not! What is wrong with this kingdom, Noah? Hah? Surely, it is sick. *Sick!*" Jonathan begins breathing heavily, much deeper and faster than normally. Noah has heard of grief like this, but he's never encountered it before, and has no idea what to do.

Jonathan rips the front of his linen smock apart with both hands. "Maybe they'll kill me now, too! Come and kill me!" He laughs. "Come down here. Fill me up with poison, and throw me in the deep. You piece of *shite!*"

Noah is at a complete loss, for Jonathan is no longer addressing *him*, but rather someone who's not there. Jonathan's eyes are rapidly growing wild and red, and his respiration continues to accelerate.

"Come on! Come get me, too! You demon! You *MISCREANT FILTH!*" Jonathan looks at his fingers in evident amazement. Noah has heard that, when one breathes too deeply for too long, the fingers tingle.

Arden enters, alarmed.

"Jon! Jonny! It's me, Arthur! Please, Jon! Calm down!" He runs to Jonathan, who stares and points into thin air. Arthur hugs him firmly. "*Please,* Jon!"

"See?" says Jonathan, pointing at no one. "You see him there? He's there, Arthur. *Look!*"

Arthur's eyes are red, and tears stream down his face. He looks where Jonathan is pointing. "*Who* is it, Jon? I see no one there. *Who* is there, Jon?"

Jonathan shoves him away with a force that would have toppled a smaller man. "Look! Look there!" His breathing accelerates still further. "It's *Graves! Oh, God. LOOK!*" His eyes agog, he plops down on the edge of the bed, quaking in terror.

Lopez enters in determined fashion, and stands before Jonathan, whose eyes still focus on some faraway point.

"Jonathan, I am Doctor Lopez. Please look at me!" Jonathan's expression is unreadable, unchanging. "Jonathan, do you remember me from last evening? Do you know who I am?" Lopez points to Arthur. "Jonathan, do you know who this is?" Still, no change. Jonathan just stares unblinkingly at the same vacant point, cringing in terror.

Henry somberly appears at the door holding a wooden cup filled with fluid, which Lopez accepts and hands to Arthur. "You must get Jonathan to drink this draught down. Can you do this?"

At first, Arthur himself is transfixed, staring at Jonathan. But he snaps out of it and looks to the doctor. "I don't know if I can. Give it to me, and I will try." Slowly, he approaches Jonathan, who remains seated, an occasional whimper of fear escaping him. "Jonathan, drink this down, will you?" But Jonathan makes no response. Lopez motions for Arthur to bring the draught up to Jonathan's lips, and spill it into his mouth. Arthur follows the wordless instructions, and is amazed to see Jonathan swallow the draught thirstily until the cup is empty. He hands the cup back to Lopez, his hand shaking.

In a few seconds, the elixir begins to have an effect. Jonathan's breathing returns to normal, and his eyes resume their blinking, first as though trying to clear his vision, and then torpidly. Finally, he lies back on his bed staring at the ceiling, and then mercifully closes his eyes.

Arthur weeps into his hands. "Oh, dear God! My friend's mind is overthrown!" He turns to Lopez. "Is he gone to madness?"

Lopez puts a reassuring hand on his shoulder. "No, Master Arden. Your friend is not mad. He will sleep now, and will be *much* better when he awakens."

Arden looks impatiently at Lopez. "How do you know?"

"Because I am a physician of forty years' experience. Believe me, this is *not* how madness begins. At least, not in people so young as Jonathan. You will see. His mind will be fine. He will be sad, as anyone would be under like circumstances, but that is to be expected. Sometimes, grief starts off very badly like this. But it passes."

Arden seems to take only small comfort from Lopez's words. "Will he continue to see people that aren't there?"

Lopez shakes his head emphatically. "No, he will not. Let us put him to bed, so that he sleeps comfortably."

Together, Arden and Lopez turn Jonathan, placing his head on the pillow facing sideways and his feet at the base of the bed.

"Do you truly wish to help him?" Lopez asks Arden.

"Of *course* I do!"

"Then, sit in this chair for the next four hours, and make sure that he does not vomit. I expect he will not, but, if he does, you must come and get me right away. I will be up in Master Ames' room for a short while, and then right next door at Mountjoy's."

The door swings full open, and the other three young men appear. "We'll take shifts, Arthur," says Salazar. "You take an hour, then each of us will take an hour's turn." He turns to Lopez. "Will that be satisfactory, Doctor?"

Lopez smiles to see such good friendship. "Quite satisfactory." He turns to Henry. "Come, Master Neville, let us see to your foot. I might as well finish our business now, so I needn't return later." He walks up the stairs ahead of Noah and Henry, who appears surprised that he has no real trouble climbing.

Noah watches as Henry sits up in the bed in his side room, with Lopez examining his naked foot using a magnifying lens of some kind.

Lopez peers carefully at the top of Henry's foot. "Laudanum is very addictive," he says. "You should avoid telling Hawking or anyone else that there was something medicinal in the draught I gave him. In my experience, people do not seek out more of something they never learn they have taken."

Lopez snaps the lens shut, and sits on a wooden chair beside the bed, staring impassively at Henry's face.

"Well?" demands Henry. "Don't just sit there. The suspense is killing me."

Lopez looks down and shakes his head. "You already know you have gout. It is not *suspense* that is killing you, Master Neville."

"Well, whatever *is* killing me, can ye stop it? And stop this damned *pain*, as well?"

Lopez smiles sagely. "I can stop both with the same treatment."

Henry looks pleased. "You can?"

"Yes, but I warn you. It will take some effort on your part."

"Just tell me, and I'll do it."

"All right, there are a few things you must do. The first is, you must stop drinking spirits."

"By 'spirits,' you mean … ?"

"I mean spirits, in all its forms. All wines, whether they be red, white, or any other color, including ports, sherries, brandies, cognacs, liqueurs, mead. Also *sack*, of which we all know you are exceedingly fond. No whisky, no ale, no beer."

"Even *weak* beer? I shall die of dysentery! You can't expect me to drink unpurified water."

"Weak beer is acceptable. Boiled water would be better, however."

Henry's face goes white. "God, man! You take my *life* when you take my reasons for living." He pouts, and adjusts the sheet. "What else?"

"You must cut down your consumption of food to a bare minimum, so that you lose nearly half your weight."

Now Henry is downright flustered. "How about breathing? May I *breathe*?"

"As much as you like."

"And women?"

"But you are *married*, Master Neville."

Henry scowls. "Oh, don't make me repeat the question, you little prig."

"Women may pass you other diseases, but they will not aggravate this one, unless … "

"Unless … ?"

"Unless they give you spirits or overfeed you."

"Do you have anything in that little black bag that will put me out of my misery permanently, like an old warhorse?"

Lopez laughs, and shakes his head. "Strictly forbidden."

"Oh, yes. I recall something about that in the Hippocratic Oath: 'I will never give a deadly drug to anybody if asked for it.' What about that stuff you gave me before? That seemed to work."

For a moment, Lopez seems bone weary and lost in thought. He sighs. "Are you telling me that you will not follow my prescribed course of treatment?"

Henry looks to Noah. "What do you think, Ames?"

Noah rubs his chin and pretends to weigh matters. "I think you will deviate from this course of treatment before Doctor Lopez leaves the *room*."

Lopez ventures, "Master Ames, perhaps you could help enforce these strictures?"

"Oh, but I assure you I hold no such influence with Master Neville." He looks at the ceiling smugly. "I know someone who'd give it a good try, however."

Henry glowers. "Ames, if you ever mention this treatment to Mistress Anne, you shall never be invited to my home again."

Noah shrugs silently at Lopez, who sighs and relents. "All right, Master Neville. You are too entrenched an adversary for me. I will leave you some tablets. The medicine is called 'colchicum.' But you must use it only when you are in terrible pain, and only in the number of tablets I shall write down for you. Are we in agreement?"

"*Now* you're using the good sense that God gave you!" says Henry.

"They will not always work, at least not always *well*, but you must not take more than the prescribed amount even if they do not work. This medicine is not a case of the more the merrier, and it can be dangerous if too much is taken. Meantime, if you feel an attack of gout coming on, you should drink clean water, preferably boiled, as much as you reasonably can, as gout is made worse by dehydration."

Henry nods. "Good to know. Thank you, Doctor."

"Now, if you gentlemen have no further crises requiring my immediate attention, I thought I might have dinner with my family."

"Thank you, Doctor Lopez," they say, and watch him go.

Once they're alone, Henry returns to the events of the previous evening. "You were there last night?" he asks.

"I was."

"Then tell me what happened, as best you can recall."

Noah recounts the events for Henry, avoiding as well as he can any personal comment or opinion. Henry does not interrupt, and raises an eyebrow only once or twice. At the end of the tale, Noah observes: "It's difficult to imagine that suppressing news of the beating given this 'Bob' person could have been of such importance as to justify the elimination of two witnesses."

"I was thinking the same thing. The beating took place in public. No matter how quickly it was over, it was surely seen by other patrons, and it would scarcely have been possible to eliminate them all. Just out of curiosity, did Skeres ever mention that drunkard Bob's last name?"

"No."

"No matter. I expect I can find out more about Bob from a number of sources. So, that leaves … Tinoco. What did the drunk say to him, exactly?"

"When Tinoco first entered, the drunk pointed him out to Skeres, referring to him as an 'old friend' or something like that, and observed that permitting

Tinoco to enter the Boar's Head was somehow proof that the tavern will admit 'just anybody.' Then later, the drunk shouted something about a red … jewel? I *think* it was 'jewel.' And he implied that Tinoco had been searching for someone to earn the jewel by killing another person of Spanish surname … which name escapes me at the moment."

"Was it 'Don' something? 'Don Emanuel,' something like that?"

"No. It was a single word: Suarez. Cortez, perhaps."

"Perez?" suggests Henry.

Noah recognizes the name immediately. "Perez. That's it! Do you know of him?"

"I've met him. He came to England after fleeing the Spanish court some months ago. Always has the most peculiar combination of strong odors about him. He's known by them. Musk and … amber. Yes, that's it. That's what they call him behind his back, Old Musk and Amber."

"Ah," says Noah, "now that you mention it, the drunk implied that Perez had a preference for young men. I did not recall it before, as such slurs are commonly hurled by drunkards, regardless of truth or falsity."

"In this case," says Henry, "it is most certainly true. Perez has 'befriended' the Bacon brothers, especially Sir Francis, if you take my meaning. Their mother has threatened to cut them both off from the family's money if Anthony does not keep Perez away from Francis. Perez nearly killed one of Essex's secretaries with his musk and amber concoction."

"Seriously?"

Henry nods emphatically. "It took the secretary several weeks to recover properly. Perez is a menace when it comes to that sort of thing. He fancies himself a physician, which Lopez can only laugh at."

"He is known to Lopez?"

"Oh, yes, the Spanish community in England is quite close-knit. A lot of Jews and half-Jews. One never knows what *they're* plotting, as they speak a language only they understand. And Lopez has a way of placing himself at the center of it all, in pursuit of his own profit. He himself is a Jew by birth, although he's converted."

Noah scratches his head. "Having watched the good doctor practice his profession," he says, "I find it difficult to imagine him at the center of anything but a hospital."

"Indeed, he once *was* at the center of Saint Bartholomew's here in London, but found international intrigue far more to his liking. Eventually, he neglected his duties so completely that the hospital refused to let him reside in the only house on the grounds. He seems to have no real interest in medicine as a career, except as a well-paid physician for the rich and titled, upon whom he lavishes his medical attention."

"How much medical attention can the rich and titled require, I wonder?"

"Oh, you've no idea! He's told me that their diet is so rich that they often develop obstruction of the bowel. From notable to notable he travels with his little enema device, which he calls a 'clyster.' I shouldn't be surprised if the Queen were to issue him a coat of arms with a clyster as its escutcheon," Henry jokes. "She's one of his patients, you know." He looks down at his foot. "You know, I'm beginning to believe the good doctor knows what he's doing. My foot barely hurts at all any more."

"Why don't you try walking about a bit?" suggests Noah.

Up and down the hall they march, and then return to Noah's room.

"Much, much better," says Henry. "I really must write Doctor Lopez a thank-you."

Noah is reminded of Henry's abortive discussion of Lopez's other life. "You said Lopez is a man of intrigue. When we went to Creechurch for the autopsy, you mentioned something about his participation in the English Armada."

Henry explains. "Portugal's international status is currently in jeopardy. The monarch having died a short time ago, several people now contend for the Portuguese throne. Depending upon who prevails, Portugal will either retain or lose its character as a sovereign country. The question is very serious to the Portuguese, of course. To us English, it may be even *more* serious."

Noah considers the situation. "From what you've said, I conclude that one of the competing claimants is the King of Spain, Philip the Second."

As ever, Henry seems intrigued by Noah's intuition. "That's correct. But what makes you say so?"

"Really, Henry. That's easy. If the King of Spain were to become King of Portugal, the result would very likely be unification of the two countries."

Henry nods. "Just as England and Spain might have been unified if Philip had been recognized as King of England when he married our late Queen Mary. His father died trying to bring that about. Gives one shivers to think about it."

"Amen. Who are the contenders for the Portuguese throne, besides King Philip?"

"One resides here in England, at the invitation of the Queen under Crown protection. His name is Don Antonio. He's been living on the grounds at Eton."

Something clicks in Noah's mind. "Wait!" he commands, and lapses deep into thought, his eyes randomly focused on a fixed point on the floor. A few seconds later, he seems to regain awareness of his surroundings. "I *do* apologize, Henry. I meant no offense speaking to you so presumptuously."

"None taken," Henry assures him.

"I just realized that certain things I learned from Marie may have a direct bearing on this situation. If I'm right," begins Noah, "for at least the past several months this Don Antonio has resided in a building at Eton College, and has argued vociferously with his son there. Don Antonio drinks heavily, and corresponds with important people in the Netherlands. In his capacity as ostensible King of Portugal, he employs as his ambassador to Queen Elizabeth … " Noah furrows his brow incredulously, "Doctor Lopez? Can this be *true*?"

"The widow told you all that?"

"Of course not! I doubt she even *knows* it all. Why, it was *you* who told me Lopez is the Portuguese ambassador to England! What Marie *did* tell me was that she'd seen a drunken Don Antonio arguing with his son in a building at Eton where her late husband went to pick up certain letters intended for the Netherlands."

"Why would her husband have been accepting letters destined for the Netherlands? Unless … " Henry's eyes open wide, "unless his ships had secretly been *going* to the Netherlands, and not just Spain as she told us in the hearse. Has she told *you* that his ships had been going to the Netherlands?"

Noah nods. "Yes. When she was in the hearse, she didn't realize it might be important for us to know. But that's not the most interesting thing."

Henry waits silently.

Noah eyes him conspiratorially. "The man who handed the letters to Marie's husband … "

"Yes?"

"Was *Doctor Lopez*."

Henry seems lost in wonder.

"Who are the other contenders for the Portuguese throne?" asks Noah.

"Not important. Except to know that there is a competing family favored by the Earl of Essex." Henry rises and begins to pace, his gout evidently forgotten. "The Queen wants Don Antonio here in England. And so does the Privy Council, but … especially Essex, for he wants war with Spain. For the advancement of *his* faction, it would be most advantageous to drive as thick a wedge as possible between Portugal and Spain, to divide their strength. To see Portugal united with Spain would be Essex's nightmare. So long as Don Antonio has a foothold here in England, Portugal's sovereignty will likely remain separate from that of Spain."

Noah finds Henry's tale most enjoyable, as this is the first time Henry's really opened up about such a politically sensitive affair. "And the Cecils' peace faction? How would *they* feel about such an eventuality?"

"Well," says Henry, "Spanish-Portuguese unification would tend to *strengthen* the Cecils' peace faction, because a unified Spain and Portugal would enhance the possibility that an eventual invasion would go badly for England. Unification of Spain and Portugal would make *peace* England's order of the day. So, the Cecils would prefer that the Queen cut off any support for Don Antonio, and boot him out of England." He wags a finger of admonition. "And do not forget the separate interest of the Queen, who rules by *advice*. Her interest is to keep the Portuguese succession unresolved for a long time, thus preventing either faction of the Privy Council from gaining an edge over the other. Any other brilliant connections to draw, Ames?"

"Nothing brilliant. But I do have a question about the way the letters were to reach their addressees in the Netherlands."

"What question?"

A silent moment passes between them, broken at last by Noah.

"Who was the messenger?"

CHAPTER 14

JONATHAN SLEEPS THROUGH the rest of that day and all of the next. He awakens mid-morning on the third day, choking from dehydration. Noah, who's dozed off on the chair next to his bed, awakens when he stirs.

"Here's some water," says Noah, elevating Jonathan's head and raising a wooden cup to his mouth. "The doctor said you would be extremely thirsty."

Jonathan takes a sip. "What happened?" he asks groggily, looking up at Noah's concerned face. "I remember that Graves is dead. But how long have I slept?" He gratefully accepts the cup from Noah's hand, and takes another sip on his own.

"You reacted to the news very badly, and then collapsed into a deep sleep. Two days."

"Is everyone else all right?"

Tentatively, Noah begins to feel relieved. This seems like the former Jonathan. "Everyone else is fine, Jonathan." He pauses. "When you're feeling better, we can visit the gravesite together."

Jonathan nods appreciatively. Suddenly, his eyes open wide. "Did I miss any court dates?"

"No, no. I checked your calendar, and would have covered for you. There's no shortage of barristers about. You have two days before your next court date."

Jonathan sits up, finishes the first cup of water, pours himself another, and finishes that, as well. Slowly, he places his feet flat on the floor.

"What are you doing?" asks Noah.

"I have work to do."

"Are you feeling quite yourself?"

Jonathan rubs his face with his hand. "I expect I will be, as soon as I clean up."

"Very well. I need to relate some things to you, but I must go now. Family business. You think you'll be all right?"

"I'm a long way from all right, but I feel rested, for a change."

"Let Arden or one of the other jesters know if you need something. They've been worried about you."

"The 'jesters.' Is that how they're to be known now?" Jonathan rubs his eyes. "Did the doctor give me something to make me sleep?"

"Nothing of consequence," says Noah, mindful of Lopez's admonition. He rises from his chair, and assays his friend's condition. "I'll be back later. Get something to eat, and avoid drinking anything stronger than weak beer for the rest of the day. Doctor's orders."

"Yes, Doctor." Jonathan nods heavily, shuffles to the water closet, and closes the door behind him.

Noah finds Arden and one of the Bennetts deep in conversation in Arden's apartment. He tells them Jonathan is awake. "We'll keep an eye on him," says Arden. "Never worry."

* * *

Noah arrives at Marie's house to find that her children returned home the previous evening, and the place now bustles with family and servants. He knocks on the door and waits. A moment later, he's greeted by the good-looking young fellow who opened the door for Marie the first time he walked her home.

"Master Ames?" he inquires with a smile.

"At your service," says Noah, bowing cordially. "Are you Stephen Junior?"

"I am, sir." The young man bows, and extends his hand in friendship. "Pleased to make your acquaintance, sir. Won't you come in? Mother will be down in a few minutes ... if we're more fortunate than usual." Stephen leads him into a small sitting room on ground level. "Mother has told me a great deal about your courtroom exploits."

Noah strains to recall which courtroom exploits Marie might know about. "Oh!" he laughs. "That day with the silly dog." He frowns humorously. "I wouldn't recommend such course of conduct to anyone your age, Goodman Rodriguez. Got me in a bit of hot water."

"Yes, mother told me. Hot water, and a dinner invitation to Serjeants' Inn."

"Oh, told you *that*, did she?" He changes the subject. "She told me that she will soon be traveling abroad with you to make an introduction to your late father's associates."

"End of April, sir. I must confess I've been spending more time in scholarly pursuits than learning the export business, but after I graduate Merton this Yuletide, I plan to devote all my waking hours to the business."

"Ah, another Oxford man! Eton or Harrow?"

"Eton, I should hope."

"Pleased to make your acquaintance, Goodman Rodriguez. Noah Ames, Eton, Merton College '75."

"Well, your advisors showed excellent discretion in choosing your schools."

"As did yours, sir."

"My schools were chosen by my late father. Who chose yours?"

Although Noah is accustomed to framing an evasive reply to this question, he is grateful to be relieved of the need by Marie, who descends the stairs in her black widow's weeds, looking sharp as ever, her veil pinned away from her face.

"Well, I heard that!" she says. "I'm surprised I haven't discovered you two sharing cognac in my parlor." Noah and young Stephen rise as she enters. Noah takes Marie's hand, and bows deeply. "Why, Master Ames," she says, "it is good to see you, for I have not done so since that day in court." She gives Noah a meaningful look.

"And it is good to see *you*, madam. The separation has been far too long."

Stephen goes to the front door and opens it for his mother. "Shall we go?" Marie nods, moves the veil to cover her face, deftly pins it into place, and walks out ahead of them.

The carriage moves off at a brisk clop. A pleasant breeze streams through the open windows, and they enjoy it in silence for a time.

"So, Master Ames," says Marie, "if it would not be violating a confidence, do tell us the occasion upon which we are delivering you to Southwark. Is it to be the theater with Master Neville today?" Her smile wavers briefly, which Noah attributes to her natural association of the theater with the recent loss of her husband.

"No, madam, although I hope to be attending the theater later in the week. One of the *Henry the Sixth* plays."

"Ah, yes!" interrupts young Stephen. "I understand they're staging that whole cycle of plays in the coming weeks. I hope to see one or more myself before we depart."

"Then, perhaps you might be my guest at some such showing — with your dear mother, of course, should she feel up to it."

Stephen leans forward and confides: "I think he has an extraordinary genius." Noah is unsure whom Stephen means.

So is Marie, who laughs prettily and says, "Stephen. It is customary to identify the person about whom one is speaking."

Stephen continues in the same posture and tone. "I mean Shakespeare. He far surpasses Marlowe, do you not think, Master Ames?"

Marie laughs again. "Oh, leave the poor man alone. He was telling us why he is going to Southwark today."

"Yes, and I shall be pleased to tell you, madam." Turning to Stephen, he says: "And I shall be sure to tell Goodman Shakespeare how highly Goodman Stephen regards his talents."

"You *know* him?" Stephen nearly shouts.

Noah can see they have already reached London Bridge on their way south. "I have met the gentleman, and expect I shall see him again," he replies. He can see the young man has a thousand questions for him, but decides to observe accepted decorum by replying first to his mother. "Today, madam, I shall be dining with Lady Burlington, who is staying with a cousin of my deceased wife, one with whom I have remained in touch."

Marie sits up very straight and expressionless, pointedly avoiding eye contact with Noah. To him, the image is that of a sentry hearing an unwelcome sound in the night.

"Lady … who?" she asks without apparent emotion.

Noah hides a smile. "Jessica, Lady Burlington, madam. She is my daughter."

Marie relaxes visibly. "How delightful! Perhaps I shall have the pleasure of meeting her someday."

"The pleasure would be hers, I'm sure, madam. And where will Goodman Stephen be accompanying you today?"

"We're attending to some odds and ends in preparation for our voyage abroad," she replies. "We shall be visiting several clothiers and a luggage merchant."

Stephen, who has been staring out of the window, suddenly gasps. He leans out the side and says something to the driver. As he resumes his seat, the carriage slows considerably.

Noah looks out the same window as Stephen. It appears they are about to pass a fashionably dressed young woman standing with her back to them, conversing with an older woman, also dressed well, but not so fashionably.

"Stephen, this will not do!" admonishes Marie. "It is *vulgar!*"

"Just one moment, *mamain*. Perhaps she will turn 'round again. She is an angel. An *angel*."

All that can be seen of the girl is her shoulder-length brown hair partially bound up in a French style Noah has seen only in portraits, half curls and half straight. She wears a vertically striped dress cinched tightly at her waist, which is almost unnaturally thin, making her bosom and hips even more protuberant. A thought runs fleetingly through Noah's mind that a woman having curves such as this is no Anglo-Saxon or Viking princess. Italian, perhaps. Perhaps … The face of the older woman now becomes visible. It's years since he's seen her. Is that … *Beth*?

When the young woman turns around and shows her face again, Stephen is quite smitten. "She is a *goddess* sent from above," he whispers longingly, much to his mother's exasperation.

Noah's heart goes out to him. "I assure you she is no such thing. She's my daughter."

"*Papa!*" shouts Jessica, spying Noah and waving the carriage to a halt with one white-gloved hand. Instead of sprinting over to Noah as she was wont to do as a child, she approaches the carriage with mincing steps, her right hand raised slightly before her, as though guiding her graceful movement. Beth, longer in the tooth and carrying a bit more heft, lumbers a few steps behind.

Unable to take his eyes off Jessica, Stephen says, "Master Ames, I am beginning to think you know quite everyone *worth* knowing!"

As Jessica approaches the side of the carriage, she acknowledges its other occupants. "Good day!" she says to Marie and Stephen, smiling brightly.

Although it irks Noah to observe protocols of title with his own daughter, he has no choice. "Lady Burlington," he says to his daughter, "may I present to you Goodwife Marie Rodriguez-Miller and her son, Goodman Stephen Rodriguez." Stephen shoots to his feet and bangs his head on the soffit. He grimaces, and sits down immediately, shaking his head to clear his vision.

Jessica reaches for Stephen's shoulder through the open window, but the carriage is too high off the ground. "Goodman Rodriguez," she says, "are you quite all right? That was a *nasty* blow."

Stephen forces a smile. "The worst of the blow was to my manly pride, madam."

"In that case, I am glad to hear it," says Jessica, "as such blows will heal quickly with feminine attention."

"I hope I am not too forward in saying, madam, that any amount of attention from you would surely speed the healing process greatly."

Marie is dismayed yet again. "Stephen, when *will* you learn how to speak with your betters?"

Jessica looks to Noah. She told him long ago that she detests the locution "betters," which, Noah pointed out, appeared somewhat hypocritical on her part. Now, he merely smiles and shrugs.

Marie turns to Jessica. "Please forgive him, Lady Burlington. As you see, he has received a knock on the head."

Jessica replies, "There is nothing to forgive, Goodwife Rodriguez, I assure you."

"Ahem," says the older woman outside the carriage. It's Beth.

Jessica opens her eyes wide and gasps. "Oh, my word!" she exclaims. "I am *so* sorry to have neglected your introduction, Auntie Elizabeth!" She takes a moment to compose the introduction in her mind before proceeding. "Goodwife and Goodman Rodriguez, this is my beloved aunt, Miss Elizabeth Fernandez."

"Enchanted," says Marie. Stephen only smiles at Beth through the pain.

"Don't bother to get up," says Beth indignantly. Noah recognizes this as vintage Beth. The poor young man nearly knocked himself cold showing courtesy to Jessica, yet Beth implies that his failure to do the same for her is somehow disrespectful.

"Well," says Noah, "it's probably best if I leave off here, as Lady Burlington, Miss Fernandez, and I will be going to the same place. We may as well reap advantage of the lovely day, and stroll together." He smiles. "Thank you so much, Goodwife Rodriguez. Goodman. I look forward to seeing you both soon in Holborn." He steps out and closes the door behind him.

Marie rises from her seat and curtsies to Jessica, who acknowledges with a smile. Marie resumes her seat, and gives the order for the carriage to resume its journey only after Jessica has turned away.

The three begin walking. "You know, *I* could have used the lift," mumbles Beth. "Not that anyone cares."

Noah smirks. "How have you been, Beth?"

"Oh, well enough, I suppose. Aren't you going to say something to your daughter?"

"Yes, I am." He stops walking. "Come here, Jessica. Let me look upon you."

Jessica turns gracefully, her skirt whorling away from her body and collapsing perfectly back into place. She offers Noah her hand in the most genteel manner, and he takes it in his, if only to hold her still long enough to study her sculpted face. Perhaps Stephen was right, and she really is an angel from above. Or perhaps it's a trick of the light that makes her seem so perfect for the role. Either way, she certainly *looks* the part. His eyes grow misty.

Jessica shakes her head sadly. "Oh, *papa*. You still see a ghost when you look at me. Do you not?"

He answers truthfully. "I see two people: one a beautiful, intelligent, young woman, and the other the ghost of a woman I once knew who had all the same qualities … and whose loss I still cannot fathom."

Jessica regards him sympathetically. "I miss her, too, *papa*."

"And I must tell you that I am *very* sorry for your loss of Lorenzo. How long has it been?"

She stands to his side, and they resume their walk. "The doctors said it was consumption. It has been just slightly more than six months now. I only stopped wearing the widow's black and veil this past Saturday. I know *you* were never convinced of it, but he was a wonderful man."

"Don't say that," he protests. "I never doubted that he cared for you, Jessica, or that he had many other fine qualities. I am sure he rests comfortably with the Lord."

"He just wasn't … *Hebrew* enough for you."

"Jessica, he was not Hebrew at all."

"I have thought often of your desire that any children of the marriage know of their Jewish heritage. Alas, there will not — " She chokes back her tears.

He stops again and pats her hand. He never could abide her crying, always feeling that he'd failed in his duty to rearrange the whole world, if need be, so that a creature so perfect as this would never have need to weep.

"Well," she sighs, "there shall *be* no children of the marriage, so I suppose it doesn't matter now. Perhaps God was telling me — "

"Jessica, stop! *No one* believes that. As for my part, it grieves me greatly that there were no children. Has the … cause been determined?"

She wipes her eyes. "There was no need to seek a physician's assistance on that question. Lorenzo was not … carnally given."

Noah nods sympathetically. "I see."

She sighs wistfully. "But he *has* left me well provided for, bless his soul. So long as I do not turn gambler, and my luck does not turn Turk, I shall never want."

"I am very glad to hear it," says Noah.

Beth snorts.

"Is there something on your mind, Beth?" he asks impatiently.

"Just that I think you'd rather have Jessica dependent upon you, so you might more closely guide her choices."

Noah shakes his head. "Same old Beth. No, dear, I have come to appreciate Jessica's position. She is finding her way in the same complex world we all face, and has seen fit to comply with the world on its own terms. We all do, to some extent."

Beth snorts again. "I suppose *Marie* has had a hand in persuading you of such?" Every Jew is taught that "Marie" and "Maria" are names given only to Christian girls, and that the Hebrew mother of Jesus, after whom such girls are named, was actually called "Miriam."

"I don't know what you mean, Beth," he replies.

Jessica pats his hand. "Daddy, women are born with the gift of knowing when another woman has staked her claim in a man. Marie has pasted her flag firmly on your doublet."

"Has she?" he asks, only too happy that Jessica has once again called him "daddy."

Jessica draws him aside, out of Beth's hearing, and whispers. "It's best you not talk about other women. Beth has been waiting for you her whole life. She even cared so faithfully for Mother throughout those last terrible months out of love for *you*. Did you know that?"

Noah is mortified. He shakes his head almost imperceptibly.

Jessica intimately adjusts his collar. "Whenever another woman has your attention, she feels unrequited and cheated of her birthright."

"Her birthright?" he asks skeptically. "As though she were next in line?"

Jessica smiles, kisses his cheek, and brings him by the hand to rejoin Beth. "Come," she says. "Let us all have a wonderful repast!"

The remainder of the afternoon is spent in fond reminiscence, and by the end of it Noah can no longer remember how he could ever have been angry with Jessica. He has also resolved never to be so oblivious to Beth's feelings, and so caught up in his own.

*   *   *

Early that evening, Noah returns to the apartment at Gray's Inn, where Henry has already taken up residence.

"Oh, Ames! Just the man I'm looking for," says Henry, arranging the contents of a small portfolio.

Noah sniffs. "*Imagine* finding me here in my room!"

"Have you spoken to Jonathan this evening? He seems sound as a fiddle now."

"No," replies Noah. "I passed his room on the way up and saw the door open, but didn't want to disturb him."

"Well, I advise you to go and see him now. It will help you sleep tonight, believe me. I have never *seen* anyone as overcome by grief as he was the other day. The improvement is quite heartening."

Noah returns to Jonathan's room, knocks at the door, and sticks his head in.

"Noah, please come in," says Jonathan. "The jesters told me how far out of myself I was the other day. I deeply regret it. As you can see, however, I'm quite well now. I've been hard at work all day." He indicates the papers neatly arranged on his desk.

"Have you time to hear what Henry and I have thought through about this whole Rodriguez affair?"

Jonathan gives him a peculiar smoldering look. "Yes, please. Sit down. Tell me everything you two discussed."

Twenty minutes later, it's full dark and the room is lit by only a single candle which sits directly before Jonathan. Behind him, the room is pitch dark, so that his face appears to float eerily in space as he speaks. "And

Master Neville remains of the opinion that Essex's men may have been acting on their own, without their master's consent?"

"Well," Noah equivocates, "we haven't really discussed that question directly."

"I can imagine," says Jonathan. "It would be very difficult for an honorable man such as Master Neville to ally himself with Essex's faction while believing him to be a common murderer. Don't you think?"

Noah nods. Jonathan seems about to say something, but then reconsiders.

"What is it you wish to tell me?" Noah asks.

Jonathan sighs. "I'm not sure how you will take it."

"Please, Jonathan, there should be no secrets between us on the Essex affair."

Jonathan nods weighingly. "All right, but I must have your oath as a barrister that you shall never repeat what I tell you now."

This is a little alarming, and Noah begins to wonder whether Jonathan's pacific demeanor does not mask some residual madness. "All right," he says.

Jonathan looks down at his desk, and then up again at Noah. "I have no need to deceive myself or, as Master Neville is doing, to pretend there is room for doubt, when in fact there is none. I have *no* doubt that Essex's men have been authorized to do everything they've done, and *will* be authorized to do much more, and much worse."

Noah sighs with relief. "I'm inclined to agree with you — "

Jonathan interrupts. "There's something more I wish to tell you about the earl, and I will hold you to your oath."

"What more is there?"

Jonathan's face floats forward conspiratorially and looks Noah dead in the eye. Where grief once prevailed, there now remains only a frighteningly calm resolution.

"It may take me ten years … but I will see that man taken to the knacker's."

Noah shivers to see such a change in this young man. "Lawfully?" he ventures.

Jonathan smiles with warm assurance, which Noah finds unnerving in light of what he's just said.

"Lawfully is how we do things."

CHAPTER 15

WITH MARIE'S HOUSE REPOPULATED, Noah resumes spending his evenings at Gray's Inn. As much as he misses her soft caress and the warmth of her body next to him on the sofa, he sleeps much more soundly now, and longer. Since his unnerving talk with Jonathan, however, something has haunted his dreams — something he's intended, but avoided doing.

By the time Noah awakens late this morning, Henry is already gone to Westminster. Before dressing, he searches his desk for the papers bearing his assailant's vague warning. He soon finds them, and forces himself with dread to read the warning once more: *Caveat causidicus.* Lawyer, beware. His stomach turns in anger as he realizes that he has actually come to live by those foul words, albeit not as intended by their author. Something about the tiny handwriting, and the intimately violent way in which the message was delivered, makes the words even more insidious.

He considers what he'd like to say back to Essex. While Essex can cosset himself in his grand residences, and insulate his person from harm by dispatching surrogates to do his dirty work, his mind is no less vulnerable than Noah's. Intuitively, Noah realizes that the time has come to retaliate in kind for the unwelcome warning, to do *something* to ensure that Essex's repose will be no less troubled than his own. He inks his pen and carefully draws a line through the tiny inscription. What should he say?

As Essex is not a lawyer, Noah's reply cannot be framed in purely reciprocal terms. But he and Essex do have *something* in common. They are both the Queen's subjects. And to remind Essex of his faithlessness as Her Majesty's subject would be sure to unsettle someone with such absurdly high self-regard. Then it comes to him. He gave me a warning. I'll give *him* a warning. Not a toothless threat, nor simply a refutation of his own warning, but a *new* warning calculated to place him in fear for his very soul.

Now he has it: "It is not the faithful subject, but the faithless subject, who needs warning." While Noah's Latin is imperfect, he translates the phrase as best he can, and inscribes it in an equally intimate hand immediately adjacent to Essex's now-stricken warning.

Non servus fidelis sed perfidus debet cavere.

There's no question in his mind how his message will be delivered. He cleans himself up, puts on a fresh set of barrister's robes, places the inscribed papers in his pocket, and heads out to the stables.

"Morning, sir!" says Tom, as he passes. "No need for you to get your boots soiled back here. Would you like me to bring your mount around?"

"Oh, no, Tom. Thanks. Just came to get some papers I left in the saddlebag." He goes to his horse's stall, opens the saddlebag that's remained empty since it was pillaged, and deposits the newly inscribed papers. He expects they will not be there long.

*   *   *

A few days later, Noah sits at his desk preparing argument of a motion in a criminal matter when a letter is slipped under his door engraved with the name "Jessica, Lady Burlington," and scented with a musky perfume that makes his eyes tear. He sneezes and reads the note, holding it as far from his nose as possible.

Dearest Father,

I thought it prudent to mention to you that Goodman Stephen has come to see me socially on two separate occasions. I hope you do not mind. Auntie Elizabeth was kind enough to prepare fine dinners for us both times.

Stephen really is a dear. (And, though I would never mention this to anyone but you, he really is *very* good-looking, and most respectful.) Anyway, he and his mother will be leaving for many weeks next Thursday morning. (Did you know that?) Stephen has asked me to join him and his lovely *mamain* for supper on the Wednesday evening immediately preceding their departure, and he has also asked me to extend an invitation to you. Isn't that lovely? This will give you a chance to explore any feelings you may have for his precious *mamain* (who is now privately referred to by my irreverent Auntie Elizabeth as "the *shikse*." I really *must* speak with her about that.)

As you are so close to the Rodriguez home in Holborn, you may wish to express your acceptance or regrets directly. (Oh, *do* come, if you can!) Either way, I would greatly appreciate your letting me know as soon as you have decided.

Your Loving Daughter,
Jessica

Unbeknownst to Jessica, Noah has already been invited by Marie, but Jessica's note provides him with a perfect excuse to trot over there unannounced a bit later, hoping against hope that Marie will be alone, and at liberty. They've spent little time together the past week or two, as Marie always feels the need to maintain the outward appearance of utmost rectitude to set an example for her two younger children, especially her daughter. From Noah's fleeting glimpses of the little girl, he expects her to become every bit as beautiful as her mother, which is quite something.

By early afternoon, it has become a sultry day. Most doors and windows at Gray's Inn have been left open, allowing a warm breeze to pass gently through the sleeping rooms. Any hope that the excess heat will be wafted out, however, has dwindled as the day has grown warmer. And, while warmth is always welcome after a cold winter, everyone knows that its arrival as early as Easter Term often presages a long and intense outbreak of plague.

A nearby door closes firmly downstairs, and the voices of Jonathan and Arthur carry up into Noah's room, their words unintelligible. The two have been seen together a great deal lately, exiting the inn at all hours of the day and night and shutting their doors as soon they return, saying nary a word to anybody. It is commonly known at the inn that Jonathan has begun to carry a dagger with him at all times, and that he has been spending considerable time with Arthur at Eton's firing range, learning to use a musket and pistol. Considering that he is the only survivor of the Boar's Head incident whose identity is known to Skeres, no one can fault him for it. The wordless voices recede.

Noah lies on his bed with his hands behind his head and closes his eyes, listening to the soothing sounds of the afternoon. Far away, a dog barks. As the breeze picks up, a whirlwind whirs past his window and dissipates as it moves onto the open square. The hallway clock ticks rhythmically. He drifts off.

He sits alone on a pew, a congregation of one, in a small, dimly lit synagogue illuminated by a few widely dispersed candles. Behind the altar stands the ark where the Torah scrolls reside, concealed by a blue satin curtain embroidered with ancient Hebrew inscriptions.

The candles flicker in the breeze. Outside, the wind gathers strength, rapidly growing into a gale, setting off another whirlwind. Unlike the one that just dissipated over Gray's Inn Square, this one maintains coherent form just outside, its inarticulate susurration swelling from a whisper to a murmur. The shutters clatter against the walls outside.

In the near total darkness, a brief, flowing movement on the dais coalesces into a robed, hooded figure standing with its back to him. Before the figure is a small table upon which sits a silver pitcher of sacramental wine. The wind outside groans.

Noah's unease becomes a dread that churns in the pit of his stomach. Something is happening here. Something that needs to be remembered.

Voices call from far away, from beyond the grave. His parents? He was so small when last he heard them that he cannot be sure. What are they saying? It sounds like a warning of some kind. The voices are fearful, and frustrated that they may not be heard beyond the veil.

The groaning whirlwind, still growing in intensity, comes to rest just outside the synagogue, amplifying the thready voices of the dead. It is a warning.

Get out! Get out! Menachem!

Hearing his own name spoken by the dead sends chills up his spine. This is no general warning, either. It is personal to him, from those who know his birth name. And he has a sickening feeling that it's not a dream at all.

He desperately wants to run, but finds himself frozen in place. The wind seeps through the synagogue, which grows damper and chillier by the second. His eyes dart around, but there's nothing to reinforce the fear that the voices are trying so desperately to instill in him.

Then the cowled figure on the dais moves, frightening him out of his wits. It turns, face concealed by the cowl. Does it even have a face? Where its face should be there appears instead a deep, black emptiness. The figure slowly carries a silver cup of sacramental wine toward the altar, as though preparing to commence some strange service that Noah has never seen. It grows in size and power. In the dark vacancy under its cowl, Noah can see ... lightning, small and distant. But there is no thunder. And this is no man. Whatever it is, it is both elemental and malign.

Noah whimpers with dread. The figure opens a book on the altar, and the whirlwind objects violently. The whole building now shudders from floor to rafters, as shingles and shutters are ripped off by the wind and hurled silently into the night. If this continues much longer, the wooden synagogue will be torn into countless pieces, and Noah with it. It will be worth it, he thinks, if only the abomination at the altar is obliterated.

Just as the figure is about to address its blasphemy to its congregation of one, there comes the sound of approaching horses. Many horses. Coming here now! "Run, Menachem!" say the voices one last time.

There's a boom.

Noah opens his eyes with a start.

All is quiet. He's relieved to be awake, but unsure he's actually been asleep. He wipes perspiration from his brow, and blinks several times to clear his vision. Looking around for the source of the sound that awakened him, he begins to wonder if it was merely part of the dream. Then he realizes that something in the room has indeed changed. A prayer book he keeps in the locked cupboard with his skullcap lies on the floor.

If anyone were to see it, his secret would be out. Quickly, he goes to the open door leading to the hallway. There's no one in sight. A deathly silence has fallen on the inn, in which he would easily hear anyone approaching or absconding. He closes the door quietly and steps back into the room.

He picks up the fallen prayer book, intending to put it back and relock the cupboard door, when he realizes the little door is still closed and securely locked. He peers at the lock. It's a flimsy affair, but effective to frustrate the casual snoop. It offers no sign of prying, twisting, scratching, or other untoward force. The key ring in his pocket holds the only key. He draws out the ring, and there's the key. He experiments with prying the cupboard open using his fingernails, but it will not budge. He strikes it several times with the meat of his hand to see if that will cause it to spring open. It does not.

He inserts the key into the lock, which turns smoothly, and opens the door. His eye lights at once upon the candlestick, and he resolves to bring it to Marie's home, as he promised. Everything inside the cabinet is exactly as he left it, except the prayer book which is now, inexplicably, in his hand. He puts it back in its accustomed place, closes the little door, and locks it.

There comes the sound of many horses approaching from the south in close formation. His eyes go wide. Mindful of the warnings and hoofbeats in his dream, he steps near enough to the window to see out, but stays far enough back to be concealed in shadow from anyone peering in from outside.

A grandiose carriage, opulently drawn by four large black horses and surrounded by several individual riders, pulls up in front of the building. Everyone, including the horses, wears the same shades of tangerine and cream, the distinctive livery of the Earl of Essex. Two riders approach the side of the carriage, stop momentarily, and quickly ride out across the square, having evidently been dispatched by its occupant.

Noah is relieved that he's closed his door, as he now hears numerous footsteps heavily descending a set of nearby stairs. Someone bursts out through the inn's main door, striding confidently toward the carriage, followed by several others, all in barrister's robes. It's Anthony Bacon, doing his sickly best to appear robust. His brother comes up close behind, followed by several others whose faces are only vaguely familiar.

As Bacon and his men emerge from the building, Noah can hear Essex's men shouting to each other and taking up positions at various points on the way up to Bacon's apartment. Noah finds this vaguely frightening. That is no doubt its intended effect.

A footman wearing Essex's livery dismounts and holds his horse's reins in one hand while opening the carriage door with the other. Essex emerges resplendently attired, followed by Southampton, who wears a gold chain around his neck, a sign of his own livery. Essex exchanges a few words with Anthony Bacon, nods to his brother, and removes his gloves, an item of clothing that seems more than a bit impractical to Noah in light of the warm day.

While the barristers talk among themselves, Essex himself silently peers up toward Noah's window with a curious expression. At first, Noah feels sure he's standing far enough back to avoid being seen, but, as Essex continues to look in his window, eventually he is overcome by the eerie feeling that Essex is actually staring him in the face. He considers whether, on the off chance that he really *can* be seen, he ought to nod to the earl, but feels insolently disinclined to do so. No, Essex does not appear to expect any acknowledgment, and will not get one.

Essex follows the Bacon brothers up the external staircase, and can be heard tromping into the inn proper, followed by several of his men. Perhaps two minutes later, Essex and the Bacons lumber down the stairs and outside again, getting into the carriage. With one more military shout, Essex's men abandon their posts in the building and depart at once, remounting quickly and following the coach south toward High Holborn, then west past Marie's house toward Westminster.

It seems strange that Essex would make such a grand show of stopping by to pick up Anthony and Francis Bacon, but apparently he's making a point about just how important the Bacons are to his future intentions.

Whatever Essex's purposes, Noah has no doubt that his horses were those signified by the dream, and that, peering out at Noah through Essex's unseeing eyes was the very malignity that gave form to the robed figure.

While he will not heed the entreaties of the dead by running away, he will certainly stand on heightened guard from now on.

* * *

Late that afternoon, after the day cools down, Noah has nearly decided to visit Marie on the pretext of accepting Jessica's secondhand invitation when Henry shouts up from downstairs.

"Master Ames, care for a walk?"

This is a surprise. Henry's gout must have improved a great deal for him to *suggest* a walk. Noah sits up and shouts a reply.

"Certainly, Master Neville. Give me a moment!"

He dresses as quickly as he can and goes downstairs. Henry is smiling, dressed in light colors for the warm weather. He looks … different, somehow. "You're looking *well*, sir!" Noah says.

"I'm *feeling* well, thank you."

Noah looks at him incredulously. "You *didn't*!"

Henry smiles smugly. "Didn't what?"

"You took Lopez's advice?" Noah takes a step back and looks closely at his friend's form. "Yes, you did! You've lost significant weight, and in less than a fortnight. And I'll warrant you've cut down your drinking, as well."

Henry puts his finger to his lips. "Shhhh. Don't let it get around. I have a reputation to uphold."

"Your secret is safe with me. Come. Let us walk in the sunshine together."

Although Henry still moves a good deal more slowly and carefully than Noah, he appears not to be suffering at all. They walk along the front of the inn.

Henry breathes deeply in the warm sun. "Well, I've discovered little about the incident at the Boar's Head. One thing I did find — "

"Wait!" Noah whispers hoarsely. "We're nearly underneath Bacon's windows," he points up discreetly, "and they're open." Even though the Bacons left with Essex, it's possible that the room remains occupied. Henry takes the point at once and shrugs, looking as mousy as anyone can while being so big and naturally outgoing.

Something occurs to Noah, another thing he's long *thought* of doing, but has never quite got around to. It occurs to him that if he looks to his left and walks from here to the oak on the square, he can detect whatever it was Bacon's man was watching this past winter. As he now stands directly beneath Bacon's window, the object of surveillance should come into view as he walks to the oak where the man was standing for all those hours.

"Come with me," he says. "Just two friends, walking and talking." Henry arches an eyebrow, but follows his lead nonetheless.

Together, they stroll toward the oak. While, to any casual observer, Noah would appear to be looking at Henry, in fact he's looking *past* him. And there it is. There's no doubt. The only thing that cannot be seen from Bacon's window but can be seen from the oak tree is … the servant's entrance to Mountjoy's Inn. He keeps walking, and Henry strides to keep up.

Noah frowns as he begins to factor this new information into the small quantity already known, forming and rejecting one hypothesis after another.

"What are you thinking?" asks Henry.

Noah looks at him gravely. "I'm thinking Doctor Lopez is in deep, deep trouble. Remember the man in brown riding clothes who was once standing by the oak we just passed?"

Henry searches his memory. "Oh, yes. Bacon's man."

"Well, it took me until now to realize what he was spying on. Please continue to look at me as I tell you."

Henry huffs along. "All right. What was he watching?"

"Mountjoy's Inn, servant's entrance."

Henry ponders a moment. "Lopez?"

"More precisely, the entrance that would be used by someone wishing to come and go unseen from Lopez's residence. Essex, or at least Bacon, appears to be investigating comings and goings at the good doctor's residence." He makes a mental note to examine this information more closely a bit later on. "What were you about to tell me?"

"Oh, not much. But I think I know who the drunkard Bob was. His name is, or at least I think it is, Robert Poley."

"Have you seen him?"

"Oh, yes. A few days ago. His face was still badly bruised from the beating, although the contusions were all mottled and yellowish, as though fading. Essex's attendant Gelly Meyrick was deriding him mercilessly. Kept saying he looked like a pig with rings around his eyes."

"How did Poley reply?"

Henry snorts. "I thought the barnyard reference ironic, as one might actually mistake *Meyrick* for a pig. But Poley avoided replying in kind. He did say one thing that might be of interest, though."

"What's that?"

"He asked Meyrick how he'd like to have a poker stuck in his eye, and said he could arrange it."

Noah stops, and so does Henry.

"This is the quality of conversation one hears at Essex House? Why on earth would you spend time there?"

Henry waves off the question. "Oh, please! They're *lackeys*, those two! There are lackeys everywhere! Besides, one can hear some of the most intelligent conversation in all England there. Philip Sydney ... "

"He's been *dead* six years!"

"... Southampton, every poet and notable you can imagine!"

Noah shakes his head. "I must be lacking in imagination. In any event, what do you make of Poley's threat?"

Henry shrugs. "If he wasn't just blustering, I expect he knows who murdered Rodriguez."

Noah nods thoughtfully.

A cheerful expression comes over Henry. "Essex is having a party at the end of May. I've received an invitation."

"Oh?" Noah sniffs. "I haven't received *mine*, as yet. But I shan't hold my breath until it arrives."

"Don't be so sure you won't receive one. If Essex holds true to form, he may well invite you."

"You're joking."

"Oh, but I assure you I am not! As I've told you, alliances at court are almost exclusively made for advantages. It would be much cheaper and easier for Essex to make you his friend than his adversary."

Having walked a circle around the square, they come once again to the building where Noah lives.

"If you saw the way he stared at my window on his brief visit to the inn this morning," says Noah, "you would know that his mind is quite made up as to which side I'm on, and it's certainly not his."

"You drew such a conclusion from a look through a window?"

"I did."

"Then you must have far better intuition into such matters than I, Master Ames."

"Perhaps, Master *Neville*."

Someone inside the inn knocks on a window as they pass. It's Master Treasurer, who signals them excitedly through the window to wait. He's not as spry as he once was. In a long minute, he appears at the front door and opens it, a bit winded.

"Good afternoon, Master Neville!" he shouts down.

Henry shouts his reply, as Master Treasurer's hearing is also not what it was. "Good afternoon, Master Treasurer!"

"Excuse me, sir," says Master Treasurer, who turns to Noah. "Master Ames, Lord Essex has sent the inn a list of invitees to his upcoming gathering." He waves the invitation energetically. "Your name appears on it." He smiles.

Noah glances aside at Henry, and shouts back to the old man. "Thank you, Master Treasurer!"

Master Treasurer smiles as though he's just delivered the most wonderful news of the season. He squints down at the paper in his hand. "Oh, and your youthful friend, Master Arthur, has also been invited." He closes the door and disappears from view.

Henry laughs derisively. "What an *intuitive* fellow you are, Master Ames!"

"We shall see, Henry," says Noah, his heart filled with portent. "Would you accompany me to the stables? I need to check on something."

"Certainly."

As they enter the stable, they spot Tom blissfully asleep on a bale of hay. Noah holds his finger to his lips, and they pass in silence. The horses remain quiet as they approach the stall where Noah's mount is kept. He opens his saddlebag.

It's empty.

"Let me repeat, Master Neville. Essex knows my mind, and shall soon learn that I know his black heart."

CHAPTER 16

THE LEGAL YEAR IS DIVIDED into four terms, between which court is in recess, and its personnel and barristers are expected to take their holidays. The two chilliest terms are also the longest, Michaelmas Term running from October to Christmas, and Hilary from January to a date in April.

Noah strives to complete as many of his cases as possible during the beautiful spring days of Easter Term, ending in May, to avoid the need to revisit them during Trinity Term in June and July, when courtrooms can swelter and the term itself can be truncated by plague.

Courthouses are places of public assembly not unlike theaters, which are commonly suspected of being prime sites for the spread of deadly infection. No solicitor wishes to prepare a case in the summer, knowing that his witnesses might be forced to flee the city prior to trial. No barrister relishes the thought of occupying close quarters with a client who might be coming down with plague. A lawyer having any choice in the matter will flee both London and Westminster at the first sign of an outbreak, for an epidemic, once begun, can spread like wildfire through the town, sometimes overtaking even a rapid exodus.

Because Noah's caseload is extensive and his work often interrupted, he never manages to steal a visit to Marie on the pretext of accepting an invitation to her *bon voyage* supper. All he can do is send her a note accepting the invitation, and his daughter a letter notifying her of his acceptance.

While Noah looks forward to the supper, where his family and Marie's will unite around the table for the first time, he dreads the indeterminate weeks without her that will follow.

"When will you return?" he would ask repeatedly.

"When God and the seas allow," she'd reply, mimicking a commercial disclaimer oft used in the shipping business. As she would always follow this discomfiting answer with a passionate kiss, he would inquire often.

When the day of the supper at last arrives, it dawns bright and clear. All morning long, work that Noah ordinarily would find enjoyable seems unbearably tedious. His thoughts drift repeatedly, and he finds himself gazing out of the window, his heart yearning for an early sunset. While he tries to keep up his spirits about his upcoming separation from Marie, the lingering loss of Rachel many years earlier fills him with anxiety bordering on despair.

If the weather is good, as it clearly is, the plan is for Jessica to meet him at Gray's Inn, and for the two of them to walk together to Marie's house.

Supper is scheduled for six. At five-thirty, Noah waits outdoors for Jessica's arrival. She pulls up in a closed coach. Noah opens the door for her, and pays the driver.

"Oh, *papa*, that really is not necessary."

"Nonsense. My pleasure, dear."

Jessica steps out of the carriage looking very elegant and very young in a simple full-length satin dress of jade green that brings out the color in her eyes. She thanks her father and kisses him on the cheek.

"So, young lady," says Noah, as they start off for Holborn, "just how serious is this business between you and Master Rodriguez?"

"Oh, not so serious at all," she says dismissively. "At least not for now."

"Are you sure *he* feels the same way?"

She cocks her head coquettishly. "That I cannot say. What I *can* say is that I have given him no *reason* to feel otherwise. A young lady cannot be too careful in treating every suitor according to his tenor." Noah nods sagely, having no idea what she means. "But we shall see if he writes while he is away — and *what* he writes."

"Keeping one's options open, I see. You were ever the careful girl, my sweet."

"How is your work, Father? It has been rumored that there was some bad business a few weeks ago involving a colleague of yours at Gray's Inn."

"Oh? What have you heard?"

"Nothing, other than what I have said. Is this person known to you?"

"He is. In fact, I am quite fond of him. An excellent barrister in the making. Unfortunately, he lost a good old friend, and was very distraught. And how is your Aunt Beth?"

"She is well … but lonely, I fear. She has no one to grow old with. I mean, it's not that she cries herself to sleep every night. Not at all. She goes about her business, and seems content to live within her means. I have been helping her a bit in that regard, making sure to bear my own freight, and a bit more."

"'Bear your own freight?' That's *shipping* talk. I perceive you have been spending more time with this Rodriguez fellow than you've let on."

"No," she laughs, "but it is very contagious, the *patois* of commerce. One must *ever* be on guard against its incursion into genteel speech."

"Indeed, one *must*," he jibes.

She looks at him askance. "Oh, *Daddy*," she says, and pokes him in the shoulder.

"Well, it looks as though we've arrived."

They climb the steps to Marie's house, and knock. There's some giggling and scrapping on the other side of the door. In a moment, Marie's younger son opens it, standing more formally erect than usual, and seems about to speak when he's playfully struck from behind by his little sister. He turns as she bolts up the interior staircase, following in hard pursuit, abandoning the door and leaving it wide open.

Noah and Jessica share a smile. He motions for her to enter first. "Please go in. I'm fairly certain we're expected."

She hesitates. "I shall, but only if I have your utmost assurance that you shall not strike me from behind."

"I extend to you my gravest assurance as a barrister."

She makes a show of weighing his words, and harboring some continuing reservations, despite which she deigns to enter first.

*   *   *

The meal is wonderfully prepared and served (by what must be *at least* five servants), and the hours fly by. Each time Noah looks at Marie, he is again surprised by her beauty, as though he's never looked upon her before. And each time he contemplates her upcoming absence, his heart leaps into his throat, depriving him of both the desire and the ability to speak.

Jessica and Stephen chat as though they're old friends. It's in moments such as this, when Noah can spy Jessica in unguarded conversation, that he most loves his daughter. He thinks how lucky Stephen is to have her attention, and how heartbroken he would be if she were to turn away.

And then he thinks how foolish his own thoughts are. She simply cannot marry every young man he likes. No, she needs to be governed by the rules of womanhood, rules he only dimly understands, that seem to slip beneath his awareness until such times as he's rigorously reminded of them, having committed some infraction or other.

When time comes for the toast, he rises, at something of a loss for words to express the depth of his feelings. As the assemblage rises, he clears his throat. Twice.

"I must confess I do not recall sharing a more enjoyable meal in my life. I love you all so dearly that I shall count the hours until your return. Madam," he says, turning to Marie, "I trust you shall not forget your humble servant, and that, during your absence, you shall nurture his place in your heart, as he shall do yours in his own. I trust you shall write me — you, too, Stephen, although I think you have found a lovelier correspondent than I" — this is met by general mirth — "and that you shall all return to me safe and sound, 'as soon as God and the seas allow,' as you have assured me so often."

Marie, deviating from convention, rises with her glass and smiles. "And *we* are confident, sir, that during our absence you shall acquit yourself in conformity with the highest standards of professionalism, as well as general tomfoolery." The youngest two think this hilarious.

Before the hubbub dies down, Noah adds: "God bless us all."

"God bless us all!" they intone.

"And — " he says. They were about to drink, but stop suddenly, and hang on his words. For reasons that are only beginning to seep into his consciousness, he adds: "God save the Queen."

"God save the Queen!" they echo jauntily.

Although it seems at first that they all laugh and drink heartily, Noah realizes over the general tumult that Marie is studying his face closely, and she's not smiling. She takes one short sip, and places her cup down on the table. Forcing a smile, she says, "You children, behave yourselves a few minutes. I have something to discuss with Master Ames outside."

The two youngest smile at each other and intone *oooooh* to suggest that something romantic is about to transpire between Marie and Noah. Jessica and Stephen, despite themselves, cover their mouths and laugh to see such childishness.

Once outside in the moonlight, Marie ushers him away from the house, putting some distance between them and the salon window, making sure that the children's view is blocked. "Noah," she says quietly. Before he can reply, she kisses him square on the mouth. He responds ardently. It seems like very heaven to him.

"Yes?" he says at last.

"I've seen many people toast the Queen's health before, but never someone who evidently believes that her welfare has become his personal responsibility."

"I — "

She puts her fingers to his lips, and turns away before resuming. "She has always been your personal benefactress, has she not?"

His eyes open wide. No one has ever guessed that before. Or perhaps they simply never ventured it aloud. "*What?* How — ?"

"A woman can *tell* how a man feels about another woman. Do you not know that?"

"But ... she's not just a *woman*."

"Yes, I know. She's the Queen. But she's *also* a woman, and we all detect your loyalty to our sex, Noah." She adjusts his collar. "I want you to promise me something. A few things."

"Anything."

She snorts. "We shall see." She begins gravely. "I perceive you are in serious trouble, or expect that you soon *shall* be. I want you to promise me that you shall accept help from others, specifically, from such young men of Gray's Inn as are willing to lend a hand."

"I shall."

"And from Master Neville, as well."

"Yes."

She shifts uncomfortably. "And I want you to promise me that you will seek and accept such help as may be available to you ... from Her Majesty."

"Oh, but *Marie* — " She tries to stop his mouth again, but he resists. "Marie, she has not seen me since I was a small boy. She probably has no recollection of me whatever, and would not recognize me if I were to stand before her."

Marie shakes her head patronizingly. "Oh, dearest Noah. You have *so* much to learn about us." She kisses him again. "Will you do as I have asked?"

He nods. "I shall, so long as you promise to return to me as soon as you can."

She holds up her right hand, as though taking an oath. "I so promise," she says. "And now that I have sworn: Have *you* been completely honest and forthright with me about all matters of importance, aside from client matters?"

He wishes he'd already shared with her his concern that she might be in communication with Southampton, and also told her that he's a Jew. But she's leaving presently for several months, and this does not seem the time.

"Certainly," he lies.

She kisses him fondly, but he cannot shake the uneasy feeling that she's kissing him goodbye for a much longer time than her present voyage.

*   *   *

Henry quickly accepts the invitation to Essex's party, and informs Noah that an invitation to one of the earl's parties is as compulsory as a summons to Queen's Bench. "While I'm aware that the word 'invitation' connotes an opportunity that one may choose to accept or decline, the earl's invitations are known to be rather mandatory."

"For *you*, perhaps," replies Noah. "But then, your invitation arrived at your house all nicely engraved and sealed. Your lovely wife has been invited, and, after all, you are a gentleman by birth." He smirks. "My invitation was extended by appending my name to a scribbled list of eight barristers. So long as one stays out of court, I expect we barristers are persons of no particular importance."

Henry strokes his beard contemplatively. "Have you ever been invited by the earl before now?"

"No."

"Then, is it not safe to say your absence would be noted?"

Noah snorts. "By whom?"

"Well, there's the earl." When Noah shows no reaction, Henry adds, "And then, of course, there's your lovely daughter."

Noah is shocked. "I beg your pardon? Has — has Jessica been invited?"

"I saw the list. Unless there's another 'Jessica, Lady Burlington,' she *has*."

"Do you suppose he's invited her deliberately," asks Noah, "to twist my arm?"

Henry shakes his head emphatically. "That's unlikely. I doubt the earl deems it possible you'd decline. No one else in your position would. Also, he probably doesn't realize that the two of you are related."

"Unless someone has told him," says Noah.

"If someone has, it certainly wasn't I."

"I suppose now I have no choice but to go." Noah sighs. "Too bad. I was preparing to send my regrets on grounds of an ailing relative who has requested my presence during his final hours."

"Oh, I'm sorry to hear that. Who is it?"

"I'm unsure which one I'd have chosen but, if pressed, I was prepared to come up with one." He mutters under his breath. "Too many relatives anyhow."

*   *   *

Arthur and Jonathan jog past the Deptford docks on a sunny mid-morning in late May.

"Who told you there was a murder out here?" asks Arthur.

Jonathan looks at him askance. "Too busy for a little frolic?"

"No. It's just that I have a lot of gear to pack before Essex's party tonight."

"Moving in with the earl?"

"Be serious. I'm accompanying Master Henry to Windsor afterwards."

"Oh, that's right!" says Jonathan, wiping the sweat from his brow. "Sorry, I'd forgot. Well, can't be helped now. Let's learn what we've come to learn." He recalls Arthur's pending question. "You wanted to know who told me about the murder. I was up and out at dawn, and heard an alarum at Lincoln's Inn, so I ran down there. Some residents were scrambling to their horses. As they rode past, I asked where they were heading, and one shouted: 'Someone's been stabbed through the eye at Eleanor Bull's.'"

"Who's Eleanor Bull?"

"She owns an inn near here." He shields his eyes from the morning sun, and points straight ahead. "In fact, it's right … there."

"How d'you know that?"

Jonathan smirks to think how astounded Arthur would be to learn of the tawdry places he frequented before taking up the law. "Master Graves introduced me to Goodwife Bull some years ago. Anyway, it seemed an unlikely coincidence that someone would be stabbed through the eye so soon after Stephen Rodriguez. I need to know whether there's any connection."

"But why did you decide we should not wear our barristers' robes?"

"*Shhhhh!*" Jonathan tugs Arthur behind a thick hedge and struggles to peek through it at the inn. He soon discovers that the hedge consists solely of thorn bushes. Sucking the blood from his finger, he turns to Arthur, who apparently still expects an answer to his inane question. "Because I don't want anyone to know we're barristers," he says impatiently. "In fact, it would be best if no one recognizes us at all." It's not a full answer, he knows, but it's as much as time allows.

Several robed barristers emerge from the inn's front door, gravely led by an unfamiliar, dour-looking barrister of some years. Jonathan turns to Arthur. "The older one in front. Do you know who he is?"

Arthur peers through the hedge, careful not to prick himself as Jonathan did. "I forget his name, but he's Queen's coroner."

"Recognize any of the others?"

"No."

Jonathan plops down onto the ground. "Let's wait here 'til they're good and gone."

Once the Lincoln's Inn contingent has departed, he rises. "Wait here." He ambles nonchalantly to the front of the inn, and steals a peek through the open doorway. Squinting, he can make out Gelly Meyrick standing in the taproom, looking down at the corpse of a small man lying on the floor. As Meyrick has only recently been humiliated in court by Noah and Jonathan, he's sure to recognize Jonathan, should he catch sight of him. Meyrick exchanges a few final words with the tapster, and walks purposefully toward the doorway through which Jonathan now peers.

Jonathan's heart rises into his mouth. He races back to the hedge and leaps over it, landing directly on Arthur, leaving them in a tangled heap, each with his share of scrapes, bruises, and torn clothing. "Sorry," says Jonathan perfunctorily, and peers back through the hedge. Meyrick emerges, mounts his horse, and trots off toward London.

"What was that all about?" asks Arthur, brushing himself off indignantly. He vainly attempts to match up two pieces of shirttail that came unseamed during the collision, and smooths back his tousled hair.

"That was Meyrick," replies Jonathan, slowly catching his breath and pointing toward the departing horseman. "Glad he didn't spot us." Before his heart has even resumed its normal pace, he emerges from behind the hedge, leading Arthur by the elbow.

"Wait," Arthur protests. "What else is there to learn? If we go inside, we're sure to be seen."

Jonathan is losing patience. "Look, Arthur. I ... *we* ... came out here to investigate whether the perpetrator could be the same man who killed my client's husband. If you think I'm just going to skulk away — "

"*Who said anything about skulking away?* But why appear in the guise of a pair of homeless ruffians? Let's put on our robes and come back here, dressed as proper barristers."

Jonathan turns to him indignantly. "Look, Arthur. As Master Ames pointed out, this case is a bit of rough trade. Now, I'm going in there to talk to that tapster, and things might get ... exciting. If you choose not to come, I'll understand."

Arthur sniffs, as though a bit insulted. "I'm coming with you, Jonathan. But let's not make a habit of sinking to their level."

Jonathan grins. "That's a bit of Oxford starch right there." He hugs Arthur roughly, and they proceed to the front door, donning their war faces before entering.

Jonathan walks straight to the corpse as though he belongs there and begins examining the scene, careful not to touch the body. The corpse lies face up. There's no mistaking it. It's the playwright Christopher Marlowe, who seems to have fallen down dead, leaving little or no sign of struggle. There's no blood to be seen, but for a small pool around a punctured eyeball. There's also no broken crockery or overturned furniture, although the scene might have been cleaned up.

The tapster, a slight fellow, is putting clean glasses away when he turns and sees Jonathan. "'Ey! Who are *you* now?" He spots Arthur. "And you, *too*? What are you, *another* pair of investigators? Already been three or four through here this mornin'. I got some o' me own work ta do, y'know." Jonathan tosses him a coin, which he deftly catches.

"Well," says the tapster with a smile, "you're the kind of investigators they should've sent all along. Aren't ye?"

"What can you tell us about the man who did this?" asks Jonathan.

"Well," says the tapster. "There was three of 'em. The drunkard, um, Poley. And the one with the scarred face. Skeres, I think. The third one, what actually killed the poor bugger lyin' there? That was Frizer. Yeah, Ingram Frizer."

"Did you see the fight?" asks Jonathan.

"Can't say's I did. I was in the storeroom fetchin' more ale for those fellas. Sure could put it away, too."

"And they kept paying?"

"Aye. And I needed to know nought else."

"Did you hear them talking about anything before the fight broke out?"

"Well, I put together that the poor bugger lyin' there was arrested a couple weeks ago, and then released. The other three was botherin' 'im fer sumpthin'. Couldn't rightly 'ear what it was."

"Money? Papers?"

The tapster shrugs. "Dunno."

"And what was this 'poor bugger's' response to hectoring by the other three?"

The tapster sneers. "I think ye got yer money's worth. Now, if you two'll leave me here to do my job — "

Jonathan frowns and shakes his head. "You haven't earned that yet," he says to the tapster, indicating the coin. "That's sixpence."

The tapster draws himself up. "Well, look, now, young man. I've told ye what little I know. Missus Bull don't want no trouble."

Jonathan strides up to the tapster, grabs him by the collar with one hand, and picks him off his feet, pressing him against the wall. "I don't believe you've told me all you know, Goodman Tapster. If Missus Bull 'don't want no trouble,' you'll tell me what Master Marlowe said to the others in reply to their hectoring."

The tapster is aghast at Jonathan's confident strength. Eyes wide, he struggles to recall. "Look, I … wait. Now I remember, he *did* say sumpthin'. Oh, what was it? Kept sayin' the same thing over and over. It was a … a woman's name. From the Old Bible. Marlowe kept sayin': 'Tell *this person*, he can't 'ave it.'"

"A woman's name from the Old Testament?"

"Aye, a Jew name, though I've heard some Christians go by it." The tapster waits patiently while comically suspended from the wall like an awkward, low-hanging bear's head, evidently persuaded that any attempt to right himself could send Jonathan into a dangerous fit.

Jonathan raises his free hand, but, instead of making a fist, as the tapster clearly expects, he says calmly, "This is half a crown … if you can remember that name."

The tapster's eyes grow wide with thought, as he now has every conceivable inducement to remember. At first, his eyes betray that he's weighing whether to conjure up a false name, just to get the half crown and see the last of this dangerous young ruffian. But apparently he thinks better of it, no doubt lest his deceit be detected and revenge exacted. "I can't recall, I tell ye. Wait!" he says in a flash. "It was one of them *judges*!"

Jonathan's eyes flash with recognition. "Was it … Deborah?"

"Yeh, that's *it*! 'Tell Deborah he can't 'ave it.'" The tapster's recognition of the name is laughably ingenuous.

"'*He?*'" says Jonathan. "Are you sure Marlowe said 'he'?"

"Yeh. Didn't make no sense to me when he said it, neither."

Jonathan plants the tapster firmly on his feet, straightens his collar, and opens the hand holding the coin. The tapster gazes down on Jonathan's palm with surprise, as though half expecting it to contain nothing, or worse. He accepts the half crown for his pains.

Without another word, Jonathan strides grimly out the front door, followed by a confused Arthur.

*   *   *

Noah has at last completed his caseload, but for a few lingering matters unlikely to be heard until Michaelmas, some time in early autumn. With ample time to dress for Essex's party tonight, he kicks his stockinged feet up on his desk. Although he's received no letters yet from Marie, he expects that most of her time until now has been spent at sea, a setting that offers little to write about and no practical way to post a letter until landfall.

Henry's clothing and books are spread all around his rooms, especially in the small room that doubles as his study. He's been packing his things to take home to Lothbury, in East London. From there, he's to attend Essex's party tonight, and then move off for the summer months with Mistress Anne to Windsor, site of his ancestral home of Billingbear. To placate the Arden side of the family, he's invited Arthur to come along with him after Essex's party.

A note from Jessica slips under the door, and Noah opens it at once. No "dear father" today. The greeting is "daddy," which he finds portentous, for there are only two types of occasion upon which she'll call him that. One is when she's feeling inordinately fond of him; the other when she's in trouble. From the opening lines, this looks to be one of the latter.

Daddy,

I hope you will not think me a silly girl for writing to you based upon nothing more than hunches, but you have always told me to trust my fears, and to speak rather than remain silent. Aunt Elizabeth heard this morning of two widely separated cases of plague in Southwark. If the reports are to be believed, each of them occurred in a poor dwelling near an open sewer, none of which is near to us here. I told Aunt Elizabeth that she should not take such reports too seriously until she hears them from someone having direct knowledge, but she says that is often too late in such matters. She is fretting about it, and very fearful for my sake. What shall I do?

Jesse

This is most disturbing. It's the first he's heard of plague this year, although he's been dreading the rumor of it for more than a month now.

And she signed the note "Jesse." Either her character has radically changed overnight, or she's telling him that his little girl is in trouble.

Henry lumbers in, carrying an empty clothing bag. "What's the matter? What are you reading?" he asks.

Noah sits down hard on the edge of the bed, feeling as though he needs to do something immediately. "It's from Jessica." His expression evidently has Henry worried.

"Yes?"

"She says the plague has hit Southwark," says Noah.

There's a moment's silence, broken by Henry, who looks out of the window toward Southwark. "I'm afraid I have no salve for your worries about the plague. Damned thing."

Noah is still too dismayed to shake off his indecision.

Henry smiles. "Cheer up, my lad! You're bringing my 'niece' to Billingbear. Come on, pack your bags!" He tosses an empty one to Noah.

Noah shakes his head. "Oh, that's most kind of you, Henry, but I *couldn't*."

"Why not?"

"It's such an imposition. What would Mistress Anne think?"

"Nonsense. Do you know how many vacant rooms we have up there? And as far as Mistress Anne goes, she would be delighted to have Lady Jessica stay the whole summer, if she could arrange it. To have that, I'd warrant she'd even put up with *you*!"

Could it be that, with a snap of his fingers, Henry will save them both from the danger of this outbreak?

"But we're both attending Essex's party this evening," says Noah.

"Then, come first thing tomorrow. If there's any change, just send a note by way of Cheerful."

"'Cheerful?' You mean 'Cheerful *Killigrew*?'"

"Do you know another?"

Noah furrows his brow skeptically. "His given name's not really 'Cheerful,' is it?"

Henry laughs. "Now that *would* have been a long shot, wouldn't it? For you to have guessed his given name to be 'Cheerful' and to have it turn out you were right. No," he chortles, "that's not his given name."

Noah waits expectantly, but in vain. "You're not going to *tell* me his real name, are you?"

"No point. Ever since you dubbed him that, it's what everyone calls him. He calls *himself* that now."

"Isn't he a bit young for such a long ride alone?"

"It's only just past Windsor, but I'll send an adult to accompany him. You would not even ask if you'd seen him ride. He's quite the accomplished equestrian." Noah makes no reply, and Henry seems to be losing patience. "Look, old man. If you want to stay here and take your chances with the plague, there's nothing I can do about it, but you shall *not* expose Jessica to this scourge. I'll fetch her *myself*, if I must."

"That won't be necessary, Henry. I shall write her immediately. Thank you so much! Still, I expect Jessica will wish to spend the night at Southwark, so she can pack in the morning, and I'll stay here at the inn. We'll follow you to Billingbear tomorrow." He picks up a pen and a sheet of writing paper, when something occurs to him. "Oh, no!"

"What now?"

Noah cringes. "Jessica's Aunt Beth."

Henry shrugs. "Bring her along."

Noah wipes his eyes with both hands, and regards Henry plaintively. "I think I'd rather chance the plague."

"Can't be *that* bad."

"I think I'd rather *catch* the plague," Noah mutters. He sighs, and begins writing.

A closed coach pulls up outside. Noah and Henry look out of the window. From a remote door of the inn, Anthony and Francis Bacon emerge in barrister's garb that looks so fine it might be fashioned of silk. But that cannot be, as only a Serjeant is permitted to wear the silk, and neither of the Bacons has yet qualified. Still, the visual effect is striking.

Francis turns momentarily toward the inn, beaming like a man who's been relieved of some awful burden, and whose time has come at last. They climb into the carriage and pull away south, turning east toward Essex's lodge in Wanstead, where the party will take place.

As Noah dispatches his note to Jessica, the entrance door downstairs bursts open and Jonathan and Arthur tramp in, talking excitedly. Noah and Henry look at each other.

"You keep packing," says Noah. "I'll go and see what's happening." He goes downstairs.

Arthur's door is open and he's ransacking his closet, evidently preparing for the journey to Billingbear. Jonathan, who's gone out of the inn, now comes back into Arthur's room, acknowledging Noah's presence with a quick nod.

Both Arthur and Jonathan look as though they've been up all night, and spent most of it in the woods. They're sweaty. There are brambles in their hair, and scrapes on their faces. A few of their garments are torn. When Arthur turns away from his closet, his face appears scratched and slightly bloody, although he appears neither to know nor care.

"Noah! Good to see you," says Jonathan energetically.

"Where have you two been?"

Jonathan snorts. "*Deptford!*" he says, as though Noah's question is amazing in some way.

"At the docks?" Noah asks. Perhaps that explains their ruffled appearance.

Jonathan pauses, and looks Noah up and down, with a look of combined surprise and pity. "You have not gone out today," he declares.

Noah shakes his head curiously.

"Oh. Well ... Marlowe is dead," says Jonathan matter-of-factly.

"*What?*"

Although the news is having trouble penetrating Noah's mind, it's obviously got through to Henry, who must have been listening from the top of the stairs. "Oh, my *God!*" Henry says, and rumbles down the stairs so fast Noah thinks he might lose his footing and tumble. Instead, he strides right past Noah into Arthur's room. "Marlowe is *dead*? Are you quite sure?"

Jonathan looks at Henry with a kind of sulking anger. "Oh, *quite*, Master Henry! I saw his corpse lying on the floor. No mistake."

"But ha – how? How did it happen?"

Jonathan turns on Henry with barely concealed fury. "I'll tell you that, Master Henry. But I have a *puzzle* you might help me with first."

"Jonathan!" shouts Noah. "Show some respect."

Henry waves Noah off. "*Which* puzzle, Jonathan?"

"Well, Marlowe spent all afternoon yesterday drinking at an inn at Deptford. There were three men with him. They spent all day together, talking and drinking. Incidentally, did you know that Marlowe was arrested a few weeks ago, then released?"

Henry shakes his head.

"Well, he was." Jonathan turns his back to Henry and watches Arthur pack. "Anyway, these three men were apparently demanding something from Marlowe all day. The innkeeper couldn't hear what it was, but he didn't care, so long as they kept drinking and paying. So, I asked the innkeeper whether he heard Marlowe's response to all this hectoring."

Noah can hold his tongue no longer. "Jonathan, why are you and Arthur so *weatherbeaten*?"

Jonathan smirks at Arthur, who turns away, chagrined. "Well," he says, "I had to ask more than once, didn't I?" He tosses Noah a conspiratorial smile. "So, I asked the innkeeper whether he heard Marlowe's response. He insisted, for a while, that he hadn't. Then, he suddenly remembered Marlowe repeating the same phrase over and over. 'Tell … some woman whose name the innkeeper couldn't recall … *he* can't have it!' He *suddenly* remembered that the woman's name was from the Old Testament, 'a Jew name' — one of the judges — so I put the fear of God in him and offered him half a crown, and he came up with the name, just like *that!*" He snaps his fingers.

"What was the name?" asks Henry.

Jonathan stands defiantly before Henry. He lowers his face and looks up insolently. "Deborah!" Jonathan spits out, studying Henry's reaction. "'Tell … *Deborah* … he can't have it!'"

The air in the room is stagnant and warm. In an instant, all the blood drains from Henry's face.

Noah breaks the silence. "I don't understand. Who is *Deborah*?"

Henry looks as though he's been slapped in the face, and says nothing.

Jonathan smirks. "Why don't *you* tell him, Master Henry?"

Henry turns to Noah. His voice cracks. "The innkeeper misunderstood. It wasn't a woman's name. It was 'Devereux.'"

To Noah, the two names sound nearly identical. "Who's *that*?"

Henry turns back to Jonathan, as though pleading to be relieved of the burden of further explanation, but Jonathan seems to be perversely enjoying himself. "Devereux," resumes Henry gravely, "is the surname of the Earl of Essex."

Noah is infuriated by Jonathan's trouncing of Henry's feelings. His face reddens and he moves it up against Jonathan's, so that they nearly touch. "I've had about enough of this, Jonathan. Don't you know that Marlowe was a *friend* of Master Henry's? Now, you will answer me without further ado. Who were the three men with Marlowe yesterday?"

Jonathan's smile falls away, and he answers. "Nicholas Skeres, Robert Poley ... " he studies Henry's face again, "and *Ingram Frizer*."

Henry stands deathly still, winces, and closes his eyes. For the first time, Jonathan's expression shows a hint of sympathy.

Noah asks, "How was Marlowe murdered?"

Jonathan passes the question along, this time calmly. "Master Henry?"

Henry turns to Jonathan, shakes his head, and speaks with apparent certainty. "A stiletto through the right eye. Ingram Frizer. Is that right?"

Jonathan nods.

"Well, Jonathan," says Henry sadly, "it looks as though you've found your man. Stephen Rodriguez was almost certainly murdered by Ingram Frizer."

"I suppose you and I have *both* lost one to the earl's men now." Although Jonathan had evidently hoped for some type of apology from Henry for his refusal to acknowledge the earl's responsibility in Graves' death, he obviously doesn't have the heart to seek it now. Instead, his face is pure pity, and his eyes well up with tears. "I'm deeply sorry for your loss, Master Henry."

Henry nods gravely. "Thank you, Jonathan. I'm sorry for your loss, as well. Sorry for Graves. Sorry for Marlowe. Sorry for all England. Here was a *poet*. When comes such another?"

CHAPTER 17

"WHAT A *FOOL* I'VE BEEN!" says Noah. "The whole picture didn't appear to me until just now, when Jonathan told us that Marlowe had been arrested and released."

Noah and Henry are briefly alone in Noah's apartment, where the meeting that assembled unprompted in Jonathan's room will soon reconvene behind closed doors.

"*What* hadn't appeared to you?" asks Henry.

Noah ignores the question. "I know from my law practice that people who are arrested, then quickly released, are often known to be former Walsingham agents."

"Yes, that's true. They're often picked up for information, or to be given instructions."

He turns to Henry. "Marlowe was a former Walsingham agent, wasn't he?"

Henry nods.

"Just as Rodriguez was! And, as it turns out, both those former Walsingham agents were murdered by the same man, who happens to spend time in the company of the *same* attendants of the *same* earl. What's more, the only two *surviving* Walsingham agents I know are you and Lopez. And you two are each aligned in some way with Essex! Am I right so far?"

Henry nods again.

"All right, Henry. That seals it! *The Earl of Essex is appropriating Walsingham's former spy network to his own purposes. Isn't he?*"

There's a moment of silence, in which Henry appears to consider how to respond.

But Noah cannot wait. "Those who join Essex are put to work. Those who don't ... are put to *death*!"

Henry seems confounded. "Until just now, I would have called you mad to say so ... but no longer. However, without proof presentable to a magistrate for adjudication, it's mere suspicion."

Noah snorts. "Suspicion bordering on a *certainty*. You've been fighting off this conclusion yourself, Henry! *Haven't* you? How could you neglect *for so long* to 'call the constable' on this? Don't you realize what a threat Essex will be to Her Majesty, once he assembles his own international spy network, leaving her with none?" He smacks his forehead. "*Ach!* As soon as we realized that Essex was involved, I felt in my *bones* that we'd stumbled onto a plot! Why did it take me until *now* to trust my instincts, and see it for what it is?" He mutters, almost to himself: "I *must* stop him!"

There's a hesitant knock at the door.

"Please, wait outside a moment!" says Noah, with more irritation than he would have liked. He turns back to Henry and suppresses his voice.

"Didn't you say some weeks ago that Cecil is Walsingham's successor?"

Henry nods, but then wavers. "Yes, but Robert succeeded him in name only. In fact, Robert was never able to recover Walsingham's files, nor his contacts."

"I'll give you odds Essex has both." Noah glowers at Henry. "This information must be given to Sir Robert Cecil. If you won't do it — and promptly, Henry — *I will.*"

Henry nods somberly. "Yes. Cecil must be warned."

Noah rubs his temple. "I don't know how I can possibly withhold this from Marie."

"There's no need for her to know until she returns from the Continent, is there?"

"I suppose not. And it's not the kind of thing one could safely put in correspondence, anyway. Not in *these* suspicious days."

Henry agrees. "Besides, Marie has no interest in affairs of state. She's interested in prosecuting the man who murdered her husband. When she returns, you or Jonathan can surely tell her that you suspect Frizer, without dragging this whole Essex business into it."

"Tell her about Frizer *without* telling her that Frizer may have committed her husband's murder at Essex's urging?" Although Noah's voice has subsided, his mind still works feverishly, and he begins to pace. "Perhaps you're right. Perhaps she need *not* know yet. Oh, I hate like the devil to involve her in this Essex affair more than absolutely necessary. It would only exacerbate her jeopardy."

He stops pacing, as he realizes there's no more to be accomplished with Henry alone. He seizes the doorknob, then pauses a moment, lost in thought. At last, he opens the door. Jonathan and Arthur enter meekly, their eyes darting about, obviously aware that excited words have been exchanged.

Henry takes a seat on the upholstered chair, while Noah rests on the edge of the bed. Jonathan and Arthur, mindful of their soiled clothing, sit on the wooden floor with their legs folded.

"I don't understand," says Arthur. "Master Henry, how did you know it was Frizer who killed Marlowe?"

"As I told Master Ames some weeks ago, Robert Poley, whom you two know as the drunkard Bob, had said he knew the right man to punch a hole in Meyrick's eye … "

"Too bad he didn't *do* it!" interjects Jonathan. "Meyrick, that sallow sack of pus, was standing over Marlowe's body when I first saw it."

Henry resumes. "I learned only two days ago that the stiletto man's name was 'Ingram Frizer,' and that he could sometimes be found in the company of Skeres and Poley. It was just bad luck you didn't encounter him at the Boar's Head."

Arthur chimes in. "Or *good* luck. If Frizer had been there, as well, they might have fought it out, and we'd all be under investigation, in prison, or worse. It was only after Skeres realized he was outnumbered that he gave up Jonathan and … Goodman Graves, may he rest in peace."

Jonathan sniffs. "Graves lived only a few hours more. It wouldn't have made much difference to him if there'd been a wholesale slaughter."

Noah scowls. "Don't say that, Jonathan. It made a *world* of difference to him that *you* survived. And who knows if you would have, if there'd been, as you say, a 'wholesale slaughter?'"

"How would you know that Graves felt that way, Master Ames?" asks Jonathan.

Noah weighs whether Jonathan's use of 'Master Ames' is intended as a jibe, but he can see that he's simply lapsed back into his old form of address. "Do you forget, or did you not know? I went to speak with Graves at Creechurch, and arrived just after you left. He told me he regarded you as the son he never had." He watches Jonathan walk to the window and stare outside to conceal his grief. "He asked me to watch out for you, so please avoid getting yourself killed or disbarred. He helped save our lives, and I owe his memory quite enough already."

Henry chimes in. "In that case, Noah, why don't we bring Master Hawking to Billingbear with us, and get him out of London during this blasted plague season?"

Arthur is surprised. "Is there plague about?"

Noah nods. "Two cases in Southwark."

Arthur rises and goes to Jonathan. "Jon, it's too dangerous for you to remain in London, with Essex's men all about. I have to go with Master Henry, and you shall have no one here to back you up. Now there's *plague*, as well. Why don't you come with us?"

Jonathan shakes his head slowly and turns toward the others, his face now composed. "Thank you very much, Master Henry, but, as you said, I know my man now, and I will not willingly hold the Rodriguez investigation in abeyance."

"But what can you accomplish here alone, Jonathan?" reasons Henry. "Just knowing who did it is insufficient. You must prepare to *prove* that Frizer committed Rodriguez's murder. How likely are you to accomplish anything now, with Frizer being investigated for the murder of a much more famous man? Let things calm down first. Besides, Frizer could get the gallows for Marlowe's murder, even without a conviction for an additional murder."

Jonathan shakes his head in disbelief. "Master Henry, your faith in criminal justice mystifies me. The murder of Christopher Marlowe will not be investigated. Not *really*. And even though Frizer is clearly the one who did it, he'll not be prosecuted for it."

"Why not?" asks Henry.

Jonathan rolls his eyes. "Because there's someone having great influence with the Queen who will prevail upon her to *forego* such prosecution ... just as he's frustrated my investigation into the murder of Stephen Rodriguez *by the same man*. Do you think me dense? I strongly suspect that the murders of Rodriguez and Marlowe were ordered by Essex. If that's correct, then these were both *state* murders, for which the state will not willingly prosecute itself, nor its own henchmen."

"Jonathan," says Henry, simulating the very voice of reason, "while we genuinely admire your tenacity and courage in wishing to remain here to investigate, it simply makes no sense in light of the plague. What if you come down with it? Who is here to nurse you? What if you fail to survive it? Who will avenge Rodriguez's murder *then*?"

Jonathan shakes his head. "I cannot contract plague." He lowers his voice, as though recalling a difficult time. "I have come through it already. The doctors say I am immune."

The others look at each other, stunned, realizing that the debate is rapidly slipping away.

"Will you come to Billingbear if you cannot find out anything in a week?" asks Noah.

Henry scotches that idea. "I'm sorry, Noah. I cannot allow it. As we do not know how the plague is carried, I cannot have Jonathan come up to Billingbear if he may be transporting the disease, even though he cannot come down with it."

Jonathan agrees wholeheartedly. "Nor would I *ask* you to put everyone at risk on my account, Master Henry. No, I'm afraid I'm in London for the duration."

Henry points to Noah and Arthur. "I assume you two will be corresponding with Jonathan while you are away?" With little hesitation, both Noah and Arthur nod. "Then, there are some things you must know. First and foremost, the secrecy of your correspondence cannot be assured."

"Why not?" asks Arthur.

"Arthur, it's time you realized that *no one's* correspondence is reliably secret. At least, not while the papists are dispatching a dozen murderers each year out of France to assassinate Her Majesty, all of whom correspond with their co-religionists in Britain."

"*Are* the papists doing so?" asks Arthur, aghast.

"I'm sorry to say, they are. Moreover, as you know, there is a certain … *interest* at the Queen's court in whatever the three of you may be corresponding about."

Jonathan, Arthur, and Noah look at each other. Not for the last time, they share a creeping sense of being watched.

"So, how shall we communicate with one another?" asks Noah.

"If you can manage to get a message directly to Cheerful, he is completely reliable. Otherwise, you should ideally communicate in code. Do you know how to create a cipher?"

All three shake their heads.

"Well, we haven't time for instruction in that art," says Henry. "You'll just have to be very discreet, and name people and events as ambiguously as possible. While someone reading your letters may be able to guess at your true meaning, it's much more difficult to *convict* someone based upon an ambiguous message."

"*Convict*?" exclaims Arthur. "We're *barristers*, for heaven's sake! Doing our jobs!"

Jonathan snickers. "*Now* who's being naive?"

"And one more thing," says Henry. "You must not assume that my servants are loyal to me. To the contrary, you must assume that any one of them could be reporting to someone else on affairs at Billingbear. And, rest assured, some of them *are* doing so."

"How can you know that?" asks Arthur skeptically.

"Because, in several cases, I know who they *are*."

Arthur's mouth falls open. "Well, if you know who they are, why don't you *dismiss* them?"

Henry smiles darkly. "Because I know who they are! If I were to dismiss them, then they would be replaced by others, and, for a time at least, I would *not* know who they are. That would place us in far *greater* peril."

"But, on whose behalf do they spy upon you?"

"You know, Arden, for a man learned in history and the law, who is himself distantly related to kings, you have not given this very much thought," Henry sniffs. "They spy for *different* people. Some for Burghley, some for the Queen ... "

"Some for Essex?" asks Jonathan.

Henry nods almost imperceptibly.

"Oh, grand!" says Jonathan in disgust.

"Welcome to the nobility in the time of the Tudors," says Henry.

Arthur asks, "And do *you* have spies in the service of other noblemen?"

Henry hoists himself out of his chair. "Fortunately, you've no need to concern yourself with any such possibility. Now, I really must be going. Keep your wits about you, all of you. Arthur will accompany me to Essex's party, smiling and saying *nothing*. Arthur, please carry these bags down to the front, would you? I shall see Noah and Lady Jessica at the party tonight, and Billingbear late tomorrow. Jonathan," he says, extending a hand that Jonathan grasps firmly, "be *doubly* careful. Trust no one. If you're in *real* trouble, write a note addressed to Noah, leave it at the front door tied to a stone, and knock loudly. Then, hide until he comes looking for you. We'll put you up secretly in one of the outbuildings. But make sure no one suspects where you're going, and, for *heaven's* sake, make sure you're not followed. God bless you and keep you."

"And you, Master Henry," replies Jonathan.

Jonathan helps Arthur carry down Henry's bags. A few minutes later, Henry and Arthur are off with their own luggage, leaving Noah alone. It makes him uneasy to think that, for a time, the fellowship will be scattered.

* * *

At Essex's party that evening at Wanstead House, Noah and Lady Jessica mill about the lobby with sundry other guests waiting to be called into the great room in order of rank.

"Don't forget," Noah reminds her, "we must leave early. We've a long ride to Henry's home at Windsor tomorrow."

When Lady Jessica's name is called early on, she scrupulously apologizes for leaving her father's side, and evidently fails to notice the throng of male admirers that parts like the Red Sea to make way for her entrance.

Peering around the door into the great room, Noah sees Jessica being inundated by an even larger throng ... of higher rank. On the far end of the room, the Earls of Essex and Southampton converse with a grizzled, richly dressed

Spanish gentleman and, unexpectedly, Doctor Lopez. To avoid seeming the voyeur, Noah withdraws from the doorway, but not before he inadvertently catches Southampton's eye.

He reports what he's seen to Henry, who has just arrived with both his wife Anne and Arthur Arden.

"The older gentleman," says Henry, "would be Don Antonio, the claimant to the Portuguese throne of whom we've spoken."

Arthur steps forward. "Well, if we're being admitted by rank," he says, "what's Lopez doing in there already? I'd no idea a physician is more highly regarded than a barrister."

Henry shakes his head. "Lopez is serving as Portuguese translator here, Arthur, not as physician. His participation is necessary for Lord Essex to communicate with his royal guest."

"Oh," says Arthur, obviously unimpressed. "It wouldn't surprise me if we lot were admitted dead last. A barrister's rank probably falls somewhere below his lordship's favorite horse."

"As one who's seen him in battle," says Southampton, springing with unnerving suddenness from behind Henry's substantial girth, "I can say with confidence that, in his lordship's regard, *none* of us holds a higher place than his horse."

Noah, Henry, and Arthur smile and bow low, and Anne curtsies. Southampton confers a courtly nod upon Anne, and turns to Henry. "Master Neville, what news from London?"

Henry shakes his head glumly. "Nothing good, m'lord. There's rumor of plague in Southwark ... and I regret to inform you that Marlowe's been murdered." Southampton seems unperturbed. "But I suppose you've heard as much."

Southampton's smile is unwavering. "Tragic," he says blithely. "And who is this *barrister* friend of yours?" he adds, nodding toward Noah with exaggerated interest.

Henry adopts a formal posture to make a proper introduction. "Lord Southampton," he says, "may I present to you Master Noah Ames, barrister at the Queen's Bench."

Noah bows, quite sure that Southampton already knows precisely who he is.

Southampton strokes his beard. "Perhaps we shall have a lawyerly diversion after the masque."

"I'm afraid I've nothing prepared for the occasion, m'lord," says Noah, his stomach suddenly all butterflies.

Southampton waves away the objection, and then, as only the well connected can, he ushers them all inside together, quite out of turn.

*   *   *

Supper consists of too many courses to count, each more exotic than the last. During coffee, a brief play is presented on the opposite end of the room. Noah hears no more than an occasional rhyming couplet, followed by a roar of appreciation. As near as he can guess, the playlet has something to do with the virtues instilled by military leadership. The players take their final bows to warm applause.

Suddenly, a sharp scent of musk fills the air. His nose tingles. He sneezes.

"Bless you, Master Ames," says a Spanish-accented voice over his right shoulder. Noah turns to see a swarthy, diminutive dandy with slick hair and a curled mustache too large for his face. Before Noah can think of what to say, the man says dubiously: "You *are* Master Ames, no?"

Noah clears his throat. "I am," he confirms, "and I have the pleasure of meeting — ?"

"Antonio Perez, at your service," the man says with a theatrical bow.

So *this* is Perez. Noah turns in his chair to look on the bearded face of the man whose presence in England has caused so much trouble. This is the man Tinoco was accused of plotting to kill, whose assailant would be paid with a red jewel — the man accused of buggering Francis Bacon until he was nearly cut off by his family, and who daily drinks a toxic concoction of musk and amber. His skin is slightly jaundiced. Noah can't help but feel that, for such a problematic individual, his face is disappointingly mundane.

Perez smiles, apparently flattered by the perusal of his features. "His Lordship of Essex has sent me to escort you to his table to take part in his ... legal exercise, I believe he called it. If you will accompany me."

Reluctantly, Noah rises. "A ... a *legal exercise*?" This must be the "lawyerly diversion" foretold by Southampton. But legal exercises are dry affairs, with students bumbling about, imitating their seniors in like circumstances who were themselves more than likely bumbling about.

What kind of legal exercise would amuse a partygoer? Noah expects that the partygoers are nothing more than a captive audience for Essex's attempt to humiliate him, or disgrace him altogether. He recalls with dismay the accusatory note he left in his saddlebag for Essex's man to find. *So, this will be Essex's revenge.* His heart pounds as he's led across the great room by the little Spaniard.

Perez, evidently recognizing his dread, offers some comfort. "Please, my friend. You are a *master* of the law, not one of its victims, as I am, who have been falsely accused of plotting to murder. You have no reason to fear it as I do. I am sure His Lordship intends only a brief diversion for his guests." Noah wishes he could share Perez's benign expectation. And *Perez* has been accused of plotting a murder?

The assembled, unaware of the nature of the coming "amusement," rise from their places and gather near the center of the room. Men jostle for position nearest Jessica, in case Essex calls for a dance. Perez bows to Noah, and takes his leave to join the others.

Essex's dining table has been removed, and replaced with three benches in the configuration of a barebones courtroom, with a witness box and a judge's bench with a small desk, but no prisoner's dock. The more Noah considers the matter, the more his reckless note appears the likely cause of all this. *Oh, what had I to gain by writing it?*

From the side of the room, two men enter, carrying a long table, which they position before Noah, leaving him at the end customarily occupied by defense counsel. At the opposite end, in the position of prosecutor, stands Essex himself, avoiding Noah's gaze. Noah bows. Without turning to acknowledge, Essex smiles to himself.

And who should step into the imaginary witness box, but Henry Neville. His eyes likewise avoid Noah's, as he puts on a good show of enjoying his part in the proceedings, all the while betraying a hint of concern.

The crowd whispers excitedly. Noah glances behind him, and sees an uneasy Jessica gently push aside a fawning gentleman to secure an unobstructed view.

As Noah wonders who's about to assume the makeshift bench, there's a banging on the door, which swings open. In walks Southampton. "Oyez, oyez!" he shouts, obviously relishing the role of bailiff, as it is so far beneath his true station.

Behind him enters the man who'll serve as judge at this mock proceeding, an uncomfortable-looking Edward Coke. One look at his forced smile tells Noah that, if Coke is "in the know" about his patron's joke, he's not amused. Coke takes his seat at the "bench." It occurs to Noah that, as Coke is commonly believed to have no sense of mirth, he'll have no choice but to play his part squarely, which gives Noah some hope, however small, of emerging unscathed from this farce.

The bailiff Southampton addresses the partygoers. "For your next amusement, his lordship thought you might wish to see a bit of courtroom antics. For that purpose, his lordship shall play prosecuting Crown counsel."

The crowd meets this with cheers for their generous host, who nods with false humility. "To lend some *verisimilitude* to our exercise," says Southampton, "we also have with us two well-regarded barristers. The distinguished Master Coke will serve as our judge." Coke rises briefly to a smattering of applause. "And our defense lawyer shall be played by Master Noah Ames of Gray's Inn."

"*Papa!*" comes Jessica's feminine voice from the floor, followed by a resounding cheer joined by her many male admirers. Noah bows humbly and glances at Essex, who exudes a barely disguised resentment.

"M'lord," says Essex. "This witness is being offered for the purpose of translating a document from the Latin." He takes a paper from his doublet.

Noah's certain that the paper is either his accusatory note or a transcription of it. "The defense objects, m'lord!" he shouts instinctively, while mentally piecing together an argument as well as he can with his pulse pounding in his ears.

Coke holds up a hand, stopping Essex in his tracks. "What is the nature of the objection, Master Ames?"

Noah bows. "Although we do not wish to make a mockery of the oath, and have no objection to foregoing it for the sake of this exercise, the witness has not been so much as *identified*, nor has the Crown demonstrated his expertise as a translator from the Latin."

"Very well," says Coke, as he turns to question the witness, obviating the need for Essex to embarrass himself by stumbling through an attempt to lay his own foundation. "Who are you, sir?" Coke asks the witness.

Henry straightens his doublet. "I am Henry Neville, of Billingbear."

Coke continues. "And what is your position, sir?"

"I am a Baron of the Cinque Ports, a manufacturer of cannon for Her Majesty's forces."

"Hear, hear!" come shouts from the patriotic spectators.

Coke turns to them indulgently. "While this is merely a moot exercise, perhaps the spectators might choose to behave with somewhat greater decorum." The crowd laughs at its own folly, and eventually quiets down.

Coke resumes. "And are you fluent in the Latin language?"

"I am," replies Henry, "having studied it at Oxford University, and having passed all my examinations."

"Very well," says Coke, turning to Essex. "Counsel may proceed."

"Master Neville," says Essex. "I show you this paper — "

"Objection, m'lord," says Noah. "As we don't know the facts — or even the *object* — of this case, it's impossible to assess the paper's relevance."

Coke looks with concern to the seething Essex, and evidently decides that a bit more sportsmanship is what's needed. "That is true," he says indulgently, "but, for purposes of this exercise, let us *presume* the paper to be of some relevance. Otherwise, distinguished Crown counsel would hardly be offering it as evidence." Essex nods gratefully.

But now Noah has had time to think of a way to frustrate Essex's intention: compel him to choose between abandoning this misbegotten exercise or revealing his own criminal actions leading up to the paper's discovery.

"Very well, m'lord," says Noah, "but the defense must object on even more fundamental grounds." He thrusts his hand toward the paper for emphasis. "We know not the *provenance* of this paper. *From whence has it come?* For aught we know, a common dustman found it blowing in the breeze outside Essex House."

Although the crowd cannot see it, Essex's face is red, and he's grinding his teeth. Coke turns to the witness. "Master Neville, did you provide this paper to his lordship of Essex?"

Henry shakes his head. "No, m'lord."

Coke rubs his eyes and does Essex another good turn. "Perhaps we should change the order of the witnesses. Master Neville should rather serve as the Crown's *second* witness. The Crown's *first* witness must be the person who produced the document to the Crown. Is such person available to the Court?"

Essex nods. "Yes, m'lord. The Crown calls the page known as 'Peter' to the witness box."

Essex's chief page appears. As Henry steps out of the makeshift box and the page takes his place, Noah's eyes fix on the page's golden hilt that was so much in evidence at The Rose, and that glinted at him just before he was struck unconscious that day at Creechurch. He concludes that Essex hasn't a clue that, by putting this young man in the witness box, he's doomed either this exercise … or himself.

"Peter," says Coke, "are you the person who brought this paper to m'lord of Essex?"

"I am," says the witness.

Noah pounces, shouting: *"Voir dire, m'lord!"*

Coke sighs, and busies Noah with an assignment while he decides what to do next: "Perhaps learned counsel for the defense would explain to the spectators what *voir dire* means."

"Certainly," Noah replies, turning to the spectators, who, to his amazement, seem riveted by this amateurish courtroom display. *"Voir dire* is Old French for 'to tell the truth.' It has two principal applications, one in jury selection, which is irrelevant here, and the other in an ongoing proceeding such as this, where it is invoked by opposing counsel to test the competence of evidence before it's admitted. In this case, I have invoked it to ask the witness whether he's ever seen this document before, whether he knows who wrote it, who it was intended for," he turns subtly toward Essex, *"how he came by it, whether it was written in response to another writing* ... and so on."

Noah is relieved to see that his point is not lost on Essex, whose apprehension reflects the realization that he'll never have the paper translated until Noah elicits all the details about the illicit manner in which he acquired it.

Coke turns to Essex. "If the Crown wishes to proceed further with this exercise, the Court must grant the defense's request for *voir dire* on this point." When Essex makes no immediate reply, Coke says, "It's up to Crown counsel."

Essex, his back turned to the crowd, is patently furious at Coke and Noah, when the only one he *should* be upset with is himself. Essex catches the eye of Southampton, who confers with him a moment and then turns to the crowd.

"His lordship calls for a dance!" announces Southampton gaily.

There's a confused smattering of applause for this abortive exercise, which even the crowd must know has gone badly for Essex. But the initial confusion quickly dissipates in the gentlemen's earnest competition for the most attractive dance partners. Jessica extricates herself from a group of such supplicants and approaches Essex, who forces a smile.

"M'lord," she says. "I am so sorry, but I must be going now, as I have a long journey to undertake tomorrow. Please accept both my profound gratitude for your incomparable hospitality, and my sincerest regrets for departing too early from such a delightful opportunity to converse further with your lordship and your many dear friends."

Essex nods his approval. Her beauty seems to have pacified even this beast. "Thank you for attending, m'lady," he replies. "I hope you shall come again."

Jessica curtsies and extends her hand toward Noah. *"Papa?"* she says, requiring him to offer her the crook of his arm.

As Noah approaches, for a brief moment, Essex's eyes lock with his. From Essex's glower, Noah learns two things: One, Essex is a sore loser.

And, two, by no means is this over.

CHAPTER 18

AT PRECISELY NINE the next morning, Noah receives a note from Jessica informing him that she's helping her Aunt Beth pack for a visit to Beth's relations in Brentwood, northeast of London. Jessica reports that when she extended Henry's invitation to Beth, the response was: "No, dear. You go ahead and have a good time with your father and the *goyim*. I'd rather spend the summer with my own kind."

Jessica's message concluded with the assurance that she'd arrive at Gray's Inn with a cart no later than ten. It's now eleven, and Noah still awaits her, sitting on his trunk in front of the inn, his patience wearing thin.

About ten minutes after the hour, Jessica drives up in an open carriage drawn by two horses, both of whom look as though they've seen better days and would rather be *anywhere* else, even if that means the knacker's. The stable boy begins to water and feed them, but it does little to raise their spirits.

Preparing to lift his trunk and place it onto the floor of the cart, Noah looks into the cart's bed just in time to realize there is no room. Jessica has packed a trunk easily thrice the size of his. He tries to shove it aside, but it will not budge.

"What did you pack in here? A *corpse*?"

Jessica places her hands on her hips. "Yes, Father. I packed a corpse in my luggage. I *always* pack a corpse in my luggage. Don't you pack a corpse in *your* luggage?"

"No. I usually gouge the teeth out as a keepsake. Much lighter." He shoves her trunk again, and huffs. "You know, we're not moving *in*. It's just a summertime visit." Jessica folds her arms and turns away, her pert little nose in the air. "Oh, *this* should be loads of fun," he says.

He hoists his trunk atop Jessica's and drops it with a hefty bang. "We'll leave as soon as the horses are watered. Billingbear is a fair distance from Gray's Inn. At this rate, we'll be lucky to get there before midnight." As Noah has never been there, he's unfamiliar with the way. Fortunately, the moon is full, and the weather clear. He takes out two oil-cloths and lanterns, as well as a map, and ties a cover over the luggage.

* * *

As it turns out, the trip progresses more smoothly than Noah expected, until they reach the small town of Waltham St. Lawrence a few hours after sundown. Their map says they're a mere two miles from their destination.

Beyond the little town, the road narrows drastically, and is closely flanked on both sides by thick woods. Just ahead of them, a slow-moving convoy of two carriages comes into view. In the moonlight, they can see a large baggage wagon being hauled by the hindmost carriage. Over its contents, a sturdy cover has been stretched and tied down. Corners and sharp edges jut up from beneath the cover, revealing trunks so bulky and numerous that they threaten to pierce it at various points.

"Look, Father. A whole *graveyardful* of corpses!" says Jessica.

As they reach the convoy, two things become clear. First, they cannot get around it. Second, it's not moving at all, as it's stuck in a rut. Noah stops the cart, grabs his lantern, and steps down, rolling up his sleeves, preparing to lend a hand. As he walks past the rear carriage, he sees two well-dressed young ladies inside, who smile and titter as he passes. One holds a young child in her arms.

The front carriage is vacant. Noah assumes that its occupants got out to help pull the carriage free. As he reaches the front, there's a strange assemblage of men. One, young and brawny, has lodged one end of a long stick under a stuck wheel, and now hangs by his hands from the free end of the stick in a failed attempt to pry the wheel loose.

As his weight has clearly proven insufficient, two small men (one old, one young) have wrapped themselves around the young man's legs. What little weight they can add clearly hasn't done the trick, as the wheel has not budged. The two small men spot Noah, jump to the ground, and brush themselves off. Small as they are, they carry themselves with dignity. The older man is bearded and sage looking; the younger man, small and stooped over, is slightly hunchbacked. Although Noah can't be sure in the moonlight, he thinks he recognizes him as Sir Robert Cecil.

Behind them, the robust young man lets go of the stick with relief, and comes down on his feet. He rubs his hands together smartly, as though they've been gripping the stick a long time.

The older man says, "I am Lord Burghley. This is my son, Sir Robert."

Noah smiles, and bows vigorously. "A genuine pleasure to meet you, gentlemen. I am Noah Ames, barrister at the Queen's Bench." He had no idea these two famous men were quite so diminutive. Sir Robert looks even smaller face-to-face than he did in the courtroom gallery that day. Although it's indeed a pleasure to meet such strong adversaries of Essex, especially since the ordeal of last night, he wishes there were more, and larger.

Lord Burghley and his son look at each other, Burghley appearing quite surprised. "We were just *talking* about you, Master Ames, before we hit this rutted stretch."

"Talking about me? I cannot imagine why. If you don't mind my asking, where are you gentlemen headed with your lovely ladies?"

Sir Robert speaks. "We're bound for the same destination as you, Master Ames. Billingbear. Like you, we've been invited by Master Neville." He leans close to whisper to Noah, though there's so great a difference in their heights that there remains more than a foot between Sir Robert's mouth and Noah's ear. "'Til the plague lets up."

"Very prudent, Sir Robert," replies Noah quietly. "That's precisely why *we* were invited, as well."

"'We?'" asks Lord Burghley.

"Yes, my daughter awaits me in the cart."

"How delightful! And your wife?"

"I'm afraid she passed away some years ago, m'lord."

"Oh, how awful for you! My own second wife departed some years ago, and I know the harshness of it."

"For me, it was a long time ago."

"Robert's wife Elizabeth has been a great comfort to me, of course," says Burghley. "She and Robert's cousin have come with us. They're in one of the carriages you passed on your way here."

"I look forward to speaking with them, and introducing my daughter to them," says Noah. "In the meanwhile, may I assist your coachman?"

"By all means, Master Ames, but please do not injure yourself."

"No, indeed! I shall do my best to avoid that."

The coachman is only too delighted to accept his help. Together they hang from the stick, which tugs the wheel up out of the rut, at last. The horses do the rest, pulling the carriage free.

Noah bows to the Cecils. "I very much look forward to talking with you gentlemen in the coming days." He picks up his lantern, and returns to his cart, tipping his hat to the ladies as he passes. They titter again, right on cue.

In the lantern light, he detects concern in Jessica's face. "What's the matter, my dear?"

With a puzzled expression, she looks to her right, then her left. "I thought I heard something moving back there. I was about to call to you, when it scurried away."

Noah takes the lantern and explores the area behind the cart, but can find nothing. "Probably just a fox," he says upon his return.

She says nothing, but pulls her cloak more firmly about her shoulders.

The moonlit darkness, which formerly seemed protective, now seems to close in. But for the good fortune of running into the Cecils, Noah and Jessica would be completely alone on the road, and the darkness would provide any adversary with cover. To anyone intending harm, Noah's brief absence from the cart surely presented a moment of maximum opportunity. While he suppresses his imagination before it can conjure up every horror capable of being inflicted upon Jessica, he resolves never again to leave his only daughter in such an exposed position.

Perhaps conversation will shake off their shared sense of danger. "You know who that is up there?" he asks, pointing with his chin toward the Cecils' convoy, which has begun to move.

"No, and I'm tired. Do I really care?"

"I'm sure I can't answer that." He shakes the reins, and they begin to move again. "Still, you'll be spending time with them. Aren't you the least bit curious?"

"Oh, all right." She pouts, shifting around uncomfortably on the hard bench. "Who are they?"

"William and Robert Cecil," he replies. When this draws no reaction, he adds, "Who happen to be England's Lord High Treasurer and Secretary of State."

She sits up, wide-eyed. "You jest, Daddy!"

"No, it's true. They're father and son."

"Are they ... married?"

Noah laughs. "The son's wife is in the second carriage. The father is twice widowed, and old enough to be your grandfather."

"Oh, I see," she says with disappointment.

"They said they were discussing me when I showed up to help dig them out." No response. Same old Jesse.

They follow the convoy for a time. Soon, it halts before the gates of a giant house whose shape vaguely suggests a church or monastery, at least in the moonlight. Jessica, who has been drifting off to sleep, now awakens. "Are we there?" she mumbles.

"I'd imagine so. Let's wait to see what happens up front." He glances around nervously in the darkness. As they've halted outside the gates of their destination, anyone seriously looking for him would now know precisely where he is. He's reminded of Henry's admonition about the disloyalty of some of the servants at Billingbear, and expects this would be a perfect site for an ambush. He wonders if he'll ever again feel secure, whether at Billingbear or anywhere else.

From here, the main house appears to be at least three stories high, topped by twelve soaring gables. The layout appears much like that of Gray's Inn, that of a proscenium stage flanked by two thrust aprons.

A man's voice at the gate wafts toward him on the breeze. It sounds as though it belongs to Walker, the Nevilles' footman from town. Several men noisily approach from the front of the convoy. As Noah awaits their appearance, he pats the dagger in his vest.

He's relieved to find that it is indeed Walker, leading the Cecils back to their trunk-laden cart. "Let's take a look," says Walker, untying the cover and tossing it back to reveal the massive trunks. He whistles softly.

Jessica thrusts her face into Noah's. "*See?*" she exclaims in a whisper.

"I'll do the best I can, gentlemen," says Walker, "but I'm afraid we won't have a full complement of menservants for another day or two. The really heavy trunks'll have to wait for their assistance."

Noah thrusts his face into Jessica's. "*See?*" he retorts.

Over the ladies' protests, Burghley decides that all but three of their trunks will remain in the stable overnight.

Walker smiles broadly at Noah's approach. "Why, Master Ames!" He bows genially. "We were told to expect you, as well. It's good to see you." Fortunately for Jessica, her single behemoth will be brought up tonight.

In a moment, the gate opens and Walker directs the newcomers to a carriage house near the rear entrance of the main building. Once the Cecils' train has been disassembled and stowed away, a young stable boy disengages the horses from Noah's cart and, with Noah's assistance, rolls it back into a stall, with Jessica in the driver's seat.

Noah looks up at his daughter and is surprised to find her sound asleep. Once again, he feels a sudden sympathy for her. After all, she began her day helping her aunt pack for a long trip, then packed for herself and took a long, bumpy ride to Billingbear in an open cart. All the bustle seems to have quite worn her out. For Noah's part, he's simply relieved to have delivered her from any suggestion of plague. He wonders in passing how Beth is faring. Well, he's out of her reach now, and will remain blessedly so for some weeks.

Instead of waking Jessica, he picks her up in his arms and carries her down off the cart. She is surprisingly light. As he brings her toward the rear entrance, she awakens, dismayed to find herself being carried.

"Please put me down, Daddy," she mumbles. "This is hardly the entrance I was hoping for. I'll walk the rest of the way, thank you." He puts her down. Instead of entering the house immediately, she starts fussing like an actress preparing for her first appearance in a dramatic work, taking a jeweled hairband from her pocket, placing it in her mouth, smoothing her hair with her hands before binding it tight, and fastening it with the band at the nape of her neck. And all without a mirror.

"How do I look?" she asks.

"You look every bit my beautiful daughter," he replies.

"*Tsk!* I can never rely on you for an objective opinion."

"That *is* my objective opinion," he huffs.

She half smiles, gives him a peck on the cheek, and goes into the house, where she's immediately met by a lady's maid who engages her in conversation about her lodgings.

Noah is shown to his room by a chambermaid.

Preparing for bed, he glances out of his second-story window, which provides a good view of the whole grounds. Something in the distance catches his eye. All the outbuildings are silhouetted in moonlight, but in a solitary upstairs room, a single candle burns. It's so distant and so lonely that he imagines it a sickroom. His heart goes out to its occupant, whoever it might be.

He changes into his bedclothes, falls back on the bed exhausted, and sleeps.

CHAPTER 19

ON NOAH'S FIRST MORNING at Billingbear, he's awakened by the rhythmic sawing of a great oak being felled outside his window. Luxuriating in the softness of his pillow, he dreams of a sawyer blissfully happy in his work. Then he remembers that his window was left shut the night before. For the sawing to be this loud, the oak would have to be inside the room. Reluctantly, he opens an eye, and identifies the sawyer as a fully clothed Henry, snoring with abandon on a soft chair opposite the bed.

As he considers awakening his slumbering host, there comes a knock at the door.

"Come in," he says quietly. The knock comes again.

"Come in!" he repeats, a bit louder. Henry snorts, and opens his eyes.

The door swings open slowly, and in walks a pretty, dark-skinned maidservant with chestnut hair, carrying a tray of coffee and sectioned tangerine oranges. The delicious scents mingle together, an exotic, pungent liqueur. She smiles at Noah, who modestly pulls the blanket up around his torso.

"Good morning, Master Henry," she says. "Mistress Anne said I might find you here with your friend."

"Master Noah Ames," says a groggy Henry, "this is Lucy, our household treasure."

Lucy curtsies at the compliment, and hands Henry his coffee in a china cup. She places several slices of tangerine on a plate, and puts it on a small corner table by his chair. She does the same for Noah, and turns to her employer. "Will there be anything else, sir?"

Henry looks to Noah, and raises his eyebrows inquiringly.

"Nothing more for me, Master Henry. Thank you. This coffee is wonderful. What a delightful way to wake up in the morning!"

"If it *is* still morning. Thank you, Lucy. That will be all."

She curtsies again, smiles discreetly at Noah, and closes the door behind her.

"I wonder where the Cecils have got to," says Henry, as he goes to the window overlooking the square behind the main building. "Not yet returned from their walk in the garden, I see."

Noah shifts uneasily. "How did you enjoy Lord Essex's party, night before last?"

"Well, he really outdid himself, don't you think?"

"I might have done without his little ... 'legal exercise,' I believe Perez called it."

"After you left with Lady Jessica, he asked me to step into a private room, handed me a paper bearing a Latin phrase, and asked whether I could translate it into English."

"Whatever did it say?"

"*Non servus fidelis sed perfidus debet cavere.*"

Noah puts his hands behind his head and lies back on the pillow. "Scintillating, I'm sure."

"The Latin is imperfect, but you do know what it means?"

"I? I believe it was *you* who got the 'first' in Latin Studies in our class. How did you translate it for his lordship?"

"'It is not the *faithful*, but the *unfaithful* subject who needs to beware.'" Henry shrugs. "But you already know what it means."

"Why do you say that?"

"Because you *wrote* it."

"Did I? I assure you I correspond with neither his lordship nor his attendants. My Latin is not good enough to use in correspondence. In any event, it would be pointless to use it with his lordship, as he obviously requires a translator. Besides, why would you think *I* wrote it? Did he tell you it was from me?"

"No. I knew it had to be you, because it's a clever response to the warning *'caveat causidicus'* you received some weeks ago, which was reinforced, as I recall, by a knock on the head. It was also obvious, to me at least, that you were desperate to avoid its being read aloud at the party."

"But, when would I have had occasion to write to Essex? And by what means would I send him such a message?"

"I was hoping you might tell *me* that."

Noah is concerned that Henry might take his obtuseness as a sign of ingratitude. He is, after all, Henry's houseguest. "I never wrote it to his lordship. Indeed, I never wrote it to *anyone*." He plants his tongue firmly in cheek. "I suppose I may have inscribed it on the back of some personal papers and left them in my saddlebag, secure in the knowledge that his lordship would *never* violate the sanctity of a barrister's papers, or (heaven *forfend!*) have such papers *purloined*."

"Which papers?"

"I struck out his warning and wrote those words on the same sheet of paper, next to the stricken line. His lackey then stole the same papers again."

Henry frowns, and shakes his head. "Do you have any idea how he could have you punished for such insolence?"

Noah brings his hands down to his sides, and sits up indignantly. "*Which* insolence, Henry? I told you, I never wrote those words to him. As was demonstrated at the party, if he wishes to prosecute me, he'll have to produce the original papers — *my* papers — and explain how he got them. How he instructed his attendant to club me over the head, invade my saddlebag *twice*, threaten me in the conduct of my duties, and *steal* my personal papers. At the very least, he'd be confessing to battery and multiple counts of larceny. It would be still *more* entertaining to watch him explain why he believes the words were meant for *him*. That might even send him to the *gallows*!"

Henry sighs. "So you think you've outwitted him? He's a very powerful man, Noah."

Noah leans back on his pillow again. "Indeed, he is. If he weren't, I'd have him in prison already."

"Why are you so protective of the Queen that you would expose yourself to such hazard, when you're uncertain she's even the object of his plot?"

"*Beside* the oath I have sworn to Her Majesty?"

"Beside that."

"Because the Queen should remain our monarch for her whole life. The descent of the Crown by accepted rules of primogeniture assures the peaceful succession of power. Without it, there would be no end of civil wars, with Englishmen slaughtering Englishmen. Strict adherence to primogeniture is England's finest tradition, and its oldest."

"Its *oldest*?" Henry laughs darkly. "If that's what you believe, then perhaps there's something you can learn while you're here at Billingbear. Why don't you put on some clothes? I'll show you some of my ancestors."

"Ancestors?" asks Noah warily.

Henry chuckles. "Not their remains. Their portraits!"

"Ah! I'll be down in a few minutes." As Henry leaves, Noah eats the last of the tangerine slices, and rises to wash and dress.

* * *

A short while later, they amble together along the main hall, which is lined with portraits in gilded frames.

"This is the tuppence tour," says Henry. "Let me know if you recognize anybody. Otherwise, I'll just tell you about the more famous ones."

Noah spots a portrait of a crowned male figure with brown hair and wide-set eyes. "Is this — ?"

Henry emits a low laugh. "That is King Richard the Third. Ironic that you should recognize him first. His reputation has hardly cast a good light on this family."

"Was he a Neville?"

"I'm afraid so. Right next to his portrait is that of his mother, Cecily Neville, Duchess of York."

"She was also the mother of King Edward the Fourth."

"Indeed, she was!"

"And the *grandmother* of the Princes in the Tower, who were murdered by her son King Richard," says Noah.

Henry nods sadly. "The elder of whom was the uncrowned King Edward the Fifth."

Noah can see that this hoary tale of national tragedy is still a fresh wound to Henry's soul. "I'm so sorry, Henry. I was caught up in the history of it all. I ... should have realized that, for you, this was a family tragedy."

"Indeed, sometimes I need to remind myself that it was a tragedy for the rest of England, as well."

"So, you're a Yorkist."

"Do not rush to judgment! On the other side of this great door, we have a few *more* kings. See if you recognize *them*."

They continue down the great hallway, past the main entrance door. At the base of each portrait is an engraved plaque naming the person depicted. Noah avoids reading them, so Henry will tell their story in his own way.

"Who is this lovely lady?" Noah asks, indicating a portrait that appears about as old as the others he's seen.

"That is Lady Anne Neville, the first wife of Edward Plantagenet, who was heir to the throne by his father King Henry the Sixth. Prince Edward was killed in the Wars of the Roses, probably by the Duke of Gloucester, who eventually became Richard the Third by capturing and then murdering Henry the Sixth in the Tower. Lady Anne remarried not too long thereafter."

"And I know *whom* she remarried. I begin to discern a pattern in your choice of narrative." Noah has the feeling he's one in a very long line of people with whom Henry and his forbears have had this same conversation. "She married Richard the Third, the man who'd murdered both her husband and his father the *king*!"

"That's precisely what she did," confirms Henry. "The point I'm demonstrating is that the English tradition of which you are so exceedingly fond, that of assuring the peaceful transfer of power by primogeniture, is only the bright side of the coin. Its tarnished and bloody reverse is that people have always done literally *anything they can* to seize the Crown, regardless of the niceties of primogeniture, or even the laws of nature."

He points to Lady Anne's portrait. "They will marry the murderers of their spouses." He points to Richard the Third. "They will murder their brothers and their nephews ... even *children*." Indicating a joint portrait of the Princes in the Tower, he says darkly: "Even children who are already *kings*."

"So, what you're saying is: That sad tradition is as hoary as primogeniture."

"It goes back all the way to the Garden of Eden." Henry nods sadly. "And the right for which Cain killed Abel was not even so much as a crown."

"I see your point," concedes Noah. The portraits lure his curiosity back to the many Neville appearances in the royal line. "So, you're not just a Yorkist. You're a Lancastrian, as well. You wear both the white *and* the red rose, just as the Tudors do. Why, you're quite as English as the Queen!"

"*Shhhhh!*" Henry draws Noah into a small room off the hall. "Don't say that aloud!" he says quietly. "Didn't I tell you the walls have ears?"

Noah's face reddens, as he's evidently been found guilty of some gross error he fails to understand. He replies in hushed tones. "But Henry! We have discussed nothing that is unknown to the general public. Hundreds of thousands of people know these things!"

"Ah, but we Nevilles are Plantagenets, and so must act as though we know no such thing about ourselves. Walk up and down these aisles with your eyes open, Noah, and you will find that Nevilles have also been Queens of Scotland, France, Bohemia ... even *Spain*, for heaven's sake! Our beloved Queen Elizabeth may trace her ancestry back to William the Conqueror, but, after all, he was French. And though Nevilles accompanied him from France, invaded England by his side, and were rewarded for their victory in the Battle of Hastings in 1066, *we* intermarried with the families of Anglo-Saxon royalty who had ruled England since King Canute. As English as the Queen?" He smirks. "We Nevilles are *centuries* more English than she."

"Then — " Noah stops himself, his eyes wide.

"Stop!" says Henry, placing his fingers against Noah's mouth. "Never say it. And, for heaven's sake, *stop thinking it!*"

Noah nods, although he's never been able to stop himself from thinking about something once it's entered his mind. What Henry forbids him to say is that the Nevilles' claim to the throne might well be superior to the tenuous claim of Henry the Seventh, whose granddaughter Elizabeth now occupies it.

"Come to the library, Noah. I have something to show you there."

They go down the hall to a huge library lined by darkly stained oak, containing hundreds of bound volumes and numerous parchment scrolls. Henry searches through a bookshelf just higher than his head, and selects a particularly battered book to take down and hand to Noah. Although it's a handwritten transcription, the title page dutifully identifies it as *Leycester's Commonwealth*, and says it was published in Antwerp in 1584.

"What's this?" asks Noah.

"Most of it is a worthless piece of vicious libel scribbled by an unidentified papist expatriate, probably Paget. It's been set in type since that transcription was made. The book's basic thesis is that the Earl of Leicester, whose given name was 'Robert Dudley' and who happened to be the Queen's favorite prior to Essex, was a murderer whose sole purpose in life was to gain the Crown for himself. It is, incidentally, a banned publication. Why, 'tis treason for you simply *to hold it in your hands at this very moment!*"

Noah gasps, and tosses the book back to Henry, who catches it and collapses into a soundless fit of laughter. Noah is mortified, and takes a step toward storming out of the library. Henry restrains him by the arm, and says, "Wait, Noah! Wait. Let me show you something. Two things, really. First, if you will leaf through the latter pages of the book, you will see that it contains a history of the Wars of the Roses. I've placed a mark next to the mention of everyone who was a Neville. Look!"

Noah first glances around the library to make sure no one is watching. Seeing no one, with some consternation he accepts the book back, and leafs through page after page. "Almost everyone *here* is a Neville."

"That's what I've been trying to tell you. And, whatever the book's deficiencies, it is *accurate* on that score."

As Henry is about to take back the book, he snaps his fingers. "Wait! There's one more thing I want you to see!" While Noah holds the book, Henry flips through it. He has obviously been through the volume many times, as he recognizes the pages upside down. "Here, look." He points to a paragraph stating that Dudley still has agents in place to inform him of new intelligence and act on his behalf, principal among whom is "Lopez the Jew for poisoning and for the art of destroying children in women's bellies."

Before Noah can digest the passage, two sets of light footsteps approach the library. Henry grabs the book out of Noah's hands, snaps it shut, and deftly restores it to its former place on the shelf. Together, Henry and Noah stroll to the center of the library, pretending to have been deeply involved in conversation there.

Henry says, a little too theatrically: "And, so you see, Master Ames, that many whom the general populace mistakenly regard as demigods are, to me, simply distant ancestors."

Lord Burghley and his son Sir Robert appear at the door in their robes of office, Lord Burghley smiling broadly. "Oh, Master Ames, do not fall prey to Master Neville's disparagement of the divine rights of kings. Most of them have proven worthy of such rights, even those bearing the tragic mark of being related to our Master Henry."

"Gentlemen!" says Henry. "Have you completed your pillaging of my rose garden? *Hmmm?* Shall I dispatch Goodman Walker to extinguish the many fires you have set, and provide alms to those you've left destitute?"

"There shall be no need, Master Henry," says Sir Robert. "We were quite vanquished and left in utter confusion by the clever device of a hedgerow maze, from which we barely escaped with our lives."

Henry laughs. "How long did it take you to find your way out?"

The Cecils exchange a glance, as neither seems sure how to reply. Sir Robert speaks. "We would *like* to inform you that we found our way out in the process of saving a fair damsel in distress. But, alas, it was rather *we* — in distress — who were guided to freedom by a damsel, in the person of fair Lady Burlington."

"You should indeed feel exalted that the Lady of the Forest deigned to heed your miserable cries," sniffs Henry.

"And so we do, Master Neville, especially as she herself had been commanded by the Lady of the House to summon us to dinner. She has, however, charged us with a nearly impossible quest, that being to drag the two of you with us, overcoming all resistance."

Noah steps into the fray. "I think it prudent, Master Neville, to recognize when one is overpowered."

"Indeed," agrees Henry. "The better part of valor is discretion." He looks grimly at Noah. "I'm afraid we have no choice but to dine. Ames, follow me with your head hung suitably low."

As they dine on mutton and potatoes, as well as some early greens from the garden, Henry offers the Cecils advice on numerous affairs of state, sometimes humbly, sometimes haughtily, always in the best of humor. Much of the discussion goes over Noah's head, most topics having no apparent connection to him. After a while, he notices that everyone is pointedly avoiding the slightest mention of Essex or his party. Even when one would expect Essex to come up, he never does.

After a while, Noah gives up on the men's discussion and begins attending to the ladies' conversation, which centers around women they all seem to know well, but Noah has never so much as heard of.

When they leave the table to disperse to diverse activities, Noah still has no clue why the Cecils have been speaking of him so often in weeks past.

* * *

At bedtime, Noah retires to his room. As he prepares to light a candle so he can undress, somewhere in the night, a light in an upstairs room catches his eye. In a remote window, a sheer white curtain sways gently, and a candle flickers on the same warm breeze. He feels sure it's the same room he spied on his arrival late last evening.

He places a candle in the candlestick, but does not light it. The night is quiet enough that, through his open window, he can make out a subdued conversation taking place just below his window, at the rear door. There are two voices — one belonging to a man, the other an older woman.

"Do you have the fresh water, as well?" asks the woman.

"Wait, let me see," replies the man. Noah is almost sure it's Henry, although, if it *is* him, something about his voice sounds uncharacteristically humble, or perhaps resigned to performing some uncomfortable duty. "Yes, here it is. You have packed quite the basket here, Julia. Thank you."

"It's my privilege. Please convey my humblest respects, sir."

"I shall certainly do so, Julia. Thank you, again."

Noah steps back from the window, lest he be seen. The rear door shuts, and, mere moments later, Henry's stout form appears outside. Henry proceeds slowly away from the house in the general direction of the outbuilding where the candle burns in the window. Noah chides himself for failing to get a better look at the building while there was still daylight, but finds that if he blocks the moon from his view, he can make out at least some detail.

It looks to be a small brick cottage of two stories, in the same architecture as the main house. If the main house was once an abbey, then the cottage might have been its rectory. He wonders about the origins of Billingbear as he observes Henry bracing himself before the cottage's side entrance.

As Noah's view of that entrance is blocked by a thick willow, his gaze naturally returns to the upstairs room, where the bottom of the sheer curtain suddenly flaps out of the window, and the candle gutters in the draft wafted by Henry's opening the exterior door. A few moments later, the interior door of the candlelit room opens and Henry enters, forcing a smile and talking, much too far away to be heard. He puts down his basket, and proceeds into the room, out of Noah's view.

Evidently, it *is* a sickroom. Although it did not occur to Noah until this very moment, he suspects that the invalid is Henry's father, whom Noah has not seen since spying him through a window one fateful night at the Tower of London.

*   *   *

The next morning, Noah awakes earlier and far more well-rested than usual. He washes and dresses, and heads downstairs to the kitchen area. No one is stirring but a few servants beginning preparations for breakfast.

"Hello, Master Ames," says Walker in a hoarse morning voice, coming in through the rear entrance with a few fagots of wood under his arm. He closes the door behind him. "Up early, *you* are. Especially for a barrister."

Noah smiles. "Yes, well, I did something barristers rarely do. I went to sleep without reading into the night. Not very good for lining the pockets, but excellent for one's outlook."

"I catch your meanin', sir."

"Tell me, have you seen Arden about? I didn't see him all day yesterday."

"Saw 'im just this mornin', sir, going out to the stables, same as yesterday. He was ridin' all day yesterday, and I expect he'll do the same today … and *every* day till the novelty wears off. It's not every fella gets to ride through the Windsor Forest." He winks confidentially, and comes over to Noah, still carrying the wood. "Uncle 'enry's approval may be enough to ride his best horses about, but *no one* goes into Windsor Forest without Her Majesty's approval '*in each instance*,'" he says, as though quoting a deed of easement. He steps over to the fireplace and puts the fagots down one at a time.

"I see," says Noah. He shrugs. "Well, at least we know he is well."

Walker wipes his hands together to brush off a few flecks of wood. He frowns with obvious concern. "And why *wouldn't* he be well, Master Ames? Is there trouble about?"

"No," says Noah pensively. "I suppose not."

"Well, if yer missin' the young folk, sir, I hear yer Master Cheerful will be up from London again this mornin'. Considerin' how fast he rides, I'm surprised he's not 'ere already."

There are heavy footfalls at the top of the staircase that Noah descended shortly before.

"Good morning, Ames. Care to go riding until breakfast?"

"Delighted, Henry!"

Henry leads him back to the stables, where they pass the pathetic horses that brought him and Jessica to Billingbear. Although they seem to be improving in the care of the Nevilles' stableman, they remain a sorry sight by comparison to the sleek beauties in the other stalls.

The stableman opens a stall, and leads out one of the larger horses.

"They *have* to be that big to bear my heft comfortably," confides Henry. He mounts with the assistance of a stepladder.

"Shall I saddle one of Master Ames' horses, sir?" the stableman asks dubiously.

"No. Give Master Ames the black one my daughter calls 'Bucklebury.'"

The stableman smiles. "Yes, sir!"

A moment later, he leads in the most beautiful black steed, young and strong, of medium build, with a sleek, well-tended coat. Better still, he seems content to allow Noah to mount him.

Henry observes rider and mount. "Master Ames, that horse was *meant* for you. You look positively dashing together."

"I'm afraid I'm not much with a horse," Noah confesses.

"We'll see."

Henry leads the way to Windsor Forest, first at a lope, then a canter. Each acceleration serves to convince Noah that Henry is right about this horse. It will be painful to part with him.

When they've gone deep into the forest, Henry leads the way up a steep slope. "My father is Forester of Windsor Park," he says. "I used to come here all the time as a lad. I know every nook of it."

They come to rest at the top of a high grassy knoll where the view is breathtaking, looking down upon endless treetops in every direction. Windsor Castle stares down at them from a commanding hill.

A fond faraway smile lights upon Henry's face. "I do love it so. I recall one time my father instructing the young Princess Elizabeth in archery, trying to teach her how to shoot a deer. Bless her soul," he laughs quietly, "she didn't have the heart for it. She talked so long that, by the time he'd prepared her to actually *do* it, the deer had long fled."

He looks up at the castle, shielding his eyes from the sun. "Well, what do you know?" He points to the castle. "You see that pennant? The one by the main entrance?"

Noah shields his eyes, and peers up. There are several pennants, one near the main entrance. "Yes, I think I do."

"That means the Queen is in residence. I wonder how long she'll be there."

A long cloud of dust rises from the incline approaching the distant castle, signifying the arrival of some dignitary or other.

"I wonder who that could be," muses Henry.

As the train pulls up to the closed gate, the tangerine-and-cream livery of the Earl of Essex becomes visible in the distance. While its bright design was no doubt fashioned to seem uplifting and heroic, to Noah the colors seem muted by the dark shadow of the lingering dust cloud hovering over them. He finds himself fervently hoping that the gate will refuse to yield, and protect the Queen as it was designed to do. Instead, it stupidly gapes wide, and the train passes through unimpeded, drawing the black cloud deep inside the castle keep. Noah looks at Henry, who appears to have been studying his face.

And then Henry says something truly unexpected. "You amaze me. I think you're in *love* with her."

"With whom?"

"With the *Queen*! You've never so much as seen her, have you?"

Noah shifts on his mount. "I did see her. Once. Long ago."

"I would have expected our little discussion of yesterday to clear your vision somewhat. They're not gods, Noah. Some of them are not even good *people*."

"*She* is, though."

"She *is* that," Henry admits. "One of the best, in fact. Not to change the subject, but the other day I found something unnerving about Hawking. I remember only too well how distraught he was about Graves' murder. I understand why he is so fanatical about prosecuting Frizer. Even without more, *that* bastard should rot in hell for what he's done to the English theater. But what disturbed me most was that I began to realize Hawking's not out for Frizer alone, is he?"

Noah looks down at the reins and says nothing.

Henry nods. "As I thought. He's not even out for Skeres. He wants larger game."

"I cannot discuss it, Master Neville." Noah looks up at him. "It's not *my* secret, or I would disclose it."

Henry arches an eyebrow. "Would you? Have you told me your secrets? You know plenty of mine."

"I suppose everyone has one or two."

"That's true. But I'm not asking idly. The Cecils are considering placing you in a most sensitive position. In light of their long-running rivalry with Essex, any blot on your past could ruin them, and change the course of English history very much for the worse from your viewpoint, judging by your expression whenever Essex's name or livery appear. I shall leave it to you to choose the precise moment to tell me, but, before you return to London or Westminster, I need to know what secrets you may have."

Noah hesitates. "And if I were to decline the proffered position?"

Henry laughs darkly, and shakes his head. "Noah, are you a trueborn Englishman?"

"Aye." To Noah, his Polish birth is a mere accident.

"One who loves his Queen?"

"Aye!" says Noah sternly.

"Then you have no choice. If you fit the Cecils' bill, you're in it up to your neck. And it won't come by invitation. It will take the form of a command signed by your earthly deity herself." He tilts his head to indicate the distant castle.

Noah nods and stares absently at his horse's mane.

Henry grabs his reins, as though to trot off.

"Wait, Henry, please," says Noah. "I'm prepared to disclose to you my only serious secret."

"Now?"

"Whenever I'm permitted to accompany you on your nocturnal pilgrimage to your father."

Henry's eyes go wide. "You don't miss a thing, do you?"

Noah is pleased that he's guessed rightly about the occupant of the sickroom. "I wish that were true. I'm afraid I do miss things, from time to time. And the consequences can prove fatal. In any event, may I accompany you?"

At first, Henry equivocates. "Oh, all right," he says. "But have you ever *seen* my father?"

Noah nods. "Once. A long, long time ago."

Henry shakes the reins, trots down to a wide path, and turns onto it, bringing his mount to a full gallop. Bucklebury easily keeps up, the ground flowing under him like a great river. Noah is exhilarated. For better or worse, a huge weight will soon be lifted from his chest. He hopes that it will all turn out for the best, but wonders how a leak of this secret might threaten the fortunes of Marie and his daughter, who so values her social standing.

CHAPTER 20

WHEN HENRY AND NOAH ARRIVE back at Billingbear, there's a full complement of guests for breakfast, and servants to assist, and the place teems with good cheer. Henry beams as he and Noah enter the dining room.

Mistress Anne sidles up to Noah. "Look at Henry," she says intimately. "He's in his glory. This is just the way he likes things: a world of good food and good company, all revolving around *him*." She goes to greet the Lord Treasurer and his son.

Jessica leaves the table to greet Henry and Noah. "Oh, *papa!*" she says for all to hear. "We were beginning to worry about you! Where did you spirit Master Henry off to?" She stands between them, facing the assembled, and takes them both by the hand. "*You* look just fine. I hope *Master Henry* is none the worse for wear." She kisses them each on the cheek.

"I assure you," replies Noah, "I have returned Master Henry in good condition — or, at least, in no *worse* condition than I found him."

The rest of the company shouts its approval and applauds as Henry takes his seat at the head of the table.

From the corner of his eye, Noah spots two people in different parts of the room waving to him. One is Lord Burghley, who signals an invitation for Noah to take a seat to his right, a place of great honor. The other is young Cheerful Killigrew, smiling as ever, pointing to his leather pouch. Evidently, he has at least one letter for Noah.

If Noah were not thinking diplomatically, he would simply go directly to Cheerful, as there's a good chance he has a letter from Jonathan, whose welfare weighs heavily on Noah's mind. But he simply cannot snub Lord Burghley. As Mistress Anne is passing at this very moment, he seeks her as a go-between to her kinsman.

"Mistress Anne, I must go and speak to Lord Burghley, but evidently a letter has been brought to me by ... " He indicates Cheerful.

"By whom, Master Ames?" she asks blankly.

"By the good-looking young Killigrew fellow over there." He points with his chin.

"Well, you'll have to be more specific, Master Ames. *All* the Killigrew men are good-looking."

"The one with the ... " He stops cold, as he realizes she's having him on.

She scoffs. "Well, if you're going to find out his given name, you're going to have to do better than *that!*" She smiles and walks away.

Noah goes to Lord Burghley. "M'lord, you do me great honor to seat me there. Just now, however, I really must see that young fellow, whom I believe to have an urgent letter for me."

Burghley peers down the table at Cheerful. "I quite understand, Master Ames. You take *all the time you need* to read and to collect your thoughts."

Noah bows. "Thank you, m'lord. Sir Robert."

Noah sidles up to Cheerful at the opposite end of the table. "Hello. What have you got for me?" he asks.

"I have but one letter for you, sir," says Cheerful in his spirited tenor voice, "but I thought you'd like to see it right away. A scruffy young fellow brought it to me. He seemed very tired, as though he'd not got much rest for days." He hands Noah the letter.

"Thank you very much." Noah takes a coin from his pocket and drops it in the boy's hand. "Here you go, Master ... ?"

"Thank you, Master Ames." The boy smiles broadly, and takes the coin.

Noah takes the letter into the hallway, looks around to ensure he's not being observed, and slits it open roughly with his finger. It's from Jonathan.

> Dear Master Ames:
>
> The coroner has completed his brief inquest into the death of Marlowe and, as I predicted, has issued a formal acquittal of Frizer. Evidently, killing someone by stabbing him through the eye with a stiletto is, in the coroner's view, insufficient to give rise to an inference of possible wrongdoing. See if even your host can rationalize such a vacuous finding.
>
> As it turns out, Frizer is a servant of Sir Thos. Walsingham, brother of the late Mister Secretary, and good friend of the tangerine crowd. (Sorry, but I'm sending this by Master Cheerful and, if he's turned Turk, we're all in the stews anyhow. Burn this immediately after reading.) I've got some jesters researching whether a coroner's acquittal prohibits a later criminal trial on grounds that it would impose double jeopardy in violation of the English constitution. Unless we find out that a criminal trial *is* forbidden, I will continue to investigate the scoundrel with the icepick.
>
> Hawk.

P.S. After writing the above, I sided the coroner in the street, and he advised me that he strongly suspects Frizer murdered Stephen Rodriguez, too (although that murder was outside the scope of his inquest). He told me to use his report as evidence that Frizer stabs people through the eye. He says that, notwithstanding his finding that Frizer lacked the requisite state of mind to make him criminally responsible in the case of *Marlowe's* death, his report should help in convicting Frizer of the *Rodriguez* murder. I think he's right. Not a bad old chap, really, but he is scared to death. Someone has gotten to him. He's not the type to accept a bribe, so I'm pretty sure he's been threatened. So, the inquest was all theater, precisely as I foresaw.

P.P.S. Have an extra pheasant for me! *Somebody* might as well enjoy this bloody summer. Plague rampant in Southwark, although nothing around Gray's, as yet.

Noah folds the letter neatly and places it firmly in his pocket, resolving to burn it at first opportunity. He takes a deep breath, dons a smile, and heads in to breakfast. The table is already thinning, as a tennis match is being organized outdoors, and no one wishes to be chosen last.

"Here is your seat, Master Ames!" says Lord Burghley. "As you can see, we have faithfully retained it for you. Please join us."

"Thank you, m'lord," says Noah, helping himself to two slices of toast and spooning a few chicken's eggs onto his plate from a communal serving dish. "I'm famished!"

No one remains at this end of the dining table, except Henry, the Lord Treasurer, and Sir Robert, all sipping coffee. When Noah looks up from his plate, he sees that all eyes await his.

"Has your correspondent sent you any news of general interest, Master Ames?" asks Burghley.

"Hmmm, well, let's see." Noah looks to Henry, who regards him with interest, albeit as inconspicuously as possible. "I have learned, unfortunately, that plague is rampant in Southwark."

"Oh, that's terrible! Master Henry, do you think, as Doctor Lopez has suggested, that it's because of all the open sewers down there?"

Henry coughs. "While I can't say I understand such things well, I think it undeniable that filth and contagion travel hand in hand."

"And I have also learned," says Noah, swallowing some toast, "that Marlowe's killer has been acquitted by the coroner after inquest."

Henry cannot mask his perturbation, but he says nothing.

Noah tries to recall Jonathan's phrase exactly, and comes fairly close. "Evidently, killing someone by stabbing him through the eye with a stiletto is insufficient to give rise to an inference of possible wrongdoing."

Burghley frowns. "Oh, that *cannot* be right!"

Sir Robert is even more overset than Henry. He slams his small fist down on the table, rises, and walks away red-faced, embarrassing his father.

"Master Neville, Master Ames, you will have to forgive Robert, as he has far less experience than you in the inevitable frustrations of legal affairs."

"Not at all," says Noah. "It does Sir Robert credit to detest injustice, nor does it require a great deal of legal practice to see it in this case. He's right to be upset."

Burghley sighs. "Still, I suppose that the death of one playwright, in the grand scheme of things, is not so great a loss."

Henry's face reddens and he turns aside, tears forming in the corners of his eyes. He clears his throat. "Marlowe was a first-rate poet, Lord Burghley," he says calmly. "England is the less without him."

Burghley evidently realizes he has spoken cavalierly. "Oh, most certainly he was, Master Neville. I spoke out of turn." Henry nods indulgently.

Sir Robert returns to his chair and apologizes for his outburst. He bows to Henry, who nods in understanding and bids him be seated.

Until now, Noah has waited in vain for some sign that Henry will tell the Cecils of Essex's designs. He now looks pointedly to Henry, who understands immediately, glances around the empty table, and beckons his footman.

"Walker, please close both sets of doors, and instruct the wait staff that no one is to enter until we have dispersed." Walker nods gravely, closes one set of doors, then closes the other set from outside.

Henry and Noah are now alone with the Cecils, who seem a little surprised and regard Henry expectantly.

"As you know," Henry begins, "there was a murder outside The Rose some weeks ago." The Cecils both nod. "Under Master Ames' guidance, one of his diligent young colleagues at Gray's Inn has been investigating on behalf of the victim's widow. Master Ames has recently made some very disturbing observations. Master Ames?"

All three sets of eyes are now fixed on Noah, who is surprised that it will be he, rather than Henry, who will inform the Cecils of the danger.

"Gentlemen," says Noah, "I strongly suspect that Lord Essex is in the process of converting Secretary Walsingham's spy network to his own use, and murdering those former spies who refuse to come along."

The Cecils are speechless, but they exchange a glance that can only mean he's touched upon a point of long concern. Burghley speaks softly and slowly. "Master Ames, you do understand the gravity of this accusation?"

Noah gulps. "I do, your lordship. I am a barrister of more than twenty years' experience. I do not take allegations of this kind lightly, and while the case is far from certain, the evidence to date all seems to point in the same direction. The man who was murdered at the theater and Christopher Marlowe were both assassinated by the forcible insertion of a stiletto through the eye into the brain." Burghley winces, and Sir Robert's face goes white. "Both victims had been agents of Secretary Walsingham while he lived, and they appear to have been murdered by the same man, who is one of Lord Essex's attendants, and who has now, as you know, been acquitted in Marlowe's murder, in questionable manner. Other former agents of Walsingham, who are in good favor with Lord Essex, remain untouched."

Sir Robert looks to Burghley. "I told you, Father. He doesn't miss a thing."

Burghley nods thoughtfully. As though he still needs to test Noah's mettle himself, he leans forward to pose a question.

"Tell us, Master Ames. How did you learn that the two victims had been Walsingham's agents?" As Burghley probably already knows, a straightforward answer would require Noah to reveal Henry as the source of that delicate information.

Noah is careful not to glance in Henry's direction. "I was told this in confidence, m'lord — "

"*I* told him," interrupts Henry.

Burghley smiles at Sir Robert, as though Noah has passed the test. "Discreet, as *well* as observant."

Sir Robert asks: "Why have you come forward with such a grave accusation before developing all the evidence?"

"I would rather risk my own life than Her Majesty's," Noah replies, and it's all the more persuasive for being true.

Burghley asks: "And you feel that Lord Essex's plan, if it is as you suspect, may present a threat to Her Majesty's well-being?"

The tension is thick as Noah replies. "I am no one to pass judgment on the character of a peer of the Crown, m'lord. But Mister Walsingham's successor — of undoubted loyalty — should have been given charge of all such agents." He glances at Sir Robert. "As this apparently has not been done, the inference might readily be drawn that whoever has prevented it from being done is … not so loyal."

"We will begin looking into this question immediately, Master Ames. Please accept our thanks, and the thanks of Her Majesty, for your perspicacity in her interest. And do not speak of this to anyone else." Noah bows his head respectfully.

Burghley changes the subject, lightening the mood. "Tell me, Master Ames, is it your experience that many of the people acquitted after trial at Queen's Bench are genuinely innocent, or are most acquittals simply the result of lawyers' wiles?"

"Well, some are indeed innocent — at least of the charges against them." This draws an unintended laugh. "Some are innocent *altogether*, as far as I can tell. Just the other week, I counseled a grain merchant who was acquitted of murder. As far as I could detect, he hadn't done a blessed thing seriously wrong in his life. Family man, God-fearing, and so on."

"Oh, that's *right*!" says Burghley, glancing at Sir Robert. "You bested Sir Edward Coke in that case, did you not? Remarkable!"

Noah is abashed. "Oh, I don't know, m'lord. His principal witness was Essex's man, Gelly Meyrick, who appeared to have seen … shall we say … a crime in another *district*?"

"Ah, but still! To defeat an adversary as learned as Coke must be quite a feather in your cap at the bar, no?"

"I suppose." Noah sips his coffee, searching his mind for an analogy. "But it's like besting a chess champion at a game of loggats. They're simply different sports."

"How so?" asks Sir Robert. "Are you not both barristers at the Queen's Bench?"

"Well, yes, we have that in common," says Noah. "But a trial is only partly about scholarship. To a large extent, as I have been reminded of late, it is about showmanship and amiability. Coke has a problem putting people at ease. He finds it difficult to persuade them that he is … *just like them*, in a sense. You know, that he puts his robes on one at a time, and that he occasionally may sneeze, or even *fart*."

Lord Burghley's face turns red, and he laughs despite himself. Sir Robert and Henry do the same, although more at Burghley's reaction than Noah's remark.

Noah continues. "Coke's strength — and it is formidable, I can tell you from experience — is in the depth of his legal learning. He is a *scholar's* scholar." He takes a bite of a small muffin. "Although it doesn't matter much at trial, he also has an unquestioned dedication to justice through the Common Law. *Brilliant* man!"

Burghley is momentarily speechless, and he looks to Sir Robert and Henry, as though Noah's remarks have in some way touched upon a prior discussion among them. Burghley turns to Noah. "You may be surprised to learn, Master Ames, that he heaped as much praise upon you, as you have upon him."

Noah is taken aback. He puts down the muffin, sits upright, and clears his throat. "I am *indeed* surprised, as I was always under the impression that he does not much like me."

"Nonsense," says Burghley. "It's *losing* he cannot abide."

"Well, then," says Noah, "he should be offered a position where he's not required to play at loggats."

*   *   *

Several beautiful days pass uneventfully. While there's still no word from Marie, it has not been so long yet as to be worrisome, especially as several of the countries to be visited are under the control of forces hostile to England. He trusts that, when she finally writes to him, she'll be careful to avoid giving prying eyes any cause for suspicion.

Although Noah greatly enjoys the company on this visit, all the bustling has deprived him of any opportunity to contemplate the loss of Marlowe. Late one afternoon, he takes a walk in the garden alone to sort through his feelings on the subject. True, he met Marlowe only once, and that with uncomfortable results, yet he *will* miss Marlowe the *playwright*. Of that he feels sure. And he'll feel it all the more poignantly for Henry's loss.

"Noah!" He's being called by Henry. It's as though the man has been conjured by his own thoughts. Henry waves, emerging from the main house. "Let me show you the labyrinth!"

Although he initially thought he'd prefer to be alone, if there's anyone who can cast light on the significance of Marlowe's death, it will be Henry. Besides, how can he deny attention to this wonderful host who has singlehandedly saved Jessica from an outbreak of plague?

Henry catches up with him, the very pink of health, neither short of breath nor showing any sign of pain.

"I must tell you, Henry, that your improved diet and Doctor Lopez's tablets have done wonders for your health and appearance."

"Oh, you needn't tell *me* that. I feel like a new man. But it's all been diet and less drinking. I haven't taken a single one of Lopez's pills since the day he gave them to me." Henry grows a bit more serious. "I don't mean to intrude on your solitude, old man, but when I saw you from the doorway just now, you didn't seem to be thinking happy thoughts."

"Well … *some* were happy. I was thinking how fortunate I am that you invited Jessica and me to Billingbear. I must tell you, I don't think I've been this happy or well rested in many years. And my mind is at ease now she's out of Southwark. I've also enjoyed meeting the Cecils, and Jessica enjoys their company immensely. She finds Sir Robert's baby adorable."

Henry smiles. "Yes, a very handsome chap, isn't he?"

"He is. You caught me thinking about something else, though. I was contemplating the loss of Christopher Marlowe, which I haven't had a moment for."

Henry sighs. "I know just what you mean. The thing of it is, it's mostly an artistic loss. He was no great contributor to the society of men."

"True. I met him only the once, and he didn't seem very interested in *talking* with me, if you take my meaning."

"No, indeed. They accused him of being everything from a pederast to an atheist. For all I know, it's true. I can't help but wonder if his … preference did not have something to do with his murder."

"How do you mean?"

"Well, I suppose he might have 'come on' to one of the men he was with that day."

"Implausible, in my view," says Noah. "No, they must have known from Walsingham's brother that Marlowe was a sodomite. A man doesn't get angry about such an invitation unless he's surprised by it. And they could not have been." Noah suddenly remembers something Marie told him. "Before Marie left England on business, she mentioned something that seemed unimportant at the time. Did you know that her upstairs parlor looks out upon Gray's Inn Square?"

Henry stops and closes his eyes. His face assumes a faraway look. "Now that you mention it, I can see *her* window."

"See her window? Where?"

"In my mind's eye, Noah."

"Ah! Well, as you know, she lost her husband shortly before leaving for the Continent. She told me that, like many a grieving widow, she'd pace the floor half the night sometimes. She said she saw Francis Bacon and Marlowe in amorous embrace at a place on Gray's Inn Square that can be seen from her window."

Henry looks only mildly interested. "And?"

"And she saw Francis Bacon pass Marlowe a letter there." Noah stops and turns to Henry. "Suppose we were to think deviously."

"Is there any other way?"

"Suppose there was something in that letter that incriminated Bacon."

Henry seems dubious. "Why would Bacon give an incriminating letter to Marlowe? Wouldn't that enable Marlowe to extort him at will?"

"It would, precisely, but suppose it would have incriminated Marlowe equally, so that Marlowe would not dare to disclose it."

"In what crime?" asks Henry.

"Perhaps the pederasty that has been rumored about the two of them. Anthony Bacon, who is Essex's candidate for Attorney General, becomes ill … too ill for the job. Now *Francis* becomes Essex's prime candidate. But there's this incriminating document out there, in Marlowe's possession. Francis tells Essex about it, and Essex decides to get it back, just in time for his big party, the one we attended. Yes, it would give Francis something to celebrate. So, Essex, or Thomas Walsingham, doesn't matter which, sends those murderous wretches Skeres, Poley, and Frizer to fetch the document."

"I'm following you so far. But those three were with Marlowe all day. Why wouldn't they have just taken the letter from him right away?"

"Because Marlowe would still once have had the letter, and he could always turn informer," Noah speculates.

"Without written evidence?"

"Why not? He may have been an eyewitness to the *act*, for all we know, as reprehensible as that seems. Such testimony is admissible, and can be very persuasive. Besides, it's possible that Marlowe had hidden the letter, and they could not find it. In that case, they would have to … "

Henry completes the sentence. "To badger Marlowe until he produced it."

"And Marlowe would have replied, as we know he repeatedly did: 'Tell Devereux he can't have it.'"

"If they could not find it, why would they take all day before murdering Marlowe?"

A shiver shoots up Noah's spine. "We've been missing Marlowe's fatal mistake!"

"What is that?" asks Henry.

"He *gave* it to them. After refusing all day, he turned over the letter! And that sealed his fate. Don't you see? Though they had recovered the only *written* proof, they still had to eliminate the possibility of eyewitness testimony. And there was only one way to do that."

As Henry completes Noah's thought, he looks stricken. "They had to *kill* him, as they may have been ordered to do regardless, because he'd also declined to serve as one of Essex's spies."

"Yes, and they couldn't kill him until he turned it over, for then it might yet have been found by someone else." Noah glowers. "Did you see the look on Francis's face as he and Anthony left Gray's Inn for Essex's party?"

Henry nods grimly. "Like the cat who ate the cream, exactly as he *would* have felt if he knew that a threat posed by Marlowe had been … removed."

Henry points to a gap between the hedges. "This is the maze. Shall we enter?"

"Why not?" says Noah. "It can't be any more confusing than the one we're caught in out here."

After making a few turns in the maze, Noah says, "Why do you suppose Marlowe was such a successful playwright?"

"I suppose he loved playing off the old conventions, and adding his own touch."

"Conventions?" asks Noah.

Henry nods. "It's a creaky old profession, playwriting, is. It has its clichéd forms, mostly based upon audience expectations. To some extent, the playwright is stuck with those expectations, and he either conforms to them, or plays off them at his peril."

"How do you mean?"

"For example, there are some hoary old sayings among players. Here's one: 'If a pistol appears on the stage at the opening curtain, it must be fired before the end of the first act.'"

Noah laughs. "What other expectations?"

"Oh, there are so many. How about this one? It's positively *ancient*: 'If there's an arras onstage, a high nobleman must be concealed behind it.'"

"An arras?"

"Yes, you know, like a tapestry. The more ornate, the higher the nobleman's stature must be. An ordinary arras may conceal an earl, possibly even a duke, but an intricately detailed one … well, *that* requires a king or queen."

"Seriously? Why?"

"Because the audience knows that a play is a game of make-believe, and enjoys these little conventions. Part of the fun is guessing what will happen next. It's so much more engaging for them if they have some built-in clues. All theater — in fact, all *fiction* — is a game of concealment and revelation, of masking and unmasking, of seeming and being. But Marlowe's strength was in *punishing* the audience."

"Punishing?"

"You know: 'You're all bad little boys and girls for wanting to see this forbidden, wicked thing. So, I'm going to shove your noses in it until you cringe.' Even so, at times his poetry *soared*. It *ennobled* the audience, despite themselves."

The sun is beginning to set.

Henry asks, "So, can you get us out of this maze unassisted?"

Noah smiles and quickly leads him out. "I don't see what the Cecils found so puzzling."

"Neither did I."

CHAPTER 21

AFTER SUPPER THE NEXT DAY, Noah finds himself next to Henry again, walking in the moonlight to the cottage whose upstairs room is occupied by the slowly failing Sir Henry.

While Henry holds the lantern, tonight it's Noah who carries the basket. He glances back at the main house, and locates his own room just above the rear door. So dark and inviting. Though he might have remained there in comfort, he's chosen instead to visit Sir Henry. In truth, he has two reasons: to reveal his great secret, and to close a circle opened at the Tower so many years ago.

"It took me a fair amount of persuading," says Henry, "but my father ultimately agreed that you could accompany me tonight. I had to send one of the maids up to make him presentable, something he rarely bothers with any more. Bear in mind, when you see him, that he's in a great deal of pain. His temperament is not what it once was. And he spends so much time alone, albeit by his own choice, that he's lost a good deal of the social grace he once had."

"I'm not going there to judge him, Henry."

"I haven't a clue what your 'great secret' could possibly have to do with my father, but we'll do this your way."

Noah smiles. "Spoken like a true friend. I will do my best to avoid upsetting him. Indeed, I cannot imagine why he would become upset. And I trust you will not be disappointed. Tell me, is his pain caused solely by gout?"

"Solely? I'm not sure. But I believe it's preponderantly so. I have tried to persuade him to lose weight and stop drinking, but it's a hopeless cause."

"Have you given him any of Doctor Lopez's tablets?"

"I asked him if he'd take them, but he has a very low opinion of physicians. I told him they worked for me, but still he seems uninterested." At the side door to the cottage, Henry comes to a halt. "I always stop here a moment," he says, "to put myself in the proper frame of mind. He can be quite irascible sometimes, and I must remind myself of the respect he is due. Come on."

Henry knocks at the outside door. Although there's no answer, he opens it, and they enter. Closing the door behind them, he turns as if to speak, then evidently changes his mind and leads the way upstairs. He takes a deep breath and opens the door to his father's room. They step inside.

The room is illuminated this evening by two large candelabras, and one small candle in an uncovered glass case that apparently burns all night. At the opposite end of the room is a large bed with a carved and polished wooden headboard. In the bed sits an old man, nearly bald, propped up against several pillows, his broad shoulders supported by extra pillows at his sides. A blanket has been wrapped around him from his lower torso to his feet. His face, though unsmiling, seems alert and interested.

"Good evening, Father," says Henry.

"Good evening, Sir Henry," says Noah.

"Good evening to you both," replies Sir Henry in a voice much like that of young Henry, but more gruff and seasoned. He beckons to Noah. "Come over here, young man. Let me see your face in the light."

Hesitantly, Noah approaches Sir Henry, who reaches up with both hands to touch his face. After a moment's contemplation, Sir Henry moves Noah's head around to view it from various angles, as though he were a horse for sale.

"Nope, never saw you before in my life. You're a barrister?"

"Yes, sir. Queen's Bench."

Henry says: "Father, Noah is one of my oldest friends. He and I went on the same European tour with Sir Henry Savile many years ago."

"Intelligent fellow, Savile. A bit too chummy with the Essex crowd nowadays, if you ask me." He turns to Noah. "What were *you* doing on the tour?"

"I'd been reared in the home of Master Savile, and he brought me along to converse with the many Hebrew scholars whom he intended to consult along the way. It has always been a dream of his to rewrite the Geneva Bible to reflect the beauty of the original language. He has not done it yet, but hope remains."

"And you were fluent in Hebrew?"

"I had become so under Master Savile's tutelage, Sir Henry."

"Why have you come here this evening?"

"Well, sir," says Noah, "I was wondering whether you would recall the single occasion on which I saw you many years ago." He's more than a little embarrassed. What *is* he doing here? Why *is* he bothering this sick man?

"Sorry, I don't recall seeing you at all."

"You did not see *me*, Sir Henry."

"How long ago?"

"Oh, this was many years ago, sir. More than thirty."

"*Thirty?* Why, you cannot be much older than that *now*."

"I was but a small boy at the time."

"I see," says Sir Henry. "And what was the occasion?"

"It would not be memorable to you, sir. You were at the Tower of London."

"Well, you'll have to be a bit more specific, I was often at the Tower at that time."

"On this occasion, sir, although Queen Elizabeth had been named successor to Queen Mary, as yet she had not been crowned."

Sir Henry nods gravely. "She was under close watch at that time, for there were many papist assassins about." Sir Henry snaps his fingers. "I remember one time when she 'slipped the collar,' so to speak." His eyes fix on a point by his feet. "Cold autumn night. We must have placed a *dozen* guards about her chamber. *More*, perhaps. She was in the middle of undressing for bed, *surrounded* by ladies in waiting, when the next thing anyone knew ... *poof!* She was gone!" He chortles. "I finally found her in one of the outbuildings. A little cottage. I think it was used as a kitchen at the time." He turns to Noah. "Was that the occasion?"

Noah smiles to see the old man's total recall of the event. "It *was*, sir."

"And you were there?"

"Aye, sir. I watched you through a window as you discovered Her Majesty safe in the cottage."

Sir Henry nods. "But what would you have been doing there?"

"I'd been helping my uncle deliver groceries. He heard the shouts and went to offer assistance, leaving me alone. I was in the cottage but a moment when Her Majesty entered and quite surprised me. I'd no idea who she was."

"Your uncle? Come to think of it, I *do* recall the grocer asking if he could help. But he was wearing ... black ... " Sir Henry drifts off for a moment, and returns to Noah with a puzzled smile. "You're not that little *Jew-boy* she raved about, are you?"

Henry intercedes. "No, Father — "

Noah smiles, and tenderly pats Sir Henry's hand. "Yes, Sir Henry. I *am* that little Jew-boy."

Henry's eyes go wide. He's dumbstruck.

Sir Henry continues. "Oh, so that's who you are! Oh, my! She went on and *on* about you. Didn't stop talking about you for *days* after that! You were so bright, and so ... *English!* Tell me, Master ... "

"*Ames*, sir."

The old man cocks his head skeptically.

"That was not your *uncle's* name. He was a little Spaniard. *Añes*, wasn't it?"

"Right, sir. That *was* his name. Avram Añes, Queen's grocer."

"Tell me, young Master … Ames. How have you fared upon the path chosen for you by Her Majesty?"

"Well, sir. I attended Eton and Merton College, Oxford, where I was fortunate to meet your son Henry. As you can see, I am a barrister now."

"But, *family*, man. *That's* what's important. I have often wondered what happened to those few whom the Queen saw fit to favor, especially the one or two who were Jews."

"I am widowed, Sir Henry. I have a daughter. She is here at Billingbear now. Oh, but her Jewish heritage is a *secret*, sir. Please be sure not to give it away. She has married into the nobility."

"Hah!" laughs Old Sir Henry. "Good for her! Now *that* would open a few eyes, wouldn't it, Henry?"

"It would, Father. It would open *your* eyes to see her. She is a great beauty."

"Well, bring her here so I may look upon her, for heaven's sake. My waning life has few enough pleasures."

"I shall bring her tomorrow, Father."

Sir Henry turns back to Noah. "Henry tells me that Marie Miller has caught your eye. You seem to have an eye for beautiful women, but be careful. *This* one has a sharp sting!"

"So I have been told, Sir Henry, although I have seen no real evidence of it, as yet."

Sir Henry regards Noah suspiciously. "You're not a moneylender, are you?"

Noah smiles. "No, Sir Henry. I'm afraid I haven't the money to *lend*."

"Ah! England's only honest lawyer."

"Perhaps, sir."

"My son tells me that you may be in trouble with Essex."

Henry tries to interrupt. "Father — "

Sir Henry waves him off. "No, no. Let us not mince words. If this fellow is an adversary of Essex, I very much wish to help him, and so should *you*." He turns to Noah. "I do not know how the Queen could favor someone like Essex. Yet, she seems to have unbounded affection for that self-aggrandizing lout."

"Father!" says Henry.

"Oh, please, Henry. I am an old man. If I cannot speak my mind now, then I may never speak it at all. Master Ames, you are precisely the opposite of Essex. You were favored with a small royal grace and have turned out true to the Crown, where he has been lavished with every royal advantage, and yet refuses so much as to acknowledge the authority of the one who showers her bounty upon him."

He grumbles, "I'm not a believer in all that 'God's anointed on earth' nonsense. Some of these royals are no better than what the Italians call *onorevole*. Have you heard the term, Master Ames? It means 'honorable man,' but it is often used sardonically to mean quite the opposite. Some of the royals are simply *ruthless* in their pursuit of power and money."

"Father, *please!*" begs Henry.

"Don't you try to stop me from speaking my mind, Henry!" Old Sir Henry is becoming exercised. "My father was put to *death* by that monster Henry the Eighth. My father Edward Neville had been Esquire of the Body, and overseer of the king's entire household most of his life. He even *looked* like Henry, to the point where he was *taken* to be the king when he appeared at a masquerade dressed as him. And yet, when my father was overheard pointing out that there may have been a technical imperfection in Henry's title to the throne, Henry had him put to death. *My father!*"

"Father," interrupts Henry. "We've been through this countless times. Edward's careless talk had more weight behind it than mere idle chatter." Henry turns to Noah. "The 'technical imperfection' my esteemed father mentions was the supposed illegitimacy of King Henry's forbear Edward the Fourth, whose father may ... I say, *may* ... have been cuckolded by his wife, whose name happened to be Cecily *Neville*."

Sir Henry sits up with a bulldog expression. "This was *your grandfather*, Henry. So both their names were 'Neville.' So *what?*"

"Edward Neville and Cecily Neville *knew* each other, Father. Although she was much older, she survived until he was twenty-four years old. She may very well have *told* him of her faithlessness, which would have upset the entire line of succession, and would incidentally have placed Edward's own *sister* in the new line. Our Queen Elizabeth would never have become Queen."

Before his father can respond, he continues. "And, regardless of whether Cecily in fact confirmed her cuckoldry to Edward, people *suspected* that she had. When Edward said it, they *believed* it! And with good reason."

Sir Henry relaxes onto his pillows, and directs his closing remark to Noah. "And for *that*, they take a man's life!" he says with disgust.

Noah changes the subject. "Sir Henry, have you tried the new medicine for gout? It works very well, they say."

But Sir Henry is not quite over his outburst. "Physicians. Bunch of quacks!" He waves dismissively.

Noah decides to make a personal appeal. "Sir Henry, would you do me a great favor? Would you please *try* the medicine for a few days? You see ... " Noah allows his voice to trail off.

"Out with it, young man!"

"You see, in light of my problems with Essex, I am concerned for my daughter's welfare, and would truly appreciate it if I might entrust her to *your* care, in the event … there is any violence."

Sir Henry regards him skeptically. "And you believe that this medicine may enable me to assist in this?"

Noah nods grimly. "I've little doubt of it, sir."

Sir Henry equivocates. "Very well," he says, at last. "I shall take the medicine for her sake. Henry, please bring me some tomorrow."

"I shall, Father. You rest now." Henry touches his father comfortingly on the shoulder.

"I shall. I'm sorry I get so upset whenever … "

Noah says, "I can *well* understand, Sir Henry. Please try to rest."

Sir Henry closes his eyes, ready to nod off. Henry signals Noah to the door, and extinguishes every candle but the small one in the glass jar beside the bed. They creep out, descend the stairs, and depart quickly and quietly.

They've walked halfway back in silence when Henry stops in his tracks. Noah turns to him.

"Good lord," says Henry, "you are such a *fraud!*"

"How do I offend, Master Neville?"

"He's to take care of your daughter, is he? He can barely *sit up!*"

"Yes, Henry," says Noah, doing his best to look guilty. "And I shall have to carry on my conscience to my dying day that your father's pain was relieved in his final years by medicine I *defrauded* him into taking. Oh, how *foul* am I!" He beats his breast, though very lightly.

Henry laughs, and resumes walking. "Did you know that there was a rumor that my father was an illegitimate son of Henry the Eighth? In fact, it gained such currency that Queen Elizabeth, upon seeing my father, once stopped an entire procession to greet him, calling him aloud 'my brother Neville.'"

Noah laughs. "Do noblemen ever have relations with their *own* wives?"

"Not if they can help it!"

Noah regards Henry quizzically. "So *that's* the deception you're preoccupied about. The medicine. *Not* my being a Jew. Did you already know?"

Henry shakes his head. "You could have knocked me over with a feather. I hadn't a clue! I still don't know what to make of it. I've always thought of you as one of us, but that perception has been knocked off its axis, and is spinning out of control. And since the moment you said it, I've been trying to figure out how you've passed for one of us all this time. Without a hitch! Did you attend religious services every morning?"

Noah laughs. "As you would have known if *you* had ever attended," he says pointedly, "I assisted in the conduct of the service."

"Oh, that's right! I saw you there once."

"Must have been Christmas. *I* was there *all* the time."

"And you became a barrister, as well."

"There are some very important initials on the waivers in support of my admission to Oxford and the bar. Eton, too."

"I would imagine." A moment of silence ensues as Henry thinks deeply. "You know, Burghley *must* have known all this time, yet never said a word to me."

"I suppose he may have forgotten. The Exchequer finished paying my tuition and rooming bills a long time ago."

"Burghley *forget*?" Henry chortles. "Not likely. Knowing him as I do, I think you may be of interest to him *because* you're a Jew who has passed as one of us."

With this cryptic remark, they bid each other good night and go up to their separate rooms, Noah wondering just how much his world will soon change.

CHAPTER 22

A FEW DAYS LATER, Cheerful delivers three letters to Noah in his room. One is from Jonathan.

The other two weather-beaten letters were picked up by Cheerful from Noah's pigeonhole at Gray's Inn. They're from Marie. As they bear no outer markings disclosing which was sent first, he selects one at random and slits it open. It provides sparse news of the seas, and of Marie's arrival at Antwerp with young Stephen. Apparently, Stephen is being heartily accepted into the field of international shipping in place of his father.

As the letter is short, he rereads it a few times. It contains a few odd phrases. Instead of saying that one of the museums in Antwerp is unimpressive, it says "the museum did not walk well." It also contains a few careless transpositions, such as "this would not have made much anyhow difference," instead of "difference anyhow." Beneath each row of text is a thin broken line made with a straightedge, as may be used to guide one's handwriting.

The second letter is dated about a week later than the first. According to Cheerful, the two letters arrived at Gray's Inn less than a day apart, so the first must have been delayed by rough seas. By the time of Marie's second writing, she and Stephen had traveled north to Amsterdam. This letter contains a few archaic spellings, as well as a couple of transpositions, much like the first. And yet, she took the same care to keep her writing straight with a thin line under each row of text.

Before turning to Jonathan's letter, Noah refolds Marie's and stares out of the window, imagining the joy he would have felt traveling alongside her to all these foreign cities. It saddens him greatly that she wrote no *private* things. No oaths of love, no little intimacies, almost as though she expected her letters might be read by others, as indeed they might. Still, it might have mollified the misgivings he's harbored since their parting, if only she'd given him something to hold onto.

Then he remembers the guidelines and the strange wording. Could they be a cipher, a code? But she never mentioned she'd write in code, and she and Noah never agreed upon an encryption method. On the other hand, perhaps she happened upon information that she needed to convey secretly. If she'd become privy to secret matters, wouldn't she improvise a simple cipher, and expect him to recognize it? Perhaps her bizarre usages were adaptations of her *clear* message that were necessary for her to conceal a *secret* one.

He shuts the door quietly, sits at the desk, and withdraws pen, ink, and a single sheet of paper. He carefully examines the outside of Marie's letters. When he's satisfied they're devoid of markings, he turns them over and spreads them out on the desk, placing a small weight on each to prevent it from wafting away on the breeze. He examines them side by side.

He expects that the letters which are most heavily underscored will spell out a message. After deciphering a paragraph, he realizes that, although the cipher is not quite so simple, it is nearly so. The letters spell out something backwards, so he decides to begin the deciphering process from the end of the later letter and work his way backward all the way to the beginning of the earlier letter.

A few minutes later, he puts his pen down and reads the message. As he turns it over to consider its significance, there's a knock at the door. It's Henry. Noah places his fingers before his lips and ushers him inside, closing the door behind him.

"I was going to ask you about your correspondence," whispers Henry.

"Marie's letters were *encoded*," Noah whispers softly.

"What's the message?"

Noah hears a slight rustling in the hallway. He signals Henry to be silent, creeps to the door, and opens it quickly. Although no one's there, a sound comes from down the hall, like a slippered foot skittering along a polished floor. Ah, well, the culprit's escaped ... for now. He reenters and closes the door. "Whoever it was is gone," he says, and turns over the decrypted message for Henry to read silently:

MESSENGER TINOCO, BUT FOR DOC RL, NOT DON A

"Let's go for a private walk," says Henry. "But first, you must choose whether to keep these letters on your person *at all times*, or invoke the safer alternative of burning them. Do they hold sentimental value for you?"

"Oh, I suppose not," says Noah regretfully. In fact, he'd hoped to reread them many times, a practice in which he often indulges, but which has become a luxury in this new day of boundless suspicion.

"We'll burn them, then, but not in this room. Let's go elsewhere, perhaps out of doors, so no spy can be confident you've burned anything."

"Wait. I've not yet read *Jonathan's* letter."

"Go ahead. I'll wait. Just don't read it aloud."

Noah slits open Jonathan's letter, and goes to the window for better light.

Dear Noah:

You and I might deem it pointless to seek a pardon for someone who's been acquitted of a crime, as he may never be tried for it again. But less than a month — a little *month* — after being acquitted of murder, Ingram Frizer has been pardoned by the Queen for the death of Christopher Marlowe.

As Frizer's acquittal by the coroner might have prevented his later criminal prosecution for Marlowe's murder in any event, the purpose behind pardoning Frizer for Marlowe's murder must have been to complicate my investigation of Stephen Rodriguez's murder. While I have been trying to act the part of the intuitive Noah Ames during such gentleman's absence, I have been having a devil of a time coming up with an alternative explanation. Pray, if you run into Master Ames, please ask him to assist me in this!

Plague has receded. In case you cannot tell from this writing, I am frankly exhausted. In light of the Queen's pardon, there seems little point in my remaining in town for the next few weeks. (Trinity Term is already a shambles.) Look for me when least expected.

Hawk.

P.S. I've learned from Arthur that Lord Burghley and Sir Robert Cecil have been there with you since shortly after Marlowe's murder. Perhaps you might ask them whether Her Majesty is accustomed to signing pardons that they have not first approved. On the other hand, if they *did* approve this pardon, I hold out little hope of obtaining justice for Goodwife Rodriguez, as then everyone of importance is against us.

P.P.S. Doctor Lopez says that he has exhausted every means of determining whether Graves was poisoned, but that the results are inconclusive.

Noah hands the letter to Henry, who reads it silently, stacks up all three letters, as well as Noah's decryption sheet, folds the stack, and forcibly stuffs it securely in his pocket.

"Come on," says Henry. "Outside, where there are no ears. Doctor Lopez will be showing up in an hour or two, and we should digest this new information fully before he arrives."

Once outside, by force of habit Noah begins walking toward the maze, but Henry leads him another way that will keep them in wide open spaces, avoiding any hedgerows or other plantings that might conceal a spy. When they reach a secluded spot, Henry sets the letters ablaze.

"As I mentioned," says Noah, "Marie formerly believed that her ships had carried letters to and from the Netherlands at the request of Doctor Lopez, acting on behalf of Don Antonio. Now she tells us that Lopez was in fact acting on his own behalf. However, I am quite certain of two things. One, I never mentioned Tinoco to her by name, as I had no clue he was *anyone's* messenger. As far as I knew, he was simply another murderous associate of Skeres' at the Boar's Head. So, she discovered Tinoco's name independently of me. Two, she has also somehow discovered that Lopez has been corresponding with the Netherlands, or perhaps Spain, *on his own behalf.*"

Henry nods. "As you know from our discussions, that is entirely in keeping with his character."

"So it appears. The night of the Boar's Head fiasco, Graves was likely murdered, and Jonathan very *nearly* murdered because they heard of Tinoco's attempt to secure Perez's murder in exchange for a red jewel. We can say with confidence, then, that by that night the secrecy of Tinoco's mission was *already* of such importance to Essex that Skeres knew, without consulting Essex further, that the immediate suppression of such information was absolutely essential."

"Yes, but what does it add to know Lopez was dealing for himself?" asks Henry.

"That's it!" says Noah. "Don't you see? Essex was not investigating Don Antonio's correspondence with the Netherlands. He was investigating *Doctor Lopez, possibly his participation in the plot to murder Perez!*"

"So," Henry observes, "even *before* the incident at the Boar's Head, Essex had instructed Skeres to ensure by any means necessary — even murder — that no one should learn of his secret investigation of Lopez. But *whose* knowledge of the Lopez investigation would be so damaging to Essex that he would suppress it by murder?"

"Whose, indeed," says Noah, "but that of the two most powerful men in England? And they're both here at Billingbear. The Cecils! We must broach this with them."

"All right," says Henry, "but what of Jonathan's letter?"

"What do *you* think of that?" asks Noah.

"I expect that Essex placed the pardon before the Queen, and she signed it without consulting the Cecils. Very disturbing. Let's go and tell them. I see no advantage in withholding news of the pardon from them even for a moment, as it's already publicly known. Perhaps we'll mention Tinoco later on. Let's wait and see about that."

"Agreed."

*   *   *

They find the Cecils at work in the spare upstairs room that Henry has set aside for them. The doors and windows are wide open, and a steady breeze passes through. As the Cecils are ostensibly on summer holiday, they're dressed far more casually than is their habit at court, and they've pared down their pool of secretaries to a mere two. Even with the reduced workload, stacks of papers are strewn about the room, covering nearly every surface. In a lighthearted concession to their holiday, atop each pile sits a colorful, highly polished stone they've found somewhere on the Billingbear grounds, serving as a paperweight.

Lord Burghley sees their approach and interrupts his dictation. "Gentlemen, how are you on this fine day?"

"Very well," replies Henry, unsmiling. "And you?"

"Also well. You seem preoccupied," observes Burghley.

"Would you two gentlemen be available to walk with us briefly outside? We should like to discuss one or two things with you."

Burghley looks to Sir Robert for any objection.

Sir Robert asks, "Would it be just as well for you to speak with us here in this room? Messieurs Cranch and Johnson have *more* than earned a break."

Henry nods.

"Gentlemen," says Sir Robert to the secretaries, as he ushers them out of the door, "we'll see you at dinner." He shuts the door firmly behind them.

Henry begins. "You have heard that Marlowe's killer has been pardoned by Her Majesty?"

Burghley and Sir Robert gape at each other in horror. There's no feigning *that* look. Sir Robert begins pacing, staring sternly at the floor.

"We've heard no such thing, Master Henry," replies Burghley. "Oh, my! This *does* cast a pall on things, does it not?"

Noah asks, "Upon whose advice would Her Majesty sign such a pardon, if not yours?"

"It can *only* be Essex," says Sir Robert. "I cannot believe he would undercut us so brazenly." He turns hesitantly to Noah. "Master Ames, I hope it is understood that you are not at liberty to repeat anything you hear from us. It would be not only a breach of your honor as a gentleman, but a crime against Her Majesty. You understand this?"

Noah is taken aback to be so forewarned. "I *do* understand."

Henry looks at Noah. "That must be what Essex was doing at Windsor Castle yesterday morning." He turns to Burghley. "Master Ames and I went riding in Windsor Park yesterday morning just before breakfast, and saw a train dressed in Essex's livery enter the castle gate. By the pennant, Her Majesty was in residence. He must have got her to sign the pardon then and there."

Satisfied that it was not the Cecils who approved the pardon, Noah wishes to broaden their report. "May I, Master Henry?"

Henry nods. "Please do."

"Gentlemen, we believe that Lord Essex has been secretly investigating Doctor Lopez's dealings in the Netherlands and possibly Spain for some time. At first, I thought Essex was investigating Lopez simply to assure himself of Lopez's loyalty as a former Walsingham agent. Then, it appeared that he was investigating Don Antonio's correspondence with the Netherlands. But I have only today received information that it is Lopez's *own* contacts with the Netherlands that are of interest to Essex.

"In addition, we have begun to assemble some facts we've learned from disparate sources. It appears that Lopez's messenger to the Netherlands is a Spaniard named 'Tinoco,' and that this Tinoco may somehow be involved in a plot to poison a visitor to the English court, one 'Perez,' whom I met briefly at Lord Essex's party the day before arriving here. Tinoco has been seen with Nicholas Skeres, one of Lord Essex's attendants, and apparently has been attempting to arrange the poisoning of Perez in exchange for a ruby."

The Cecils seem more perplexed by Noah's having assembled these disparate facts than by the facts themselves. In fact, his comments appear to strike them more as confirmation of existing suspicions than as news.

"He is making his move, Father," says Sir Robert. "This is about disgracing us, so that he can secure the Attorney Generalship for one of the Bacons."

"Slow down, Robert," says Burghley. "Master Ames, what sense do you make of all this?"

It's Noah's turn to be perplexed, and he does something he's rarely done in the presence of anyone in a position of authority. He reasons aloud. "Honestly, m'lord. Although I cannot tell whether this is a plot by Essex, or by Lopez, or whether those two are working *with* or *against* each other, this intrigue seems to be entirely separate from the one involving Essex's attempt to take over Walsingham's spy network. Indeed, it was only Lopez's involvement in both intrigues that made the two seem one."

Sir Robert looks to his father. "What have we to say to *that*, Father?"

Burghley strokes his beard. "Tell me, Master Ames. What is the feeling at the Inns of Court concerning Francis Bacon for Attorney General?"

Noah is amazed at the revolutionary pace at which the subject has been changed. Or has it? "Essex has made no bones about wanting that office filled by any Bacon he can get," he says. "He has visited them several times at Gray's Inn, rather ostentatiously. A few weeks ago, he made a theatrical show of picking them up at the inn, and giving them a lift to Westminster as a conspicuous part of his retinue."

"Do you have a sense how the barristers generally feel about that?"

"The Bacons are more feared than liked. Anthony is the more respected of the two, but he is often ill with stones. I would not wish such pain on a dog. Francis is generally believed to be the more intelligent of the two, but he is quite inexperienced in court."

"And if it is a choice between Francis and *your* candidate?"

"*My* candidate?"

Burghley smiles. "Yes, your esteemed competitor at loggats."

"Oh! Actually, I hadn't even thought of Coke for that position, as I believe he's about to be appointed Solicitor General, which is regarded as being just one step *beneath* Attorney General."

"Oh, he's *already* Solicitor General," says Burghley. "Her Majesty signed the papers some days ago."

"Well, then, m'lord, if it's Francis Bacon or Coke, it's Coke, and by a long shot. Not only has Francis never won — or even *played* — a round at 'loggats,' but he is quite young to aspire to be Attorney General right now."

Burghley shoots a commiserative glance at Sir Robert. "Unfortunately, we have one or two candidates of our *own* for senior positions who are not quite as seasoned as they might be." Evidently, as Henry suggested weeks ago, young Robert is being groomed to fill his father's position upon retirement.

"I see," says Noah. "Well, I have additional reservations about Francis Bacon."

"Tut — " says Henry, raising his hand, then dropping it. He clearly wishes Noah had stopped before saying that, but it's too late.

"What *is* it, Master Ames?" asks Burghley.

Henry throws up his hands in consternation. "Well, you've started it now, Ames. Go ahead. Just be careful to distinguish known fact from suspicion."

"Well, I believe — and others at Gray's Inn also believe — that Francis Bacon was … intimately involved with Christopher Marlowe, whom we suspect was murdered by the same person who murdered Stephen Rodriguez at The Rose — "

Burghley turns to Sir Robert. "Rodriguez? Is that the Rodriguez who married Southampton's sister?"

Sir Robert interrupts hesitantly. "Begging your pardon, Father, I expect that your question inadvertently conflates two persons into one. The earl's sister 'Mary' is quite plain. The beautiful one who married Rodriguez is named '*Marie*,' and she is *not* the earl's sister. At least, not his *full* sister."

Noah's head swims. Sir Robert is the second knowledgeable person to suggest openly that Southampton's father was also Marie's! Why has he neglected to investigate whether Marie is more involved in this whole Essex affair than he knows? Has he been blinded by beauty? Although he supposes that he deserves whatever comes his way on account of his own blindness, he prays that his neglect will not redound to the detriment of Jonathan, or any other innocent.

Burghley says: "Permit me to stop you right there, Master Ames, as to continue would drag you much deeper into this affair than you might wish to find yourself. Suffice it to say at this point that the ... connections ... you have detected between the Marlowe murder and the murder at The Rose are already the subject of speculation at court. There may well be one mind behind both murders, and the Lopez investigation, as well. And *all* those affairs may in turn be related to the Attorney General contest. That is all we really should discuss with you about the matter now." He looks sheepishly at Sir Robert and Henry. "Actually, it's considerably more than we'd planned."

Noah bows. "Gentlemen, I am at Her Majesty's service, and yours, at *any* time. My loyalties are quite undivided in this."

Burghley nods. "We have every confidence that such is the case, Master Ames, or we would not have discussed these matters with you at all."

Walker knocks at the door and opens it unbidden a moment later. He sticks his head in, and curtly bows three times in rapid succession. "Gentlemen, Doctor Lopez has arrived." As he's about to close the door, Henry grabs it and follows him down the hall, talking all the while.

Noah is left in awkward silence with the Cecils, and decides to make the most of it in a way they'll remember. He earnestly looks each of them in the eye in turn. "Please do not *hesitate*, gentlemen." He bows low, walks out through the open door, and closes it behind him.

* * *

Dinner, which consists of a summer version of mince pie with garden vegetables, passes in small talk. The wine flows freely, and even Henry overindulges in a manner that has, for him, become rather the exception than the rule. Afterwards, Mistress Anne leads Burghley, Sir Robert, Henry, Noah, and Doctor Lopez up to the parlor for cognac, smiling at each of them as she leaves. She closes the double doors elegantly on her way out.

Doctor Lopez has already had well more than two full bottles of wine, which seems rather to have agitated than relaxed him. He enters the parlor unsteady on his feet, and badly out of breath from climbing a single flight of stairs. Henry pours a small cognac for Burghley, Sir Robert, Noah, and himself, but a full goblet for Lopez.

"Oh, *thank* you, Master Neville!" Lopez slurs. "You are too generous."

"Not at all, Doctor Lopez. Thank you for coming all this way to examine my father."

"Oh, it's my pleasure, Master Neville. I only hope that I am able to help him."

"So," says Burghley, full of bonhomie, "how have things been going for you down in Creechurch? Or are you staying at Mountjoy's full time now?"

Lopez swallows another indelicate swig of cognac, and speaks entirely too loudly. "I spend my time in each place about equally. Although in Holborn, I have a little, you know … " His hand signals equivocation, suggesting a sexual dalliance.

"Oh, a *swordsman*, are we?" asks Henry. "I might have known."

"Well," replies Lopez, "nothing so indiscriminate as might end me up with hollow bones and lunacy like … Lord Essex."

Noah looks to Burghley and Sir Robert, both of whom stand behind Lopez, outside his field of vision. They're horrified. This is Essex's *physician* talking unreservedly about his having a venereal disease, an egregious breach of the confidential relationship between doctor and patient. And, what's worse, Lopez has been physician for each of the Cecils and even the *Queen*! What might he reveal about *them* under the influence of spirits?

Yet Burghley sees an opportunity he cannot decline. Noah cannot help but admire how he avoids addressing Lopez in a manner reminding him of his professional status. "Surely, Roderigo, you are not saying that Lord Essex suffers from the French disease!"

"Am I not!" Lopez replies. "Tell me, do you think it the behavior of a man in control of his faculties to disobey the Queen's express command to remain in England, out of harm's way?"

"Oh, but surely, Roderigo, there are reasons other than madness for such disobedience."

"Are there? I can think of none." Lopez looks at Henry and points to his cognac. "This is *very* good, you know. *Very* good." He takes another large swig, and gazes at an indeterminate point on the wall. His speech is so slurred that it's becoming difficult to make out. "Is it 'normal' for an earl to bang on the gates of Lisbon with his fists, challenging an entire city to individual combat in defense of the Queen's honor ... which, to *my* knowledge, had never been besmirched by said city? I don't think so." His voice begins to subside, as though his energy is nearly spent and his eyelids weigh heavy. "No, this is rather indicative of his physical and mental condition. Why, once ... " He drifts off. His eyes shut. In a moment, he snores loudly.

Henry mutters, "And *he* says *I* shouldn't drink."

Ordinarily, Noah would expect people to ignore such drunken talk by a professional man, and to take what he's said with a grain of salt. But what Lopez said is truly reprehensible, even if some of it might be turned to the Cecils' advantage.

Henry opens the double doors, where Walker stands ready with another manservant to carry Lopez to bed. Walker takes Lopez's shoulders and the other man his feet. Together, they lift him up and carry him out, feet first.

Henry closes the doors and sits down again. "I heard that Lopez had said such things in a drunken state before," he says, "but I wanted to be certain."

"Who was his audience last time?" asks Sir Robert.

"Don Antonio and his son. They immediately ran to Essex and told him about it."

Noah speculates. "*That's* enough for Essex to hold a grudge against Lopez."

Burghley shakes his head. "But not enough to convict him of a crime. No, when Essex gets the goods on Lopez, it will be for much more than a besotted rant. Heaven help him. And I fear Essex's real target will not be Lopez at all."

"Who will it be?" asks Noah.

"Robert and I." Burghley shakes his head. "I am sorry, Robert. Sorry, Master Neville. But there is nothing for it; Master Ames might as well know. Master Ames, I'm about tell you something that Lord Essex believes about his own ancestry."

Noah nods.

"We have no way of knowing whether what I'm about to say is true or not," says Burghley, "but both Her Majesty and Essex believe it. And the information evidently came down to them from separate sources." He pauses before revealing his great secret. "Her Majesty's father was Lord Essex's great-grandfather."

Noah is perplexed. "Mary Boleyn had an illegitimate child by Henry the Eighth?"

Burghley nods. "As *they* both believe it, it might as well be true. The child was Catherine Carey, whose eldest daughter was Lettice Knollys, who in turn gave birth to Lord Essex."

"So, since his youth," says Noah contemplatively, "Essex has been fired with the belief that the blood of the English lion courses through his veins." Now he's even *more* perplexed. "But what has this to do with what we've been discussing?"

Lord Burghley nods indulgently. "Patience, and you shall soon see. Until a few months ago, Essex thought Lopez was *his* man. It was incredibly stupid of him. Essex, more than anyone, should have known that Lopez was, is, and ever shall be for sale, not merely to the *highest* bidder, but to *every* bidder. Lopez never got over losing his fortune in the failed English Armada expedition.

"For a long time, Essex thought himself to be the sole recipient of all Lopez's fresh intelligence from Spain and the Netherlands, and I'm sure he was paying commensurately for it. But whenever Lopez would come off a ship, or receive new intelligence, we Cecils were always the first to know. It went on like that for years, with Essex none the wiser, but none the worse for it, really.

"Then, one day, some time ago, Essex made a grand show of bringing fresh intelligence to the Queen. When he presented it to her, she laughed and said she'd known it for months. He's not a stupid man, and it didn't take him long to realize she could only have got it from us, and that *we* could only have got it from Lopez."

"So, it *is* Lopez he's after," says Noah.

Burghley smiles indulgently, and shakes his head. He resumes his tale in the most melancholy voice. "No. That is not the way Essex thinks. Once he knew that Lopez was mainly *our* man, he realized that by discrediting Lopez, he could discredit us. With *us* discredited, he could get Bacon as Attorney General and, with that, control of the Crown's criminal prosecutions. With control of prosecutions, he can be rid of us for good and all.

"Her Majesty has no heir. So, with *us* gone, there will be but an aging and childless woman between Essex … and the Crown."

CHAPTER 23

THE REMAINDER OF THE SUMMER passes with little tribulation. In late June, there's a Midsummer's Eve celebration at Billingbear that attracts every country nobleman and merchant within twenty miles. Four families travel from as far away as York, two from Paris, and one from Edinburgh, in Scotland.

Five earls are in attendance at different times, although neither Essex nor Southampton makes an appearance, for which absences Noah and the Cecils are especially grateful. Noah remains at a complete loss to think what he'd say to Southampton about his possible half sister Marie, if she were to come up in conversation.

Jessica is in her splendor at the Midsummer celebration, and all the rest of the summer. As she regards it as her womanly duty never to appear publicly in the same outfit more than once, it takes her less than three weeks to run through every item of clothing she packed in her gargantuan trunk. When that supply is exhausted, she adopts the costly expedient of having the Nevilles' seamstresses fashion her new clothing on a nearly continuous basis.

Although the seamstresses are well housed and well paid by the Nevilles, such personal services are performed for *visitors* only as a courtesy by the staff, so it all ends up costing Noah a small fortune in gratuities, called "vails." He ends up wishing Jessica had brought a far *bigger* trunk. Her repeating refrain of "*see?*" reverberates cruelly in his mind.

On two separate occasions that summer, there are many-colored fireworks. On the latter occasion, Billingbear entertains a walloping demonstration of bright brass cannon manufactured by the Nevilles at the Gresham works, and Henry appears in a cannoneer's uniform, igniting the long fuse on the opening cannon himself. He makes quite a sight covering his ears and running away before it goes off.

Late-summer news is that the plague has passed for the time being, and it's reasonably safe to return to London. Reliable solicitors and attorneys have brought Noah a goodly number of interesting and lucrative cases for Michaelmas Term. Jessica has received so many social invitations for the autumn season that she needs to borrow two large portfolios from Mistress Anne merely to transport them back to London for sorting out.

Yet, as the end of August inevitably rolls around, and with it the day when Noah and Jessica will have to say goodbye to Billingbear, a wistful sadness pervades their thoughts. Although there is undeniably much of interest to be done at home, both Noah and Jessica know that nothing can compare to their time at Billingbear, and that a wholly unexpected experience such as this summer's can never truly be repeated.

In the house, Noah and Jessica bid goodbye to Mistress Anne and her children, the Cecils having left two weeks earlier to attend to Her Majesty's affairs. Noah is careful to leave each of the servants a vail large enough to say that he or she is much appreciated. Although, to be sure, his gratuities cannot approach the size of many left by the wealthy, they're nevertheless more than he can comfortably afford.

The stableman brings Jessica's open cart around. It's been cleaned and polished so well as to be unrecognizable as the one they arrived in. Noah's initial confusion is compounded by the replacement of Jessica's horses with different ones, much younger and larger.

Noah looks inquiringly at Henry. "Whose horses are these?"

"They're *yours*. I hope you don't mind, but I've exchanged them for the two you brought up here, who are now safely out to pasture. My stableman says that one of them is actually good for breeding, so we're putting him to the most pleasurable kind of work. Neither of them has very much time remaining on earth, I'm sorry to say."

"Henry, you're joking! Why, I could *never* accept — "

Henry laughs. "Of *course* you could. And here's someone I know you could *never* turn down."

As Noah turns to look, Bucklebury is led out, the black beauty he's ridden many times this summer through Windsor Forest. All saddled and ready to go.

Noah turns to Henry, gratitude welling up in his breast. "I — I don't know what to say to such generosity."

"Well, a simple 'thank you' might do."

"'Thank you?'" Noah seizes Henry's hand and shakes it energetically. "*Thank you* so much, my good friend!"

Jessica, who's overheard all this sitting in the driver's seat of the open cart, shouts: "Thank you, Uncle Henry!"

Henry shouts back: "You're both most welcome! Thank you for being such wonderful guests." He leans in to Noah, and speaks in hushed tones. "I expect that, before all is said and done, you'll *need* these horses more than you know. Especially Bucklebury. So, take good care of them."

A frisson of fear rides up Noah's spine. Abandoning the temporary haven of Billingbear, he feels more uneasy than ever, as though disturbed parts of his mind have returned to their highest state of vigilance.

"I shall take the best *imaginable* care of them, Master Henry. And thank you again."

As Noah and Jessica depart through the gate, Henry waves to them and they wave in return. Once through the gate, Noah's stomach begins to churn. Just as he begins to contemplate that he'll be unable to offer Jessica any real protection on the upcoming journey, five young horsemen sidle up to them.

It's Jonathan and the four jesters.

"Well, bless my soul," says Jonathan in his best imitation of a North London accent, "if it ain't that Ames fella from the courthouse!"

"What are *you* all doing here?" Noah demands sternly, though in truth he's never been so glad to see anyone.

"We thought we'd escort you home," says Jonathan.

Noah suddenly realizes each of them is armed with a full-length sword, and all but the Bennett twins are wearing pistols. "Expecting company?" he inquires.

"Always," replies Jonathan jovially. "But, arming ourselves like this is mostly intended to avoid company altogether. Let's enjoy the ride." He tips his hat to Jessica, with whom he seems quite smitten.

"Why, Master Hawking," she says, "you look most dashing."

He bows in the saddle. "And may I say, Lady Burlington, that you are the loveliest thing your humble servant has seen since you left London?"

Jessica pretends to give it some thought. "I suppose you may say that. Yes," she decides, "you may say that whenever you wish."

Jonathan smiles, and leads the way to the road.

As they turn east toward London, with the late morning sun reaching its zenith, their heads and shoulders begin to overheat, disinclining them to much conversation. Noah shakes off his torpor to pull Bucklebury up alongside Jonathan.

"Any news of note?" asks Noah.

Jonathan shrugs. "Not much about the Essex affair since early July. Since then, I've even taken a holiday of my own. I've begun broadening my education beyond weapons, to include such things as medicines and poisons."

Noah raises an eyebrow. "Idle reading?"

Jonathan laughs. "Hardly. As the earl has Walsingham's whole network at his disposal, he has numerous ways of getting at people. I just want to stay a step or two ahead of him. Your Doctor Lopez has been one of my best sources, incidentally."

"Indeed?"

"Oh, yes. Not just of reading material, either. *Supplies*, as well. He put me in touch with an apothecary in London, and another in Spain."

"Supplies? Are you planning on becoming a physician? Or a *poisoner*?"

"Neither," sniffs Jonathan. "Rather, a defender of myself and a more senior barrister ... and his lovely daughter."

"Well, you needn't go polluting your brain with such nonsense on our account."

Jonathan shrugs off Noah's comment. "I'm studying the effects of certain drugs on dogs and horses."

"Which drugs?" asks Noah.

"Laudanum, and other calmatives. Small quantities of foxglove derivatives, which are really toxic only in larger amounts. It may someday help me spot another case of poisoning, so that I can steer my investigators in that direction. Also ... laxatives."

Noah laughs. *"Laxatives*? Why?"

"No reason, except that Lopez is so knowledgeable about them, his enthusiasm is really quite contagious. You know, much of his medical practice is devoted to such ... problems."

"So I have heard. You'll be well-advised to keep such things away from *these* horses, please."

"Sacred, I assure you."

"How is your schedule shaping up for Michaelmas Term?" asks Noah.

"Not bad, really. I was already working up a fairly full caseload before I left town a few weeks ago. I imagine there'll be a few more things waiting for me at Gray's Inn. And yours? How is *your* autumn looking?"

"Very busy. I must confess, however, that I cannot *wait* for Marie to return."

"I can imagine. When is that promised?"

"'As soon as ... '"

"'God and the seas allow.' Yes, I know, but what is her best estimate?"

"October first."

"So, she shall arrive at the beginning of the new term." Jonathan smirks. "You'll have your hands full."

"I'll ignore that, young man."

* * *

When Noah discovers that Marie and Stephen will arrive at Dover a full week earlier than expected, he's elated. The same winds that initially drove them north away from the Continent have swiftly driven them north to

England, and home. The evening before their expected arrival, he makes sure that his note will be awaiting Marie when they arrive. It's quite prim, requesting leave to pay a call at her earliest convenience.

The following morning, he keeps vigil from the window of his room at Gray's, watching High Holborn for a carriage large enough to hold two passengers with heavy luggage. Around nine o'clock, he spots one moving unhurriedly toward Marie's house and out of sight.

While he expects she's received many letters seeking her immediate attention, he'd hoped that his would wend its way to the front of the queue. Yet, dinner comes and goes with nary a word. Though he considers walking nonchalantly past her house, his note has made it impossible for him to convincingly feign surprise at their early arrival. No, Marie would not like the appearance fostered by a surprise visit, so he resolves to wait.

Finally, at four, a boy arrives with a brief note from Marie requesting the pleasure of his company at dinner the following day. The following day! He thinks of all the nights he's lain awake pining for her return. And now, to have his company dispensed with entirely on the day of her arrival? Evidently, his deepest feelings are no longer reciprocated by Marie, if they ever were, and he can't help but wonder whether she's found someone else. Perhaps someone she's known a long time, who's been waiting year after year for his opportunity to pounce. His blood boils.

Oh, why did he not take selfish advantage that first evening and make her his bedmate? Why did he take matters so slowly? Perhaps she doubts his ardency, or his self-confidence. And now all is lost. He passes a restless night, and braces himself for the worst.

Next day, he climbs the steps at Marie's house right on schedule — not early, which would betray his eagerness, yet not late, which might appear uncaring. He's admitted by a servant, and escorted to the upstairs parlor to await the lady of the house. In due time, she appears. Though her smile is sincere, it's reserved, as well.

"Master Ames," she says pertly. "And how have you been these past months?"

Her undeniably pleasant, but off-putting, primness strikes him as a slap in the face. She might as well have stuck a dagger into his heart. Yet, what choice has he but to play along? Better that than to be excluded from her company, which prospect does not bear contemplation.

"I have been well, madam. I was glad to learn from your correspondence that Master Rodriguez has been well received by his late father's business associates. And I was most grateful for the additional information you so kindly provided."

She nods. "I trust you've given thought to the conversation we shared immediately prior to my departure?"

Basking in the glow of her shapely face and form, he hasn't a clue which conversation she's talking about. "I believe I have mulled over every conversation you and I have ever had, the memories of which have lent me great support during your overlong absence."

She regards him skeptically, but he's sure she knows perfectly well that he has no idea which conversation she means. *Which* blasted conversation? The one about mutual trust? She asked whether he was being honest and forthright, but he's *still* never lied to her. That can't be it.

She leads him down to dinner with Stephen and the other children. Although he's greeted by the children as an old friend, Marie's coolness is evident, and he has barely any appetite.

Yet, when they are again alone and she bids him goodbye, she smiles warmly and says, "I hope that I shall ever be most deserving of your trust, Master Ames."

"And I of yours," he says. He bows, and leaves on foot for Gray's with a great deal to ponder. He vows to regain her full affection. *But how?*

* * *

It's mid-October, and the term is in full swing. The air is becoming crisp again, especially in the evening, and the leaves have begun to change their color.

Noah has not yet hinted at eventual marriage with Marie, as the reserve she exhibited upon her return from the Netherlands has never quite dissipated, and, in his lowest moods, he fears she'll turn him down. Besides, he rationalizes, it would be inappropriate to broach the subject foursquare until a year has passed since her husband's death.

Although Jessica is still favorably disposed toward young Stephen, her social schedule has left her with little time to spare for him. He seems quite crestfallen, at a loss for a way to compete with men of higher rank who shower attention and endless gifts upon her. Jessica has confided in Noah that she's decided to remain unattached for a time. Although Noah has tried to convey this to Stephen in every way possible that will not entail a breach of confidence, Stephen has been little comforted.

One evening around sunset, Noah shuffles through the dead leaves, returning to Gray's Inn on foot after a successful trial at Westminster. As he approaches the inn, at first he's alarmed to see a candle burning in his own window, but quickly realizes that someone hostile wouldn't have lit a candle that might signal his presence.

Jonathan's door is closed, which can only mean he's out. Noah passes by, and goes upstairs. Before opening the door to his own apartment, he knocks quietly and steps back out of the doorway, lest anyone leap out at him.

"Who's there?" asks a muffled Henry.

Noah goes inside. Henry's clothing is spread about the room, as though he's packing.

"Leaving so soon?" asks Noah.

Henry is folding clothing in the room he used earlier in the year. He peers around the door at Noah. "Leaving? I just *got* here."

"Oh, it looks like you're packing to travel."

"Very astute," says Henry. "In fact, I must appear at Westminster tomorrow, in Parliament. I'll be meeting Burghley and Robert immediately afterwards. We're going to Windsor in the evening, to meet with Her Majesty the following morning."

"Well, it's nice to know I'm living in your closet."

Henry snickers. "No time for mirth, Noah. You know why I'm going up there."

"No, why?"

"It's about the earl's great matter."

"The Attorney Generalship?"

"Yes. There's been a change. This is all secret, yes?"

"Of course."

"Anthony Bacon is too ill for the job. He was supposed to go up to Windsor on October the ninth, a week or so ago, but he was in so much pain from the kidney stones that he couldn't even get into the carriage to go. A few days later, though he managed to get *into* the carriage, he had to turn back. In fact, he couldn't even go home. Instead, he went straight to his physician, Parmant, at Eton. Poor man."

"So, it's Coke for Attorney General?"

"Remains to be seen. Essex went up that Saturday and apologized profusely to the Queen. You'll never guess whom he's pushing for now."

"Francis, of course."

"You're shocked, I see," says Henry drearily.

"And Her Majesty is seeking *your* advice, as well?"

"Mainly indirectly, through Burghley. The Cecils are quite at a loss as to how to win her over to Coke."

"How about the other matter?"

"Lopez? The more the rivalry heats up for Attorney General, the more you'll see Essex putting the screws to Lopez."

"I've no doubt."

"It's unfortunate that the Cecils are Lopez's only champions, as they need to appear impartial in the matter."

*   *   *

At Christmas, Jessica graces a party attended by the most eligible noblemen in London, while Noah goes to Marie's house for a traditional supper of Christmas goose and pudding. All the Rodriguez children are there. Stephen pokes at his food and, after a respectful interval, asks to be excused. Marie allows him to go upstairs to his room.

"He's been despondent for weeks," she tells Noah privately. "I'm afraid Jessica has turned away."

After dessert, the young children are put to bed, although with all the excitement and anticipation about the gifts they'll find the next morning, they take longer than usual to drop off.

After an hour or so, Noah accompanies Marie to a small windowless room on the second story that he's never seen used. It's lined with oak, and appears to be furnished as a private study. He sees that Marie has given his candlestick pride of place in this most intimate room. With his encouragement, she lights a candle mourning her deceased husband on the occasion of Christmas. After a few minutes' silence watching the candle flicker gently, they leave the room together.

Marie is about to lock the door behind them when they hear a knock downstairs. "Who could be calling at this hour?" she wonders aloud.

Noah descends the stairs to find out. When he opens the front door, standing in the early snow is a very worried, very old-looking Doctor Lopez, who appears to have left home without his coat. Although his rooms at Mountjoy's are only a stone's throw from Marie's house, the snow has already accumulated on his shoulders, and frosts his hair and mustache.

"Oh, Master Ames, I am so relieved to find you here! I'm afraid I interrupted the revels at Gray's Inn so that I might prevail upon the residents to tell me where you could be found. I hope you will forgive me ... and them." He looks positively ashen. Noah nods reassuringly.

Marie peers down from the top of the stairs. "Won't you come in, Doctor Lopez?"

"Thank you, madam," he replies, bowing. He steps into the vestibule, but will go no further into the house. "I will detain Master Ames for only a moment," he says. Marie, who'd been about to come down, takes this as a request to be left alone with Noah, and returns to the upstairs parlor.

"What's the matter, Roderigo?" asks Noah. "What's happened?"

Lopez seems to equivocate about whether to reply, and apparently decides against it. "I have only one question, sir."

"All right, but I have no books here to help me find the answer. You *know* that."

"Yes, sir, and I would not disturb you with work on the evening of this great feast, in any event. But I *must* ask you: Can an ambassador of a foreign power be tried in an English criminal court?"

Noah doesn't know why, but he's shocked by the question. Certainly, he should long have expected it. But Lopez's downfall has always been something that *might* happen. Only *eventually*. Never something that will *definitely* happen. Never *right now*.

"Well, Doctor Lopez, I will give you the best answer I can recall from my legal training, but I beg you not to rely on it. As best I remember, an ambassador of a foreign power present in England at the request of his Sovereign *cannot* be tried in an English criminal court."

As the old man looks so relieved, Noah regrets having to finish the thought. "However," he resumes, "the privilege against prosecution belongs not to the ambassador, but to his Sovereign. If the Sovereign consents to the prosecution in a writing to the Queen, or if he informs the Queen in writing that the ambassadorship has come to a definite end, then the ambassador *can* be criminally tried here. Do you wish to come see me at Gray's tomorrow morning? You can tell me what's happened, and we can discuss this thoroughly."

Lopez appears to be searching his memory, the worry having returned to his gray face. "That will not be necessary, Master Ames. I'm sure I am unduly concerned about nothing. That would be just like me. Good evening. Please pay my respects to Goodwife Rodriguez." He smiles weakly, stumbles out into the snow, and turns down High Holborn back toward his residence at Mountjoy's Inn.

Noah leans through the doorway, peering after him into the night, and his heart sinks. Where once strutted a proud physician, a coatless old man now drifts along a path of treacherous sleet, a lone and soundless figure buffeted by a menacing blizzard.

Just as the snow seems about to block Noah's view, the muffled clop of horses' hooves striking snowy pavement approaches from the same direction. A covered coach flanked by two horsemen comes to a halt athwart Lopez's path. Noah races out of the door toward him, but, before he can reach him, one of the horsemen dismounts, and the coach door is flung open from inside. Noah freezes in place.

"Suspicion of high treason," says the horseman, in response to a mumbled question from Lopez. The horseman roughly escorts the old man into the coach, slams the door behind him, receives softly spoken instructions from inside the coach, and remounts.

The carriage and horsemen clop slowly toward Noah, and, to his amazement, stop right beside him. Though he can make out the silhouettes of several occupants, he cannot identify them through the blowing snow.

"Happy Christmas, Counselor," a voice says sardonically from inside.

Though Noah shudders to hear that voice, he has no choice but to bow. "M'lord of Essex," he says. "And to you, also."

The horseman turns his head toward the coach. "This one too, m'lord?" he asks impassively, evidently referring to Noah.

"No," replies Essex wearily. "Just the Jew."

With a shake of the reins, the carriage resumes apace, and disappears from view. A moment later, the clopping dies away.

Just the Jew. Essex was unaware that he'd distinguished between Lopez and Noah on specious grounds. If he'd arrested *all* the Jews on the street just now, Noah would have been taken, too. And Essex's tone made it seem that Lopez was being arrested *because* he was a Jew. Not for the first time, Noah's stomach churns with guilt derived of the knowledge that he alone has escaped the treatment suffered by all his tribe.

Gradually, it dawns on him that he's being coated with wet snow, just as Lopez was. Glancing back toward the shelter of Marie's house, he sees her standing in the doorway watching after him, sadly chafing her hands in the icy breeze, evidently aware of what just happened. She is the very embodiment of home and hearth, everything he's been missing all these long years. He's sickened to think what harm might befall her on his account, should his faith ever be discovered by someone wishing him harm, someone like Essex.

And what if she's not as she appears? What if she really *is* in cahoots with Southampton, who, for all he knows, was sitting in the carriage with Essex just now? Better she herself never learns of Noah's faith. Better for them both that he lives out the rest of his life in the same self-loathing and self-pity he's been living in up to now. He even wonders for the first time whether Uncle

Avram made the wrong choice in delivering him up to an "important" life. He trudges up the steps, feeling very *unimportant*. All that welcoming warmth inside, all that bounty, even this good woman's great beauty ... is not meant for *him*, but for someone he's merely pretending to be.

Though Marie takes Noah warmly by the hand and shuts the door on the freezing wind, he shivers to think that he is, and always will be ... alone.

Happy Christmas, indeed.

CHAPTER 24

NOAH WALKS OUT OF A COURTROOM at Westminster on the first day of Hilary Term. Across great Westminster Hall, he spots Henry, evidently on a break from proceedings in Parliament, and waves him over.

"You've heard about Lopez?" asks Henry.

"I *saw* it! A frightening thing, to have a man just scooped up like that, without notice. No reason given his family. Poor man. Can *anyone* save him?"

Henry smirks. "Not just *anyone*. Will you accept service of legal papers from me?"

"*Legal papers?*"

"Yes, from your good friend Lord Burghley."

"I don't suppose he's *suing* me," says Noah.

"You may eventually wish that's all these papers were about. No, it's a commission." Henry looks furtively around the hall. "It's in my pocket."

"Isn't legal process from the Privy Council supposed to be served by an imposing figure in Queen's livery?"

"That can be *arranged!*" threatens Henry. "It's a bit conspicuous, however. When you see the nature of the commission, I think you'll be relieved no one saw you served."

"I see," says Noah with growing unease. "Yes, of course I will accept service of papers."

Henry discreetly slips a letter out of his pocket and into Noah's. Although Noah manages only a fleeting glimpse, he spots a red ribbon and large red seal on its exterior.

"Open it at Gray's Inn," says Henry. "Privately. Don't discuss it with anybody, except Hawking, if you like. But *he's* not to discuss it with anyone yet, not even Arthur."

"You're frightening me."

"Sorry for all the hugger-mugger." Henry smirks. "Think of it as an early valentine from God's elect on earth." He walks away as quickly as his girth allows.

* * *

Noah sits at his desk, thoughtfully gazing out of the window. Before him lie a letter opener and a parchment, its red seal broken.

There's a knock on the door. It's Jonathan, in barrister's robes. He enters without awaiting a response. "Just got back from court. You wanted to see me?"

Noah nods grimly.

"What's the matter?" asks Jonathan. "You look like a man condemned."

"Close the door." Noah waits until he hears the click. "I've been sitting here contemplating how much torment I've brought to your life ... and how selfish it would be to impose upon you any further."

"Master ... Noah, you have brought nothing ill into my life. Besides, who ever said that *ease* was life's purpose?"

"Oh, it's not the *work* for which I apologize. Work is the lifeblood of any barrister's practice. But *this* kind of ... " His voice trails off, and he shakes his head.

"Does this involve Essex?" asks Jonathan.

"I'm afraid so."

"Well, in for a penny, in for a pound. You know *my* feelings on the topic."

Noah sits up in his chair and faces Jonathan. "I know your feelings, but I will never again deprive you of *choice*. I think that's been my principal failing as regards you in this whole affair. Unfortunately, in this profession, it's simply impossible to provide someone with choice, without also burdening him with dangerous knowledge." He points to the parchment. "Go ahead and read it."

"Aloud?"

"If you wish, but quietly, and you may discuss it with *no one*, not even ... the boys."

Jonathan begins to read softly: "'By the Privy Council,' etcetera, 'Year of Our Lord,' and so on." Jonathan searches downward, using his finger as guide.

"*Here* it is! 'Whereas, one Roderigo Lopez, an alien to the realm, has been arrested on suspicion of high treason against the Crown; and further whereas, to promote the interests of justice and in the exercise of clemency, Her Majesty sees fit to ensure that said prisoner shall be afforded in his defense every right and privilege to which an English subject may be entitled, though he be none, now therefore, it is hereby highly resolved that the barrister at Queen's Bench known as Noah Ames, resident at Gray's Inn without the City of London, shall be and hereby is appointed to meet and confer with said prisoner in strictest privacy at the Tower of London for the purpose of providing said prisoner with his good counsel in defending himself against said charges, and it is further ordered that said barrister Noah Ames be granted the assistance of one additional barrister of his choosing, the reasonable costs and disbursements of both such barristers' services to be defrayed by the Crown upon application to the Exchequer,' and so on, 'signed this day, William Cecil, Lord Burghley.'"

"What do you think?" asks Noah.

Jonathan is evidently too enthralled to have heard the question. "Did you see the initials at the foot of this?" He points to the bottom of the document.

"E.R.," says Noah. "*Elizabeth Regina.*"

Jonathan whistles softly. "Elizabeth the Queen. My, but you *have* come up in the world!"

"*You're* named in there, too, if you want it."

"*Me?* Oh. Yes, very flattering. I'm the barrister to be designated later." Jonathan refolds the commission and tosses it on the desk. "*I'm* in," he chirps.

* * *

Tom the stable boy brings the horses around. Noah pats Bucklebury on the flank, mounts, and starts off with Jonathan to the Tower.

"They just issued your commission yesterday," says Jonathan. "I hope they're expecting us."

"I hope they're *not*," replies Noah. "If I'm guessing right, Essex will want this matter tied up in a bow without delay, and he's already weeks — probably *months* — ahead of us in gathering information. He might not know of my commission at all yet. When he finally learns of it, I want him to envision us already athwart his path."

"I wonder what resistance the Cecils will offer to this prosecution."

Noah makes no reply, as he's still sorting out how much information that he's learned from the Cecils can be shared with Jonathan without breaching confidence.

They pass London Bridge and bear left, now picking up the path taken by Uncle Avram's oxcart all those years ago. In the intervening years, the trees have overgrown Tower Street from the north, further obstructing the view of the Tower approach. Although they will have to pass hard by Tower Hill, the site of numerous infamous hangings, Noah is relieved to know they won't have to enter from Thameside through the ominously named Traitor's Gate. He marvels that his Uncle Avram was not too frightened to enter the Tower, filled as it is with nightmarish names and places.

As they round the last turn, he can see that the entrance is still guarded by men with pikes. Although the pike heads look a bit more elaborate than they did when Noah was a boy (now perhaps what are called "partisans"), they're clearly intended for the same purpose. Noah and Jonathan ride up to the gate, and a grizzled old guard approaches them, his voice commanding and hoarse.

"Now, what would two barristers be doin' here on this chilly mornin'? I suppose you two are not o' Gray's Inn."

The voice is familiar. Incredibly, it's the same guard who admitted Noah and his uncle so many years earlier.

"Oh?" says Noah. "Why would you choose that particular inn to remark upon?"

"Oh, I dunno, sir. Just that they had their Twelfth Night revels a few nights ago, and it's common knowledge they take a few weeks to recover."

Noah smiles at Jonathan, who looks abashed, having taken part in the revels and imbibed more than his share.

"Sorry to disappoint," says Noah. "We are indeed of Gray's Inn. Between *us*, however, its residents are seldom seen at this time merely because the courts are out of session until Hilary Term commences mid-January."

"Thought sure you'd still be huddled 'round yer fireplaces in the nice warm inn. Makes a nice picture, anyhow."

"Tell me, sir, how long have you been a Yeoman of the Tower Guard?"

The guard searches his memory. "Well, let's see. I reckon I've been at this post, man and boy, around forty year."

Noah hands him his commission. While the guard studies it, Noah recalls all the changes he's seen over those same years that seem to have flown by: Eton, Merton, Gray's Inn, Queen's Bench. And yet, every day of those years, this man has stood guard at the same gate, rain or shine, heat or chill, daylight or darkness. He cannot but admire such dedication.

"I see this commission's in order, suh, but we weren't expectin' nobody to interview this particular prisoner for a few days, except … "

"Except Lord Essex?"

The guard nods. "Or Sir Robert Cecil, sir."

"But you do intend to allow us in?"

The guard laughs. "With those initials on yer commission, sir, you could have the run of the guard tower and my bunk, to boot!" He returns the commission to Noah, and raises his hand. The portcullis groans open.

Noah folds the commission and replaces it in his pocket. He puts a half crown in the guard's hand.

The guard nods. "That's Administrative Expenses, sir."

"I beg your pardon?"

The guard leans into Noah, and jingles the pocket in which he deposited the coin. "On the application to the Exchequer, sir. You bury that in Administrative Expenses. He'll know what it means, but won't give you no trouble about it."

"Tell me, Goodman Guard, if you would. What is your name?"

"Gardner, sir." He smiles. "I would ask for yours in return, sir, but it's on the commission." He puts a bit of extra huskiness in his voice, and says:

"Welcome to the Tower o' London, Master Ames."

Evidently, this is the theatrical voice he reserves to remind visitors of the Tower's bloody history. As though they need reminding.

Noah enters the Tower with Jonathan, wishing nothing more than that this morning's errand was to deliver groceries.

*   *   *

Lopez's dark, stone-lined cell at the Tower is no larger than ten feet by twelve. Although, upon entering, Noah is not hit by the overpowering stench of urine and feces that confronts a visitor to Newgate Prison, this cell could use a good cleaning and drying out nonetheless. The jailer lets them in, enters after them, and slams the door shut from inside.

Noah glowers, and speaks softly. "Goodman Jailer, you must not remain inside the cell during the interview."

The jailer smirks. "Sorry, sir. But I take my orders from the Queen."

"So do I!" Noah shoots back, and thrusts the commission up to his view. "And here are your orders. It says 'in strictest privacy.'"

The jailer turns sullen. "I dunno that's how I read it, suh."

"Shall we go to the Queen for an interpretation? Or, perhaps ... we could simply double the Administrative Expense?"

"The Admin — " The jailer's eyebrows rise. "I'm sure that would be just fine, suh."

"I'm pleased we see it the same way. Please wait down the hall. We'll summon you when we've finished."

"Certainly, suh!" says the jailer, who leaves with a spring in his step, shutting the door from outside this time. Noah feels satisfied, as he's thus far given the jailer only half what he originally intended, anyway.

Lopez lies motionless on his cot, facing the stone wall, which glistens with moisture. Jonathan has already failed several times to persuade him to turn toward them.

"Doctor Lopez," says Noah, "is this the greeting I deserve?"

Lopez turns and sits up at the sound of his voice. "Not at all, Master Ames. It is a relief to see you. Have you come to post bail?"

Noah shakes his head dolefully. "Alas, Doctor. No bail shall be set in this case. I'm afraid we have come bearing only our advice."

Lopez regards him skeptically. "Are you sent here by Master Cecil?"

"After a fashion. Her Majesty has appointed us to assist you with legal advice. Although Lord Burghley *has* signed my commission, I shall not report to him … or anyone else, for that matter. I am *your* counsel. This is Master Hawking, whom you've met at Gray's. I've known him for years and trust him implicitly."

A gleam of hope shines in Lopez's eyes. "I see. But why … why should Her Majesty appoint counsel to assist in my defense? Do you know what I stand accused of?"

"Not precisely, and we'll get to that later. But you do understand, Doctor Lopez, that all communications between you, on one hand, and Master Hawking or myself, on the other, are privileged. That means we can never repeat what you have said, nor can we lawfully be compelled to do so. You understand?"

"Yes, I see."

"And you understand that means that you must never lie to Master Hawking or me, or withhold any part of the truth from us?"

"Truth!" Lopez scoffs, but then nods. "Yes, I understand."

"You have not been tortured, have you? Or threatened with torture?"

Lopez shakes his head unequivocally. "I have not. No."

"Very well, Doctor Lopez. I have asked Master Hawking to interview you. For today, I will be mostly listening."

"I understand."

Jonathan already has his pen in hand, and his journal open on his lap. "Doctor Lopez, of what country are you a citizen?" Lopez appears not to understand. "Perhaps this would be a better phrasing: To what Sovereign are you subject?"

Lopez appears confused, and looks to Noah for help.

"Perhaps you should ask for the client's birthplace," says Noah, "and his residence since that time."

"Oh," says Lopez. "I see. I was born in Crato, in Portugal, in the Year of Our Lord 1525."

"Is Portugal a country independent from Spain?" asks Jonathan. Lopez again appears not to understand. "What I'm trying to find out — "

"No, no. Your question is clear," Lopez assures him, "but the answer, I'm afraid, is *not*. When I was born in Portugal, it was an independent country. But, many years later, the king died, and there are now several different claimants to the Portuguese throne."

Now it's Jonathan's turn to look confused.

Lopez resumes. "One claimant to the throne is Philip the Second of Spain. If he wins the throne, then perhaps Portugal is not an independent country. You see?"

Jonathan scribbles something, and nods. "I believe so. All right, then, when you were born, you were a subject of the King of Portugal. Correct?"

Lopez looks to Noah again, pleading mutely.

"Jonathan," says Noah. "I do not wish to interrupt, but I must explain to you what it means to be born a Jew in Christendom."

Jonathan waits expectantly.

"A Jew born in England, for example, is not an Englishman. In fact, he is not even a subject of the Crown. He stands in a strange, in some respects, *unique* relation to the Sovereign. For most purposes, he's an alien, a kind of long-term visitor. Unlike Christianity, although Judaism is a religion, it is also a *race*, as its members are supposed to marry only other members of the race. In a sense, then, the Jews are a separate nation. You see?"

Jonathan nods uncertainly, and turns back to Lopez. "But you became a Christian in Portugal?"

"Not exactly. We were forcibly converted to papism. And we openly practiced it, but it did not really matter, because we were still regarded as Jews. And, inside, many of us were still believers in the Hebrew religion."

"But, if you converted, *then* you became Portuguese?"

"If we *professed* to convert, yes. But then came the Inquisition, and we were not *believed* to be real Christians, so many of us were put to the sword as heretics, or expelled."

"All right. Where did you go after leaving Portugal?"

"To Spain, to study medicine."

"And did you become a subject of the Spanish … ?"

"No. Same as Portugal. Not a subject. A Jew. But I was a papist, really. I'd converted, and accepted Jesus Christ as my savior. I did not stay very long in Spain. I came to England shortly after Her Majesty … God save her … was crowned."

"And you joined the reformed Church of England?"

"Yes, just as all you English did."

Jonathan daubs perspiration from his brow. Evidently, this is proving much more difficult than he anticipated. "So, then, now you are a subject of the English Crown."

"No, I am not. I am a Jew."

"So, you're *not* an Englishman?"

"How could I be?" replies Lopez. "I am an ambassador to Her Majesty from a foreign country."

"From which country?"

"Portugal."

Noah holds up his hand in exasperation. "Jonathan, stop!"

Noah's head is spinning as wildly as Jonathan's. This man is being accused of violating his natural loyalties. But how can a man be expected to know where his natural loyalties lie, if he never knows who he is? If he never knows his true relation to the country of his residence?

And worse, it's beginning to dawn on Noah that this whole line of questioning is equally salient to *him*. If *he* had not been figuratively "adopted" by the Queen, how would *he* answer Jonathan's questions about *himself*? What nationality is he? Polish? French? English? Jewish alien?

Even now, having been a lifelong beneficiary of the Queen's largesse, what *is* his relation to the Crown? He has held himself out to be a loyal subject of the Queen all his life, and feels such loyalty deep within his bones. But is this sufficient to make him the Queen's subject? What if his Jewishness were to become generally known? Would he still be taken as the Queen's loyal subject? Or as a Jew? Or, worse, as a fraud?

Has he in fact become what he's purported to be for so long? Or is his Englishness mere *theater*?

* * *

After all questions are put aside concerning citizenship and loyalty, as well as professed and actual religion, that day's interview reveals a portion of Lopez's story.

Besides being a practicing physician to the very poor and the very rich, Lopez worked for Walsingham in gathering intelligence for many years. After a time, Walsingham authorized him to act as a "projector," that is, an agent who purports to be something he's not, so that he may gather additional intelligence and ensnare foreign agents.

Sometimes Lopez would pretend to act for a power other than England. Sometimes, he would pretend to be a double agent serving (and collecting fees from) two or more Sovereigns.

Once an agent becomes a projector, the number of permutations in his possible roles boggles the mind, as he might pretend to be more than one thing to different people at the same time. And he might be dealing with others who are themselves projectors doing likewise.

From such devious practices, a seductive world of shadow and illusion springs into existence, devoid of substance, in which a player never knows the truth about anyone but himself, and is often tempted to forget even that.

According to Lopez, one of the two principal hazards imposed by "projecting" is that one need *always* act consistently with the expectations of those being duped. One slip-up can, and often does, cost the projector his life.

The other main hazard of projecting is that, whether by need or greed, a projector can be tempted to "freelance," interjecting his personal interest in an affair when, for a fee or personal advancement, he will mislead his real sponsors. He might secretly share his sponsors' information with others, also for personal advantage. Such things as these Lopez did, and all because he wanted the money.

When the Portuguese monarch died without apparent heir, Lopez backed one of the contenders for the throne whom he had known most of his life, Don Antonio. Although Don Antonio's claim was not unimpeachable, at Lopez's urging Queen Elizabeth provided him a foothold in England. Lopez put him up at Eton along with his eldest son, Don Emanuel, who now wishes to capitulate to King Philip of Spain. These are the "dons" that Marie heard arguing from her carriage at Eton.

Lopez personally helped to organize and finance the disastrous English Armada that was intended to prevent King Philip from reconstituting the Spanish Armada and to install Don Antonio on the Portuguese throne, ensuring that Portugal would remain independent of Spain. This was the expedition which the Queen forbade Essex to join, but which Essex joined nevertheless, on which he had proven both his courage and his irrationality by challenging all denizens of the City of Lisbon to individual combat.

Lopez lost his entire considerable fortune in the expedition. Although he was getting old, he was eager to resume his life of espionage in order to regain some portion of his personal fortune for his family. But Walsingham *died,* and no one stepped into his shoes as Her Majesty's spymaster. Lopez now had no wealth, no significant income, and no English sponsor. So, he became a freelance "projector." This man without a country then became a *spy* without a country.

Riding away from the last interview with Lopez at the Tower, Noah contemplates the near futility of defending the man. The Cecils know that if they lose the battle for the Attorney Generalship and Essex's man Francis Bacon is appointed, Bacon will be in the perfect position to prosecute them as accomplices to any crime committed by Lopez. Once they learn — as soon they must — that Lopez has committed treason, the only way *they'll* be able to avoid a charge of treason at Essex's hands will be to let Lopez die before he can be compelled to give testimony against them in court. The sooner he's dispatched, the better for them.

When Noah and Jonathan leave the Tower that first day, they've learned only half the international part of the story. In the coming days, they learn the rest: how King Philip of Spain engaged in his own "projection," ensnaring Lopez to participate in a plot to assassinate his former minister Perez, who'd betrayed Philip and come to live in England under Crown protection.

What Noah finds most astounding is Lopez's utter failure to recognize the close in-fighting between factions of the English Privy Council, foolishly treating them as though they were warring sovereigns separated by great oceans.

Lopez stupidly began a projection with Essex as dupe, providing intelligence, bought and paid for by Essex, first to the Cecils. Once Essex saw that he was Lopez's dupe, he realized he could easily prove to the Queen that Lopez was the Cecils' man. After that, all he would need to show in order to disgrace the Cecils was that Lopez committed treason under their protection, which Lopez stupidly *did* by assisting in the plot to assassinate Perez.

This man without a country, who became a spy without a country, is now a *treasonous* spy, poisonous to his former sponsors. He has no constituents. He is a fatal liability to his erstwhile friends, and a disposable asset to his deadliest enemy.

Lopez is as good as dead.

And the only people who want him to receive a fair and public trial are Noah, Jonathan … and the Queen.

CHAPTER 25

BY THE TIME NOAH IS FREE to visit Jessica again, it's already the last day of January. In the morning chill, he dons his robes, mounts Bucklebury, and rides toward Southwark. As he leaves London Bridge, the wind suddenly picks up, and The Rose comes into view in the distance. He's heard it will be opening for the season tomorrow.

It occurs to him that February will begin tomorrow, and that it was late February last year that he and Henry went to see the debut of Marlowe's *Jew of Malta*. That was the same day Marie's husband was murdered, and Essex, having been roundly applauded by the crowd, lied to the constable about witnessing the murder.

So much has happened in the past year. Some things have come together. He has arrived at a new unspoken concord with Jessica, and fallen in love with Marie. He's cemented his professional relationship with Jonathan, and his friendship with Henry. Yet many important matters remain out of joint. The murder of Marie's husband Stephen remains unavenged, as does that of Jonathan's father figure Graves. Marlowe is in the ground, too, with no one to mourn him, or even investigate the circumstances of his death. And, of course, the fight for Lopez's life has barely begun.

In the distance, Noah espies workmen posting bills all around The Rose announcing the upcoming show, and he decides to pay the theater a short visit. Dismounting some distance away, he leads Bucklebury toward the entrance. As he watches work progress, the top bill flies off a pile carried by one workman, who lets it go lest he lose the rest while chasing the errant paper. It falls face down at Noah's feet. He picks it up and turns it over.

"The Jew of Malta!" screams the headline, with the word "Jew" printed in a lurid typeface that appears to drip blood. Although the print is all in black, the intended effect is unmistakable. "Come see the heathen Jew!" says the bill, "Poisoner of good Christian souls!"

So, amidst newly sprung rumors of a real Jewish doctor plotting to poison the Queen, new life is breathed into Marlowe's play about a Jew who takes pleasure in poisoning Christians. Although Marlowe may have hinted to the discriminating viewer that his play was intended to parody the very notion of the wicked Jew, in times of public fear and outcry such subtleties are bound to be washed over. On its face, the play is an indictment of all Jews, and that's how it will be taken. And how satisfying it will be for the panting crowd to learn that the wicked Jewish plot has been foiled by its beloved Earl of Essex!

He folds the bill absentmindedly and puts it in his pocket. He wonders in passing whether Jessica might be in danger amidst such bigotry, and chides himself for taking comfort in her Christian guise.

Just then, a commotion breaks out across the lawn, mere paces from the spot where Stephen Rodriguez was murdered. A mother is trying to lead her two young children past a menacing crowd of perhaps a dozen people, although it appears to be growing rapidly.

The old fishwife at the head of the crowd brandishes a crooked switch at the children, a horrid glee on her wizened and toothless face.

"Pay no attention to them!" cries the mother to her children, and turns on the angry old fishwife. "What's the matter with you? We're your neighbors! We've lived here all our lives! Will you turn on us because of a foolish stage play?"

"Aaaohh! A foolish stage play, is it? When you Jew devils 'ave tried to *poison the Queen*? Oughta throw the 'ole lotta ye into the Thames, they ought!"

Noah runs over to stand by the mother, who acknowledges his assistance gratefully. The fishwife, even more decrepit than she seemed from across the lawn, looks him up and down skeptically.

"What are *you* doin' round 'ere, Master Barrister? Come lookin' fah clients, 'ave ye? Ye'll find plenty criminals 'round 'ere, but none as can pay fees enough to satisfy *your* sort!"

The voice of another old woman comes from the rear of the crowd. "Mebbe ye can spring me old cadger outta Newgate Prison. Old sot oughta be dried out by now!" The crowd laughs broadly.

Noah holds up his hands. "What seems to be the problem with this woman and her children, madam?" he asks in his most dignified courtroom voice.

"She's a Jew bitch, this one!" spits the fishwife angrily. "She's probably teachin' those little Jewlings 'ow to murder Our Lord again, next time he shows up!" The crowd cheers and applauds.

"Please, madam. Can't you live peacefully alongside these people now, as you always have?"

"Whadda *you*? Some sorta Jew lover? Mebbe we oughta take a switch to you, too." She swings the stick halfheartedly at his head. Although he draws back out of its reach, the way it whirs past him shows it to be much heavier than he thought.

A familiar male voice comes from a few feet behind him. "Now, Alice, I *could* take you in just for swingin' yer switch at this gentleman's 'ed. So calm down right now!" It's Constable Barnstable, who looks curiously at the mother and her children, and then turns back to the fishwife. "What kinda bug ye got up yer arse about this one, Alice?"

Alice seems abashed at this inquiry by the constable, and by being singled out by name.

"She's a heathen, Constable. A Jew devil."

Barnstable looks the mother and her children up and down again. "Nope, Alice. Don't see no 'orns. No devils 'ere." He turns back to Alice. "I don't suppose ye got some kinda commission to root out all the Jews in Her Majesty's kingdom, do ye?"

Alice spits over her shoulder. "You know I 'aven't. But why you takin' the side of these 'ere pagans, Constable?"

Barnstable ignores her and addresses the whole crowd loudly.

"Now, listen up, you crew! It's my job to protect the Queen's peace, and that's exactly what I'm goin' to do. I will not allow you lot to break the peace because somebody don't believe exactly the way you do! Ain't we 'ad enough of that 'round 'ere to last a lifetime?" As the crowd realizes that he's referring to the bloody strife between the reformed Church of England and the papists, groans of agreement rise from the back of the crowd. The constable nods. "Now, if any o' you see this fine lady or 'er two lovely children breakin' the law, you come to me, and I'll see about it right away. That I promise ye. Don't be takin' matters into yer own 'ands, neither, or it'll be *you* I'm cartin' away in manacles. Is that clear?" The crowd sounds a reluctant but unanimous agreement. "Awright! Now, be on yer way! Y'all got work of yer own to do. Be about it!"

As the crowd disperses, the fishwife shoots Noah a filthy look. He stares her down, and she slinks away without another word.

The young mother comes over to him and bows low, her children doing the same in imitation. "Thank you, sir. You have been a godsend to us. Bless you. You are a *true* Christian!" Before Noah can even think of correcting her, she kisses the hem of his robe, grabs her children's hands, and scurries away.

Barnstable misinterprets Noah's horrified expression. "Oh, don't be too upset, suh. I know these people. Poor but honest, most of 'em. I know who the troublemakers are, and keep an eye on 'em."

"Thank you for coming along at such a propitious time, Constable Barn-Stable. And for acting so responsibly."

"Tweren't nothin', suh. Just another part of me job. Truth is, I don't get why so many of these people are eager to follow such bent, twisted folk as Old Alice. But that young Jewess was right about you, suh. That was a right Christian thing ye done. May the peace of Our Lord be upon you, suh."

Mortified again, Noah conceals it better this time. "God's peace be upon *you*, as well, Constable Barn-Stable," Noah replies. He absentmindedly fishes a coin out of his pocket and hands it to the constable, who backs away with much bowing, and leaves Noah alone with his thoughts.

As he resumes his ride to Jessica, he's overcome by several emotions, foremost of which is shame. *That mother and her children are my people! Who am I to live apart from them, and conceal my religion, so I may live comfortably at Gray's Inn and be taken as a Christian, even by my own kind?*

In which of these two worlds do I truly belong? he wonders, and then concludes, as he always has, that he's an equal misfit in both.

*   *   *

Returning to Gray's Inn after dinner, Noah finds Henry in his room.

"A plot to poison the Queen!" exclaims Noah. "First, Essex arrests Lopez on suspicion of treason. Then, he searches Lopez's house and finds no papers at all. How does this transform itself into a plot to poison *the* Queen?"

Henry smiles. "Your client had been released for a time, got there first, and prudently burned every piece of paper in the house. By the time Essex's men arrived, they found nothing but soot in the flue, and hot embers in the grate."

"Soot and embers? In late January? I cannot imagine what might have been burned in a fireplace in January other than inculpatory personal papers!"

"Please, counsel, save the theatrics for the jury. I'm sure he burned wood there, too. The important thing is: They found no papers."

"And when Essex informed the Queen that Lopez was a traitor, how did she reply?"

Henry searches his memory, and clears his throat. "'Rash and temerarious youth,' she said, 'to enter into a matter against the poor man which you cannot prove, and whose innocence I know well enough!' She also accused him of proceeding against Lopez out of malice."

"And then Essex spends two days in isolation, and returns to the Queen directly to inform her that Lopez has not only committed treason, but his intention was to murder *her* by poison?"

"That's right," confirms Henry.

"Has anyone asked Essex how he found this out, notwithstanding his two-day isolation?"

"Evidently, they have not."

"And what evidence has he of this poison plot?"

"Well, he found a ruby in Lopez's house. Lopez admitted receiving it from King Philip, but said that he'd told his wife to sell it."

"And that proves ... ?"

"It proves that Lopez was in contact with a hostile Sovereign, and accepted from him something of value. As even kings generally do not part with things of value without expecting something in return, one permissible conclusion would be that Philip expected Lopez's cooperation."

"Why would Lopez lie about still having the jewel, after he's already admitted receiving it from King Philip?"

"Beyond me, too," says Henry. "He probably *did* tell his wife to sell it, but she decided not to do so. Wives do that kind of thing sometimes, you know."

A knock at the door. It's Jonathan. Seeing Henry, Jonathan seems uncertain whether to enter.

"Gentlemen," says Noah, "there are things we cannot discuss openly, even among ourselves. As Master Neville is not counsel in the case, Jonathan and I cannot discuss with him communications with Doctor Lopez, as that would render them unprivileged. Also, as I have been party to confidential conversations with the Cecils and Master Neville on the Queen's business, Henry and I cannot reveal *those* discussions to *Master Hawking*. In short, we are all walking a razor's edge here. Now that the formalities have been taken care of, let me say that, if either of you repeats anything said in this meeting, I shall simply shoot myself, and leave you to deal with the consequences."

Henry and Jonathan laugh darkly.

Henry asks, "Assuming this whole scenario of poisoning the Queen is a figment of Essex's imagination, what would his motive have been in concocting it?"

Noah sits down and pulls off his boots. "I can help you there. Essex is not a trial lawyer. He's a soldier, so he does what a soldier does. He broadens the field of battle to his advantage, slants it in his favor, and seeks powerful allies. He needs a jury that will enter the courtroom inclined to convict. So, he taints the view of the community from which they'll be selected." He withdraws from his pocket the bill he picked up in Southwark this morning, and hands it to Henry. "Here's a bit of his handiwork."

"Are you suggesting he's mounting a revival of a stage play in order to influence public opinion?" asks Henry.

"I would not put it past him. More likely, though, he tipped off the theater operator Henslowe that a Jew had been thrown in the Tower for plotting to poison the Queen. Henslowe would require no prodding after that. He would realize that such a revival could prove quite profitable, especially as he would no longer need to compensate Marlowe."

"And to think," says Henry, "Essex was reminded of the old libel — that Jews poison Christians — by a stage play he saw the very day Stephen Rodriguez was murdered, where we ourselves were in attendance. This is life imitating art at its worst. Did you know that Marlowe actually mentioned Lopez by name in his play about Doctor Faustus?" He shakes his head. "And to think that, by doing so, Marlowe was unwittingly drumming up his posthumous theatrical revenues."

Noah tosses his boots into the corner. "So that's how Essex expands and slants the field of battle. And he also gets allies on the jury that way. But he hopes to get an even more powerful ally by changing the narrative of the case to one of poisoning the Queen. And that's ... "

"The *Queen*," says Jonathan.

"Of course," says Henry. "If he has the Queen on his side, he doesn't *need* the Cecils. She can direct them to stand out of Essex's way."

"But — " begins Noah. Aware how close he is to violating the Cecils' confidence, he decides against finishing his thought with Jonathan present. "Jonathan, why don't you change out of your robes, and give me a moment alone with Master Neville?"

"All right," says Jonathan. "Shall I come back up when I've done?"

"Absolutely. There are some things we must discuss."

Jonathan closes the door behind him, and can be heard trudging down the stairs to his room.

"Anything you'd care to tell me, Henry?"

"Regarding ... what?"

"The Cecils."

"Nothing to tell," says Henry.

"As depressing as it seems, I think Essex may already have the Cecils cornered," says Noah. "If they believe he can prove that Lopez committed *any* treason on their watch, they have no choice but cooperate in anything Essex wants to do to Lopez. And for Essex to defeat the Cecils, the treason would not have to be so dramatic as an attempt to poison the Queen; the plot against Perez would suffice. In fact, the Cecils would probably *prefer* to indulge Essex's inspired lunacy about poisoning the Queen, as any trial on that charge would swerve clear *around* Lopez's actual treason. Yes. A deal has been made. I can feel it in my bones. So long as Essex agrees not to pin Lopez's treason on the Cecils, they'll let him prosecute Lopez for *anything*." His shoulders sag. "Even a crime he did not commit."

Henry shakes his head. "Doesn't sound right. Burghley has already told the Queen that Lopez's actions were aimed solely against Don Antonio."

"*Don Antonio?*" says Noah. "I thought Lopez lost his fortune trying to put Don Antonio on the Portuguese *throne!*"

Henry sighs. "Sometimes it seems there are more plots than plotters. And affections can change. The Privy Council has learned that Don Antonio's son has organized a conspiracy among more than a hundred expatriate members of the Portuguese aristocracy in which they have joined together in seeking a pardon from King Philip of Spain in exchange for their forswearing any allegiance to Don Antonio. Lopez dislikes Don Antonio, and I wouldn't be surprised if he were promoting the effort."

"But that's not criminal," observes Noah, "and it has nothing to do with the Queen's person. Does that plot involve killing Perez?"

"To the contrary," says Henry, "as Perez is suspected of providing intelligence to Don Antonio, Perez's death may be the object of a counterplot by *King Philip*." Henry scratches his head. "But as far as the Cecils are concerned, I have personally heard Sir Robert tell Her Majesty that Lopez is not guilty of plotting against her person."

"Well," says Noah, "that's something, at least. But I fear Lopez's fate may already be sealed."

Henry bucks him up. "Don't be so sure. And so long as we fulfill the roles assigned to us, we can look the Creator straight in the eye and say so. I have faith in you, Master Ames. If anyone can affect the outcome of this, it's you." He takes his coat and opens the door. "I'm off now. I'll send Hawking up on my way out."

Noah is lost in thought when Jonathan comes up a short while later.

"Master Neville tells me you are doubting your own powers," says Jonathan.

"So long as Essex has no choice but to drag Lopez before Queen's Bench, we can force him to produce his documentary evidence of this non-existent conspiracy, and we shall *have* him. There's only one problem with that."

"What's that?"

"He *knows* it," says Noah. "After all, he knows that's where I *live*, at Queen's Bench. I know every corner of the field, everywhere he may hide, and every way to smoke him out."

"That's more the spirit," says Jonathan, breathing easier. "We *shall* best him."

Noah shakes his head grimly. "No. He cannot afford to walk onto a battlefield where he's likely to be bested, Jonathan. The stakes are too high. I fear he may engage in desperate measures to avoid such a showdown."

"Such as?"

"Having Lopez killed in the Tower. Or … having *me* killed."

Jonathan downplays both possibilities. "But surely either of those would be traced back to him. They're too obvious."

"You're probably right." Noah sighs. "I think I've known all along what he's going to do."

"What's that?"

"Now that he's got Burghley at gunpoint, he's going to avoid Queen's Bench entirely by convening a Court of Oyer and Terminer 'to hear and determine' the case against Lopez."

Jonathan reacts as though Noah has said the most outlandish thing imaginable. "*That* creaky old thing?"

"There's a reason it creaks like an old gallows," replies Noah. "Think of the times it's been used in the past. They cranked it up to get rid of Archbishop Cranmer and Lady Jane Grey. No one of note or name is ever acquitted in Oyer and Terminer."

"Why's that?" asks Jonathan.

Noah smirks. "Well, have *you* ever practiced there?" Jonathan shakes his head. "I didn't think so. Neither have I, for *there* the accused has no right even to have a lawyer present. He has no right to examine the evidence against him, to cross-examine witnesses, or even to make a full statement to the court. And the selection of jurymen absolutely *assures* conviction."

"How so?"

"In London, a Court of Oyer and Terminer is convened by the Privy Council. Neither the grand jury nor the petit jury is chosen by the usual method of random selection. They are, rather, appointed by commission issuing from the Privy Council itself. If the Commissioners, sitting as grand jurors, hand up a bill of indictment, as they *always* will, the same Commissioners instantly become the petit jury. And they are effectively above challenge on grounds of interest in the proceeding."

"How can *anyone* be 'above challenge'?"

"As you say, it's an archaic forum. Commissioners are selected by virtue of high office, such as the Lord Chief Justice, the Chief Justice of Chancery Court, and so on, all of whom are dependent upon the continued good will of the Queen's Privy Council. Even the Sovereign ensures that she has an individual there as her representative 'in person.' In short, the Privy Council creates the appearance that every important part of government is aware of the proceeding and is present to ensure that justice is done."

"When in fact they've been selected to ensure a guilty verdict," says Jonathan. "That's an outrage. Why, it's a violation of Magna Carta! It's — it's — "

"It's what Essex is going to do. He has free rein now, and since the Cecils cannot effectively stand in his way, they may rather assist him."

The room is silent for a full minute before Jonathan ventures a particularly sensitive question. "Is there a reason you did not mention this in the presence of Master Neville?"

Noah sighs, as though he's been asking himself the same thing. "I'm ashamed to confess, the answer to your question is 'yes,' to avoid making a suggestion that might be passed along to Essex, one he might otherwise miss." He waves dismissively. "*Ach!* If Henry has been enlisted by Essex, we're finished anyway. But I perceive a glimmer that the Cecils have retained some shred of decency, and are prepared to assist us in some way. I do not think we would have been appointed if they hadn't requested us. That probably means that the Queen wants to avoid a horrendous miscarriage of justice. In any event, we shan't go down without a fight."

"Amen," says Jonathan gravely. "And what a fight it will be!"

* * *

As neither Noah nor Jonathan need appear in court the next day, they spend all night in the inn's library, taking copious notes, reframing the limitations on Oyer and Terminer's jurisdiction into readily understandable phrases.

They move into the dining area. Noah rubs his eyes as, for the third time, he silently reviews the letter they've drafted together. In addition to preparing a clean original, Jonathan has made a verbatim copy for them to retain.

"This is about as good as it gets," says Noah, "and — " He loses his train of thought, cocks his head, and turns suddenly toward the window.

"What is it?" asks Jonathan wearily, as such looks have been known to result in several additional hours in the library.

"Where's that little dog?"

"Little — ?" Jonathan furrows his brow as though he's concerned for Noah's rationality. "Oh, *Finerty!*"

"Yes. Wasn't he in the window for several weeks?"

Jonathan chortles. "Yes, he was. I don't know what's happened to him. Salazar pointed out a few days ago that he'd gone missing."

A servant's voice from the hallway: "Master Ames, you have two visitors, a Master Neville and a Master ... *Cheerful*?"

Noah blinks several times to clear his vision. "Please escort them here. Thank you." As Henry and Cheerful are brought in, Jonathan rises and bows.

Noah is simply too tired, and nods his head. "Good morning, gentlemen. What can we do for you?"

"I'm afraid we bring some bad news," says Henry. "As it turns out, the Privy Council has convened a Court of Oyer and Terminer ... "

Noah completes his sentence: " ... to hear and determine the matter of the guilt or innocence of Roderigo Lopez in the plot to poison the Queen. Court will be convened at Guildhall, in ... *three* weeks," he estimates.

Henry's mouth hangs open, his eyes wide. "How did you — ? Did someone — ?"

Noah is exhausted, but still he cannot resist. "And you have considerately brought Master Cheerful Killigrew with you to await any urgent message I may have for Lord Burghley."

Noah picks up a pen, inks it, and signs the letter he and Jonathan just completed. He folds it and writes on it: "To William Cecil, Lord Burghley." While Henry watches in amazement, and much to Jonathan's mirth, he hands it to Cheerful, gives him a shilling, and says: "There you go, m'lad. Thank you for your pains."

Henry seizes Cheerful by the arm before he can run out to take horse, and regards Noah as though he's lost his mind. "Don't you want to read the notice?" he asks, handing it to Noah.

Noah takes a few moments to read it silently. "Very well. Thank you, Master Neville, I have read the notice. Master Killigrew, please deliver my letter to Lord Burghley."

Henry releases Cheerful's arm. "How did you know?" he asks in amazement.

"Don't worry, Henry. There is no leak of information at the Privy Council. Having been in this profession for many years, I've seen it *all*. Thank you so much for coming. Now, if you will excuse me, I would like to go to bed."

"Wait!" says Henry. "I have other news." He regards Noah skeptically. "Considering how swollen your head has become, however, I shall require your assurance that you will receive this news with reserve and humility — feigned, if need be."

"Very well," says Noah, yawning.

"Sir Henry is up and around. It appears to be mostly due to his undertaking to take care of your daughter, and Doctor Lopez's medicine."

Tired as Noah is, he stands up and does a little jig in place. He pulls Henry out of his chair and hugs him like a brother.

"Old Sir Henry!" Noah cries. "Why, that's *wonderful!*"

Henry regards him with irritation. "What happened to feigning reserve and humility?"

"I *did* try," says Noah, crinkling his nose. "I'm just not very *good* at it."

Noah tramps upstairs, slams the door, collapses on his bed, and sleeps.

* * *

It's just after supper on Sunday evening a few weeks later. As yet, Noah has received no reply to his letter to Burghley. He's about to write another, this one directly to the Queen, when he hears a commotion downstairs.

"Yes, sir," he hears Jonathan say obediently.

Heavy footfalls make their way up the stairs, followed by a knock. "Ames. It's me. Neville. Open up. I need to speak with you right away!"

Noah opens the door. "Come in, Henry. What news?"

Henry shuts the door behind him. "I instructed Jonathan to collect Arthur and his other friends in his room, and to tell them to wait to be summoned up here. I told Jonathan to come up alone as soon as that was done."

"Sounds serious."

"As plague. I came straight here from an audience with the Queen at Windsor, attended, of course, by Lord Burghley and Robert Cecil. This was their opportunity to review your petition with Her Majesty."

"My letter?"

"Was it not a petition?" asks Henry. "That's what they called it."

"Doesn't matter. I have no idea what it should be called, as there's no precedent for it. I've never seen anything like it in a book. Please continue. I'm sorry to have interrupted."

Jonathan flies up the stairs, lets himself in, and sits down, out of breath.

Henry gives him a moment to catch his breath, and resumes. "The Cecils told the Queen that you wish to address the Commissioners as soon as they have been empaneled and the charges read, which will be this coming Wednesday, incidentally. Two days from now. She asked Robert what you intended to speak to them about, and he said you wished to move them to transfer the Lopez matter to Queen's Bench, and dissolve the Court of Oyer and Terminer.

"Her Majesty asked what your grounds might be. I must say Robert did a *masterful* job of articulating them to Her Majesty, largely based, no doubt, upon the petition you and Jonathan wrote, but they seemed to make a great deal of sense.

"Her Majesty asked whether it would be *lawful* for the Commissioners to do as you'd propose. He told her that it would be lawful — if unorthodox — for Commissioners to dissolve their court voluntarily. She asked Robert whether it would be 'prudent' to allow such a motion to be made."

Noah places his hands over his eyes and grits his teeth. It could all be lost right here. "How did he reply?"

"He said that the points underlying your motion are important, and that it would be a good idea to have such arguments made — but perhaps not by *you*."

Noah's stunned. "But *he's* the one who had me appointed in — "

Henry smirks. "Stop! You must understand that we're talking about *Sir Robert Cecil*, the world's foremost expert in handling Her Majesty."

"Sorry for ripping into your narrative."

"Mended again," says Henry indulgently. "So, Her Majesty asks why it might be better to have a *different* lawyer make the motion. And Robert says: 'Because Master Ames is a *real* lawyer, madam. He is not a sycophant currying favor with a faction of the Privy Council, but more like a common tradesman, whose single-minded aim is to help his client, in this case, Doctor Lopez. There is no telling *what* he may say to the Commissioners, or how indignant they may feel.'"

Jonathan chimes in, incredulous. "He said that? A common *tradesman*? What did she say to that?"

Henry smiles. "Her Majesty said, 'How refreshing! You will instruct the Commissioners to hear Master Ames out, until *he* feels he is good and through. There shall be no interruptions, no reprisals or threats thereof. I expect my Commissioners to treat him with the utmost courtesy, and to give good heed to everything he says.' Of course, that is precisely what Robert *hoped* she would say.

"Robert then said, 'But, Your Majesty, the Commissioners are the most strong-willed men in the realm. They'll not take kindly to being told what to do by a mere *barrister*.' At that point, Her Majesty, who was becoming more than a little irritated, said: 'They will hear him out just as I have said. Let me be clear. I do not care *what* he says. I do not care if he blows out a wall of Guildhall with a Gresham cannon.'

"'But, Your Majesty,' said Robert, 'you *cannot* be in earnest!'" Henry's face turns bright red, and he laughs. "And the Queen turns to me and says, 'Master Neville, fetch me a cannon!'"

Noah's jaw drops, and Jonathan doubles over in laughter.

"So, we're *on*, then!" says Noah, a hopeful light in his eyes.

"Wait!" says Henry. "I'm nearly done. Her Majesty then said: 'I place Master Ames and his assistant under the protection of Lord Burghley and yourself.' As we were being dismissed, Robert said, 'Majesty, you have said that *all* the Commissioners shall hear him out. Does that include *Lord Essex*?' Her face turned quite to stone, and she said: '*Especially* Lord Essex!'"

Jonathan gloats at that most of all.

"One last thing," says Henry, almost as an afterthought. "Robert persuaded the Queen to issue a writ of safe passage ordering all subjects to assist in keeping you safe and on your way. I tried to talk him out of it, but he wouldn't hear of it. Anyway, I'm suppressing it. It's in my pocket to stay."

"Why suppress it?" asks Noah.

"Because if Essex learns of it, he'll know he cannot be seen to arrest you."

Noah cocks his head. "Is that not the *point* of the writ?"

"Of course. But, if Essex cannot arrest you, he may see no other way but to *kill* you. Either way, we should now bring up your young brothers at the bar, to make sure that doesn't happen."

Any residual relief has left the room. "Thank you, Henry. You are a true friend. However, I would just as soon refrain from participating in my own funeral arrangements. Jonathan, please take care of such measures with Master Neville in your own room, and leave me here with my thoughts. I have a great deal of work to do between now and Wednesday. And please, Jonathan — no lethal force. If I cannot escape Essex's men without ruining all your lives, I'd rather be taken, and, if need be, face my end alone."

Jonathan nods reluctantly.

Noah continues. "Henry, there is one more thing I would beg of you. Whatever you may be able to find out about the composition of the panel, as well as the identity of Crown counsel at the hearing, I would be much obliged."

"I shall let you know tomorrow," says Henry. "On one point, however, I can tell you right now. Crown counsel for the Court will be the Solicitor General, Edward Coke."

Noah nods gravely. "Then it is to *his* conscience we must make our most strident appeal. There's no way I can persuade the panel myself. But Coke will remain with the panel long after I've left, and they'll be inclined to credit what he says. If we can enlist *Coke*," he says, hoping he's not fooling himself, "we might have chance."

CHAPTER 26

THAT WEDNESDAY AFTERNOON, at quarter to three, Noah, Jonathan, and Arthur don their barrister's robes and depart Gray's Inn together on foot. Although it's less frigid than it's been, it's still nearly freezing, and crystalline moisture nips at their faces. As they walk toward Guildhall under a leaden sky, Arthur tells them what they'll do if a contingent of Essex's tangerine-and-cream assembles outside while Noah's addressing the Court of Oyer and Terminer, as the purpose of such a gathering can only be to lie in wait for him. In that case, the plan is for the jesters to remove Noah and Jonathan from London until they can arrange a prompt return under Crown protection.

The consensus among the jesters is that, once Noah's argument has been made, Essex will be supremely furious, making it the likeliest occasion for him to have his men forcibly "escort" Noah to Essex House, ostensibly for a consultation, but really to begin repaying him for several public humiliations. The Queen's issuance of a writ of safe passage at the request of Sir Robert Cecil only reinforces their view.

Noah, for his part, has never been so frightened in his life. The most important men in England are now assembled in Guildhall, fully expecting to participate in a legal proceeding. As the Queen has instructed them to hear him out, in approximately half an hour he'll tell them that their services are not needed and that they should disband and go home.

"Noah," says Arthur urgently, "have you heard a word I've said?"

Noah has been so focused on his upcoming task that he hasn't taken in what Arthur's been saying.

"Noah!" Jonathan says sternly. "If anything unsavory is happening outside Guildhall, Arthur will send us a message inside. If that happens, then, when you leave the hall, you must fly out of the door like *Até hot from hell.* Understand? *Or they will have you!*"

Noah nods absently.

Jonathan shakes his head in frustration. "Not good enough. Say it back to me, Noah!"

Noah looks him straight in his eye. "If there's a problem outside, Arthur will send a message to us. That means, when it's done, I fly out of the door, and … what?"

Jonathan is exasperated. "We run like hell on horseback!"

Guildhall is on the same street as Henry's town home, and only a few hundred feet from it. As they reach Lothbury, Noah feels the urge to turn right, and pay the Nevilles a social call. It takes every bit of determination he has to turn left instead.

The sun emerges as Guildhall comes into view. Arthur stops, and holds the others back firmly by the arm. About a dozen people mill about in front of the hall. Two appear to be vendors of food, perhaps sausages, judging by the smell. The aroma of roasting chestnuts also wafts toward them on the cold breeze. Most of the others appear to be gentlemen.

"How many do you see, Jonathan?" asks Arthur.

Jonathan's eyes scan the scene. "One, two … three in livery. Probably another one or two in plainclothes, somewhere. Can't be sure."

"Who's that fat ugly one in peaches and cream?" Arthur asks. "Looks like a bulldog who got loose in the dairy. Still, he looks familiar."

"That's Gelly Meyrick. You've seen him before, giving perjured testimony against Granger. He's made of filth and dirty tricks. Watch out for that one."

"They'd better watch out for *us*," Arthur says, and quickly turns back to Gray's Inn without a parting word.

Noah and Jonathan proceed to the main entrance.

"Hey! Who are *you* two?" says a gruff voice behind them. It's Meyrick, evidently failing to recognize either Noah or Jonathan.

Noah turns, looks Meyrick up and down, and snarls with contempt. "Who the devil are *you*, presuming to interfere in the Queen's business? On second thought, stay right there. I'll call a constable, and have you arrested for perjury."

Meyrick recoils, and slinks away with a sneer. Jonathan seems surprised that Noah, even in his distracted state, can call up the reserves needed to face down that ugly hulk.

The doorkeeper examines Noah's commission, and allows them both to pass. As they traverse the vestibule into the main hall and walk toward the well, Noah loses all awareness of the world in general, focusing solely on the panel and what he has to say. No sound is heard in the cavernous room but the clopping of their feet on the wooden floor, echoing distantly in the rafters. The afternoon sun that slants through the clerestory windows onto the eastern wall feels like a palpable weight on Noah's heart.

On the dais sit some of the most accomplished men in the land. To Noah's right are the familiar Lord Burghley and Sir Robert Cecil, as well as Solicitor General Edward Coke, who serves as Crown counsel in the case. Burghley holds the scepter symbolizing the presence of the Sovereign, which is a good sign, as it means that Noah will address the panel through Burghley, and can watch his face for any sign he's overstepped.

To Noah's extreme left sits the dour and angry Robert Devereux, Earl of Essex, blatantly resentful that he has been required to entertain a defense motion, his lips taut, as though he's just been forced to eat a particularly sour fruit.

Between these two extremes sit several judges whom Noah recognizes on sight. One is the Chief Justice of Queen's Bench, also known as the Lord Chief Justice of England, who briefly joined Lord Bleffingham and Noah as they dined with Master Neville at Serjeants' Inn many months ago. There are additional justices of Queen's Bench, too, as well as of the Courts of Chancery, Common Pleas, and Requests. Also seated on the dais is the Chancellor of the Exchequer, to whom Noah will be submitting his bill for legal services provided to Doctor Lopez.

There is another warrior up there who would be recognized by anyone in England. It's Admiral Howard, who, along with Francis Drake, is credited with destroying the Spanish Armada mere hours before its scheduled invasion of England. He's flanked by several knights of renown, though none of comparable stature.

A sneeze comes from the gallery, which is supposed to be vacant on grand jury occasions such as this. He looks up to see the sole representative of Parliament sent to observe the proceedings, namely, Henry Neville. Henry nods without looking at Noah, evidently satisfied that his presence has been duly noted by the defense.

Lord Burghley bangs the scepter on the floor three times. "Commissioners in the matter of *Regina versus Roderigo Lopez*. As we have discussed heretofore, we have been commanded by the Queen to hear and consider various motions to be made by Master Noah Ames, counsel for the prisoner. Her Majesty has commanded that there shall be no answer or comment from the Commissioners nor Crown Counsel during the presentation. Counsel will proceed."

"M'lord." Noah bows, his heart pounding. "Gentlemen Commissioners." He bows again. "Distinguished Crown Counsel." He bows to Coke. "May it please the Court, my name is Noah Ames. This is my assistant, Jonathan Hawking. We are both counsel at Queen's Bench, representing the prisoner Roderigo Lopez in this Court by special commission of Her Majesty. We beg the Court's indulgence for the robes we wear, as we have earlier today appeared at Queen's Bench, which court is very much in session at Westminster. Never having appeared before an extraordinary Court of Oyer and Terminer, we are neither of us aware of any customary accouterments expected of counsel admitted to this Court.

"On behalf of the prisoner, it is my duty to move that the Court transfer the matter of Roderigo Lopez to Queen's Bench for all purposes, including, but not limited to grand jury deliberations, which have not yet commenced in this matter."

Noah surveys the reaction thus far, which seems reasonably temperate.

"The Queen's Bench finds its origin in the *Curia Regis*, which was the original court where King William the Conqueror heard all matters, regardless whether they were of concern to the Crown. When jurisdiction was first divided between matters which were of no concern to the Crown, and those which *were*, it was Queen's Bench (known at the time as King's Bench, of course) which was granted jurisdiction over all matters of concern to the Crown, including cases of high treason.

"I mention this only for those Commissioners who might otherwise be completely unaware. By no means do I profess any expertise in such matters. Needless to say, there are Commissioners and Crown counsel among you who know far more about the origins of Queen's Bench than I, and who have struggled on occasion to enlighten me in the past … with mixed results, as you can see."

This is met with restrained laughter.

"So, we may conclude that this case falls well within the jurisdiction of Queen's Bench, and indeed would have been commenced there if this Court had not been convened. As Queen's Bench is perfectly capable of hearing and deciding cases such as this, one naturally asks: *What is the purpose of convening a Court of Oyer and Terminer?*

"To be sure, when Queen's Bench is out of session, if a matter truly must be addressed immediately, sometimes a court such as this is convened. However, as the prosecution is evidently satisfied in this case that Her Majesty is now in no danger from the alleged plot, there seems little reason to rush to indictment and trial. And, as I have mentioned, Queen's Bench is *in session* in the midst of its Hilary Term, and is perfectly capable of handling this case justly and speedily."

Having dispensed with one pretext for convening the Court, Noah moves on to the next. "In a Court of Oyer and Terminer, such as this, Commissioners are selected on grounds of their high standing in the community. Outside London, the assurance that the accused will be tried before a panel of local notables makes substantial sense, as so many potential jurors in the English countryside are uneducated and even illiterate. *Within* London, however, there is a large body of men who are literate and educated. In fact, some say London suffers from a *surfeit* of educated men.

"In London, then, there is no valid reason to require the greatest dignitaries of the realm to serve as Commissioners. Here we are *awash* in potential jurors. And I beg the indulgence of the Lord Admiral, as I am certain to be using *that* term incorrectly, as well." A few snorts and titters are heard from the dais.

"But, one may ask, where is the potential prejudice to the accused if, sitting in judgment on the facts of his case are the most learned men in the land, instead of the first twelve nobodies who can be corralled off a London street to sit on his jury? I will tell you where that potential prejudice lies, but, to do so, I must refer to first principles, that is, to Magna Carta. Incidentally, I fully expect to hear a great deal of tooth grinding by those of you who know Magna Carta better than I ... which I daresay may be *all* of you." The panel erupts into general laughter at this, as it not only demeans Noah's learning but overstates the Commissioners' learning, while at the same time doubting their patience.

"Magna Carta contains two widely separated mentions of the requisite trial by 'a jury of his peers.' Article Twenty-One provides that earls and barons shall not be tried for a serious crime except by their peers. Similarly, Article Thirty-Nine provides that no *freeman* shall be tried for a serious crime, nor will the Crown 'go upon him nor send upon him,' except by the lawful judgment of *his* peers or by the law of the land.

"Well, now, Magna Carta mentions earls and barons, whose peers must likewise be earls and barons, and the like. And Magna Carta *separately* mentions freemen, whose peers must be *other* freemen, *not* earls and barons. There can be no doubt that the prisoner Roderigo Lopez, a common physician, is neither an earl nor a baron. Yet, many Commissioners of this Court *are* earls and barons, lords, knights, and admirals. This jury is therefore *not* comprised of peers of the accused."

Noah then builds on his argument. "Those of you who have listened closely may say: *Ah, but Magna Carta says that a freeman need not be tried by a jury of his peers, so long as he be tried 'by the law of the land,' which must mean something different from a trial by jury, or there would have been no need for the draftsmen to use those words, 'the law of the land.'* And you are to be congratulated, for that is a *correct* interpretation.

"What, then, *is* 'the law of the land?' Our English Constitution is largely unwritten. It is found in what is often called the 'Common Law,' as expressed in the customs and practices of our courts of *regular session*, which Queen's Bench *is*, but which Oyer and Terminer is most certainly *not*. It is the irregular character of this Court and its composition, its *uncommon* procedure, if you will, that removes this Court from the ambit of *Common* Law."

Noah pauses to let this point sink in. "But, if this argument sounds too complex, let us go back to the words 'nor will the *Crown* go upon him nor send upon him.' And there's the crux of the argument. Magna Carta was a consensual limitation on the power of the *Crown*. (Never mind how the Crown's consent was extracted.) It is *the Crown* which is prohibited to punish a freeman for a serious crime, without first giving him *either* a trial by a jury of his peers *or* judgment according to the Common Law.

"*In the City of London, by whose authority is a Court of Oyer and Terminer created?* Why, by the Privy Council, of course, whose members are appointed by the Queen to serve at her pleasure. *And who does the Privy Council appoint as Commissioners?*" The panel leans in carefully to hear this, and not one of them is smiling. "Why, the most highly appointed men in the land, some of whom are themselves members of the Privy Council! Are they likely to be the smartest men in the land? *Yes!* Are they best able to reason? *Yes!*

"But *are their positions independent of the good will of the Crown and its Privy Council?*" Noah pauses to ensure he has their undivided attention. "*NO!*" he shouts. His voice thunders off the rafters, driving home his point. Dissension is now brewing on the dais.

Noah continues. "We are all familiar with the ancient wisdom that 'he who takes the Queen's shilling is the Queen's man.' Gentlemen, like it or not, *you are the Queen's men*! Yet, your commissions say that you shall try this freeman as his jurors, although you are no peers of his, and you shall try him according to procedures and customs *other than* the Common Law. As we have just seen, such a trial would violate Magna Carta, plain and simple."

An uproar ensues, but less than Noah expected. He looks over to Coke, who's taking copious notes. His expression ... *ah*, his expression betrays a heavy conscience. Noah has scored a major point with his adversary, who is a known champion of the Common Law.

"The simplest solution is to transfer the case to Queen's Bench," he suggests. The Lord Chief Justice peers down at Noah with a quizzical, ambivalent smirk, as it's *his* court that would receive this politically explosive case if it were to be transferred. Noah relaxes the pitch and volume of his voice. "And, you know, over there, we try cases like this *all the time*. A case of high treason in Queen's Bench is not, and never has been, a field day for the prisoner. I assure you that the path from *Westminster* to Tyburn is far more thoroughly worn than that from *Guildhall* to the same awful destination."

Noah begins sidling left toward the Earl of Essex. "But at Queen's Bench, as distinguished from *this* Court, the judge exercises great discretion. He may permit the participation of counsel for the accused. He may compel the Crown to produce documentary evidence and eyewitness testimony, and subject it to the scrutiny and cross-examination of the accused and his counsel." Noah's voice is growing louder again, and he now looks Essex straight in the eye. He makes sure everyone sees it, too.

"At Queen's Bench, unlike *this* Court, the accused has a greater role to play than to be shouted down by the best lawyer in all England. *There*, it is a *contest*! A contest *of truth*! *Yes*, a court is a place that *should* inspire the awe of every subject! And it should be a place of *terror* … but *only* for the subject who is guilty of the *very* crime of which he stands accused! For all others, it should be a place of *acquittal* … of *justice* … even of *mercy*. I know as well as every other Englishman that there is not a Commissioner on this Court who has *ever* run away from a fair fight. Let *this* be a fair fight!"

If Essex were a keg of gunpowder, he would have exploded by now. The look in his reddened eyes is nothing short of bloody murder. Noah returns to the center of the well, and looks to Burghley instead.

"If this Court denies our motion to transfer the case to Queen's Bench, then we now make the following motions in *this* Court: First, that all peers of the Crown and titled persons be required to resign their commissions, their appointment having violated Magna Carta. Second, that all members of the Privy Council be required to resign *their* commissions, their appointment having violated Magna Carta.

"Third, in the event that any Commissioner remains after such resignations, the accused hereby invokes his right to question every remaining Commissioner on grounds of possible interest in the outcome of the case according to the ancient form known as *voir dire*. Such right has been recognized by Common Law for more than a century. It applies in every court in the land empowered to try felonies, and this Court is *no exception*!"

"Fourth, we move to dismiss this case on grounds of diplomatic immunity under the Law of Sovereigns, in that the accused has been expressly received by Her Majesty as an ambassador of a foreign Sovereign, namely, Portugal, and that the unequivocal written consent of such Sovereign to the prosecution of the accused has *not* been received by Her Majesty. And, as the identity of the Sovereign of Portugal remains in doubt, no such consent is likely to be forthcoming."

It's just as well Noah has finished, as he would no longer be heard over the general clamor. Several Commissioners have risen from their seats and begun talking to others excitedly.

This last argument was directed hard at Coke, and his eyes went wide with it. He glances over his shoulder, not at his political master, Lord Burghley, nor at his political critic Essex, but at the master of his *profession*, the Lord Chief Justice of England, who returns his gaze with eyes wide and lips pursed and then rests his chin thoughtfully on his hands. Burghley raps his hand on a Bible in a futile attempt to bring the room back to order.

There is a tap on Noah's shoulder. It's Jonathan, who hands him a small stack of sundry items. While the room remains in tumult, Noah examines them, and at first finds them confusing. They're a series of playing cards: a queen of hearts, five aces, and a deuce. Someone must have raided more than one deck to cull these. On the deuce, the numerals and the suit have been obliterated, so as to be unreadable. He turns it over, and sees that the deck design is a black horse rearing up on its hind legs, looking remarkably like Bucklebury. Noah looks to Jonathan, and sees that they share an understanding.

The message is that, outside Guildhall, agents of Essex have gathered to arrest Noah immediately upon his departure, and that, arrayed against them are Marie, the four jesters, one *more* jester whose identity Noah cannot even guess at, and Noah's faithful steed Bucklebury. Noah looks up at Burghley, who is engaged in a heated discussion with two knights on the panel.

No one is paying the least attention to Noah any more. He walks up to Burghley, and waits in the well beneath him to be recognized. It's the arguing knights who first grow silent and look down at Noah; then Burghley does the same, while the rest of the hall remains in a commotion.

"M'lord," shouts Noah above the din, "may we go without awaiting decision on our motions?"

Burghley looks at him in complete exasperation, as though he'd like to throw the Bible at him. "By all means, Master Ames. Please, go. Please." His eyes shoot heavenward. "*Go!*"

"Thank you, m'lord." Noah bows.

He and Jonathan never look back. As the two robed barristers run like madmen through the vestibule, the doorkeeper's jaw drops, and he flees into the hall to escape them.

Just before swinging open the outside door, Jonathan says, "Bucklebury is right outside. Ride north as fast you can, turn right at the wall, and left up Bishopsgate. We'll regroup as soon as we're clear, but we *must* get out of the walled city first, or we'll be trapped! Don't look back. We'll be *right* behind you. I'll count to three. Ready?" Noah nods apprehensively. "One, two, *three!*"

Jonathan twists the knob and rams the door open with his shoulder, applying enough force to hurl anyone on the other side into the street.

Noah bursts out into the bright afternoon light, and there stands Bucklebury, sleek and black in all his glory. As Noah leaps onto his back and prods him forward, he catches sight of something unexpected. Three horses in Essex's livery are lying in the street, as though struck by a runaway cart. But before Noah can turn to look, Bucklebury shoots like a cannonball from a dead stop to frightening speed, forcing Noah to struggle to stay in the saddle.

"Go, go, go!" cries a woman's commanding voice a short distance behind him. It's Marie, using a vocal timbre Noah has never heard before. With every tiny maneuver, she shouts a new command to her mount. After only a few seconds, he learns to distinguish her horse's footfalls from those of the others further behind. She's gaining on him slightly, although remaining carefully back of him, preparing to pull up on his right as soon as he reaches the outer wall of the old city and turns right along it.

Bucklebury has not yet attained a full gallop, but already the buildings of London fly by at a dizzying pace. People shout and scramble out of his way, and he hears hooves, more hooves, thundering behind him, keeping up with his every shift and turn. Good lord, how many are there? And how many are *hostile*?

Both exhilarated and terrified, he turns right at the wall, and Marie remains in formation with him, as though demonstrating a routine maneuver on a parade ground. With the old city wall now on his left, Marie pulls next to him on his right, wearing form-fitting black riding clothes, her hair tightly bound at the nape of her neck in sportsmanlike fashion.

As they rapidly approach Bishopsgate Road, in the distance ahead of them appear two horsemen in Essex's livery approaching the same gate in the opposite direction, riding hard on a course designed to cut them off before they can reach the gate. At their current speed and direction, Noah expects they'll collide with him and Marie disastrously, just before they can escape.

But, in a split second, Marie is passed on her right by two young horsemen in masks, riding even harder than she, each wielding a heavy sandbag in his right hand.

"Keep going!" shouts one of them.

To Noah's astonishment, the two young horsemen drive straight at Essex's men and, without slowing down, smash their sandbags into the men's faces, unseating them both, and knocking one clean off his horse, while the other is dragged by a stirrup. One of the sandbags must have burst open, as sand flies everywhere.

Marie shouts over the wind. "Here comes the gate! Turn left when I say so. Wait ... wait ... NOW!" She drops back. Noah tugs the reins left, and Bucklebury hurtles through the gate with no diminution in speed. Once again, Marie maintains her relative position like an instructor in horse. Clearing the gate, he wonders how odd it must be to see a man dressed in the sedate garb of a barrister hurtling down the road at such speeds.

As they leave the walled City of London behind, the road quickly broadens. Instead of slowing down, however, Marie prods her horse to a full gallop and pulls into the lead, ensuring that their breakneck pace will not relent until all sign of Essex's men has receded into memory.

Having caught the enemy unawares, they have escaped an insurmountable force. But they may not have escaped every pair of eyes and ears in his pay.

CHAPTER 27

ABOUT FIVE MILES NORTH of London, with Noah at her side, Marie pulls to the left edge of the road, stops, and looks back. Evidently satisfied that those following them are all on Noah's side of the dispute, she steers her mount off the road and trots a few hundred yards into a churchyard, where she dismounts and leads her horse around to the back, out of sight. There's nothing there but grass, a few ancient grave markers, and a babbling brook.

"This is the rendezvous point," she says. "We must await the others here." She goes to the brook to fetch water for her horse, and Noah follows. Bucklebury seems happy to have a drink. In fact, he seems playful, as though he would have enjoyed running much farther than he did.

"That was a narrow escape," Noah declares. "Thank you for assisting with your expert horsemanship. Tell me. How did the boys persuade you to come along?"

She smiles and kisses his cheek. "When it became obvious they know less about horsemanship and self-defense than I do, I insisted." She glances around uneasily. "We're not out of the woods yet. In fact, we're not even *in* the woods yet. And I wish we were."

In a few moments, the stragglers lead their mounts into the churchyard, chatting in good spirits.

"Where are we headed?" asks Noah.

Arthur answers. "Oxfordshire. But I'm afraid Essex will guess that."

"How?" asks Noah.

Arthur brings a water bucket up to his horse's mouth. "We're north of London. Doesn't leave us many alternatives, and he knows it. If we turn east, we end up in his own County Essex amidst his henchmen, who would, incidentally, like to kill us all about now." He takes the empty pail away from his horse. "Straight north would get us into Buckinghamshire, which would be a highly efficient way to trap ourselves on this side of the Great Ouse River. Not smart."

"Although Essex's wealth and support are not in County Essex," says Noah, "we can't be sure what we would encounter there. You think Essex will conclude that northwest is all that's left us?"

"That, and he knows you're familiar with Oxford, having spent a few years at Merton."

"But *he* didn't," says Noah. "He's Cambridge." Overhearing this, the others hiss, as though at a stage villain. "*Tsk!* That's not why I said it!" He realizes that the fifth jester also hissed Cambridge through his mask.

"So you're an Oxford man, as well?"

"I thought we established that some time ago," says the fifth jester, removing his mask and revealing himself to be Stephen Rodriguez.

Noah smiles. "Oh, yes, over cognac in your dear mother's parlor." He turns to Marie. "Who's running the store?"

"No one, but we'll be back tomorrow, I hope." Marie turns to Stephen. "Better put your mask back on, señor. We can't afford to be recognized later."

"Once Essex suspects we're Oxford-bound," says Arthur, "he can either track us or send men there to await intelligence."

"Judging from what *I've* seen," says Jonathan, "if his morons are awaiting intelligence, they'll be waiting a long time. It would take an Act of God."

Arthur resumes impatiently. "He's sure to have help from some of his faithful followers. That's why we're probably better off passing through forest."

Marie holds her hand up to her eyes, and gazes at the horizon. "That's true only so long as the light holds. It will be getting dark soon, and the forest will be completely impassable on horseback. Besides, doesn't it feel as though there'll be a mist tonight?" There is general agreement that a thin fog will descend around dusk. "Mist is fine for concealing us. Unfortunately, it can also hide our path from us, confound our horses' footing, and provide equal aid to the enemy. We'd best get started."

They remount. Before emerging from the churchyard into view of the road, they line up on horseback behind the church, and choose Salazar to spy for any sign of Essex's men. He returns a short while later.

"No sign," he assures them. They move out in single file, and take a northwest route toward Oxfordshire.

They haven't gone far when Jonathan, who's assumed a position at the front, drops back to talk to Noah. "We'd better break into smaller units. We're just too conspicuous this way. A farmer's unlikely to remember seeing three or four traveling together on horseback, but he may *well* remember eight."

Marie overhears him and pulls alongside. "That will not be a problem. Once we pass into Oxfordshire, some of us are going home presently."

"*Who* is?" asks Salazar.

"Both Bennetts and Stephen," she replies.

Noah regards her skeptically. "Where is Stephen going home *to*?"

"Uncle Horace in Surrey, to keep an eye on the young ones."

Noah shakes his head. "That's too far to ride in one night. Those three needn't go any further with us now. We're unlikely to be in danger until reaching Oxfordshire, and they will not be going that far with us in any event. I'd feel much better if Stephen were to spend the night with the Bennetts at Gray's Inn. He can use my rooms." Looking down the embankment, he spots a stream. "Let's water the horses, and put our heads together a moment."

They trot down a dale, and canter along the stream to a glen that cannot be seen from the road. Fortunately, Jonathan thought to pack pen, ink, and paper. As Arthur is the only one who knows the precise location of their destination, a vacant barn at the edge of his family's farm, he joins Noah and Jonathan in composing a note to Sir Robert Cecil requesting a Crown escort to ensure their safe return to Gray's Inn. At Noah's insistence, they ask that the escort be headed by Yeoman Gardner, the trusty guard who admitted Noah and his uncle to the Tower so many years ago.

It's Stephen who suggests they omit the precise location of the barn, proposing instead that they appoint some public place for the next day's rendezvous with Gardner, which might prevent their being trapped in the barn by someone having either found the note or taken it from Stephen by force.

"Where are the Cecils staying tonight?" asks Stephen.

"At the Nevilles' at Lothbury," Noah replies.

Stephen's eyes grow wide. "But that's practically next door to *Guildhall!*"

"Yes, well, that can't be helped. Did you bring a change of clothing?"

Stephen snaps his fingers. "Now that you mention it, I did!"

Noah summons the Bennetts to hear the plan.

"All right," he says. "The Bennetts will accompany Stephen to Lothbury, but remain out of sight. Having the three of you appear there together after today's escapade would be foolhardy. Stephen, you may leave the note with Walker, if you tell him it's an emergency. Otherwise, find Henry. Only as a last resort, wake Sir Robert Cecil, and if you do, show some deference. After that, accompany the Bennetts back to Gray's Inn for the night. Here's my key."

"Where have you proposed to meet Gardner tomorrow?" asks Stephen.

"There's a parish church at Stanton Saint John, just northeast of Oxford. I've asked him in the note to meet us there at two o'clock, if he can."

"How do you plan to cross the Thame?" asks Stephen, referring to the river that meanders through Oxfordshire for many miles before becoming a tributary of the much wider Thames River that runs through London.

Arthur replies. "Some miles from here, there's a small ferry that rests on the eastern bank. It's little more than a raft, really, guided by a couple of long poles. It's big enough to take the five of us and our horses, but that's about the limit of it."

"Can the river be forded at that spot?" asks Noah.

"No. Although the Thame is only about a hundred feet wide at that point, it's twenty *deep*, which means it cannot be forded. There are no bridges close by, and the nearest fords are about thirty miles in either direction, which is why the ferry is there. If we cross over on it, we can leave it on the west bank for the night. There's a ferryman who tends to it every morning. As soon as he sees it on the wrong bank, he'll move it back."

"Won't Essex's men be looking for us there?" asks Noah.

Arthur shrugs. "I wish I knew. But our only practical alternative leaves us much *more* exposed, and Essex would anticipate us going that way, too. It's Holman's Bridge, by Aylesbury. If I were Essex, I'd be encamped on that bridge when we got there. We have no choice but to assume he cannot spy out every route. And, fortunately, he doesn't know precisely where we're going."

"All right, we all know our jobs now," says Noah. "You three leave us, and godspeed. See you in London tomorrow, by the grace of God."

Just before riding away, Stephen looks back at Marie, concern evident on his face. "Take good care, Mother!"

"Never mind *me*, young man. Watch *yourself*!" she replies, and watches him disappear the way they came, her face a mixture of pride and concern.

As the remaining party prepares to remount, Jonathan takes Noah aside and discreetly hands him a pistol.

"What's *this*?" asks Noah. "I told you, Jon. No lethal measures."

Jonathan smirks. "Of course not. We'll leave those to the enemy. This won't kill anyone. It's powdered up, but there's no ball in it."

Noah regards him skeptically. "No loose shot, either?"

Jonathan shakes his head and remounts. They leave the stream and rejoin the road. As they move quickly toward the ferry, Noah prays it will be on their side of the river when they arrive.

Either way, it will be the perfect place for a trap.

* * *

"It's over this hill," says Arthur. "When we reach the top, keep to the forest, and keep your voices down. If they're here, we may be able to spot them in the clearing."

Less than an hour of daylight remains. The woods are thick, but the lowest branches are high enough to allow them to pass comfortably on horseback. A thick layer of brush covers the forest floor. Though they try their best to keep silent, from time to time the quiet rustling of their movement is unavoidably punctuated by the sound of a hoof striking a rock, or the crack of a branch.

As they reach the crest of the ridge and the horses come to a halt, there's an eerie silence. They find themselves looking down on a large meadow. About a half mile in the distance, a narrow river runs across their field of view. On its near bank is a dock with a small ferry tied to it. A pair of long poles point straight up, affixed to the ferry by some means that cannot be made out at this distance. A thick fog rolls downstream, joined by a mist that rises from the river's surface.

"Something's not right," Arthur says pensively. "Look at the ground by the dock. There are fresh tracks. They seem to lead ... " He peers to his right, toward the edge of the woods but a short distance away. "Let's back up into the trees!" he whispers urgently. "I don't think they've spotted us." They move back.

"What do you mean, 'they'?" asks Noah, in an alarmed whisper. "Who? How many *are* there?"

"I'm not sure," says Arthur, "maybe only two, but I fear the worst. It may be *them.*" He peers out at a hilltop beyond the point where he expects the enemy may lie in wait. "We should move above them, and scout them from behind. You see that ridge to our right? We should be able to see them from there." He turns to Salazar. "What do you think, Andres?"

Andres looks to the spot Arthur indicated. "I don't know the terrain, but that's at least a quarter hour's ride from here, and I'm not even sure they'd be visible from there. It would take an additional quarter hour to return, so we'd lose at least a half hour. I doubt we've enough daylight." He hesitates. "Can we cross the river at night?"

Arthur shakes his head. "I wouldn't want to try it. There are some big rocks in it, and, around this time of year, the river can suddenly turn swift."

"That decides it," says Marie. "We're out of time. If they're here, we're going to have to draw them out."

"How?" asks Noah.

There's a moment's silence.

"Well," says Jonathan, "if they've tracked us here all the way from London, then they probably still have no firearms, as they would have been authorized to arrest us, but not to kill us."

"Stands to reason," says Arthur. "But there are no witnesses out here, and if they *do* have pistols and instructions to use them, we're dead. Maybe they knew about the writ of safe passage. If they did, then they surely wouldn't have brought pistols to Guildhall, relying instead upon overpowering strength.

They could not afford to kill us there. And I think Essex would still be inclined to have them arrest us, rather than kill us."

"The only way to draw them out is to show them their quarry," says Salazar. "I have an idea. Master Ames, give Arthur your cap and barrister's cloak." Noah fishes around in his saddlebag. "Goodwife Rodriguez, did you bring an overcoat?"

"Of course," she says. "Do you think I wish to freeze to death?"

"May I borrow it?" asks Salazar. She gives it to him. "Jonathan, bring your weapons to hand. If they fire on us, then fire in their direction. That should pin them down long enough for us to escape. And if they come after us, then come after *them*." Jonathan nods, and silently pats down several weapons already on his person while Arthur and Andres do their best to look like Noah and Marie from the rear.

"Masks and hoods on!" whispers Andres. "Jonathan, don't come out right away. If we're followed, we'll draw them back past the edge of the woods, and you hit them from behind." He sits up primly, turns to Arthur, and says in a high-pitched effeminate voice: "Shall we?"

"By all means, my dear," replies Arthur in a deep baritone.

Cautiously, Arthur and Andres ride side by side into the clearing. Noah and Marie watch them go.

"Do I really sound like that?" asks Noah.

She turns to him, quietly outraged. "Do *I*?"

Arthur and Salazar have gone only a short way when two men emerge from the precise location where Arthur expected them to be. The tangerine and cream of Essex's livery is plain, even in the gloaming.

"Halt!" one shouts.

Instead of stopping, Arthur and Andres pick up speed, ride briefly toward the river, then veer left with Essex's men in hot pursuit, making a great circle that brings them up to the edge of the woods, right past Jonathan. As they ride by, Jonathan spurs his horse forward, rides up behind the man nearest Arthur, and sandbags him from behind with such force that the man falls out of the saddle and lands face down on the ground with his limbs splayed, motionless.

At the first sign of commotion, Salazar turns and flashes a broad smile at the Essex man nearest him, whose shock at seeing a mustachioed young Spaniard instead of a woman provides Salazar with the brief moment he needs to leap out of the saddle onto him and drag him to the ground, pummeling his face all the while, giving him no chance to recover.

Soon both Jonathan's and Andres's men lie face down, their hands bound behind them. In a moment, they're being dragged up into the woods past Noah and Marie. Jonathan's prisoner is not moving at all. Although Andres' appears terrified, he does not struggle.

As soon as Arthur is confident their adversaries have been subdued, he dismounts and checks their saddlebags for weapons. One was carrying a dagger, the other a short sword. Otherwise, all he finds are a few coins and maps. "They have no pistols, thank heavens," he says. "Bring them a short way into the woods, and tie them up near their mounts. Someone will surely come searching for them." He leads the two horses up into the woods. In a moment, the men and horses have been securely tied to the trunks of large oak trees.

"Let's go," says Jonathan. He rides casually down toward the ferry with Arthur and Andres, ignoring Noah and Marie, who straggle behind. The fog creeps up out of the river onto the meadow before them. It's growing dark.

"Shall we?" asks Marie, mimicking the voice Andres used to imitate her.

"Why, certainly, my dear," replies Noah, in equally theatrical tones.

They leave the cover of the woods well behind the others, and have gone only a short way before the others disappear into the mist by the raft.

At that moment, Gelly Meyrick returns and finds his men missing.

* * *

Fog has rapidly billowed up from the river and now covers the entire meadow, stopping only a few yards short of the forest's edge, making sounds difficult to locate.

It's Marie who first senses the heavy approach of Meyrick's horse from behind. Instead of turning to look, she immediately prods her mount away from the approaching hoofbeats.

"Come *on*, Noah!" she yells behind her. Momentarily flustered, Noah fails to comprehend why she's lurched away.

Meyrick rides out of the mist and strikes Noah heavily in the lower back with his huge open hand, knocking the wind out of him and nearly throwing him from the saddle. Noah doubles over in breathless pain, which was evidently Meyrick's plan, as he rides right past Noah and gallops after Marie.

"Come back here, witch!" Meyrick grunts in a grating voice that brings to mind a wild boar. His strategy is apparently to capture the weakest member of the company, whom he naturally expects to be the woman. That's a mistake for which Marie intends to make him pay dearly.

Having turned just in time to see Noah struck from behind, she quickly turns and gallops away to draw Meyrick after her. He's riding a big warhorse, giving him the advantage in strength, but ceding her the edge in speed. She presses her advantage by carving a great circle around the meadow and climbing obliquely back up the hill past the spot where they first left the shelter of the woods.

Meyrick is not as stupid as he looks, however. He's anticipated her move. Instead of following in her wake, under cover of fog he goes straight up the hill, bisecting her circle, seeking to cut her off at forest's edge.

Although she initially blames the fog for her inability to hear his hoofbeats behind her, at the last second she realizes her mistake and prods her mount to a fast gallop. Just as Meyrick emerges from the fog, his grubby arm outstretched in her direction, she flies past him, her shoulder brushing his hand, knocking it out of the way.

Realizing that she has actually come within reach of the brute and nearly collided with him, she lets go a horrified shriek, putting a warlike edge on it before it leaves her throat.

She must get to the ferry, which is now their only escape, and she's probably singlehandedly delaying its departure. As she leaves the clearing and dives back into the fog, Meyrick and his monstrous horse come alongside. On a straight downward run, her speed advantage has completely disappeared, and her slight advantage in maneuverability will make no difference. Turning into the thickening fog, she realizes that neither she nor her mount can see more than a few yards ahead.

* * *

"Meyrick!" shouts Noah, as Meyrick speeds past him toward the ferry in close pursuit of Marie.

Noah can see the brute gaining on her, maneuvering to her right, and grasping for her. He prods Bucklebury, who hurtles forward into the clearing made by the two leading horses as they cut through the fog.

"Meyrick!" he shouts again, but still the brute takes no notice, fully intent on getting his filthy hands on Marie. Noah quickly searches his pockets for weapons. All he can find is Uncle Avram's dagger and the pistol that Jonathan handed him earlier. His mind races, and he curses himself. It was on his own instructions that Jonathan loaded the pistol with nothing but a powder charge. He'll have to make do as best he can.

He draws the dagger and pulls up to Meyrick's right, trying to get close enough to brandish it in his face. Meyrick takes his eyes off Marie for only a split second. Seeing the dagger, he draws his short sword and prepares to swing it, but not at Noah — at *Marie*. Noah must do something *fast*, so he lunges at Meyrick with the dagger, nearly falling from the saddle in the process.

Meyrick sees him lunge and quickly swings his short sword at Noah. Noah recoils, but not fast enough. The sword swings under his outstretched arm and grazes the left side of his torso. He shouts in agony and surprise, and drops his dagger. A warm trickle at the site of the wound cools rapidly in the passing wind.

Marie has disappeared into the mist up ahead, leaving Noah and Meyrick galloping side by side into thick fog. Their mounts scream in terror, as they can no longer see more than a few feet ahead, and, running blind, can break a leg on something as commonplace as an unexpected divot or dead branch.

Doing his best to ignore his bloody wound, Noah quickly draws the pistol. As Meyrick draws back his sword to make another thrust, in sheer desperation Noah spurs Bucklebury to still greater speed, bringing him to the neck of Meyrick's mount. His wound shrieks at him as he stretches out his left arm, brings the pistol as near as possible to the ear of Meyrick's mount, cocks it, and fires.

BOOM! The blast rings out. Even through the dampening mist, it echoes off the hills and round again. Meyrick's mount pitches and tumbles, ejecting him forward like a cannonball into the fog.

As Bucklebury slows down, Noah looks down at his wound, which bleeds profusely. He nearly blacks out, but maintains his senses and struggles to remain in the saddle. He sees Marie ahead of him, the activity around the ferry having split the fog in its immediate vicinity. He can see her hand off her mount to Arthur, who brings it on board and helps her to embark.

Noah proceeds straight to the landing. Although he tries to come to a halt at the dock, there's no stopping Bucklebury, who leaps excitedly onto the ferry, somehow landing on the small space still vacant. The ferry pitches from his weight, causing the other horses to whinny excitedly. If the other horses had not been placed precisely where they were, the ferry would surely have capsized, but instead it quickly rights itself.

As Noah dismounts and becalms Bucklebury, the pain returns and shoots through his left side like a knife. He doubles over, and lies face down on the deck, unable to move, barely able to breathe. Marie gasps. "Oh, my God! Noah, you're hurt!"

She turns him over, trembling in anticipation of what she might find. She grabs a piece of cloth from her saddlebag and wipes away as much of the blood as possible. "It must hurt like the devil," she says, "but it's not deep. You've been very fortunate, yet again."

The jesters appear shaken by the bloody wound. One of them hands Marie a fresh cloth, and she presses it against the wound. "Hold this in place without pressing too hard," she tells Noah, placing his hand over the cloth.

"Cast off!" shouts Arthur as Salazar, who's been standing by, unties the rope and shoves the ferry away from the dock.

Before Arthur can extricate a maneuvering pole from its sheath, the ferry drifts a few yards downstream, bringing them to a point barely six feet from the riverside they just left.

There, at the edge of the water, stands Gelly Meyrick, in stark relief against the fog behind him, grass-stained, weatherbeaten, and bleeding from scratches on his face and legs. He stands still as a death mask, and there's murder in his eyes.

Jonathan sees him immediately, draws out a pistol, cocks it, and aims it at his face. Arthur, who has finally mastered one of the guide poles, lodges it against the current, holding the ferry still to avoid jostling Jonathan in case he has to shoot.

Meyrick neither flinches nor shows any sign of emotion, but merely looks Jonathan straight in the eye. He speaks in a growling whisper.

"You lamed me mount," says Meyrick, as though it's the lowest accusation that can be leveled at another human being.

"Yes, I did. Didn't I?" Jonathan smiles cruelly, even though it was Noah who fired the pistol. "And *you* killed my old man, and wounded my master. Why don't you wade in and finish the job, you *filth*? Come on, you *coward*! You pig's *offal*! You bridge troll! You stinking sack of manure!" He reaches into his vest pocket, draws out a scroll with an embossed red seal at its base, holds it up to view, and lets it unfurl before Meyrick's fixed gaze.

"I've got a royal writ of safe passage here. I've got a pistol. All I need is a *pretext*! Come *on*, you lump of vomit! You putrid oaf! Take one step. Just one. Give me a reason. Come *on*!" Jonathan is growling now, his eyes red with rage, his face contorted in hatred.

While Noah's ability to gauge time is adversely affected by his pain, it seems to him that they remain in this position for about a half minute before Arthur finally takes matters into his own hands and gently shoves the ferry away from the bank.

Neither Jonathan nor Meyrick moves a muscle. Slowly, Meyrick disappears into the fog, and the ferry carries them backward toward the opposite bank. When they're safely clear of Meyrick, Arthur kneels beside Noah, but addresses Marie.

"How bad is it?"

"It's not deep at all, but the wound is long, so it's very painful. He'll have to avoid tugging on it too much." She turns to Noah, who's no longer overcome with pain. "Keep your left arm at your side, and you'll be all right, until we get you to a physician, although how we'll find one in this blasted countryside, I've no idea."

Noah forces himself to smile, which he can manage only wanly. "Won't need one. I'll be all right." He turns to Jonathan, and forces a more convincing smile. "Jonathan, I didn't know *you* had the writ of safe passage."

Jonathan plops down forlornly on the deck with the pistol in one hand and the paper in the other.

"I *don't*," he replies. Quizzical glances are exchanged in total silence.

"Then, what is *that*?" Noah asks, pointing to the paper. "Whose seal is on there?"

"Master Treasurer's. It's an overdue rent bill from Gray's Inn."

Noah gingerly sits up in surprise. Marie lets go a nervous laugh.

"And the pistol?" says Noah. "Is it loaded with ball? With shot?"

"Neither," replies Jonathan. "Just powder ... like yours."

Arden and Salazar gape at each other in silence.

"Just so I understand," says Arden. "You held Gelly Meyrick at bay with an overdue rent bill and a popgun?"

Noah laughs quietly, in defiance of his wound's painful protest.

Although Jonathan cannot join in the general mirth, he nods with a smirk. "I suppose I *did*."

As they drift across the river, Noah watches Jonathan intently. He has seen homicidal rage only a few times before, but he's quite sure he saw it in Jonathan's eyes just now. Pistol or no, he has no doubt that, if Meyrick had taken a single step forward, Jonathan would not have relented until either he or Meyrick was dead.

It wasn't the pistol that had held Meyrick at bay. And it certainly wasn't the "writ." It was the absolute certainty in Jonathan's eyes that he was going to kill Meyrick.

CHAPTER 28

NOAH SITS ON THE COLD, HARD GROUND in the dark, leaning against the trunk of a great oak, so fatigued that he's drifted off waiting for Arthur's return. Someone gently shakes his shoulder. His head jerks, and his eyes open.

It's Arthur. "All right. I've checked the barn. It's vacant, and *looks* it. There's a fireplace in it, some wood — "

"No fires," mumbles Noah. "No light, no chimney smoke."

Arthur sounds exasperated. "All right, but it's plenty cold in there. I hope you brought some warm clothes and blankets."

Noah blinks several times to clear his vision, and extends his right arm. "Give me a hand — *oooof!*" The combined pain of his wounded torso and his stiff back mercilessly remind him of the pounding they took earlier this evening. Although Marie has tied two garments together into a makeshift girdle that goes around his torso and thoroughly stanches his bleeding, it's far less effective in reducing pain.

Arthur helps him to his feet. "Best news is: The cook left a lot of food for us near the back door of the kitchen. Cold meats, potatoes, bread, beer, and so on. I even grabbed a bottle of whiskey to clean up your wound. It's all in these four sacks. Come on. Let's go inside."

The others stir from their uncomfortable resting places. Jonathan wipes his eyes. He takes the bags from Arthur, ties them into two makeshift saddlebags, and suspends them across his horse's back.

In bedraggled single file, they stumble across the rutted field. Still, conditions might have been worse on this last leg of their journey. They remain dry, and it's not as dark as it might have been. The sky is mostly cloudless, and the moon nearly full. Although the moonlight silhouettes them for any prying eyes, nothing can be done to avoid that. Besides, if any hostile eyes are near enough to see them, they'll inevitably be taken, as they're in no condition to flee.

The rough-hewn barn door creaks open in the pale moonlight. Upon entering, each traveler feels saddened in his own way that his long-promised respite from violent pursuit is nothing more than this cold and weathered old structure. Jonathan mournfully closes the door behind them.

They wait while Marie cleans Noah's wound. Although it stings badly, Noah clenches his teeth, refusing to complain or make any sound as she works and then reaffixes the girdle.

Marie takes out the bowls of food and beer, spreads the bags out as a rough tablecloth on a plank floor near the fireplace, and places the bowls atop the cloth. They begin eating and drinking in silence, but slowly their spirits rise.

Arthur and Andres concentrate on the beer. At one point, they smile broadly at each other, apparently sharing some memory of earlier in the day. Finally, Andres can hold his laughter no longer, and sprays beer out his mouth.

"Salazar!" says Arthur, in his best impersonation of a censorious schoolmaster. "You are a *pig*! There is a lady present! And we are *eating*!" Salazar just smiles.

Marie smiles at Noah in the moonlight.

"Care to share the jest, boys?" she asks.

Jonathan shifts uneasily. "Oh, *no*. I think I know what this is going to be."

"Well," begins Arthur, "Jonathan handed us his potion this morning, and told us how much to slip to Essex's horses by Guildhall. When Essex's men looked away, Andres put the measured amount in their feed bags. He also loosened the saddles."

Jonathan's brow furrows. "Why did you do *that*?"

Arthur ignores the question. "We knew that the stuff would put the horses to sleep, eventually. But what Jonathan failed to tell us was that it would also make the horses ... " he seeks the perfect word, "*gassy*."

Noah looks at Jonathan incredulously. "You gave them laudanum *and* laxatives?"

Jonathan nods. "I asked Doctor Lopez months ago how to measure the appropriate amounts. I estimated the weight of an average horse, and had these two administer a nonlethal amount. Loosening the saddles was *their* idea."

Arthur resumes. "While we were waiting for the two of you to emerge from Guildhall, we kept an eye on the horses. One of Essex's men climbed onto his horse, which immediately *sat down*! You've never seen a horseman so shocked, as he slid off the rear of the horse into the street, saddle and all. Then, another horse sat down. The rider, who had not yet mounted, watched in horror as his saddle slid right off onto the ground.

"Then the most brutish of the three horsemen saw what was happening, and got up on his mount. By this time, he suspected that someone had been tampering with the horses, but he had no way of knowing what they'd done, or who'd done it. So, he just sat there imperiously on his steed, guiding it around the square, when suddenly ... "

Andres's laughter intensifies, his breath now coming in short gasps, which draws an admonishing look from Arthur.

"So," resumes Arthur, "there was this horseman looking around suspiciously, when suddenly his mount let out the loudest and longest fart in the history of horse farts, which is all well documented, I assure you. And then, the horse did his ... *business*, and — Andres, *please!*"

Noah can barely contain his own laughter, though his side aches. "*What did he do?*"

"The horse sat down ... and the saddle came loose."

"*Oh, gads!*" says Marie, her eyes shut tight. "*Please*. No more!"

Jonathan is red-faced. "I was only trying to incapacitate their horses."

Andres sits up, and barks: "Well, you managed *that*, all right!"

Jonathan cocks his head. "The last rider. Was that — ?"

Arthur nods. "Meyrick."

"Oh!" says Jonathan. "So *that's* what he meant when he said I lamed his mount. Hah!" He claps his hands. "Good!"

* * *

Arthur fetches blankets from the farmhouse to keep them warm without building a telltale fire, although in fact it never gets much colder in the barn than it was when they first entered.

Noah awakens only once in the night, to find Marie kissing his cheek, which helps him escape a horrid dream of being chased by an ogre with a sword. He opens his eyes and gazes into hers. "I love you," he whispers. She smiles skeptically, and kisses him.

On the edge of a dream, he hears her whisper, "Do you?"

* * *

At dawn, Noah is rudely awakened by a pounding on the door, and sits up like a shot. Although neither his back nor his flesh wound is quite right, to his relief, they're already much better than the previous evening.

"Open up, in the name of the Queen!" comes an unfamiliar, very commanding voice. The others sit up in alarm.

Jonathan, who has evidently been awake for a while, comes over to Noah and whispers excitedly. "We're surrounded. They're at both doors. I could see them through the window in the hayloft."

"What livery are they in?" asks Noah.

"*ER* badges all over. The motto is *Semper Eadem*."

"That's something of a relief. 'Ever the Same.' That means they're the Queen's men. Let's just hope the livery is genuine." His brow furrows. "But how could Gardner have found us in this barn?"

Jonathan shrugs. "Neither Stephen nor the Bennetts knew precisely where we'd be."

Marie scowls. "Stephen would never betray anyone!" she says. "Gardner could easily have deduced it once he learned where Arthur's family farm was located."

Noah scowls. "No one's said anything about betrayal. The information could have been wrested from him."

Jonathan nods nervously. "They *could* be Essex's men!"

"Doesn't matter," replies Noah. "Draw no weapons. We're letting them in. If they're Essex's men, I'll try to surrender alone." He turns to the others. "Do you hear me? No violence. No attempt at escape."

The others nod reluctantly. Noah rises with some effort, draws a deep breath that causes his side to twinge, and swings open the door.

"Are you Noah Ames?" asks a tall dark man in Queen's livery.

"I *am*!" says Noah with bravado, adopting his fearless courtroom voice. "And who might *you* be?"

"I am Francis of the Tower Guard," he pronounces sternly.

"It is good to meet you, Francis of the Tower Guard!" replies Noah in stentorian tones.

The guard seems surprised to be greeted as a friend. Evidently, such things rarely happen to guards of the Tower of London.

A gruff voice comes from behind Francis.

"Let me by, Frank! We've no time to waste." To Noah's great relief, the grizzled Yeoman Gardner appears, and bows perfunctorily. This is the first time Noah has ever seen him away from his post outside the Tower. "Mornin', Master Ames. Glad we've got you now. There's some strange folk about, from over east, if you take my meanin'." Noah nods. He can only be referring to Essex's men.

"Francis," says Gardner. "I've some business with Master Ames and Master Hawking. Give these other fine people some food, and keep them here." He draws Francis aside. "*Guests*, not prisoners. Got it? And get their horses fed and watered." Francis nods.

Gardner points to Noah's shirt, which is matted with dried blood. "Looks like you run into a sharp branch, suh. You need help with that right away?"

"No, thank you, Yeoman Gardner," says Noah, pointing with his chin toward Marie. "It's been ably tended by our esteemed surgeon in residence."

Gardner glances at Marie, who nods in return. He takes a quick look around the wound, and closes Noah's shirt. "Better job than the Yeomans' surgeon woulda done." He tips his hat to Marie, and mutters beneath his breath. "But then, I'll warrant she wasn't drunk when she done it."

"Your business is with me, too?" asks Jonathan. In answer, Gardner takes him by the arm and escorts him out of the door. There are Tower guards everywhere. So much for secrecy.

The fog has lifted, but the leaves still drip with the heavy dew of early morning, and the ground is wet. A covered carriage awaits them. Noah and Jonathan get in, followed by Gardner, who shuts the door behind.

"Where are we going?" asks Noah.

Gardner takes out Noah's note of the previous night, and reads aloud from it. "My correspondent here says 'the parish church at Stanton Saint John.'"

"That's my note, but why go there now?" asks Noah. "You've already found us."

Gardner smiles smugly.

They ride for about twenty minutes, coming to a halt on a hilltop with a wide vista. A small steeple peeks out of the treetops partway down the hill, signifying the location of a chapel. Gardner steps out of the carriage, carrying a large leather pouch. He puts his finger to his lips, and beckons them to follow silently. Through a small woods, he descends toward the chapel. After a while, he stops and signals them to crouch.

"You see that little chapel through the woods?" he asks quietly.

"Yes. Is that the parish church where we were to meet?" asks Jonathan.

Gardner nods. Jonathan spies something through the trees, and whistles softly.

"What do you see?" Gardner asks, though he obviously knows.

"Gelly Meyrick, holding — " Jonathan squints, "a ... *crossbow*?" He looks to Gardner for confirmation.

Gardner nods. "Meyrick has orders to bring Master Ames to the earl, but he's got no orders about *you*, Master Hawking. So, now you know who that crossbow is for."

Noah interrupts, pressing his arm against his wound, which seems to relieve the pain caused by all this jostling. "How would Meyrick know our rendezvous point?"

"Your note passed through several sets of hands before it reached Her Majesty, sir. They're not all to be trusted ... obviously."

"Meyrick is a scoundrel!" says Jonathan, gritting his teeth.

"Aye. He's *that*, sir. Fortunately, I brought another friend of yours with me." Gardner opens the leather pouch, and withdraws a shiny, well-oiled crossbow. He cocks it deftly, hands it to Jonathan, and points out its sighting mechanism. "You just look through this notch here, and line it up with the metal blade. Y'see?" He mimes pulling the release lever, and makes a clicking sound with his tongue.

Jonathan nods. "Yes, but — "

"We'll be waitin' for you up at the coach. See y'in a few minutes, sir — unless you'd like me to assist?"

Jonathan shakes his head, looking dubiously at the crossbow in his hand, and sits on a large boulder still wet with dew. Gardner and Noah return to the carriage.

"Why would you do that?" Noah asks as soon as they reach the carriage.

Gardner smirks. "Same reason I do everythin', suh. Orders."

Noah is at a loss. "But who would give such an order?"

"That I may not say. But, tell me, suh. You think you're the only one who needs to know a man's character?"

"But what could such a thing tell about Hawking's character?"

Just then, Jonathan reappears, climbing out of the woods carrying the crossbow, still cocked. It has plainly not been used. He hands it back to Gardner, who bows curtly. Jonathan nods in return, and steps back into the carriage alone, staring pensively out the opposite window.

Gardner leads Noah out of Jonathan's earshot. As he uncocks the crossbow and puts it back in its leather case, he raises an eyebrow: "Who said anythin' about *his* character, suh?" he asks.

"You mean ... this is about *my* character?" asks Noah.

"Well, sir, you watched me hand that young man a crossbow and encourage him to kill a man, and you never said a *word*."

Now Noah is chagrined. "But I just assumed — "

Gardner laughs chestily. "Just jokin', suh. It *was* about Master Hawking's character. And don't worry. He did the right thing."

Noah looks at him skeptically. "*Did* he, Yeoman Gardner? I wonder. Under the same circumstances, would *you* have killed Meyrick?"

"In a *heartbeat*, suh," Gardner says without hesitation. Seeing Noah's surprise at his frankness, he adds: "Oh, *I* like to be right, too, sir. But I'd rather stay alive." He thinks for a moment. "On the other hand, maybe that's why I'm suited to the Tower Guard, and Master Hawking is not. But that's all right, as that's not a position he's up for, is it?"

They rejoin Jonathan in the carriage, and set off back to the barn where they left the others. There's something Noah wants to ask before rejoining them. "Yeoman Gardner," he asks, "when may we see our client again?"

Gardner obviously weighs his reply carefully. "Master Hawking will probably see Doctor Lopez in the next few days." He's pointedly omitted mention of Noah from this assurance, but he'll say no more about it.

*   *   *

Jonathan, Arthur, and Andres ride their own horses, while Bucklebury and Marie's horse are tied abreast behind the carriage, each perfectly content to take the long walk without the extra weight of a rider.

Because of the persistent pain in Noah's back and side, he lies stretched out along one of the carriage seats all the way back to London. As there's nothing to absorb the shock of the wheels hitting the road, Marie has placed several blankets under him, rolled up another, and tucked it under his knees, which seems to provide some relief. She graces the opposite seat.

They doze off several times. It's late afternoon by the time they reach London. From his reclining position, Noah can see the top of Bishopsgate, which means they're entering London along the path by which they fled it the previous afternoon.

From the tops of the few landmarks he can discern, he realizes they're turning west on Candlewick Street, near the river, which strikes him as an unnecessarily roundabout way of reaching Gray's Inn.

As he's feeling much better, he sits up and pats Marie's hand. She smiles wanly. They pass Saint Paul's on their right, and proceed through Ludgate onto Fleet Street, where they stop almost immediately. To their left is Serjeants' Inn.

Noah sticks his head out of the window, about to tell Gardner that he's stopped prematurely, when Gardner opens the door to let them out.

"I'm afraid you've inadvertently promoted me, Yeoman Gardner," Noah protests. "I reside at Gray's Inn."

Gardner smiles, and shakes his head confidently. "Wasn't *me* who promoted you, sir. And whether it's a mistake … well, that remains to be seen."

Noah is dazed by Gardner's suggestion. Can Noah have been elevated to Serjeant because of yesterday's events? Is that even possible?

Noah steps down from the coach, and then assists Marie. As he turns to the inn, he realizes there's a large group of Serjeants gathered in the vestibule just inside the outer door.

Gardner whispers in his ear. "Your masked friends never entered the walled city, sir. They left us about ten miles back. Better they're not seen with us." Gardner calls to Jonathan, who dismounts and hands off his horse to the stableman. "Master Hawking, you'll be staying here with your Master Ames until we can post some sentries outside your quarters at Gray's Inn. Meantime, there'll be two Tower guards stationed here next couple o' weeks." He whistles to two of his men, who hand off their horses to the stableman and take up positions beside the door.

"And now, Master Ames, I suppose congratulations are 'in order,' as they say, but I don't want to be stealin' too much thunder from those fellas waitin' for you inside. So, let me just say 'congratulations.' I'll be leavin' you now for a snore. I only slept a few hours last night before gettin' the call, and then I realized I'd have to get to you before … *they* did, or the whole trip woulda turned out pointless."

Noah shudders at the implication. "Thank you very much, Yeoman Gardner. I *knew* I could rely on you." He tries to give Gardner a handful of coins, but Gardner waves it away.

"Thank you very much, suh, but I've got so many men here to pay that the Exchequer's disbursin' this one to me directly. Orders from the top!" He winks. "Besides, if you tried to bury all *this* lot under Administrative Expenses, I'm afeard you'd be comin' to the Tower through that gate leadin' up from the Thames, if you take my meanin'." Noah shudders again. *Traitor's Gate.* It's commonly believed that no one who enters through that gate leaves the Tower alive. What a *morbid* sense of humor!

Relieved that he put on a fresh shirt before beginning the return trip, Noah escorts Marie by the arm into Serjeants' Inn, followed by Jonathan. As the doors open, the assemblage breaks out into applause. At the front of the pack, Lord Bleffingham beams at Noah. He's holding two scrolls.

"Serjeant Ames, it is my privilege to welcome you to the venerable ranks of the Serjeants-at-Law. We are an old French order dating from a time before the Conqueror, when — "

"Oh, let 'em in the *door*, Harold!" comes a good-humored shout from the rear. "They're exhausted and hungry, and we've got a meal waiting for them. Let 'em eat it while it's still hot!"

"Very well," says Bleffingham good-naturedly. "I hereby serve upon you this writ relieving you of your representation of Roderigo Lopez, and this second writ, which I implore you to read immediately."

So, Gardner knew that Noah was to be relieved as counsel to Doctor Lopez, which is why he referred to an upcoming meeting between Jonathan and Lopez while omitting any mention of Noah.

"M'lord," says Noah respectfully, "before opening this second scroll, may I ask what became of our motions in the Court of Oyer and Terminer? And how fares Doctor Lopez?"

Bleffingham flinches almost imperceptibly. "All in good time, Master Ames. All in good time. But, for now, we must insist that you open this scroll and read."

He opens it, and, just as Gardner has foretold, it is letters patent appointing Noah Ames a Serjeant-at-Law. At its foot are the signatures of Lord Burghley and the Queen. Noah is speechless. To think that he's spent the past day infuriating the Queen's favorite and running for his life, and now the highest honor awardable to an English barrister is being bestowed upon him by that selfsame Queen. All very dizzying.

He smiles at the assembled, who easily number twenty-five, waves the letters at them in his right hand, and shouts triumphantly: "I am *one* of you!"

A cheer goes up.

"Now," says Bleffingham, "you must come eat and drink, and tell us of your perilous exploits." He ushers them to places of honor at the head of the table.

Bleffingham rises to give the first toast. "Welcome, Serjeant Ames." He raises his glass. "You have returned to us like the judge of the Old Testament who escaped unscathed from the lions' den. But, in your case, Serjeant Ames, the lions' den was the Court of Oyer and Terminer, which is filled with lions far more terrifying than any dreamed of in the Old Testament. A neat trick, if you can pull it off, and, needless to say, one that many of your newfound brethren would like you to teach them." This is met by good-humored shouts of approval.

"To Noah Ames," says Bleffingham, "*a second Daniel!*"

"A second Daniel!" they shout as one, and drink deeply. After several additional toasts, they eat a hearty soup, and begin on a course of mutton.

Even in his relief and joy, however, Noah realizes that his stomach is churning, and it's not from eating in his famished condition. Rather, it's that glint of pity he caught in Bleffingham's eye at the mention of Lopez.

Almost as though he's been reading Noah's mind, Bleffingham approaches him from behind, trailed by Jonathan. "Serjeant Ames, will you accompany Master Hawking and me for a moment?" He bows to Marie. "Pardon us for just a few minutes, Goodwife Rodriguez." She nods patiently.

Bleffingham escorts Noah and Jonathan to a room ordinarily used for private consultations between Serjeants and members of the Privy Council. As he closes the door behind them, Henry Neville emerges from a side room.

"Master — or should I say 'Serjeant' Ames," begins Henry. "I am glad to see you looking very little the worse for wear. You will be pleased to learn that your daughter remains safe in the company of my father. Welcome back,

Jonathan. It must remain secret that I was here. As you may have guessed, it was *I* who told Gardner to look for you in the outbuildings at Arden's farm."

Noah could kick himself. Of *course* it was Henry! He's Arthur's *kinsman*, after all, and must know the farm's location. To Henry, their destination must have been obvious.

Henry continues. "As *someone* need inform you, I must tell you that your omnibus motion before the Court of Oyer and Terminer was denied, and that Doctor Lopez was tried there this afternoon, and found guilty."

Noah and Jonathan almost fall down at the news. "What?" Noah stammers incredulously. "Then why all the *celebration*?"

"Because," says Henry, "Her Majesty was appalled to hear your incisive argument that to try a commoner in such a court violates Magna Carta. She is entirely rethinking use of such courts in the future. More importantly, for your purposes, she is considering vacating the conviction, and transferring the Lopez matter to Queen's Bench. She has also instructed Robert Cecil to schedule a clemency hearing in the case."

"Where is Lopez now?" asks Noah.

"The Tower. But, *Serjeant* Ames, you are forbidden to speak with him again. Until further notice, your client ... *your sole client* ... is the Crown. The Exchequer's been notified to put you on the Crown's pay. Oh, and he tells me you'd better submit your final bill for services to Lopez right away." He smiles smugly. "Like it or not, Serjeant Ames, you are taking the Queen's *shilling*, so you are the Queen's *man*. I imagine you'll be hearing that quite a lot in the coming days."

Noah can only smile to have his own words thrown back at him. "But who will serve as Lopez's legal counsel?"

Henry points to Jonathan. "As soon as the commission can be arranged, his counsel will be Master Hawking."

Well, *that's* a relief. Then, Noah remembers Coke's reaction to several of his arguments. "And Coke?" he asks. "Had *he* no problem dispensing with our arguments?"

Henry and Bleffingham exchange a knowing look.

"I cannot afford to be seen with you just now," says Henry. "However, Lord Bleffingham has told me that he will be kind enough to escort you two to Coke's window at Inner Temple. Meanwhile, I will congratulate you both on your courage, and Serjeant Ames on the occasion of his elevation. I bid you all adieu, although I will be seeing you soon." Henry bows low, and departs through the side room.

Lord Bleffingham escorts them outside to Inner Temple, which is nearby. As they reach the side of the inn from which Coke's room looks out, the setting sun brightly illuminates the windows.

The old judge points out Coke's window. "It's there on the first story, third from the left."

Noah and Jonathan peer up, shielding their eyes from the reflected sunlight. And there he sits in Coke's window, after having changed hands so often, sometimes by force, sometimes by stealth.

"Finerty!" exclaims Jonathan.

"*Shhhh*, Master Hawking. Master Coke is surely sleeping now. He is probably the only man in England to have been awake more hours than you have for the past two days."

"I wonder what he intended by putting that silly dog in the window," muses Jonathan.

"I should think it clear," says Noah. "He was signifying to me — and *you*, Jonathan — that we had bested him, just as we had in the trial where Finerty made his first appearance."

"*Bested* him?" asks Jonathan. "How? He went ahead as Crown counsel in the Court of Oyer and Terminer, and convicted our client!"

Noah shakes his head. "But in that he was only doing his job. No, we bested him *prior* to that. Unless I'm mistaken, he argued *our* case to the Court long after you and I fled for Oxfordshire." He looks to Bleffingham, who nods gravely.

"That is correct," says the old jurist. "He argued assiduously on two principal points. First, the diplomatic immunity issue. Then, Magna Carta."

"How long did it go on?"

"I understand he returned to Inner Temple just before dawn, slept for two hours, then returned for trial."

"Are you suggesting he argued for *twelve hours*?" asks Jonathan.

"As I heard it from Master Neville," says Lord Bleffingham, "there was 'blood on the walls.' No one left the entire time. Essex had learned of your escape within minutes, and was beside himself all evening and all night. He threatened Coke with everything he could think of. I fear — "

Noah looks at him somberly. "You fear he may have ruined his chances for Attorney General?"

"I'm afraid so. Even the Cecils were furious at him, as they now had to explain to Her Majesty that two of the best practicing lawyers in the land believe the Court of Oyer and Terminer to violate Magna Carta."

After a long silence, Noah thinks to break the solemnity of the moment, saying to Jonathan: "Your nephew should really take that dog back."

"No," says Bleffingham. "It should rather be placed in the national archives. You and Coke have begun an argument that is capable of only one resolution, although your position may take many years to prevail."

CHAPTER 29

AT SERJEANTS' INN, Marie is assigned a comfortable room reserved for visiting dignitaries and the occasional female visitor. Nevertheless, as soon as her children return from Uncle Horace's the second week of March, she resumes residence at her house in Holborn. Noah has become a frequent dinner guest there, and spends as much time with her as propriety will allow.

Jonathan receives a note from Yeoman Gardner, assuring him that, although a special guard has been posted at Gray's Inn to ensure his safety, Essex's men have been called off.

Jonathan moves out of Serjeants' Inn one morning without fanfare. On his way out of the door, Noah approaches him. "I wish you the very best of luck," he says, shaking his hand, "although you've shown yourself quite capable of making your own good fortune. Doctor Lopez finds himself in very accomplished hands."

"Might you assist in preparing his case for clemency?" Jonathan asks sheepishly.

Noah shakes his head. "It's forbidden, I'm afraid. I've been summoned to serve as Queen's counselor at the hearing." He looks around to make sure he's not being overheard by others. "I might suggest, however, that you make discreet inquiries of Master Neville. And, by all means, recruit the jesters. They're not just men at arms, you know." He winks.

Jonathan leaves, looking a little unsure of himself.

* * *

Henry appears very early for supper one evening at Serjeants' Inn, before the residents have begun gathering in the vestibule. "Shall you be staying to supper, Serjeant Ames?" he asks.

Noah senses something beneath this sudden formality. Henry opens his eyes wide and tilts his head toward the room where they met surreptitiously on the day of Noah's elevation to Serjeant. Noah signals his understanding. "I shall, Master Neville," he replies blandly. "I'll see you at supper, then."

Instead of going directly to the room indicated by Henry, Noah visits the pigeonholes located by the inn's entrance, and painstakingly opens each letter in his. He slips each one into his pocket after reading it, then takes a roundabout path to his rendezvous with Henry. When he arrives, Henry is waiting, and gestures for Noah to close the door behind him.

"Essex has been investigating your past," he pronounces gravely.

Noah smirks. "Better than a sleeping draught."

"Noah, this is serious. This morning, his men took Master Treasurer off the street and escorted him to Essex House for an interview with the earl."

"'Arrested him for interrogation' would be nearer the mark. They wouldn't dare do that at Gray's Inn."

"What does Master Treasurer know?" asks Henry.

"That I have led an exemplary, downright boring life to date," Noah says. "But … he probably suspects I'm a Jew."

"Why?"

"Well, he's in charge of the roll of barristers. His records of my admission to the bar would look a bit different from those of the other residents."

"How so?"

"Although there would be an oath of loyalty to the Crown, there would be *no* certification that the Eucharist had been administered to me and that I had sworn to be faithful to the Church of England. Ordinarily, that's a requirement for admission to the bar."

"Or indeed for *any* post of responsibility in England. What is there in place of the certification?"

"In my case, there would be a Crown waiver of the oath."

"Signed by whom?"

Noah opens his eyes wide, as though to say "you know perfectly *well* by whom."

"I see," says Henry. "Is there any chance Master Treasurer would disclose that to Essex?"

"Under torture?" He's loath to think about it, and when he forces himself to, he can only shrug.

"Not torture. Essex isn't that stupid."

"No, but he *is* that ruthless, I assure you," says Noah. "I doubt the old man would *voluntarily* tell Essex anything about my admission papers, or anyone else's, for that matter. He's sworn to secrecy, and he takes that sort of thing very seriously."

"As well he should," says Henry. "Where are the records kept?"

"Good question. I believe they're kept at the inn, but I'm not sure."

"Could you remove them, if you wanted to?"

Noah is initially outraged, but then remembers that he's speaking to his dearest friend. "That would be the *worst* thing I could do. And don't *you* do it, either. Tampering with official records would be tantamount to a confession of wrongdoing. What I can't figure out is why Essex hasn't just asked Master Savile, who's one of his own secretaries. I was reared in his *house*, for heaven's sake."

Henry nods. "Indeed. Essex may not know that. I *do* know Essex has had his men polling old classmates of yours at Eton and Oxford."

"Including you?" asks Noah.

"Amazingly, no. He has not asked me, and with good reason."

"What reason?"

"He suspects I would not tell him anything useful, and I wouldn't. And my refusal might cause a rift between him and his cannon maker."

"Ever the pragmatist. Perhaps it's the same with Savile." Noah shakes his head. "I cannot, for the life of me, see why either Master Savile or Master *Neville* curries the earl's favor. It's beneath you both."

Henry looks disappointed. "There are no angels on the Privy Council, Noah, even though you may feel you know a couple from your time at Billingbear. Anyway, look for Essex to try to turn Lopez's clemency hearing into an inquisition against you."

"Forewarned is forearmed," says Noah pensively. "Perhaps I can make that work in Lopez's favor."

"Can you?"

"Depends," says Noah. "What would you say is Essex's greatest weakness on the battlefield?"

"By all accounts, he has two," says Henry. "First, he does not appreciate the degree to which a battle's outcome is determined by the lay of the land, thinking mistakenly that all things can be accomplished by valor."

"And the second?"

"Rather than to lose a single battle, he'd sacrifice his whole army, and even himself."

"Much can be done with this knowledge," says Noah, smiling craftily.

* * *

"Mother," says Stephen, "a distinguished guest awaits you in the upstairs parlor."

"Who is it?" asks Marie.

Stephen smiles abashedly. "He said it's a surprise."

She observes her son skeptically, but, as he's never wont to be taken in, she expects that the visitor, whoever he is, has some valid claim on her attention. She goes to the parlor.

The visitor stands with his back to her, gazing out of the window toward Gray's Inn. His long hair is reddish brown. He wears a black doublet with a white ruff, and stark white gloves. He turns to face her. He's still handsome, but wears a mustache and light whiskers now.

She curtsies impatiently. "May I ask, m'lord, what brings the stylish Earl of Southampton to the unstylish suburb of Holborn?"

"Why, *you* do, Marie! Or shall I address you formally, as you have me? Is it 'Mistress Rodriguez,' or 'Miss Miller,' as of old?"

"Mistress Rodriguez will do."

"The way you're glaring at me, you must remember me as some sort of ogre … and yet," he clasps his hands together reverend-like, "I never mistreated you."

"Perhaps his lordship has received a blow to the head that has affected his memory."

Southampton seems genuinely surprised by her hostility. "What have I done to earn a greeting of this foul tenor? I never laid a hand on you!"

"Nor stopped any of your friends from laying as many hands on me as they could manage."

"I — I didn't know things were so bad for you. I didn't even know where you kept yourself most of the time."

She blushes. "I slept in the stables to make sure to keep my virtue."

"I'm most sorry for it, Marie, and even sorrier that it has left you with such a sour memory of *me*."

Marie reminds him how little care he's shown her. "Tell me, Henry, if I may call you so," he nods indulgently, "when you saw my murdered husband lying on the ground that day at The Rose, did it occur to you to step down from your coach and lend me a hand? Or at least to express your *condolences*?"

"Marie, you *know* how Robert is — "

" — And what has Lord Essex to do with this?" she demands. "If you'd cared for me one whit, you would have come to my aid. I was *alone*, for heaven's sake, and my husband had just been murdered! Common *courtesy* demanded it, Henry, if not affection."

Now it's Southampton's turn to blush. "Robert had asked me to remain in the coach," he says, staring at his feet.

You bastard! she wants to shout, her heart pounding in her chest. *Your precious Robert had my husband murdered, and you did nothing to stop him!*

"What *brings* you here, Henry?" she repeats.

Southampton responds hopefully to her improved tone. "I was wondering: Do you know a barrister named Noah Ames?"

So, this is what he came for. Something to use against Noah!

"I *do* know him," she says impatiently.

He shuffles in place, looking anywhere but at her. "What can you tell me about him?"

She sighs. "He lives at Gray's Inn. Appears at Queen's Bench quite often." She shrugs.

He smiles. "Yes, but that's professional. What can you tell me about him *personally?*"

"Only that he has a daughter by his late wife. She's one of *you* now."

"One of *us?*" he asks, apparently puzzled.

"A noblewoman," she explains.

"Yes, I've met her," he says. "Anything else?"

She feels the heat rising under her collar. "Henry, if I never told anyone about the grunting coming from your room every night you spent with Robert, what makes you think I would tell *you* anything about Noah Ames — or about anyone else, for that matter? I'm not wont to tell tales out of school."

"*Marie!*" he gasps, as though it's a terrible breach of manners for her to mention such a thing, "Robert and I were both young."

"You're both *still* young, I think!" she snaps back at him. "You are *ever* by his side!"

He stiffens, and observes her coldly. "My business here is complete, I think."

She curtsies. "Do come again."

Southampton storms out of the parlor and down the stairs. As the front door slams, pride wells up in her breast. She can almost hear her old dad say, "Got a bit o' yer *own* back."

*   *   *

Noah waits alone in a silent corridor outside a great room adjoining the royal residence in Richmond Palace. His silk Serjeant's robes are surprisingly warm, and so new that he still feels something of an impostor in them. Any moment now, he'll be called into the room where Lord Burghley will preside over the clemency hearing of Roderigo Lopez. This will be the first occasion upon which Noah will act as advisor to the Crown, and he prays he'll acquit himself well.

The windows rattle and bang, making a startling racket. Although it sounds as though something alive is struggling to gain entry from the roof, it's merely the March wind blowing hard. Outside, the lowering sky portends a storm. The heavy door before him is at least twenty feet tall, painted in a mottled off-white, its every molding finely gilded. He hears footsteps on the other side of the door, and his heart pounds.

The door swings open slowly as befits its grandeur, and a man in richly colored royal livery appears. On his right shoulder is sewn the Tudor rose of conjoined white and red, symbolizing the resolution of the Wars of the Roses by the reunification of the ancient houses of Lancaster and York. He holds a white staff symbolizing the office of the Lord Steward.

Noah bows low. "Lord Steward," he says, having been prepared for this moment by Lord Bleffingham.

"Serjeant Ames," replies the Lord Steward. "Please enter, and take your seat beside the Lord High Treasurer and the Secretary of State."

As Noah enters, he's momentarily disoriented. This is the first time he's ever entered a room designed for official business from the rear. He was prepared to traverse the room to come face to face with those in power, as he did in Guildhall, yet now, in this world behind the looking glass, he need walk only a few feet, and it will be Noah himself occupying a seat of power.

As he enters, Lord Burghley and Sir Robert turn to greet him. Noah bows low, and the diminutive Sir Robert elegantly escorts Noah to his chair. The door through which he entered is on the same level as the dais, but the main part of the room, as well as the main entrance on its opposite side, lie several feet lower. Noah's seat looks down on a huge well, not much different from those in which he's tried many cases.

The wall to Noah's extreme left is covered with deeply colored paintings of many different sizes and subjects, from mythology to landscapes to royal portraits. Before the wall, a dozen or so wooden chairs have been assembled for the occasion. As no prisoner will be present, and no testimony taken, the room contains nothing resembling a fixed jury box, a prisoner's dock, nor a witness stand.

The right side of the room is dominated by a huge marble pedestal occupying the full width of the room, slightly higher than the dais upon which Noah sits. From its center is thrust an alabaster apron, upon which stands a great golden chair with dark red velvet cushions. Atop the back of the chair is the coat of arms of the royal house of England with the lion and the dragon, under which is draped a light blue horizontal ribbon bearing the words *Semper Eadem* gilded with such finesse as to resemble a golden filigree. On those occasions when Her Majesty is present, this is the Throne of England.

Curiously, the throne is situated far from the wall behind it. In fact, it's a good twenty feet into the room. Suspended from the smooth white ceiling, draping gracefully down onto the apron just behind the throne, is the largest, most ornately woven arras Noah has ever seen, its twenty feet of width concealing everything behind it from view.

Echoing through Noah's mind is an observation of Henry's, made on a summer's day at Billingbear that seems impossibly distant now: "If there is an ornate arras onstage, a Sovereign must be concealed behind it." But, alas, this is real life, and a real Sovereign is not bound by the rules of the theater. Indeed, the cold purity of the alabaster seems to belie the very possibility that a warm, living woman has ever been there.

The Lord Steward steps down from the dais into the well. A young page scurries over to him through the entryway across the room. "Please summon the Yeoman Warder first," says the older man, and the page hurries silently away through the main entrance.

A moment later, Gardner appears, arrayed in royal livery second in richness only to that of the Lord Steward himself. He carries no weapon, which strikes Noah as strange, as he's accustomed to seeing armed guards in courtrooms. But this is not a courtroom, he reminds himself. This is the royal residence, a sacred precinct in which arms are forbidden to all but a trusted few. Gardner takes up a position near the vacant throne, his face deadpan, and winks at Noah almost imperceptibly. Noah nods equally subtly in return.

"Yeoman, please escort the invited spectators."

Gardner bows, goes to the main entrance, and escorts about a dozen people into the room. The only one Noah recognizes is Henry Neville, who avoids his gaze. The others, judging by their attire, are nobles of high rank. Gardner escorts them to the wooden chairs near the paintings, and bows low.

"Guardsman," says the Lord Steward. "Please bring in counsel for the concerned parties."

No sooner are the words out than the Earl of Essex barges in through the main entrance, wearing an irritated expression, as though it was intolerably rude to keep him waiting. Noah notices immediately that he wears a sword, which is blatantly inappropriate to the place and occasion. Gardner obviously notices the sword, too, and apparently can do nothing but shrug and wait for orders.

In Essex's wake follow eight men of his retinue, including Noah's old Master Savile, carrying his accustomed portfolio containing paper, quill, and inkpot. He also seems to be carrying a black book, possibly a Bible.

Two burly men in Essex livery forcibly escort Master Treasurer into the room by either arm. The old man looks positively terrified, and shoots a pleading glance at Noah. Although Noah's heart goes out to him, he sits impassive, avoiding any show of favor.

The Lord Steward seethes at this blustering entrance. Lord Burghley and Sir Robert just seem weary, as though Essex's continually outrageous conduct has left them incapable of further exasperation.

Essex leaves his retinue behind, and strides up to Burghley. "Let's get on with it. I've been kept waiting long enough."

Burghley takes a deep breath and speaks.

"M'lord Essex, as you have sought, and been granted, leave to participate in this proceeding as though counsel for the Crown, it is particularly inappropriate for you to complain about having to wait with other counsel. Lord Steward, it might help to avoid any appearance of favor if we were to have *all* counsel in here now."

As a demonstration of evenhandedness in the face of Essex's loutish conduct, the Lord Steward signals Gardner to remain at his post by the throne, and personally goes to the main entrance to escort counsel for Lopez into the well. Noah watches proudly as Jonathan strides confidently in, just as he has been taught, followed by Arden and Salazar, all looking impossibly young, and somehow *imposing*, in fresh new barristers' robes. Jonathan waits to be addressed by Lord Burghley.

"Master Hawking, are you prepared to proceed in the clemency application of Roderigo Lopez?"

"May it please the Lord High Treasurer, we are prepared."

Burghley nods, obviously pleased with Jonathan's demeanor, which contrasts so sharply with Essex's boorish impertinence.

"Then, you may — "

"*I object to the composition of this Court ... *" shouts Essex. He sneers at Noah, adding "as seems to be the fashion."

Burghley looks down sympathetically at Jonathan and raises his index finger to suggest that this outburst will take only a moment to be dealt with. "M'lord Essex, you will have your opportunity to speak after esteemed counsel for the convicted has — "

"I have been led to believe," interrupts Essex, "that objections to the composition of the court may be *waived* if they are not made prior to commencement of the proceeding."

Burghley turns on him angrily. "M'lord, you have had a full week to submit any motion you wish. Are we to understand that you wish to make a prefatory motion *at this late hour?*"

"Yes!" says Essex.

"Well," says Burghley, more composed, "as this is not strictly a court, and as the proceeding is being conducted by the Lord High Treasurer and the

Secretary of State, what *possible* objection could you have to the composition of the 'court,' as you call it?"

Essex points to Noah. "That man is an *impostor!*"

Jonathan is about to speak, when Burghley holds up his hand and says kindly: "Master Hawking, there is no jury here. There is only us, so please bear with us."

Jonathan nods, evidently satisfied.

Burghley turns sharply to Essex. "By 'that man,' m'lord, I believe you are referring to Serjeant Ames?"

Essex says dismissively: "If he so calls himself."

"But Serjeant Ames will take no part in this proceeding," says Lord Burghley. "He has been selected to act as counsel to *Her Majesty*, and has no influence over the record we are compiling today. Nor shall he influence our recommendations in any way. His sole function is to make his own *separate* recommendations to Her Majesty at the conclusion of today's proceedings. Now, *may we begin?*"

"He is *not* a Serjeant!"

"M'lord, *I signed his commission*. As did *Her Majesty!*"

"But in err— "

Now it's Burghley's turn to interrupt. "This proceeding presents no occasion to challenge the admission of the Queen's counsel to the roll of Serjeants, m'lord. If you have such a complaint, you must take it up *elsewhere* with the treasurer of the Inn of Court by which was he was admitted to practice."

"I have brought with me the treas — "

Noah rises and stares stone-faced down at Essex, thereby shutting his mouth, a task which seemed impossible a mere moment before. The great test of Noah's faith has arrived, and there's no escape. He turns to Lord Burghley, and addresses him serenely.

"M'lord, as you have said, there is no jury present. There is only *us*. I have no objection to m'lord Essex's impeachment of my right to practice law." He turns toward Essex. "In fact, I welcome the opportunity to respond."

In the well, a wide-eyed Jonathan instinctively steps backward, clearly understanding that a titanic struggle is about to take place in which he has no part to play. Noah has just opened a door for Essex, and Essex is about to walk through it, heedless of something every barrister knows: When an adversary opens a door, it is only the fool who enters.

The clerestory windows rattle sharply in the wind.

Burghley walks over to Noah on the dais, and whispers. "I have done everything I can for you. If you insist on participating in this, I cannot control the outcome."

Noah nods, looks the old man fondly in the face, and whispers in reply. "Thank you, m'lord. I ask only that you not interfere, *though he strike me down*. Do I have your word?"

Burghley's eyes grow wide. "You have," he says with resolve.

Noah goes to the small staircase at the end of the dais, and descends into the well. Seeing the room from this familiar perspective, he immediately feels more at home. He bows theatrically to Essex, who observes him warily. "M'lord, you have some question concerning my capacity to practice law?"

"'Lord' me no 'lord,' sir. You are a *Jew*!" When the gasp expected by Essex does not materialize, he seems deflated.

Noah nods politely. "Yet I am a Jew admitted to practice before the courts of England, m'lord."

"Bah!" says Essex. "There is no such Jew. Did you not attend Eton and Oxford?"

"I did."

"And was it not then a requirement that every scholar attend religious service every day?"

"It was. And I did."

Essex is frustrated by the admission. "But you do not pray to Jesus Christ!"

"No, m'lord. I rather pray as Jesus *prayed* … and to the same God."

"Then, how did you participate in the service?"

"At Eton, I assisted Reverend Lamb in the service."

Essex is outraged. "And did he know that you were a Hebrew?"

"He did, m'lord."

"What qualifications had you to assist in a service of the Church of England?"

"M'lord, thousands of years ago, my ancestors were priests in the Temple of Solomon in Jerusalem, and assisted in services on the Highest of Holy Days. Reverend Lamb was of the opinion that this qualified me to assist in a schoolboys' service at Eton Chapel … *and* to sweep up afterwards." This carefully planned addendum brings the slightest titter from the spectators, which infuriates Essex, who is not to be denied.

"Did you *touch* the wine and bread at the Eucharist?"

Noah shakes his head. "I transported them on a tray for the Reverend, but I did not touch them."

"Ah. *Why not?*"

"Because Reverend Lamb told me that someday a bigot might ask me whether I *had* touched them, and that it might be important for me to answer truthfully that I had not."

Essex draws himself up. "Are you saying that I am a bigot?"

"Not in the least, m'lord." Noah bows respectfully. "I merely answered your question with Reverend Lamb's own words."

At this point, everyone in the room knows that Noah has gained the upper hand. And Noah intends to rely upon Henry's assessment of Essex's weakness, trusting that Essex simply cannot find it in himself to relent. True to character, Essex plods on. "But you *might* have touched them, if such had been permitted."

"If I had not been so forewarned, m'lord, I *might* have touched the wine or the bread incidentally, but it would not matter."

"To *you*, perhaps!"

"Reverend Lamb had a pet saying on the subject, m'lord. 'It is not the vintner who makes the blood of Christ, nor the baker His flesh. It is rather the true faith of the parishioner that transforms the wine and the bread into the blood and body of Christ.'"

"And did you ever *take* the sacrament?" asks Essex.

"I would not so profane it, m'lord. It is a terrible blasphemy to take the sacrament unless one's mind is absolutely right concerning its meaning."

"You mean concerning the *transubstantiation* of the wine into the blood of Christ, and the bread into His flesh?"

"More precisely, m'lord, the *con*substantiation."

Noah has deliberately guided Essex into a difficult area of reformed Church of England theology about which he's made sure to educate himself thoroughly. He's pleased to demonstrate for the assembled that Essex's grasp of the distinction is poor. But that does not dissuade Essex from further probing.

"You believe transubstantiation to be *impossible*, do you not?"

Noah shakes his head at Essex's stubborn refusal to adopt the correct term. "No, m'lord. For me to say it is *impossible* would mean that I believe I know all that is *possible*. Not even I am so arrogant as that." The spectators are well pleased with this feint at intellectual modesty. "In truth, I have seen such devotion in true believers at the Eucharist that I would not *wish* it to be impossible. Faith is all, which is no doubt why Her Majesty herself publicly declined to take the sacrament prior to being crowned, until Her Majesty was certain she had her own mind right on the subject."

Essex is flustered. "You little *Jew*," he spits out, "do you pretend to know Her Majesty's mind now?"

"I know her mind when she *expresses* it, m'lord, as she did shortly thereafter in the Religious Settlement, which addressed the very *place* of the Eucharist in Church of England theology."

"And you purport to be loyal to the Queen, even though you are no Englishman?"

It smarts for Noah to be told he is not an Englishman, but not enough to move him off his mark. Still, a suppressed anger rises in his voice. "I am *required* by Hebrew law to be loyal to my earthly Sovereign, Queen Elizabeth, *God save her*, and would be so loyal even if it were *not* required of me. And something which not many Englishmen can say for themselves, m'lord: Neither I nor any member of my tribe has *ever* been divided in his loyalty to the Crown. We have never had a Pope, nor has the Pope of Rome ever done anything to warrant our loyalty."

Essex is inflamed at Noah's impertinence. "Were you not required, as a condition to gaining admission to the bar, to swear your loyalty to the Church of England?"

"No, m'lord, although in the absence of a Crown waiver, I *would* have been so required."

Essex turns and looks suspiciously at Master Treasurer, who cowers. "So, then there *was* a Crown waiver!"

"Aye," replies Noah.

"And who signed it?"

Noah considers before replying. Essex wants the answer to be "Lord Burghley," as he wishes very much to paint Burghley as being "in league" with the Jews, such as Noah and, by implication, *Lopez*. His thrusts on Noah's religion are, of course, targeted primarily at *Lopez*, and Noah's parries are in Lopez's *defense*, and, by now, every thinking person in the room knows it. "I am *bound* not to say," he replies at last.

"By whom?"

"I have *sworn*, m'lord, which means that I am doubly bound, not only by the person at whose request I have sworn, but by God Himself."

Essex turns away in disgust. "*Your* God!"

"Yes, m'lord, *my* God, and the God of Abraham and *Jesus of Nazareth*!"

Essex turns and shouts: "But you do not *believe* in the divinity of Jesus!"

Noah glances at Henry in the gallery. "Who *some* believe to be a god, I think of as a distant relative." Henry winces to hear his words used to such suicidal effect.

Essex marches over to Noah, who stands his ground and stares insolently into his eyes, making no motion to retreat or avert his stare.

Essex slaps him hard in the face. The spectators gasp. Noah nearly goes down, but recovers, blood dripping from the corner of his mouth. He brings himself up to full stature, and resumes his former defiant posture.

The windows rattle, breaking the silence. In the corner of his eye, Noah sees both Jonathan and Gardner take a step toward coming to his defense. He shakes his head to warn them off, and both reluctantly step back.

Essex is red-faced with anger, as well as embarrassment for losing his temper. "You Jew *bastard*! Loyal to the *Crown*? When have you *ever* risked your worthless life for the Crown?"

Noah barks a laugh, despite himself: "Why, m'lord! That is precisely what I am doing right now."

Essex smacks him again, harder this time.

But this time Noah is expecting it, and braces himself steadfastly, his insolent stare never wavering. He silently recites a prayer. Knowing full well that he's about to take his life in his hands, he says aloud: "And taking the advice of my distant relative, m'lord, I turn the other cheek!" He turns his head insolently.

Essex's anger overthrows his judgment, and he draws his sword, which emits an unmistakable ring that echoes through the rafters.

"*ENOUGH!*" comes a woman's commanding voice from behind the arras.

Essex quickly puts up his sword and drops to one knee. Noah closes his eyes and mentally recites a quick prayer of thanks. He turns toward the throne, and bows.

There stands Queen Elizabeth, the Red Lady, in sharp contrast to the ivory and alabaster upon which she stands. Her auburn hair falls about her shoulders onto a velvet gown of forest green bedecked with ribbons of darkest red, her expression a stern mix of amazement and fury. The assembled bow in place before this vision of mature and terrifying beauty, every eye fixed on the floor. The room is silent once again. Not even the windows dare make a noise.

Her mouth, which was severely pursed, relaxes.

"Which of you is Master Hawking?" she asks equably.

Noah has been watching Jonathan out of the corner of his eye. When the Queen singles him out by name, he nearly pitches forward, but quickly rights himself, rises, and looks in her direction without making eye contact.

"I am Hawking, Your Majesty," says Jonathan, his voice quavering. Whatever he was expecting when he got out of bed this morning, it certainly wasn't this.

"Ah," she says calmly. "Tell me, Master Hawking. What punishment is prescribed in law for someone who draws his weapon in the Court of Queen's Bench?"

Jonathan's eyes go wide, but on his first try to speak, his tongue cleaves to the roof of his mouth.

"Calm down, Master Hawking. We rarely ask a question of one so young, unless we already know the answer."

Jonathan tries again, and this time his voice emerges. "If the Sovereign be not present, the hand which poised to strike is forfeit."

"But the Sovereign was *not* present when Lord Essex poised to strike. Is that not correct?"

"Her — Your Majesty's presence was *unknown* to us. Whether Your Majesty was *in fact* 'present' while behind the arras is a fine point. That I cannot tell for certain."

"Carefully phrased, Master Hawking," replies the Queen with exaggerated admiration. "Do you know why the law provides its warrant for punishment only in the case where the offender draws a weapon *outside* the Sovereign's presence?"

"It is unwritten, Your Majesty. But I believe I know why."

"Ah," says the Queen. "Then, here is a real test of your feel for English law. *Why?*"

Jonathan rocks anxiously before answering. "Because, Your Majesty, no warrant in law is needed for the Sovereign *herself* to take the hand of the subject."

"I *see*," says the Queen pensively. She looks over Essex's retinue. "Master *Savile*, how are you today, sir?" she asks, as though she just noticed him and no solemnity should *ever* be permitted to interfere with old acquaintance.

"I am well, Majesty," comes the aged voice of Noah's old master.

"Is that a Bible in your hand, Master Savile?"

"'*Tis*, Majesty."

"Good for you. Hand the Bible to Yeoman Gardner, if you would be so kind, sir." Savile shuffles over to Gardner, hands him the Bible, bows to the Queen, and returns to his former place.

Gardner stands there awkwardly with the Bible in his hand, awaiting instructions with obvious dread.

"Yeoman Gardner," says the Queen, "place Lord Essex's hand on the Bible, and cut it off."

CHAPTER 30

GARDNER APPEARS BAFFLED. "I haven't a blade, madam," he says with chagrin.

"No bother," says the Queen. "Use *his*. He should not have brought it here, anyway. Might as well put it to good use."

Gardner places his own hand on the hilt of Essex's sword. "Beggin' your pardon, m'lord," he says. Essex nods his assent. Gardner draws Essex's sword, and places the Bible on the table in front of him.

Although no one has been given leave to rise, everyone has done so nonetheless. At this point, all eyes are fixed on this impossible event.

"If you'd be so kind, m'lord," says Gardner to the earl. "Please put your hand on this book."

Noah is amazed that Gardner can be so cold-blooded in performing such a horrific act, but, of course, Gardner is a Yeoman Warder, one of the guards of the Tower of London, whose collective reputation for inflicting corporal punishment strikes fear into every heart in Europe.

Essex places his hand on the Bible, never taking his eyes off the Queen. There is a contest of wills taking place here that Noah can barely fathom.

"Hold off a moment, Yeoman Gardner," says the Queen, turning to Noah. "Serjeant Ames, can you offer us a persuasive reason that we should not remove Lord Essex's hand?"

"Well, madam," Noah says, "such hand would better serve the Crown slaying its enemies in battle than rotting on a pike on London Bridge."

The Queen frowns in disappointment. "A facile argument from utility, Serjeant Ames. Is that the best you can do? No, if Lord Essex has shown anything today, it is that he does *not* understand that a field of battle is independent of his inexorable will, and that he will *always* be defeated by an opponent who understands the battlefield better than he. No, Serjeant Ames, England is *not* persuaded."

To Noah's amazement, she nods to Gardner, who raises the sword to strike.

"Madam, *I cry you mercy!*" says a man's voice. It takes a moment for Noah to realize that the voice is his own. He drops to one knee.

The Queen looks at him askance. "Have you more to say on this subject, Serjeant Ames?"

"I beg Your Majesty to exercise mercy," he says feebly, his mind racing. He has nothing prepared for an eventuality such as this, and so has no choice but to speak extemporaneously, something he avoids whenever possible.

"*Mercy?*" asks the Queen skeptically. "What kind of argument is this? Do you say it is our *duty* to stay our hand?" She shakes her head. "The law is clear on this. We have it from Master Hawking himself, and from many others, as well. What duty in this regard have we failed to discharge?"

"None, Majesty, for mercy is *not* a duty, nor would its exercise prove such greatness if it were. It cannot be extracted by constraint or argument. It cannot be found in the statute books or the law reports. It resides rather in Your Majesty's heart, or nowhere at all, and it must flow, if at all, as a free act of your will."

Tears well up in Noah's eyes. "For *you alone*, Your Majesty, stand at the intersection of God and man. For most of your pitiable subjects, Your Majesty is all we ever glimpse of Him in this life. I beg you to exercise mercy in this case, not because it is your *duty*, but rather because it is your royal *prerogative* to import some small quantum of mercy from the heaven that made you and sent you here, to show it to your earthly subjects in your royal hands, and provide Christian example for millions of your subjects to follow."

The Queen takes a step back, a quizzical look on her face, and turns her back to the assembled. My God, thinks Noah, she *wants* to lop off his hand. This makes no sense, as Essex is known to be the Queen's favorite.

Essex turns his head slightly to look at Noah. If there is some emotion there, he cannot tell what it is. Curiosity, perhaps. Still, it's better than nothing.

The Queen turns. "Very well, Serjeant Ames. You have moved us. We shall leave the choice to the earl. M'lord of Essex, if you shall take an oath on that Bible to guarantee the safety of Serjeant Ames, his family, and all those in his company or service, then you may keep your hand. If not, then your hand is ours. And if you *do* take the oath and violate it, your hand is the *least* you will be missing. Do we make ourselves clear?"

Essex glowers at her. In his face, fear mixes with utmost contempt. He clears his throat. "I so swear, Your Majesty."

After a moment's equivocation, the Queen says: "Not good enough. Master Savile, please escort the earl from this room, write up the oath as we have pronounced it, and present it to him for signature before three witnesses. We want it by tomorrow. We do not wish to see the earl's face again today, nor for the rest of the *week*. Do you understand?"

"Yes, Majesty," says Savile. As he steps forward to escort Essex by the arm, Essex shakes him off and storms out of the room. Savile shrugs at the Queen, who shrugs back at him. He raises his eyebrows at Noah, who cannot help but smile in return. Essex's remaining retinue trails Savile out of the door.

The Queen turns to those remaining. "We have not forgotten you, Master Hawking, nor your client. Although you have not advanced your case today, nothing will befall Doctor Lopez until this matter is given due consideration. We shall leave it to you to decide whether you wish to have another audience with Lord Burghley, with neither Essex nor your Sovereign present, who seem only to interfere in such matters in any event. Alternatively, you may make your submission in writing. You need not decide now, but let Lord Burghley know by letter this week. We can assure you that Serjeant Ames will be consulted in our deliberations in this matter, which should be of some comfort to you."

"Thank you, Your Majesty," says Jonathan, bowing low.

"In any event," says the Queen, "you have learned something today about pleading for clemency. It is our sincerest hope that our clemency has not been wasted on an unworthy subject. You may go. In fact, you may *all* go, but for Lord Burghley, the Secretary of State, Serjeant Ames, and Master Neville."

With much bowing and stepping backward, the room is soon vacated by all except those bidden to remain.

"Serjeant Ames," says the Queen impatiently, "I seem to be spending an inordinate amount of my time signing documents and doing other things for the sole purpose of keeping you alive."

Noah winces, although he's relieved that she's suspended her use of the ceremonial "we." "I shall endeavor in all things to make such efforts worth Your Majesty's while."

"See that you do. And please do what you can to render them unnecessary in future. We have *other* business, you know."

Noah bows.

The Queen looks down upon him with grudging admiration. "My congratulations to you on mastering the weapons of the powerless, as they are not customarily fashioned of a size to be wielded by the hand of a *man*."

"Thank you, madam."

"I did not take you for a gambling man, Serjeant Ames. You surprised me. You could not be sure I was there behind the arras."

"A gambler puts his faith in *probabilities*, Your Majesty. I put my faith in God. If He wishes to take me back to Him, who am I to argue?"

She nods pensively. "A strange courage, Serjeant Ames. I was in any event relieved to see that you did not goad the earl for the purpose of gaining a pound of his flesh, as he would have us believe of all your tribe. You defended yourself, and Master Hawking's client, magnificently." She glares down at him. "And don't think for a moment that I don't know that's *precisely* what you were doing, and what you had planned *all along*."

"Some things cannot be planned, Majesty."

"Perhaps not, Serjeant, but that's the first thing you've said today that I'm not sure you believe. In any event, I think you have had enough majesty for one day. Don't you?"

"I could never tire of Your Majesty ... but this *has* been quite an exhausting experience."

The Queen smiles, with a hint of skepticism. "Return to us alone tomorrow afternoon at four o'clock. Serjeant Ames and Master Neville, you may go."

Noah and Henry bow low and step back, in keeping with the dictates of protocol for departing the royal presence. They've turned to go when the Queen says blithely: "Master Neville, please escort Serjeant Ames out through the kitchen, and give him a roasted potato, as I believe it his custom to roast every potato at hand."

Noah stops in his tracks. Tears in his eyes, he turns and makes a long sweeping bow, just as he had as a small child so many years before. "At your service," he says hoarsely, and is pleased to see tears in her eyes, as well.

*   *   *

As Noah and Henry leave the palace, the skies make good their threat and pour a heavy rain onto London and all its environs. Noah and Henry share a closed carriage back to London.

For a time, they sit in uncomfortable silence. At last, Henry makes an attempt at conversation.

"Her Majesty is quite something, is she not?"

Noah comes only partway out of his reverie. "Indeed, she is. She is one of the most perceptive people I have ever met."

"I imagine she gets that from her father."

"I would imagine," Noah replies. But he cannot bear small talk with such a close friend when there's such a point of contention between them. His mood changes swiftly and completely. He looks Henry in the eye. "How can you ally yourself with that man?"

"As I've explained before — "

"He's so full of *contempt*!"

"Oh, I don't know," says Henry. "No more than many others of his rank."

"Being unfamiliar with others of his rank, I cannot opine on that. But I *do* know that, whatever feelings he may put on display, in fact he has contempt for everyone but himself. Believe me, Henry. I *felt* it today. For God's sake, I saved his *hand*! And still he would have spat upon me like a cur, if he could."

"Oh, don't feel bad about that. Suspicion of the Jews is rampant in England. We have so few here that it's easy to attribute to them all the ills of the world."

"That's *another* question. Has anyone given a moment's thought to the vulgar Jew-hatred that Essex has deliberately ignited? There are wicked people prepared to sow the seeds of hatred for their own ends, and many credulous souls ripe for the picking. All Southwark is filled with blood libel and venom for the Jews. I fear for my daughter's life, lest someone find out her heritage, and exact revenge for imagined wrongs."

"Your daughter is safe with Sir Henry — "

"And God *bless* Sir Henry for it, and you for bringing it about. But what about everyone *else's* daughter, Henry? What about the Jewish merchant trying to do an honest business? Is it not enough we're regarded as strangers, and therefore suspect? Must we also have hatemongers like Essex drumming up demons to promote our persecution?"

"Can I ask you something?" Henry says sheepishly.

"Anything," says Noah.

"Why don't you all just convert to Christianity?"

Noah is shocked. "Why *should* we?" He shakes his head. "Henry, I know you far too well to think that you would suggest something like that to save our souls through membership in the Church of England. What you mean is 'why can't we all *pretend* to be Church of England?' No doubt, you think life would work so much more *smoothly*. Well, it *wouldn't*! Everywhere it's been tried by papism, it's been an abysmal failure. People will *not* stop regarding us as outsiders simply because we profess to be like them. They will suspect our motives in converting, as well they should. People cannot *choose* what to believe. If someone does not believe Jesus to be his savior, then it's nothing short of blasphemy to accept him into the Church, so he can mouth prayers he does not believe, in words that will never rise above the rafters."

"What about Lopez?"

"What *about* him? Has there ever been a soul more lost? He has no idea *who* he is. He willingly plays the part of Proteus, conforming to whatever shape pleases those around him. 'Just accept me, and I will pretend to believe anything you wish!' So lost a soul is he that I've no doubt he has *in fact* changed his beliefs any number of times, to conform to whatever creed was demanded by the country he resided in at the moment. Yet, *still* they said — and *continue* to say — 'You are *not* one of us, whatever you may pretend.'"

Henry nods. "Marlowe certainly did the Jews no favor writing his Jew as though he were Avarice in a morality play."

"Perhaps you know a playwright who will write his Jew as a human being with the same feelings and weaknesses as a Christian."

"Perhaps."

"But Jew-hatred aside, Henry, you must abandon any alliance with Essex."

Henry shrugs. "Easier said than done."

Noah looks pityingly at his old friend. "I was very near him today, and could see his expression. Do you know there was only one person in that room for whom he showed greater contempt than for me?"

Henry looks perplexed.

Noah is dismayed by his friend's blindness. "His greatest contempt is reserved for the *Queen of England*, Henry!"

"No," says Henry dismissively.

"Yes, I tell you! You *must* abandon him. This is no harmless dalliance, Henry. It's more like an alliance with the devil." Noah nearly shouts in frustration. "*That man will be your undoing!*"

The rest of the ride is spent deep in thought, although there could never be any real rancor between these two closest of friends. Noah worries that there may come a time when he'll be required to use every bit of his knowledge and skill to save his best friend's neck from the headsman's axe, and wonders whether he'll be up to the task.

*   *   *

That night, Noah dines alone with Marie in the upstairs parlor, regaling her with the exciting events of the day. As his Hebrew faith has now become public knowledge, he can no longer delay in telling Marie.

"When Essex accused me of being a Jew," he says, "he obviously expected the world to cave in on me and, when it did not, he was thrown off his mark for the rest of the argument." He takes her hand in his own. "So, my dear, the time has come when I must reveal to you that I am a Jew by birth, and have never converted to Christianity."

Her face turns bright red, and she turns her back to him. He's dumbstruck.

Seething, she turns to him again. "Only now that the *whole world* knows you're a Jew do you deem it safe to tell *me*!"

"But I always intended to tell you," he insists.

"*When*, Noah?" she asks, her eyes growing red. "When? Only once the whole *world* knows? Months ago, you sat on that sofa, looked me straight in the eye, and swore that *trust* is the most important basis for any relationship. Do you remember that?"

"Yes," he admits with trepidation.

"For heaven's sake, Noah!" she cries. "You confessed your faith to *Essex* before you told me. Can you imagine how that makes me feel? That it was so important to keep me in the dark? Is *that* how much you trust me?"

"But, Marie," he says, choking up. "I love you more than my life."

"How *can* you love me, if you don't trust me? For heaven's sake, Noah, I stuck by your side all the while Essex's men pursued you to the ends of the earth — or as far as *Oxford,* anyway. I was nearly killed by that beast, Meyrick. I've stanched your wounds and nursed you to health. What more need I do — what more *could* I do — to earn your trust?" She weeps.

His memory floods with all the blatant hints she's dropped after returning from the Netherlands, and he's staggered by the weight of his own stupidity and ingratitude.

She wags a finger in his face. "Noah Ames, you are a *great* fool!"

"Oh, Marie," he says. "I am *indeed* a great fool! Greater than even *you* know."

"Well, for your information, I've known you're a Jew for months!"

"But, how?"

"Oh, don't be such a dolt!" she tells him, wiping away her tears. "Do you remember when you asked if I wished to light candles for my deceased husband, and then brought me some?"

He nods.

"And you also brought me your favored candlestick, so that we could light a single candle together, as my late husband and your late wife died on the same day of the year?"

"Yes," he mutters, unsure where she's going with this.

"Did you not see that there were Hebrew letters engraved on the bottom of the candlestick?"

His eyes open wide. "Oh!" He can only imagine how comical his pained expression must appear. He shakes his head. "I always intended to tell you," he repeats, at a loss for anything new to say.

"Then, what kept you?"

Well, if there's ever to be an opportune time to ask her about it, it's now. "I withheld it because I never wanted to upset you by asking about your connection with the Earl of Southampton ... who is, after all, Essex's closest friend."

"What? Who told you about *that*?" she asks sternly.

"No one *told* me," he mumbles, "but it was suggested by Lord Bleffingham and Sir Robert Cecil that you're widely believed to be half sister to the Earl of Southampton."

"Nonsense! Typical of noblemen and politicians. They think that, just because their *own* mothers cannot keep their knees together — "

"Marie!" exclaims Noah.

"Oh, I'm sorry. But my mother was a wonderful woman by all accounts, and *completely* faithful to my father, bless her soul. Bless *both* their dear departed souls. My mother died bringing me into this fetid world, and I cannot abide hearing her name dragged through the mud. I've heard the same *stupid* things all my life!" She briefly covers her face with her hands. "Look at me," she says, uncovering her face. "Do you think I'm pleasant looking?"

Noah suspects that saying the wrong thing is likely to start a war, possibly a biblical plague, though he has no choice but to venture, "I think you're the most beautiful thing on earth, excepting possibly my daughter."

"Thank you for that." She smiles, pulls out a handkerchief, and daubs at her tears. "But I wasn't fishing for a compliment. I simply wished to point out that my father was a strikingly good-looking man, even if he *was* a stableman. And I'm the spit and image of him." She holds up her hands. "These *hands* are not more alike. Oh, maybe there's a bit of my mother thrown in for good measure.

"That little weasel, Henry Wriothesley, who calls himself the earl now? If he looks like me, it's more likely because the stableman was *his* father, too. The old Earl of Southampton was an absurdly God-fearing papist. There was more than one crucifix in every room of that house, yet not a single Bible to be read.

"It's been my experience that the truly godly are not much for the sack. It's those who merely *pretend* that you have to watch out for. The time my father was arrested and threatened with the rack ... " She's briefly overcome, but brings herself together by an evident force of will. "Every stinking one of them came after me. *Animals!* I learned the dagger and pistol just to fend them off. After a while, I started sleeping in a hayloft in the stables, where I'd removed two of the slats, so that anyone coming after me would put his foot straight through the floor up to his crotch. And, before you ask, it happened ... *twice!*"

He tries to change the subject. "Is that when you learned to ride so well?"

She regards him as though he's a bit dim-witted. "No. My father was a *stableman*, for heaven's sake!" She pulls a fresh handkerchief from her dressing gown. "Did you see how 'fondly' Wriothesley treated me when Stephen was killed? Why, he didn't even step out of the carriage! *He* obviously doesn't think me his sister."

"But *has* he a sister?"

"Mary. Poor thing. At sixteen, she looked every bit the spinster. Oh, but I'm sure he doesn't care for *her*, either. He's his *own* sister!" She laughs through her tears, and looks up at Noah. "I'm sorry, but doesn't he strike you as a bit ... *girly?*" Noah shrugs. "When he was younger, Lord Burghley hired an anonymous poet to write him sonnet after sonnet persuading him to marry Burghley's granddaughter." She laughs again. "I stole into his room one night, and read some. The poetry was excellent. But more than half the sonnets were designed to persuade him that he was interested in women."

"Is he?"

She seems puzzled. "I don't know. I'm not sure *he* knows. But, for all that, I can tell you he's the most self-concerned brat who ever lived."

"Marie, please," he pleads. "I don't know *what* to say. I'm so sorry for not trusting you, as my every instinct commanded." He places his arms awkwardly around her.

"Oh, it's all right," she sniffs. "It's my own fault. I should have made the connection myself, and put your mind at ease about it. Southampton came here the other day, looking for dirt on you. So you weren't wrong in thinking he'd try to turn me against you. I handed him his walking papers." She barks a laugh. "So, I suppose you and I are *both* great fools!"

He holds her until she calms down, then tilts her face up to his own. "A perfect match," he says softly. "Two great fools."

She laughs through her tears.

He drops to one knee, and swallows hard. "Will you, great fool, take *this* great fool to be your lawful wedded husband?"

Though she's unable to get a word out, she nods vigorously, and they embrace.

At long last, Marie extinguishes all but one candle. She leans into him, and in the midst of a kiss that steals his breath away, her hands slide up to his cheeks and stroke them adoringly. She presses her body ardently into his, molding its softness to his firm shape. In the space of a single steamy breath, her embrace is transformed from gentle adoration into urgent desire. Her ample breasts flatten against his ribcage. Her groin presses so hard against his that, even through their clothing, his thigh feels the burning heat of her female desire.

Noah wrests his arms free, and places his left hand on the nape of her neck, pressing his lips ever more urgently into hers. As he's backed up hard against the wall and off balance, his right hand seeks for purchase in the curve of her lower back. Instead of allowing it to settle there, she grasps it and lowers it to her left buttock, which he cups in his hand, kneading its softness. His maleness begins to respond, and his body writhes in unison with hers.

The air rising onto his face from the narrow space around his collar grows hot and moist as a bread oven, and his heaving chest feels as though it might actually be scalded by their conjoined heat.

He blows out the remaining candle.

*   *   *

One of the Queen's ladies-in-waiting ushers Noah into a small private room containing a single long table, and seats him at its foot in a comfortably upholstered chair.

"Her Majesty is expected in just a moment," she says demurely.

"Thank you," he says, as she bustles out.

Noah is even more nervous today than he was yesterday. At least then he was in the accustomed confines of a courtroom, however beautifully appointed, surrounded by lawyers and professional rhetoricians. Today, he'll sit and have coffee alone with the Queen, a favor rarely bestowed upon anyone in the land.

A clock on the mantel ticks loudly. At precisely four o'clock, the Queen enters, attired much more informally than the previous day, in a dress that one might see on any number of fashionable ladies in London, but more finely made, no doubt.

He rises and bows. "Your Majesty," he says.

"Do sit down, *Serjeant Noah Ames*. I *gave* you that name, did I not? Many years ago?"

"You gave me *all parts* of my name, madam —'Noah Ames' many years ago, and 'Serjeant' much more recently. I hope I have brought it credit to your satisfaction."

"Tell me, Serjeant Ames. The Exchequer informs me that, over the years, you have repaid him the full amount expended by the Crown for your upkeep and education. Is this true?"

Noah blushes. "It *is*, Majesty."

"The Exchequer is not in need of your charity, Serjeant Ames."

"No, madam. He would indeed be in pitiable condition if he were forced to rely upon what meager charity *I* can spare. But charity to the Exchequer was not my aim. I thought perhaps the Crown might use the extra funds to provide another disadvantaged boy with the wonderful opportunities given me."

She nods. "I *thought* that might have been your purpose. Very commendable. The Exchequer has assured me that your contribution will go to that very purpose."

A servant wheels in a table bearing coffee, cream, and tangerines, reminding Noah of his first morning at Billingbear, but evoking far less pleasant memories, as well.

"Is this not to your liking?" asks the Queen, evidently mistaking his woolgathering for distaste.

"It is very *much* to my liking, Majesty, although I cannot say I will ever think of tangerine and cream in quite the same way again."

At first she seems confused, then it dawns on her.

"Ah, yes. Essex's livery. My father tried to rid the kingdom of these rival liveries, but, as you can see, some things must be dealt with anew in every generation. In any event, I doubt *you* need fear Essex, sir, as you have saved him the use of his right hand."

"Indeed, madam. It is not *I* for whom I fear. I was thinking of my employer."

"But that's … me. Oh, you don't think … ? Well, we can't worry about everything at once. That's what I always say. I show Essex favor in honor of his stepfather, the Earl of Leicester."

"Old Sir Henry Neville said that the two could not have been more dissimilar."

"*Did* he say that?" she asks thoughtfully.

Noah gives a moment's thought to whether he's gotten the Nevilles into hot water by saying so, but decides that a statement so vague could be written off as small talk.

"He did, madam. His gout is much improved, incidentally."

"I am glad to hear it. He has suffered from it so long."

"Madam, if I may ask, while I am in the Crown's employ, will I be taking on private clients, as well?"

"Do you *wish* to do so?"

Noah shrugs. "It is how I've earned my keep, madam. But, in truth, I would be better pleased to serve one mistress until the end of my days."

"Then, so you shall," she says, and laughs. "Unless, what you meant is that you intend to *marry*!"

"That is not what I meant. But, madam, now that you mention it, I have heard that persons appearing in the royal presence are expected to seek the Sovereign's approval before marrying, and … well, I am planning on marrying again."

The Queen claps her hands with glee. "And who is the lucky maid?"

"Her name is Marie Miller — "

"Southampton's *sister*? I've heard she's quite beautiful."

This is awkward. "Your Majesty, although she was reared in the manor house, in fact she is *not* the earl's sister."

The Queen bows her head indulgently. "Doesn't matter. *Good for her!* Have you come to seek my blessing?"

"If Your Majesty's approval is … "

"Oh, I see. You seek my blessing only if you *need* it!"

"Not at *all*, madam. It's just that we are not Church of England, and I did not know whether … " His voice trails off.

"Do you know *why* the Sovereign's consent is required for the marriages of those in her family, and others around her?"

He considers a moment. "No."

She smiles. "Well, that's the briefest answer I've heard from *you*, Serjeant Ames. It is to give the Sovereign an opportunity to prevent those around her, especially family, from entering into an alliance inimical to the interests of England. You *do* need my consent, sir, as will Lady Burlington, when the time comes." She sits up gaily. "As for *your* choice, you have my blessing. Are you inviting me to the wedding?"

Noah's mouth hangs open in amazement.

"Briefer *still!*" She laughs.

"While we would be *thrilled* for you to attend, madam, even in my mind's eye I cannot envision Your Majesty in such a place."

"There is an arras for every occasion, Serjeant Ames."

"It's not *that*, madam. It's that there have been no fixed places for such weddings … since the expulsion."

"Ah, I see," she says with regret. "Well, how would you like to present your lovely bride and daughter to me here, after the wedding?"

"It is an honor that I dream not of, madam. I would *greatly* appreciate it, as would they!"

"Done! I have been hearing about Lady Burlington in glorious detail since last summer. Half of London is in her thrall. Where is she now?"

"She is temporarily in the care of Sir Henry, at Billingbear."

At first, the Queen seems alarmed to hear it, but in a moment she waves away her concern. "Oh, he's an old man now, I suppose."

CHAPTER 31

JESSICA IS SO EXCITED that Noah can only laugh. They've just been formally instructed how to behave in the royal presence, and now wait outside the room in which they'll meet Her Majesty. Jessica keeps standing on her toes as she did as a toddler, her eyes wide.

Marie, now Mistress Marie Ames, tries to calm her down. "Dear, Her Majesty is unlikely to be favorably impressed by such behavior."

Jessica looks at her wide-eyed, as though she'd calm down if she could. She lets go a little whimper and stops tiptoeing.

Jessica is, as always, beautifully dressed in a form-fitting outfit that looks as though it's been designed around her. In keeping with the Spanish motif of the wedding a few hours earlier, she wears a large white flower in her hair, which is bound tautly back, and a long curl pasted to one cheek. Her dress and shoes are black, and her chemise a stark white.

"Do I look all right? Not too Spanish?" asks Jessica, as Marie adjusts the chemise.

"You're adorable, dear, I assure you." Marie crinkles her nose. "Not too Spanish."

Marie takes Noah's hand, and smiles. Marie herself is beautifully dressed, perhaps a bit more gravely than the occasion requires, in observance of her widowed status.

The door opens, and a lady-in-waiting announces them.

"Your Majesty, may I present Jessica, Lady Burlington," Marie squeezes Noah's hand excitedly, "and Serjeant and Mistress Noah Ames." The door swings wide.

The Queen stands before her chair, beaming at them as they enter, her hands clasped together over her heart. Beside her stand the Cecils, beaming almost as broadly.

Noah bows, while Marie and Jessica curtsey.

"Please rise," says the Queen, "and let me look at you all." She takes a long look at them, shaking her head. "Lord Burghley, this is a tableau fit for a

Holbein painting. If this is not English stock, we would be wise to beautify ourselves with such heavenly creatures!"

"Indeed we would, Majesty," says Burghley.

"Serjeant Ames," says the Queen, "if it would be agreeable to you, we should like to confer our blessing upon each of these two lovelies separately."

"As you wish, Your Majesty."

"Lord Burghley," she says, "why don't you and Sir Robert attend to those other matters we discussed." Burghley and Sir Robert bow and depart silently.

"Lady Burlington?" says the Queen. Jessica approaches her unsteadily. As the Queen is so skilled at doing, in a moment she's put Jessica at ease, and the two chat amiably. The Queen hands Jessica a jewel box, and sends her back to Noah.

"Mistress Ames?" says the Queen, beckoning Marie. Although Noah cannot hear a word the two say, they seem to be enjoying themselves. At the conclusion of the interview, which lasts only a few minutes, the Queen hands Marie a small box. Marie thanks her, curtsies, and rejoins Noah and Jessica.

"Serjeant Ames," says the Queen, "you are a most fortunate fellow to have the love of two such deserving women. My blessings upon your marriage and your future together."

"Thank you, Majesty," Noah replies.

"You may go," says the Queen, beaming as before.

With a bow and curtsey, they step backward out of the room. Noah allows Marie and Jessica to leave before him.

"Serjeant Ames," says the Queen, "please prepare yourself to address the clemency application in one week's time."

"Yes, Your Majesty. Thank you so much for seeing us today."

As Noah backs out, the Cecils return. He bows, and shuts the door quietly behind him. He says to Marie quietly, "Care to tell me what you two discussed?"

Marie smiles at him, and smooths his cheek with her hand. "No chance," she says.

*   *   *

It's a mid-afternoon in springtime when the abortive clemency hearing reconvenes in the same room at Richmond Palace. Outside, a storm is brewing and, despite the hour, the sky darkens.

Noah has taught Jonathan never to submit a petition on paper alone if a personal appearance is permitted, so Jonathan has chosen to appear before Lord Burghley again. Both Noah and Jonathan are thankful that Essex will be absent, and positively delighted to hear that the Queen will personally attend.

Whether intentionally or absentmindedly, the Queen is perched on the throne. The effect of her simply taking the seat was transfixing. There were only a few spectators to see it, however, one of whom was Henry Neville.

Jonathan has nearly completed his presentation of legal and factual points, and finishes in good form with an appeal to humanity.

"Your Majesty," he says. "When last I spoke with Doctor Lopez, I asked him whether he would *ever* have poisoned the Queen in exchange for the ruby given him by the King of Spain. He said: 'Never. For the Queen is a virtuous woman.' Then, by heart, he quoted Proverbs 31:10, which says: 'Who can find a virtuous woman? For her price is *far* above rubies.'

"I asked him how Your Majesty could be *sure* that he would never have abused his status as a physician to poison Your Majesty, and he said: 'Master Hawking, would you ever abuse your position as barrister to send your client to the gallows for money?' I said: 'Why, no!' And he said, 'Do you know why not?' and then proceeded to answer his own question: 'Because when you have practiced a learned profession for many years, you *become* your profession. My *identity*,' he said, 'is that of physician. If I were to betray the trust of my patient, I would betray my own identity, and my God. This I could *never* do.' Thank you, Your Majesty."

"Well spoken, Master Hawking," says the Queen. "While we do not intend to arrive at a conclusion in this matter today, we will tell you that, although we do not believe Doctor Lopez would have attempted to poison our person, upon review of the unchallenged evidence, *disregarding* all evidence to which objection has been made, we believe it clear that Doctor Lopez, for at least a time, was engaged in a conspiracy, one spoke of which countenanced the poisoning death of Señor Perez, who was here in England under Crown protection. Now, this is high treason, regardless of whether Doctor Lopez would in fact have carried out such poisoning himself. We believe therefore that he is probably guilty of high treason, albeit not precisely that for which he was convicted."

Jonathan interrupts. "Your Majesty, an English court can convict an accused only of the crime *charged!*"

The Queen nods. "Be that as it may, Master Hawking, it is beyond the scope of this tribunal to dispense perfect justice. It is consequently our preliminary opinion that, in the exercise of clemency, we should remit only the portion of the sentence providing for the convicted to be drawn and quartered, but to allow his execution to take place by hanging. While this may be — "

There's a sharp rapping at the door. The Lord Steward enters, pale as a sheet.

The Queen is visibly annoyed. "Yes, m'lord. What is it? Can it not wait?"

"I believe Your Majesty would wish to know this news immediately … even under these circumstances." The Lord Steward sounds strangely hoarse today.

"Oh, very well," she accedes impatiently.

"Your Majesty, the writ of execution which you signed some months ago, that was being held by Lord Essex — "

The Queen blanches. "Oh, don't tell me he released it without my instructions!" She rises from the throne and comes to the very edge of the elevated apron.

"Not exactly, madam. However, I have learned that, together with his friend Tinoco, Doctor Lopez was in fact," he swallows hard, "tried before Queen's Bench this morning."

Jonathan turns, outraged. "How can this *be*? I am his *counsel*!"

The Lord Steward plods on. "He was tried before a jury by the newly appointed Attorney General Master Coke before Chief Justice Popham." He looks at the floor. "I regret to say that Doctor Lopez was *convicted*, madam, and — "

"Oh, no!" cries Noah in dismay.

"And executed at Tyburn by being hanged, drawn, and quartered. I am *so* sorry to inform Your Majesty of this."

The Queen, who stands near a four-foot precipice, is near collapse.

"*Look to the Queen!*" shouts Burghley, who's too far away to reach her in time. Noah bolts across the well, and positions himself to catch her should she fall.

At the last moment, she rights herself, but her wan face suddenly looks weary, old, and terribly fragile. Without a word, she brings herself up to full height, turns, and departs through the door behind the arras.

Lightning can be seen through the clerestory windows. The storm is still too far away to be heard.

But it's coming.

THE END

AFTERWORD

A Second Daniel is a work of historical fiction, a sort of "what if" winter's tale written for the reader's amusement. A great deal of research went into it, but it should not be relied upon for scholarly purposes, other than to excite further inquiry.

Although this afterword is written primarily to document the substantial modernization of English criminal procedure depicted in the story, lest the law student lend undue credence to the fictionalized account,[1] a few remarks on the rest of the story might be in order first.

Except for the involvement of the fictitious barrister Noah Ames and his friends, the progress of the Doctor Roderigo Lopez case is fairly (if summarily) portrayed, as is the deficient investigation of Christopher Marlowe's murder.

In general, I've attempted to portray the historical figures and their activities in a manner consistent with facts generally known about them. The only person whose age has been changed substantially for storytelling purposes is Henry Savile, whom I've aged a generation so that he could serve as mentor and guardian to Noah Ames. The real Henry Savile was, as portrayed, preoccupied with writing a biography of Saint John Chrysostom. Savile ultimately became instrumental in the translation and preparation of the King James Version of the Bible, a feat for the ages.

Within the bounds of what is known about people in the period, the story contains much conjecture. For example, although there were rumors of homosexual conduct about Marlowe and Francis Bacon, we know of nothing specifically linking Marlowe's murder with any secret relationship the two may have had.

For humorous reasons, I have unfairly portrayed Gelly Meyrick as porcine, and I've portrayed his manner of speech as more common than it probably was.

---

[1] The author is suspected of having served as an adjunct professor of law at a New York law school for more than thirty years.

Similarly, I scarred Skeres and made Robert Poley a drunkard because I thought it would make them more memorable. But those two were scoundrels, anyway.

I have portrayed many historical figures as more tolerant of Jews than they almost certainly would have proven, had there been more than a tiny number of Jews in England to test their mettle. If I hadn't done so, the events of the story could not possibly have occurred. I've probably portrayed other historical figures as being more virulently anti-Jewish than they were; for example, the Earl of Essex was probably anti-Jewish in about the same offhanded way as most Englishmen would have been at the time. As he was primarily responsible for the false accusation and prosecution of Doctor Lopez, however, I thought it fair to attribute to him the coarser type of Jew-hating portrayed in the novel. Concerning the Cecils' regrettable involvement in the prosecution of Lopez, see below.

The Queen did indeed have a Jewish grocer named Añes, but not Avram.[2] Many of the characters in the story are entirely fictitious, including all who are portrayed as being (or as having once been) Jews or of Jewish descent, except Roderigo Lopez. His change of religion and multifarious activities are faithfully (if incompletely) portrayed. Jonathan Hawking and all other barristers resident at Gray's Inn are likewise fictitious, except for Anthony and Francis Bacon, whose activities are more or less accurately portrayed. Lord Bleffingham is fictitious, as well.

GOODMAN GRANGER'S TRIAL

The story deviates from Elizabethan legal practice in numerous ways, some important, some less so, depending upon one's viewpoint. A criminal trial in Elizabethan England was a dismaying and terrifying affair for any accused, except perhaps for the most well-educated and well-spoken. The procedure in the trial of the fictitious Goodman Granger does not fairly resemble a real trial of the day.

The reader may well ask why it was necessary to modernize something as esoteric as Elizabethan criminal procedure. Such liberties were necessary in order to fulfill important narrative requirements, mostly to ascribe sufficient fairness to the proceedings to leave room for Noah's active participation and a plausible prospect of his success. As any lawyer who's tried a case before a judge with a closed mind can tell you: if a trial is not a contest, it's both futile and boring.

In Elizabethan times, Goodman Granger would not have been entitled to the protections now customarily afforded the accused in order to secure that

---

[2]J. SHAPIRO, SHAKESPEARE AND THE JEWS 71 (1996).

bedrock of modern Anglo-American jurisprudence, the presumption of innocence. To the contrary, it would have been incumbent upon Granger, by means of vocal objection, to put the prosecutor to his proof. In those days, many types of accused made a poor showing: the inarticulate, the bashful, the uneducated, the mentally handicapped, and the just plain bewildered, to name a few.

During Elizabethan times, an accused imprisoned prior to trial had no right to consult counsel on his own behalf, nor to participate in the preparation of his defense. While it might have been possible to compose a novel about a barrister practicing under such primitive conditions, such a hopeless setting would have provided little opportunity for a barrister's heroism. For those wishing (or, at least, willing) to delve into a fictionalized account of the horrors of the legal system as it prevailed during the reign of Queen Elizabeth's father, Henry the Eighth, I strongly recommend C.J. Sansom's Matthew Shardlake novels. Sansom's novels are uniformly engaging, but the justice system he depicts seems hopeless and dreary to modern sensibilities, enough so to make the modern lawyer thank his lucky stars that he or she need never practice under such conditions.

The few extant accounts of procedure at ordinary criminal trials of the Elizabethan period make no mention of counsel.[3] It was rather "[i]n the more important cases [that] the examination of the prisoner would be conducted by counsel, where in less important cases it would usually consist of a debate between the prisoner and the prosecutor and the other witnesses, the judge of course interfering as he saw fit."[4]

As every American law student knows, until the latter half of the twentieth century, the Government was not required to appoint counsel to represent an accused. Noah's appointment by the Queen for that purpose some four hundred years earlier would have been a sharp and historic departure from common practice.

A real Goodman Granger would likely have had no counsel with whom to confer. No Noah Ames. No Jonathan Hawking. Nobody. And if he had, it's extremely unlikely he would have been permitted to consult with his counsel while testifying. That much is still true today.

Nor were the rules of evidence as well-defined as we now know them, and their fluidity left the trial judge with great discretion in deciding questions of admissibility. The rhythm of question-objection-ruling so familiar to lawyers of

---

[3] J. STEPHEN, A HISTORY OF THE CRIMINAL LAW OF ENGLAND 349-50 (1883) (quoting at length T. SMITH, COMMONWEALTH OF ENGLAND (written 1565, printed 1584)).

[4] id. at 350.

today (and whimsically depicted in the fictitious Granger trial) would have been far from the norm in those days.

The depiction of Goodman Granger's trial is accurate to the extent that it was left to Granger himself to challenge the Crown to submit the Crown's witness for cross-examination; otherwise, the witness would have gone unconfronted. And, incredibly, Granger would have had no right to call witnesses of his own.

FRIZER'S MURDER OF MARLOWE, AND ACQUITTAL BY THE CORONER

The story's description of the coroner's trial of Ingram Frizer for the murder of Christopher Marlowe is not nearly as ahistorical as one would hope. In fact, Frizer was tried by a coroner and found not guilty. The coroner's verdict, however, expressly disclaimed that it would preclude a court of law (presumably one of plenary criminal jurisdiction, such as Queen's Bench) from trying Frizer. It's disturbing to note that the novel is accurate in showing that Frizer was in fact pardoned, which did indeed preclude subsequent prosecution.

COURTS OF IRREGULAR SESSION

That some perceived enemies of the Crown were tried at courts of irregular session, such as Oyer and Terminer, is historical fact. Noah was correct in remarking that Courts of Oyer and Terminer had been convened to convict Archbishop Cranmer and Lady Jane Grey, both of whom were convicted and put to death.

The patently unfair practice of appointing members of the Privy Council to serve as Commissioners of such courts is also historical fact. The Court of Oyer and Terminer that tried and convicted Doctor Lopez (the first time) was constituted by the very Commissioners named and described in the novel, including but not limited to the obviously partial Earl of Essex. As Noah told Jonathan, it was indeed standard procedure for the same Commissioners to sit as both grand and petit jurors.

I expect that thinking lawyers of the time must have perceived the inconsistency between the requirements of Magna Carta and the practice of detaining a commoner, such as Doctor Lopez, to be tried by a court comprised of men of much higher station. I can only surmise that this was the reason Lopez was retried at the Court of Queen's Bench before being put to death. Despite the novel's glimmer of hope that Queen Elizabeth might soon put an end to the practice, in fact the practice appears to have been reexamined no sooner than the Petition of Right in 1628, during the reign of the unfortunate Charles the First.[5]

---

[5]Some of the abuses inherent in convening a Court of Oyer and Terminer at the request of private individuals against other named individuals were recognized and circumscribed at least as early as the reign of Edward the Third. 1 *id.* at 110.

As with many developments in the evolution of the largely unwritten English Constitution, it is difficult to discern from generally available sources precisely when such abuses were finally ended. Though the evolution of the English Constitution may seem inscrutable to those living under a written constitution, there can be no doubt that English justice has, in its own winding way, evolved into a model for the world to emulate in the protection of individual rights against a sometimes overweening state.

At the time Lopez was executed, his clemency application had in fact not been decided, nor had the Queen authorized the release of his death warrant. While the evidence is equivocal, it appears that Lord Burghley — notwithstanding that he had suffered a serious stroke unacknowledged in the book — had a hand in authorizing his retrial. I regret the need to mention that forged evidence appears to have been submitted with the knowledge and cooperation of both Lord Burghley and Sir Robert Cecil.[6]

There's no reason to believe that a motion such as that brought by Noah was made before the Court of Oyer and Terminer, urging the court to transfer the Lopez case to Queen's Bench, and then to dissolve. It is doubtful that a procedure had been established for presentation of such a motion (even Noah remarks that there was none), and I have little doubt that a lawyer presuming to intercede between the Crown and its perceived enemies in such unorthodox manner would have found himself in grave and immediate peril, much as Noah did after making his highly irregular motion.

MIGHT ESSEX HAVE LOST HIS HAND?

Finally, the student may be surprised to learn of the historical accuracy of one aspect of Elizabethan law that arose during the fictionalized version of Lopez's clemency hearing. Punishment for someone raising a hand to strike another in the court of King's (or Queen's) Bench, *regardless* whether the hand struck, and *regardless* whether it wielded a weapon, was that "he shall lose his hand and his goods, and the profits of his lands during his life, and suffer perpetual imprisonment, if the indictment lay the offence as done *coram domino rege*."[7]

As the confrontation between Essex and Noah was entirely fictional, the Queen did not have occasion to decide whether to order Essex's hand cut off. But it is extremely unlikely Her Majesty would have done so, since Essex is

---

[6]D. GREEN, THE DOUBLE LIFE OF DOCTOR LOPEZ 256 *et seq.* (2003).

[7]1 J. STEPHEN, A HISTORY OF THE CRIMINAL LAW OF ENGLAND, *supra* note 3, at 93 n.2.

known to have actually raised his hand once against the Queen's person, and needed to be restrained. Yet he never lost his hand. As the faithful reader will see in a later book in the series, eventually he lost much more than that.

INNS OF COURT

Serjeants' Inn is gone, as is the order of Serjeants. Gray's Inn, however, still stands precisely where it is situated in the novel. Although, in Noah's time, that was just west of the City of London, the city has long since expanded to subsume it.

THE IMPRESS OF HEAVEN

BY NEAL ROBERTS

CHAPTER 1

GREAT ROOM OF THE LORD KEEPER OF THE GREAT SEAL
YORK HOUSE
LONDON, ENGLAND
JUNE 5, 1600

IN THE FOREMOST PEW of a hushed room packed with spectators, Serjeant Noah Ames awaits the opening of the Earl of Essex's trial on charges of high treason against the Crown. On the dais await many of the most famous officials in England. Displayed behind them is every item of colorful heraldry that can be mustered for an occasion outside a genuine throne room. An ornately woven arras bearing Queen Elizabeth's coat of arms and her motto *Semper Eadem* drapes from the thirty-foot ceiling to the back of the unoccupied throne.

From behind Noah come the overloud voices of an old man and his wife, evidently discussing him. Although spectators upon this occasion are supposedly limited to the nobility and members of the learned professions, the pair's uncultured manner of speech shows them to be no more than common merchants. Without turning around, Noah cannot be sure whether they speak so loudly because they wish to be overheard, or simply because, being hard of hearing themselves, they believe they're speaking in moderate tones.

"That's the Queen's Jew lawyer, right in front of us," croaks the old woman.

"Who, *this* one?"

"Don't point, Elias. No. *This* one, right here."

"What would *he* be doing here?" inquires the old man.

"Probably come to rejoice, if the earl's carted off to Tyburn."

"What's his grudge against the earl?"

"Why don't you *ask* him?" she says.

"*Pshaw!* Don't be ridiculous."

After a moment's silence, she intimates in a stage whisper, "They say he blames the earl for executin' that Jew doctor who tried to poison the Queen before he could plead for clemency."

The old man replies, "Thick as thieves, eh? Should never have let that snake close enough to the Queen to sting her in the first place."

Noah looks to his right where his co-counsel, the young Arthur Arden, returns his gaze and smolders at the presumptuousness of the two know-nothings behind them. Noah pats Arthur's hand comfortingly, careful to seem unperturbed.

"Anyways," says the old woman, "he's got no love for our Essex, and *that's* the truth!"

Our Essex! This is becoming almost too much for Noah himself to bear. As he considers a riposte, however, the Lord Steward pounds his staff on the floor three times, mutely ordering the assembled to rise, which they do, with a thump and rustle.

A dark-stained oaken door behind the dais swings open, and in walks the diminutive Sir Robert Cecil, Secretary of State, who glances about quickly, and strides to his place behind the elevated podium at the center of the dais. As attested by his elaborate costume, Cecil has served the Crown as its leading minister since the death of his father Lord Burghley less than two years ago. He glances down at the small satin pillow carefully positioned before the dais where, by royal command, the accused will kneel until the conclusion of the trial. "Yeoman Warder! Kindly escort the earl into the chamber," he solemnly pronounces.

Grizzled old Yeoman Gardner, long familiar to Noah, leaves his post alongside the dais, and tramps heavily to the rear portal through which the spectators entered. He shouts a command, and the door swings open.

The downcast figure of Robert Devereux, Earl of Essex, mournfully enters the chamber escorted by two burly guards. The colorful uniforms of the Yeoman Warders contrast sharply with the dark penitential garment worn by the accused earl, a monk's robe of deepest black, devoid of any color or flourish to signify his station. His face partly concealed by a cowl, his only adornment is a large golden pendant in the shape of a cross that hangs from a heavy gold chain around his neck. The guards march him respectfully to his assigned place, as marked by the pillow. His cowled face too low to be seen, he faces the dais as his escort stamps noisily to the rear, departing through the door by which it entered. He glances along the dais, pausing a moment as his eye finds Sir Francis Bacon at one end. He kneels.

Satisfied with the earl's submissive posture, Cecil intones ceremoniously: "Who shall prosecute for the Crown?"

A voice responds promptly. "Queen's Counsel Sir Francis Bacon, for the prosecution."

Cecil nods his approval. "And who shall assist the earl in his defense?"

At first, there's no response, the only sound that of a rising wind outdoors that rattles the clerestory windows. After a few moments' silence, Cecil arches his eyebrows expectantly.

Noah, his stomach knotted, succumbs at last to the expectations of court and counsel. Girding himself, he rises to answer the call.

"Serjeant Noah Ames, for the prisoner," he says, his clear voice ringing through the chamber.

An unearthly gasp arises from the spectators behind him, followed by howls of protest against the "Jew lawyer." Evidently, the spectators have been given no foreknowledge that the barrister who'll be defending the earl is the very man most commonly believed to *despise* him. Amidst the tumult, Noah silently recites a Hebrew prayer asking God's forgiveness, and recalls the events that led him to this bizarre juncture.

* * *

EIGHT MONTHS EARLIER
WESTMINSTER, ENGLAND

Outside the Court of Queen's Bench, Noah dismounts, pats his horse's muzzle, and hands off the reins to the courthouse stableman. "This mount belongs to Sir Robert Cecil. I borrowed him last night, and promised to return him this morning."

"I *thought* he looked familiar," says the stableman. "Who're ye here to see this lovely morning, Serjeant Ames?"

Noah pats the note in his pocket. "I've been summoned by Sir Robert, John."

The stableman nods. "I'll have the boy take you inside to 'im." As ever, Noah hands him a good gratuity.

An eager-looking young page appears and leads the way through the rear entrance down a labyrinth of hallways, chambers, and jury rooms, stopping at last before a closed door of dark-stained oak. He opens it a crack, and peers inside. "Sir Francis!" says the page. "I didn't expect you to be here. I was told to bring in Serjeant Ames."

"Indeed!" says the voice of Francis Bacon. "Until a few moments ago, I did not expect to be here myself. By all means, bring in Serjeant Ames." The page lets Noah in, and bows out, leaving the door ajar.

Noah is familiar with this room. It's sometimes used by judges or members of the Privy Council to view outsized documents, such as land maps. It's sizable and well-appointed, housing a large central table that can readily accommodate twenty. At the moment, however, the room holds only Sir Francis and Noah.

Noah bows. "Sir Francis, it is ever a joy to see you."

Sir Francis rises with evident pleasure. "As it is to see you, Serjeant Ames."

Noah takes a seat one chair away from Sir Francis to make use of the abundant space. "What's this all about?" Noah asks.

"I assume you've been summoned here on the same business as I. Sir Robert evidently wishes us to join him in hearing Lord Mountjoy's plans for the upcoming campaign against the Irish rebels."

"Shall we not be joined by any *military* men?"

Sir Francis shakes his head. "Only one. But he's a *good* one. Although Her Majesty *had* wished to hear this presentation personally and to have the Lord Admiral beside her, they're both a bit under the weather." He lowers his voice. "The Lord Admiral is getting on in years, you know."

Noah nods sadly. "So, who shall it be, besides us politicians and barristers?"

Sir Francis leans back, his chest swelling with pride. "None other than the Captain of the Yeoman Warders!"

Noah's eyebrows shoot up in admiration. "Sir Walter Raleigh. We lawyers shall provide a poor second chair to a warrior of such stature."

Sir Francis waves his hand. "It's all been decided, anyway. Lord Mountjoy already has the nod. Both the Lord Admiral and Sir Walter concur that Mountjoy's the best man to replace Lord Essex as leader of Her Majesty's forces in Ireland, now that Essex has returned … *prematurely…* and been placed under house arrest."

The smile drops from Noah's face and he shakes his head.

"What is it, Noah?" asks Sir Francis. "You seem almost disappointed at Essex's well-deserved disgrace. I should have thought you'd feel vindicated at last in your low opinion of him."

Noah sighs. "As you know, Sir Francis, I believe my opinion of Lord Essex to be well-founded. I have therefore never felt a need for vindication, although I'll confess it is somewhat heartening to be joined by others at last, even if they ought to have recognized his failings long ago."

"You'll pardon if I observe that you do not *appear* to be 'heartened,' as you say."

"No, I am not *preponderantly* heartened. Like everyone else, I am sorely disappointed that Her Majesty's plan for subjugation of the Irish rebels has been turned on its head by that one willful man, that he reached a truce with the rebels as he had been expressly *forbidden* to do, that he left his post in Ireland contrary to Her Majesty's command, and then compounded it all with his personal invasion of Her Majesty's closet before she could be properly attired."

Sir Francis smirks. "I take it, then, that you are in agreement with the commission's removing him from command in Ireland and ordering him imprisoned with no date for his release?"

"As for his removal, I think that the commissioners' emergency decision was absolutely necessary and completely justified. As for his indefinite imprisonment ... well, you know as well as I that no Englishman may be imprisoned indefinitely without a full trial."

"And you regard as legally insufficient the inquest conducted less than a week after his return." Sir Francis smiles. "So do I. So does Attorney General Coke." He looks at Noah appraisingly. "I have to admire your commitment to the precept that the rights of every Englishman cannot be secure unless the very *devil* is assured a full trial."

Noah snickers. "Cleverly phrased, Sir Francis."

"Page!" shouts Sir Francis. The page appears quickly in the doorway. "Has Sir Robert arrived, as yet?"

"Not yet, sir."

"Very well. In the meantime, I wish to confer privately with Serjeant Ames. Close the door behind you." The page bows and obeys.

Sir Francis leans toward Noah and speaks quietly. "I don't suppose you've heard what the Queen has in store for Lord Essex?"

"No," Noah replies hesitantly.

"His many supporters are driving her mad with their demands for his release. But he's truly exhausted her patience this time, and she'll have none of it. Instead, she's considering disposing of the whole matter *privately*."

Noah finds that prospect alarming, for when the Queen's father, Henry the Eighth, disposed of public grievances privately, the offender would never leave the Tower alive.

Sir Francis evidently perceives Noah's horror. "Oh, don't worry," he assures him. "Her Majesty merely intends that his lordship be tried in Star Chamber. Are you familiar with the procedure of that forum?"

Noah is chagrined. "I've assisted there a few times, but I must confess that, if Star Chamber has some uniform code of procedure, I've never been able to detect its workings."

"Well, Her Majesty knows you to be a quick study."

Noah squirms in his chair. "*Me?*" He doesn't like the turn taken by this conversation.

"She hasn't made her mind up quite yet, but I expect that is a mere formality. In preparation for Essex's appearance at Star Chamber, the Queen intends to commission you to investigate his conduct during past military campaigns and to report your findings to her."

Noah's stomach suddenly feels queasy. He regards Sir Francis skeptically. "Surely, Her Majesty has many alternative candidates having less ... personal history with his lordship."

"You mean ... who don't *detest* him?" Bacon's question meets with no response. "Well, whatever your feelings, Her Majesty is well aware of them, and she evidently finds them irrelevant, which is all that matters. She trusts your judgment, Noah, and your objectivity, regardless of your personal feelings."

There comes a light knock at the door, which opens a crack to reveal Sir Robert Cecil peeking in, eyebrows arched. "We're a bit late. Are we interrupting a discussion of importance?"

"Not in the least," says Sir Francis, as he and Noah rise and bow.

"Good!" says Sir Robert. He enters and takes the seat between Noah and Sir Francis.

Lord Mountjoy enters immediately afterward and strides confidently to the opposite side of the table, followed by a page who struggles mightily to hold onto an ungainly armful of long scrolls. Mountjoy removes his gloves and begins taking the scrolls from his page, one by one, and placing them on the table. He makes a handsome appearance, with his high forehead and tightly curled black hair. Sir Francis plainly follows his movements with interest. But then, Sir Francis is well known to be especially fond of the more attractive specimens of his own sex.

Just as Mountjoy is about to begin, in rushes Sir Walter Raleigh. "I *do* hope my tardiness has not made a great hash of things!"

Instinctively, Noah and Sir Francis shoot to their feet and bow, Sir Robert rising more deliberately.

Sir Walter beams at Mountjoy and shakes his hand warmly, as they exchange a few private words. Then, to Noah's surprise, Sir Walter comes 'round the table, and takes the vacant seat next to his. He leans toward Noah and whispers, "I must ask you sometime about certain events in the early Bible."

Noah smiles and nods. "At your leisure, Sir Walter." As public disclosure of Noah's religion has transformed him, as if by magic, into the court's resident expert in Hebrew history and law, over the past few years he's spent a good deal of effort actually learning the subject.

Mountjoy begins his presentation, holding up each map as he explains it. As the little direct sunlight penetrating into the room comes from behind him, the watermark of his distinctive family crest lights up at the center of each map as he holds it up, a long-horned bull behind a shield flanked by a woman and a man. As he finishes with each map, he slides it along the table toward his page, who rolls it up again, but only after unfurling and handing him the next map. In this way, the presentation proceeds seamlessly.

As Mountjoy is primarily a man of action, it takes him only about twenty minutes to outline his plans for taking the fight to the Irish rebels. Despite Noah's lack of military experience, he finds Mountjoy's concise explanation highly satisfactory in both scope and clarity. Sir Walter and Sir Francis seem favorably impressed, as well.

Sir Robert, although also apparently well pleased, leans his elbows on the table, and rests his head upon his hands in contemplation, his brow furrowed. After a long pause, he says: "Sir Charles ... pardon me, *Lord Mountjoy* ... you have very ably discussed with us *your* battle plan, for which we thank you most humbly. But now I am concerned with the *enemy's* battle plan."

"Rest assured, Sir Robert, Tyrone's battle plan is foremost in *my* mind, as well." Mountjoy arches an eyebrow. "You wouldn't happen to have a *copy* of it, would you?"

Sir Walter and Sir Robert laugh aloud. Noah and Sir Francis share a smile, as they realize at the same moment that Sir Robert has unwittingly taken on his late father's demeanor, assuming the same contemplative posture, laughing in the same way at precisely the same kind of jest. And Sir Robert is immediately lost in thought again, just as his father would have been.

Noah breaks the silence. "If I know Sir Robert, m'lord, he was not thinking of Tyrone, but rather of our Sovereign's great enemy, Spain. And the possibility of Spanish intervention on Tyrone's side."

Sir Robert lets out a jovial laugh. "Serjeant Ames, I find it unnerving that you have learned to read my mind."

"At some level, Sir Robert, all good tacticians think alike," says Noah.

Mountjoy replies. "Yes, gentlemen, I had anticipated that question. Even with Spanish King Philip dead, his daughter, the Infanta, may yet march in his footsteps. And, if the genealogists are to be believed, she may eventually make a claim to the British throne in her own right. As you know, this has been a principal concern of Lord Essex." He winces, as he realizes he should have omitted any mention of that troublesome man. Sir Walter looks away, as his own well-known disputes with Essex have caused everyone to look his way.

Mountjoy urgently mutters something to his page, who searches through the remaining scrolls. Evidently, the top of each scroll has been marked with a unique identifying number. Finding the required scroll, the page unfurls it and hands it to his master, who holds it up to view.

The left side of the map shows Ireland, its size somewhat diminished to allow Cornwall, at Britain's southwestern tip, to be shown on the right. At two places in Ireland and one in Cornwall, the cartographer has drawn symbols apparently representing an array of English forces and battlements.

Sir Francis is taken aback. "Surely, you do not anticipate a Spanish invasion of *Cornwall!*"

Mountjoy sighs. "One must prepare for *all* contingencies, Sir Francis. Indeed, it was mainly because Spain's most recent attempt went *unanticipated* that its landing in Britain, if it had been successful, might have proven calamitous to the realm."

"Once again," says Sir Robert wistfully, "we were saved by sea and wind, which was none of our doing. Indeed, we would never even have *learned* of the attempt, had hundreds of drowned Spanish sailors not washed ashore."

Mountjoy resumes. "I brought this map to show you, not so much our Cornish defenses, as the preparations we're currently making against possible interference by the Spanish in Ireland itself." He points to Ireland's southern coast, and various symbols indicating English forces. "As County Cork is a likely landing point for the Spanish, we shall set up these widespread battlements, not only to assure ourselves of early warning, but also to give us the greatest ability to contain the Spanish by slowing their movements, should they successfully disembark.

"Strange as it seems, we also need be concerned about a possible landing up *here* in the far north, in Donegal. We have intelligence that the Irish rebels have nearly *begged* the Spanish to land there, and, as you can see from these diagrams, we intend to reinforce our existing strength there, as well."

Just then, Noah notices something unusual about this latest map. He glances at Sir Walter, whose eyes meet his, as he has evidently noticed the same thing. Although Mountjoy is about to slide the map to his page to be rolled up, he stops when Noah speaks. "M'lord, it is evident that you and your page take every precaution to guard these very sensitive maps from disclosure or theft. May I ask who prepared them?"

Mountjoy seems surprised by the inquiry. "You mean, my cartographer?"
"Yes, m'lord."

"His name is John Tyler. He's been with me many years."

"Does he always use the same paper for your maps?"

Now all eyes are on Noah, as questions about such details seem out of place anywhere but in the courtroom. Sir Walter seems mildly amused.

"Yes," says Mountjoy, "he uses my bespoke Italian stock."

"And it bears the distinctive watermark of your family crest that I was just admiring."

"Yes. Why?"

"Because the paper on which this last map was prepared does not bear your watermark," says Noah.

"Of what *importance* is that?" asks Sir Francis.

Mountjoy skeptically holds up the map of Ireland and Cornwall to the sun's rays, and his eyes flash in realization. "It may mean nothing," he says, then looks toward Noah with grudging admiration. "But it may mean ... *a great deal*." Mountjoy looks to his page, who shrugs in return. "No need to speculate now. We shall investigate this question, and I will personally let Sir Robert know of any explanation I find."

"Thank you, Lord Mountjoy," says Sir Robert. "Her Majesty wishes me to extend to you her undying thanks for your efforts on her behalf."

Mountjoy bows low, and says: "That is all the thanks for which the true subject might *ever* hope."

"Amen," mumble the others, every one thinking how Essex would never have entertained such a sentiment.

* * *

As Noah leaves the courthouse, he's hailed by the familiar voice of a young man. Scanning the lobby, he spots Jonathan Hawking waving an arm.

"Serjeant Ames!" shouts Jonathan again, quickly closing the distance between them.

"Jonathan! So good to see you! What have you been up to, of late?"

"Oh, workaday matters."

"How fares your practice?" asks Noah, as he and Jonathan saunter toward King Street. "I have heard that, since the conclusion of our business with Lord Essex's men, you have become the most sought-after barrister in all England."

"So *I* have heard, as well," replies Jonathan doubtfully. "And I must confess that I *have* acquired a better class of clients and earn larger fees. Yet," he sighs, "to my mind, things have not much changed. I feel as though I am ... stagnating."

"Well," says Noah, adopting his favored pose as the voice of experience, "there is more to life — even to a *barrister's* life — than the law."

"I suppose," replies Jonathan. "Tell me, how goes the fair Lady Jessica?"

"My daughter is currently staying in the country, at the residence of the Earl of Somerset."

"Oh? Enjoying an autumnal holiday?"

Noah frowns. "I should expect you to know my daughter better than that, by now. Lady Jessica may *act* the ingenue, but she is never entirely uncalculating. She was invited by Lady Somerset in contemplation of marriage to the earl's son, Viscount ... Something-or-Other."

"Oh," says Jonathan, suddenly serious, "I had no idea that she'd rejoined the ranks of the marriageable. She seemed to withdraw from such matters permanently after your family's ... origins were publicly revealed by Lord Essex."

"She *did* withdraw for a time. In truth, I do not know what revived her interest, but I suppose it's not every day one is courted by a viscount. She has informed me that his landholdings are quite extensive."

"Naturally," observes Jonathan, his voice flagging.

Noah stops short, and Jonathan nearly bumps into him.

"What's wrong?" asks Jonathan. "You suddenly look as though you've had one of your famous epiphanies."

Noah considers a moment. "A short time ago, I left Lord Mountjoy's presentation concerning his upcoming deployment in Ireland. All his maps had been prepared on paper bearing a watermark of his family crest. Except *one*."

"Which one?"

"I'm sure I shouldn't discuss this in any detail, but, as a general matter, it showed certain coastal positions in Ireland and Cornwall."

"Was it a particularly sensitive map?"

"For *some* purposes, I suppose," replies Noah. "Perhaps I'm losing my grip, seeing Essex's hand behind everything questionable. At first, I thought that the original map might have been stolen by a spy. But it just occurred to me that I've likely been worrying about nothing, for, if the map had been copied by an unauthorized person onto paper lacking the watermark, he would simply have restored the watermarked original to Mountjoy's papers and taken the *copy* with him."

Jonathan nods. "In which case, Lord Mountjoy, none the wiser, would have shown you the original, and the spycraft would have gone undetected."

Noah waves the thought away. "Oh, for heaven's sake! The cartographer likely ran out of his favored paper, and used whatever was at hand. Any spy who would needlessly remove an original would have to be a dunderhead indeed, to enhance the likelihood of detection."

As they reach King Street, to their left, on Thieving Lane, languish numerous beggars in all states of disrepair. Although, during times of plenty, a London beggar can usually scrounge enough to keep body and soul together, the recent famine has left many to perish of hunger or disease. Despair is evident in their eyes. On this occasion, Noah and Jonathan both look the other way.

"Care to share a carriage as far as Holborn?" asks Jonathan.

Noah taps Jonathan's boots with his walking stick. "Something wrong with *those*?"

"Not at all. I just thought perhaps you'd prefer to ride."

Noah shakes his head. "Not on a perfectly clement day, such as this. Come, walk with me." They go up King Street, and turn right on the Strand. "I enjoy walking past my old haunts at Serjeants' Inn. It reminds me that there was a time when I hoped for nothing more than an eventual position on the Bench."

"Things might have turned out simpler for you, I suppose."

Noah shrugs. "Indeed. They could not be much more complicated than they're about to become."

"How so?"

Noah lowers his voice to speak in confidence. "Although it may all come to naught, Sir Francis just informed me that Her Majesty intends to commission me to investigate Essex's past conduct of military affairs."

Jonathan's eyes go wide. "Setting the sheep to guard the ravenous wolf? That *would* be complicated for you, wouldn't it? How could she expect you to be evenhanded?"

"That's just what I asked Sir Francis. Her Majesty is thoroughly versed in my history with Lord Essex. Evidently, she has greater faith in me than I have in myself."

"That says a great deal about her confidence in you, I must say." Jonathan turns to Noah with a smile. "Will you be seeking the assistance of a more junior barrister in this investigation, by any chance?"

Noah is dismayed that the question has been raised so soon. Although he expected every young barrister to vie for a chance to assist in an investigation of such importance, he expected to have more time to consider whom to choose. It's especially unfortunate that it's Jonathan who's raised the question, for, as soon as the possibility of such a commission was mentioned, Noah immediately considered Jonathan and, just as quickly, dismissed the thought.

"Jonathan, I could not possibly ask *you* to assist in this."

"Why not?" Jonathan asks, sounding hurt. "We've worked together for years!"

"And shall *continue* for years to come! Just not in this matter." He looks at Jonathan impatiently. "For one thing, I care too much for your immortal soul."

Jonathan scowls. "Oh, please. You must be England's only Hebrew *bishop*! Why, you have an animus against Essex *yourself*, as you just acknowledged."

"But *you* blame him for Goodman Graves' death."

"Only because he had a *hand* in it."

"We don't *know* that, Jonathan."

"Doctor *Lopez* thought so," Jonathan observes hotly.

"Nonsense," replies Noah. "Lopez, may he rest in peace, admitted *in your presence* that he had no touchstone to determine whether it was poison or no." As pedestrian traffic is passing nearby, Noah draws up close to Jonathan and mutters. "Do you think I've forgotten that you swore to see Essex beheaded?"

Jonathan broods. "Oh, that was said in a fit of pique!"

Noah turns on him. "Oh? You *forswear* it, then?"

Jonathan stares at the ground. "No," he mutters.

"I thought not. Jonathan, I give you all credit for your honesty. But I cannot in good conscience place you in a position of such temptation. Besides, I promised Goodman Graves to look after you, and I feel morally obligated to do so."

"Who's it to be, then?" asks Jonathan. "One of the jesters? Arthur? Andres?"

"I haven't had an opportunity to give it a moment's thought, Jonathan. You caught me quite at unawares."

The rest of the walk takes place without conversation. They soon pass the Lord Keeper's house, where Essex is lodged against his will, and an image comes to Noah's mind of a caged predator, preening for escape. As Noah prepares to turn north toward his wife's house on High Holborn, he invites Jonathan to join them for dinner.

Jonathan seems sullen. "Not today. But thank you very much ... and please extend my compliments to Mistress Ames, and, if you see her, to Lady Jessica."

"I certainly shall, Jonathan. And, as you continue on your way" — Jonathan waits attentively — "do not neglect to count your blessings. After all, you are ... "

Jonathan can't help but smile. "Yes, I know: 'the most sought-after barrister in all England.' I really should have that printed on my calling card." They part ways with accustomed affection.

Noah little suspects that he'll be seeing Jonathan again before the sun sets.

And Jonathan little suspects that he'll be seeing Lady Jessica quite soon indeed.

END OF THE SNEAK PEEK

FREE DOWNLOAD

Sign up for Neal's newsletter and journey for free to England's shores in 1558 with young Menachem in the exclusive prequel scene, *Escape*.

MORE GREAT READS FROM BOOKTROPE

A Decent Woman **by Eleanor Parker Sapia** (Historical Fiction) Set against the combustive backdrop of a chauvinistic society, A Decent Woman is the provocative story of two women as they battle for their dignity and for love against the pain of betrayal and social change.

Blue Honor **by K. Williams** (Historical Fiction) Four families struggle with love and loss during the American Civil War. The only certainty they have is that nothing will be the same.

By the River **by Jae Carvel** (Historical Fiction) Sarah Ann, a widow with three young children, arrives in the John Day Valley of Eastern Oregon in 1869, where she eventually leaves her stoic nature behind and becomes a woman of substance.

Incurable **by E.C. Moore** (Historical Fiction) Never had he laid eyes on such a lovely head so up close and personal. Reg did his best not to let his hungry eyes travel south. He recognized what was happening.

Paradigm Shift **by Bill Ellis** (Historical Fiction) A rich blend of social history, drama, love, passion and determination, Ellis delivers a powerful page-turner about the struggles and perseverance to overcome all odds.

Revontuli **by Andrew Eddy** (Historical Fiction) Inspired by true events, Revontuli depicts one of the last untold stories of World War II: the burning of the Finnmark. Marit, a strong-willed Sami, comes of age and shares a forbidden romance with the German soldier occupying her home.

Sweet Song **by Terry Persun** (Historical Fiction) This tale of a mixed-race man passing as white in post-Civil-War America speaks from the heart about where we've come from and who we are.

The Duel for Conseulo **by Claudia Long** (Historical Fiction) The second novel of the Castillo family, a gripping, passionate story of a woman struggling to balance love, family, and faith in early 1700's Mexico—a world still darkened by the Inquisition.

The Old Cape House **by Barbara Eppich Struna** (Historical Fiction) A Cape Cod secret is discovered after being hidden for 300 years. Two women, centuries apart, weave this historical tale of mystery, love and adventure.

Discover more books and learn about our
new approach to publishing at **booktrope.com**.

15200680R00213

Printed in Great Britain
by Amazon.co.uk, Ltd.,
Marston Gate.